The Time Weaver

Thomas A. Knight

ISBN-13: 978-0986843716
DragonWing Publishing
ISBN-10: 0986843717

Credits:

Cover Design and Illustration © 2011, 2013, Claire Stratford

Edited By: Alison DeLuca
Editing and Proofreading By: Claire Stratford
Structural Editor: Thomas A. Knight
DragonWing Publishing

Find the author at: http://thomasaknight.com

2013-02-17

Praise for Thomas A. Knight and The Time Weaver:

"I was caught up in this book from the moment I started reading it. It was so full of action, adventure, magic, mystery, evil, and a twist of romance that I couldn't help but keep reading."
- Angela, Angels are Kids and Furkids

"It starts good. I enjoyed it a lot. And as you read on, it gets better. And better."
- Will Knight, Bibliophilia, Please

"I haven't felt so at home inside of the pages of a fantasy novel in a long time."
- Megan Monell, Love, Literature, Art, and Reason

"Thomas A. Knight's, The Time Weaver is epic in every way. The world building is stunning and detailed, full of scary creatures, monumental landscapes and wonderful characters."
- Sallie Lundy-Frommer, Author, Yesterday's Daughter

Other books by Thomas A. Knight

The Time Weaver Chronicles
The Time Weaver
Legacy
Reprisal (Coming in 2014)

Visit http://thomasaknight.com for the latest news and
updates on Thomas A. Knight

To my loving wife Claire.
You are my heart, my soul, my everything.

Table of Contents

Chapter 1 - Once Upon a Time

Krycin and Merek stood atop the battlements, surveying the land before them. The smell of death hung in the air. Rank upon rank of the Dark Lord's vicious army waited outside the city walls. They wore black armor, and were equipped with an array of spears, swords, and pole-arms. Each soldier carried a shield with the Dark Lord's symbol emblazoned on it in red: a lily with a snake wrapped around the stem. Shouts from soldiers stationed on the city walls rose up to their heights but became mere background noise as they mingled and lost all definition. Buildings set ablaze by the Dark Lord's wizards billowed with smoke, filling the air with ash and the acrid taste of burnt wood. Constructed of dense gray granite, the castle held firm against any magic cast at it. "So this is it then, our last stand," Merek said, turning to Krycin. His ancient face was lined with concern.

"It was good knowing you old friend," Krycin said. He looked as if he faced the gallows, but Merek sensed something more in his voice. He wasn't ready to give up just yet.

The Dark Lord Gladius paraded in front of his army on a giant black warhorse. His battle cries goaded his troops into a frenzy. Their shouts and howls reverberated off the stone walls and shook the Findoor people to the bone. Krycin took a step toward the front of the battlements and paused, as though he might jump. Merek approached him and asked, "You're not going to do anything stupid are you?"

A glimmer danced in Krycin's eyes, a light in the darkness that surrounded them, and he smiled. "You know me..."

"That's what I'm afraid of." The old wizard watched Krycin take one final step to the edge of the wall and hesitate. Clothed in loose-fitting black pants and an off-white tunic, Krycin looked more like a commoner than a powerful wizard or warrior. Tilting his head to the sky, he inhaled a deep breath and held it for a long moment before letting it go.

Merek watched his friend at the edge of the wall. "Come, Krycin, let's convene with the commanders and come up with a plan. Gladius has us outnumbered and cornered, but we aren't beaten just yet." Merek's gray robes fluttered in a light breeze. A deep hood covered most of his silver hair, and the sleeves extended to the middle of his hands. Every edge of his robe was embroidered with a gold trim that gleamed in even the dimmest light.

"I'm afraid that for the first time since I've known you," Krycin said, turning to face Merek, "you might be wrong. When Gladius took our King, he took our heart and soul. The soldiers fight with little spirit, and our resources are dwindling fast. With all supply shipments cut off, we must act now, or there will be nothing left to save."

Krycin's words stung in the old wizard's ears. "You know you can't face Gladius alone," Merek said. He took a step closer to Krycin, raising his voice, "He's already taken so many of your kind. What makes you think that you will fare any better? Give us just a little more time, and we will find a way to destroy him and his army."

"Time? What would ever make you think that we had any more time? When Gladius marched from the Badlands with his army, then we had time. When he traveled across the Losteron Plains, then we had time. We had time when he killed our King, and when he destroyed so many of my people. But now? Now we don't have time." His voice grew in volume with each sentence, and by the time he finished all the commanders could hear the exchange between the two men.

Merek opened his mouth to provide a rebuttal, but before he could, Krycin turned and stepped off the edge of the battlements. He drifted down like a feather, the magical power of air keeping him from falling to his death. Dust stirred into small clouds around him as he landed just outside the castle walls. With the city between himself and Gladius, he took off running. A few quick strides later he was lost among the buildings that surrounded the castle.

Shaking his head at the display, Merek shouted orders to provide cover fire for Krycin. A small contingent of archers and shield bearers marched out onto the city walls to stave off enemy troops and provide an opening when Krycin emerged.

Krycin thundered through the city, moving past buildings so fast he couldn't tell a tavern from a smithy. The smell of burnt wood strengthened as he approached the city walls where some buildings still burned. Despite the continued onslaught of enemies, the front gates, reinforced by the power of earth, held fast.

As he made his approach, Krycin lifted his hand and summoned the power of time and space. He charged at the front gate at top speed, but the gate showed no sign of opening. Krycin continued on without a worry. Just before he struck the solid wood obstruction, he let loose the magical energy he had summoned, and disappeared, reappearing on the other side of the gate.

Scanning the battle field, Krycin spotted Gladius. He held his hand out to the side, as if holding a weapon, and summoned the powers of light and life. A sword of pure light materialized in his hand. The sword shone so bright that those looking on shielded their eyes to avoid being blinded. From the hilt of the sword, streamers of light spread up his arm and over his body. As the light encased him, it solidified into crystal creating a complete suit of armor around him. Krycin let out a battle cry and ran toward Gladius, who ignored the blinding light of his sword.

Gladius dismounted his warhorse and readied his own weapon, a sword forged of black steel that erupted into flames the moment it was drawn. The air around Gladius wavered in the heat, the interlocking plates of his black armor making him look more like a construct than a man. In his off-hand he held a large black shield that matched those of his army. Krycin saw his eyes glowing red with magic but did not stop his advance.

An instant after both men drew their weapons, they clashed together in an explosion of power. Their swords collided, raining sparks down onto the field. The blades sang as they separated and Krycin drew his sword back to swing again. His second attack connected with Gladius's shield, leaving a giant gash through the center of the emblem.

Gladius returned the attack and shoved Krycin back. With all his might, he swung the blazing sword in an overhead stroke. It crashed down on Krycin, who wielded no shield. Calling upon the power of time and space again, Krycin blinked out of existence and reappeared behind Gladius. The blade continued through empty air, causing Gladius to stumble forward. Catching himself with one foot, he used the momentum to swing his sword around the other way in a spin that would have impressed even the most seasoned gladiator.

The move caught Krycin off his guard, leaving him flat-footed to bear the full force of the attack. The black sword roared through the air and struck his left shoulder. The crystal plates gave out and shattered, allowing the sword to bite into his flesh. It seared through muscle and tendons, stopping when it struck bone. Krycin cried out, but choked back the pain and lashed upward with his sword. Having Gladius's weapon mired in his shoulder gave him the advantage he needed. His sword flashed up in an arc and caught Gladius's left arm as he tried to steady himself. The pure light of the sword penetrated his armor and separated his arm from his body at the elbow. The black shield pulled the severed arm to the ground with an ominous thud.

Gladius howled with rage and struggled to free his sword from Krycin's shoulder. "You've already lost," Gladius said as he heaved at the blade, pulling Krycin with it. "Even if you kill me, my army will wash over this land and annihilate your people. All of Galadir will tremble at their might."

Krycin dropped his sword and reached up to grab the black sword that sizzled and smoked, still cooking his flesh. The pain was almost unbearable, but he gained a good grip on the blade and looked into Gladius's eyes. Through clenched teeth he said, "What makes you think I'm going to kill you?"

A look of confusion washed over Gladius's face, and changed to terror as Krycin called upon the power of his people, the element of time and space. He drew the energy not from the world around him, but from Gladius, using the sword as a conduit. A torrent of magical energy poured from Gladius, robbing him of his strength and of all the power taken from Krycin's people. As Krycin harnessed it, his eyes blazed with inner light and the black sword glowed white-hot, fusing it with both men's armor. With a semi-permanent connection made between them, Gladius became the broken levee holding back the ocean. The magic flowed through him, and Krycin received the flood.

No matter how Gladius tried, he couldn't remove his hand from the sword. Smoke rose from his eyes, nose and mouth as the flow of magic heated his body, cooking him from the inside out. The smell of burning flesh filled the air as his super-heated armor blistered and

4

charred his skin. Still he screamed with an inhuman strength, dropping to his knees.

The flow of energy stopped and a hush fell over the battlefield. Krycin stood like a beacon, his entire body blazing with light, and stared down at his opponent. Gladius met Krycin's gaze, his eyes filled with hatred. A light breeze blew, cooling the surface of his armor. Krycin spoke, his voice strong and clear, "Goodbye Gladius."

Merek watched as Krycin's body erupted like a volcano, unleashing a wave of energy over the entire battlefield. Most of Gladius's army was caught in the white dome, but those unlucky enough to be near the edges were disintegrated, their bodies dissolving into dust. A shock wave traveled out from the energy curtain that knocked any remaining troops off their feet and shook the castle walls. Merek held the edge of the wall to remain on his feet. The energy bubble extended out from Krycin and spared nobody in its path. Panicked troops made feeble attempts to run, but only the farthest troops stood a chance of avoiding it. Merek could see nothing inside the crackling shell until it stopped growing.

For the seconds it remained, vague shadows moved around inside it. Merek could hear his own heart beat, then it wavered and shrank down to where Krycin had stood and dispersed. All that remained on the battlefield were a few scattered soldiers scrambling for their lives, and empty grass where the black mass of the army had stood.

The land remained quiet only for a moment, both sides staring in disbelief at what they had just seen. Merek broke the silence and shouted out to the remaining Findoor troops, "Attack! Purge this land of their filth. Every one of them."

"And so, flags were raised for archers and infantry, and the front gates of the city were opened. The Findoor army swept the land and chased the remains of the Dark Lord's army back to the eastern Badlands from which they came.

"Merek ruled the Kingdom until the young prince came of age, and peace settled over the land. A peace that saw the Kingdom of Findoor thrive and grow into the greatest Kingdom Galadir had ever known."

Five-year-old Seth frowned and looked up into his father's eyes. "And what about Krycin? What happened to Krycin?"

"Neither Krycin, nor Gladius were ever seen or heard from again," Seth's father said, closing the cover of the old leather-bound book. "It's time for bed now."

Seth frowned and squirmed on his bed. "Aww, but Dad! Are you sure there isn't just one more story there? Krycin can't be gone." His eyes lit up at the prospect, but his father shook his head, dashing his hopes.

"That's all there is. Tomorrow we'll go out to the library and pick out a new book to read, okay?" He smiled at his son and tousled his hair.

"Tomorrow? But you'll work late again. And if you work late," Seth said, his lips curling into a pout, "we won't have time to go to the library, and then we won't have anything to read before bed."

"I know Seth, and I won't work late. I'll get home just in time, you'll see. Get some rest." He tucked Seth in and kissed his forehead. "Goodnight buddy."

"G'night Daddy." Seth sighed and nestled down into his blankets, ready to give sleep a go despite his racing thoughts.

Seth's eyes opened but he saw nothing. His room was dark, but a nagging feeling just below his belly told him that morning or not, he had to get up to pee or he would wet the bed. Not keen on the prospect of wet sheets and jammies, he pulled himself up and climbed down out of the large single bed. A faint line of light under his door showed him the way out of his room. He squinted in the bright hallway, the light blinding him until his eyes adjusted. When he could see again, he heard voices at the other end of the hall and forgot about his mission. His parents were having some kind of conversation and his mother's voice was getting loud. He walked down the hallway toward the kitchen, passing by the bathroom door as he went. *Why is Mommy yelling*, he thought as he walked, *Mommy never yells.*

When he was around the corner from the kitchen, he was able to make out the words and what he heard made him freeze in his tracks. "Why does it have to be tonight?" his mother shouted at his father.

"I've been discovered. It's not safe for me to stay here. You knew this day would come," Seth's father said in a very matter-of-fact way.

"That doesn't make it easier, and you know it."

"Five years ago, when we came here, we discussed this, and I told you then that this was only temporary. I can't let him find you, and he's so close."

"I just wish there was another way, I don't think I can do this without you." She was crying now and Seth could hear her sobs. It pulled at his heart and made him want to cry as well.

"If he comes, use the book, and utterly destroy him. Come now, I have precious little time to waste." Footsteps approached the kitchen door where Seth stood off to the left, and then his father appeared before him. "Seth, what are you doing out of bed?"

Seth thought for a second, then remembered, "Oh! I have to pee!" He turned and ran back down the hall to the bathroom door. When he finished, his father took him back to bed and tucked him in, kissed him goodnight, and then left the room, closing his door behind him. As Seth drifted off to sleep, the last remnants of his parent's argument escaped his memory.

Chapter 2 - Twenty-Five Years Later

The alarm clock blasted out its buzzer right on time, waking Seth from a deep restful sleep. His arm swung over to his night table and batted at the alarm clock. When he managed to get it to shut up, he opened his eyes and saw sunlight flooding in through the window. A gentle spring breeze wafted in, carrying with it the scent of lilacs and cherry blossoms. The sound of robins singing their hearts out filled the air.

Why didn't I book my birthday off, he thought, sitting up in bed and stretching his arms out. *I just know Dave's going to make a big deal out of this.*

A small wood nightstand rested beside his bed against the wall, with his bedroom window above it. Across the room from his bed was a large book shelf, filled with books, and in the far corner of the room, his bedroom door remained closed over, but not latched. At the end of the bed, against the same wall, there was a wardrobe, the top of which was cluttered up with a small lamp, and various trinkets and collectibles that he gained over the years. He let out a great yawn and checked the alarm clock on his nightstand. Two minutes past seven was lit up with bright red LED numbers.

I guess I better get ready, he thought as he got up out of bed. Seth walked over to his wardrobe and picked out clothes, laying them out on his bed, then went to have a shower. Ten minutes later, he returned to his room and got dressed. He was about to go grab some breakfast when a book on his bookshelf caught his eye. In among the books about software development, operating systems, computer security, and database design, was a large volume that stood out from the rest. The book looked ancient, with a metal reinforced spine and a faded brown leather cover. *Dad's book,* he thought. With a sigh he tried again to leave the room.

On his second attempt, he found himself drawn back to the book, as if some invisible force wouldn't let him leave. His eyes found the book again, its unusual bindings calling out to him, begging him to grasp it. Seth turned to check the time on his alarm clock. *It's only twenty after seven, I guess I have time,* he thought, relenting to the compulsion. He removed the book from the shelf, his fingers wrapping around the spine as if it were a fragile antique that might crumble at the slightest touch. The feel of the cover always pleased him; its supple texture like a well-worn baseball mitt.

The metal reinforcements continued along the top and bottom edges of the cover and met in the middle. A steel band wrapped around the opening of the book, preventing it from opening. A small mechanism held the band in place, and it wouldn't budge no matter how much Seth tried. The book was the last remnant that he had of his father. Seth sat down on his bed with the book and examined the lock. "Talk to me, tell me your secrets. Why would you open for Dad, but not me?"

He sat and stared at it for what seemed like hours, losing himself in the creases and colors of the soft cover, the various levels of oxidation of the metal, and the flat plate that held the closure. The surface of the plate looked the worst, and without thinking he rubbed his fingers over it, trying to wipe the discoloration off. When he did this, an audible click echoed through the room, and the lock sprang open, startling Seth enough to make him drop the book.

"Jesus," he said, putting his hands on his knees and taking a deep breath to settle his heart. "Cripes, it's only a book."

His eyes went back to the book, now resting open on the floor with the spine up in the air like an old pup tent. A rush of emotions hit Seth all at once, seeing the book open for the first time since his father disappeared. "Why now?" Seth asked, blinking back tears he couldn't explain. "You've sat on my shelf for twenty-five years, what's changed?"

Seth picked up the old book and held it on his lap for a moment. His guts wound up in anticipation of what he would find inside. "I remember Dad reading to me," he said, "but that's all. I don't even remember his face."

As he reached for the front cover, his hand trembled. Something deep inside him told him not to open the book. His mother was fond of the expression "let sleeping dogs lie" and right now the words danced through his head. He rested his fingers on the edge of the cover and took a deep breath, trying to ease the anxiety, then lifted it open.

The book smelled musty, like an old damp basement, and the paper inside was a yellow-cream color with darker edges where it was exposed to the air. Seth felt an almost unnatural chill wash over him, sending shivers up his spine as he looked at the cover page. In the center of the page was a symbol drawn in black ink of a crown with a sword through it. He ran his fingers over the symbol and said, "It's not even faded."

More curious than ever, and with the initial fear behind him, he flipped to the next page only to be surprised again. In neat lines, hand-written in the same black ink, were symbols he didn't recognize. The entire page was filled with them, from one end to the other, giving no clue as to how they would be read or what they meant. A neat half-inch margin surrounded the symbols on the page, giving it a professional look. Rifling through the next few pages showed him more of the cryptic glyphs.

Perplexed about what was written in the book, Seth closed the cover. A loud click from the book startled him as the band slid back into the locking mechanism. "What the...?" he said, pulling at the band which was now locked tight. He considered the lock for a moment before repeating what he did the first time, running his fingers down the plate. The lock clicked, and the band came loose again, allowing him to open it again. *I'll have to take this to Dave, maybe he'll know what to make of it,* he thought as he closed the book and tucked it under his arm.

"Crap, work!" he said, getting up from his bed in a panic. He hurried out the door without checking the clock. On the face of his alarm on the table beside his bed, red numbers blazed on the LED display -- seven twenty.

Seth grabbed a quick bite to eat and searched for a way to get his father's book to work. *If I just carry it in, there's going to be a ton of questions to answer.* He spotted his laptop bag leaning against the wall beside the door and walked over to it. After a quick comparison between the book and the bag he said, "That'll do." He removed the computer from the bag and left it on the counter. When he placed the book inside, the outer edges of the bag hugged the book like it was meant to be there. Seth closed the bag and slung it over his shoulder, then ran out the door, locking it behind him.

Griffin Technologies was one of Denton, Iowa's most innovative software companies. Seth arrived on time, and was greeted with birthday wishes by every co-worker he met on his way to his office. Sitting down behind his desk, he picked up the phone and dialed his best friend's extension. "Hey Dave, come in here for a minute, I've got something to show you."

"Oh yeah? What is it?" Dave asked.

"Just get in here."

"Alright, just a sec." The other end of the line disconnected and Seth hung up his phone. Moments later, Dave appeared at his office door.

"What's up dude?" Dave said, looking anxious to see the surprise.

Seth lifted his laptop bag onto his desk and opened it. "I want you to take a look at this for me," he said as he removed the book from the bag. "You're the fancy cryptography specialist, maybe you can figure out what the writing means." Seth slid it across his desk to Dave and watched for his reaction.

For a long moment, Dave examined the book, checking out the leather and steel construction. After a thorough examination of the exterior of the book, he looked up at Seth and said, "Sure man, I can take a stab at it." Dave picked up the book and tried to pull the band from the lock, but it wouldn't budge. After taking a closer look at it and finding no easy latch or button, he referred to his friend, "Alright, what's the trick?"

"Just run your fingers over that plate, it should open," Seth said, pointing to the metal circle on the cover.

Dave ran his fingers over the plate, but nothing happened. "Okay, seriously now. No jokes. How do I open it?"

"What do you mean? I had it open this morning; first time I've ever been able to open it. I just ran my fingers over the plate," he reached a hand down and traced two fingers over the lock, which popped open with a loud click, "...like that."

"Well, apparently it doesn't like me. Okay, so what am I looking at?"

Seth opened the cover to the first page with writing on it and pointed to the symbols. "Do you recognize this? Any of it?"

Dave's eyes lit up at the sight of the black ink on the yellowed pages, "Whoa, dude, I don't know what you have here, but this is wild. Can I borrow it?"

"Yeah, just take care of it."

"You know you can trust me. I'm gonna scan a few pages and post them on-line in my cryptography group. Crowd-source it, right? Maybe we can come up with something. We're still on for lunch today, right?" He flashed Seth a smile that said he wouldn't take "no" for an answer.

"Yeah, I'll go. This better not be another one of your set-ups again."

"Would I do that?" Dave asked, giving Seth an innocent look.

"Do I need to remind you what happened last time you tried that?"

"Oh, psycho-chick? Yeah, that won't happen again." Dave picked up the book being careful not to close it and walked toward the office door. "I'll let you know if I find anything."

"Right, thanks man," Seth said, turning to start his work for the day.

At lunch time, Dave showed up at Seth's office door. "So? You ready to go or what?" he asked. Seth's book hung from his hand as he leaned against the door frame.

"Yeah, I'm ready. Did you find anything out about that?"

Dave held up the book. "What, this? No. I've got my people working on it. Where did you say you got this?"

"It was my father's. It's the only thing he left me," Seth said, pushing away from his desk. "Okay, let's go. I want to get out of here for a bit." He circled his desk and took the book from Dave, placing it back in his laptop bag for safe-keeping, then followed Dave out of the building. On their way out, Seth gave a friendly wave to the cute receptionist at the front desk.

Out in the parking lot, Dave spoke over his shoulder to Seth, "Now she's a woman you could really get into, if you know what I mean." Dave's crooked grin made Seth smile.

"It's too bad she's taken. Either way, I'm not really looking for anyone, you know that. I don't know why you keep trying to set me up with someone."

"Because, Seth, you're lonely, I can tell. My guy-sense knows everything. It's my duty as your best friend to ensure that you have at least a dozen crappy relationships before you find 'the one'. I mean, really, what kind of life would you have without our adventures in dating?"

Seth raised an eyebrow at Dave as they reached the car. "A normal one?" He opened the car door and got in, resting his laptop bag on the floor under his legs. Dave got in the driver's side and started the car. Before they pulled out, Seth looked at Dave and said, "Try to stay under the speed limit this time."

Dave shook his head and hit the accelerator. "Look, you live alone in that big old house of yours. If you didn't have me bugging you to come out all the time, you'd have no social life at all. And before you say it, hanging out with your mom is *not* a social life. As of today, you're thirty years old. You're not getting any younger, man."

Seth rolled his eyes and turned on the radio, looking for a station that played decent music while Dave drove them to his favorite restaurant. Before they got out of the car, Dave looked down at the laptop bag on the floor. "So I was thinking Seth, if that was your father's book, why don't you pay a visit to your mom and ask her about what's inside?"

"You know, that's the best idea you've come up with all day."

Dave got out of the car and stretched his legs. "See? I'm more than just a pretty face." He led the way to the front entrance of the restaurant and held the door open. From the outside, Costain's looked like many other restaurants in the city, with a simple contemporary design, lots of glass on the outside, and a sign in red script lettering that declared its name to the world. Inside, however, it looked like somebody took a sports bar and a retro diner and stuck them together. Split down the middle, the bar side was decorated with jerseys, sports equipment, and various banners and ads from popular drinks. The dining room was a mix of tables and booths, with vinyl upholstery, gingham table cloths, and pictures of old movie stars on the walls. Lighting up the entire place were neon lights that made flowing lines on the ceiling.

Dave followed Seth in, then surged past him and approached the maitre d's desk, where a dark-haired girl stood tapping a pen against a book. "Reservation for Alkirk, please."

The young girl, who looked no more than eighteen or nineteen, perked up. "Oh! Right this way."

Seth gave Dave a funny look and elbowed him. "You made the reservation under my name?"

Dave shot him a grin. "They always treat you better here."

With a snort, Seth said, "Maybe if you didn't hit on all their waitresses..."

They followed the girl to a table where two women were already seated. One with dirty blond hair and long eyelashes who looked familiar to Seth, and the other whom he didn't know. The familiar woman smiled when she saw Dave, and then looked past him to see Seth following close behind. It wasn't until their eyes met that Seth remembered who she was.

"Sophie!" he blurted out and quickened his pace to the table.

Her smile grew warm and her eyes lit up. "How are you?"

"I... I'm okay," Seth said, "It's been a long time." He sat down beside the other girl in the booth so that he could face her. Dave sat himself beside Sophie.

"Since high school. What have you been doing with yourself?" Sophie asked.

"Oh, nothing much really," Seth said, fiddling with the edge of the table. "After you left, I went to college, and then got a job at Griffin. Been working there since. Nothing really exciting. How 'bout you? How's life treating you?"

Sophie was about to speak, but was cut off by Dave, "So, Sophie, who's your friend? I know, I know, you two love birds haven't seen each other in a long time, but this lovely young woman over here is patiently awaiting an introduction." He flashed Seth a knowing smile before turning back to the other woman.

Sophie introduced the other girl as her best friend Natalie, and the group talked over lunch. They all laughed and caught up, talking about days gone by and learning about each other. Dave dropped a hint to the waitress that it was Seth's Birthday. When they finished their meal, she had the staff of the restaurant come to the table and embarrass Seth with a birthday song and a free dessert.

They were just finishing their desserts when a passing waitress, balancing a tray of dirty glasses with expert precision, stumbled over an untied shoelace. She caught herself on Seth's table, but struggled to keep her hold on the load of dishes. It played out in slow motion as the tray teetered this way and that, and one glass tumbled over the edge.

Seth watched the glass fall, its contents spilling out. Sunlight through a window glistened off the silhouetted soda as it hung in mid air. The scene fascinated him in the muted room; the glass and the soda falling so slowly he could count the leftover ice cubes. It lasted only a few seconds, but it felt like an eternity. Then the glass hit the floor with a loud *smash*.

"Damn it," the waitress said, turning to face Seth's table. "Sorry about that, folks, I'll send somebody right over to clean up."

Seth sat and stared at the broken glass on the floor, the dull drone of a busy restaurant now sounding in his ears. Dave waved a hand in front of Seth's face. "Hellooooo, Earth to Seth."

"What?" he asked, looking up at everyone at the table. His face flushed as he realized he had spent the better part of a minute staring at glass shards on the floor.

"It's just a broken glass, dude," Dave said, "Anyway, as I was saying, maybe we should all hook up tonight? Go out dancing and show Seth a good time on his Birthday? Drinks'll be on me, what do ya say?"

Sophie smiled at the idea, nodding in agreement. "Yeah, that sounds like a great idea." Her friend also agreed, then they all turned to Seth.

He looked from one face to another, trying to decide if he would agree. "Alright, I guess."

"Excellent, you won't regret it!" Dave said, then got up and paid the bill. On their way back to work, the image of the glass hanging in the air stayed in Seth's mind. It was like time had stopped, and something bothered him about that.

After Seth finished work for the day, he stopped at his mom's house on his way home to visit and ask about the book. As he pulled into the driveway, he noticed the lawn was tidy and mowed and the cedar bushes in the front garden were pruned. *Mom must have hired somebody,* he thought as he grabbed his laptop bag and got out of his car. Walking up to her front door, he admired the neat rows of flowers that edged the walkway. The old house she lived in was the same house Seth grew up in. At the age of twenty-four he bought a house and moved out on his own.

Walking in through the front door without knocking, Seth was assaulted by the scent of fresh baked cookies. His mom lived a simple life in the house all alone.

"Mom?" he shouted as he kicked off his shoes.

"In the kitchen," she said back.

He crossed the living room and walked down the hallway, turning left into the kitchen. His mom stood at the counter holding a baking sheet with an oven mitt and moved cookies from it onto a cooling rack. She looked over her shoulder at him and said, "Hi Seth, I'm just finishing these up. I'll only be a minute."

"Alright, no problem. I can't stay long, I'm going out tonight, but I needed to talk to you."

She finished removing the cookies from the baking sheet and placed it on the stove. Turning to Seth with a smile she said, "Happy Birthday, Seth." She walked over to him and gave him a hug and a kiss on the cheek. "What's on your mind?"

Seth lifted the laptop bag onto the kitchen table and opened it, taking out the book. "I wondered if you knew anything about this. I know it belonged to Dad, but I can't figure out what's written in it."

Her eyes were glued to the book the way a predator watches its prey, and her demeanor changed from pleasant to defensive. "Oh, that old thing? I thought you threw that out years ago. Why don't you just get rid of it?"

"Because it's all I have left of him. Of Dad. Watch," Seth ran his fingers over the plate on the front, and the closure came loose. He opened the book to the first page with symbols on it and showed his Mother. "In all the years I've kept it, I've never been able to open it. And now this morning, I figured it out. Do you know what this writing is? Dad used to read it to me every night before bed."

Walking over to the counter to retrieve a rack of already cooled cookies, she spared barely a glance at the book before shrugging it off. "I don't know Seth, your Dad knew a lot of things. Just get rid of it, it's probably covered in mold after all these years." She shoveled cookies into a tin, keeping her back to Seth.

"There's something you're not telling me. I can tell, because you're breaking the cookies. Come on Mom, I'm thirty years old now, I can handle it. What's in this book, and what does it have to do with Dad?"

She spun around, her eyes welling up with tears. "I don't know, Seth. I don't know what's in that book, I don't know what happened to your father, and I don't know why he got up one day, went out, and never came home. I do know that whatever is in that book, it's not good for you. Just do yourself a favor and get rid of it." Tears flowed down her face that she wiped away with a sleeve. She did her best to compose herself, and then handed Seth the tin of cookies. "Now here, it's not much, but I made them for you. Happy Birthday Seth."

"Thanks, Mom." He staggered back, taking the cookies and setting them on the table. Turning back to his mother, he reached out with both arms and gave her a hug. "Sorry I upset you, I'll get rid of it."

"Oh, I'm fine. Don't worry about me. You enjoy your cookies, and have a good night out tonight." She faked a smile for him as he closed the book and zipped it back into his bag.

"Yeah. Thanks again, Mom. I'll come by this weekend, okay?"

"That sounds good. I'll have a new puzzle for us to do."

Seth gave her a kiss and walked out of the kitchen. He left his mom's house carrying the laptop bag and the tin of cookies.

Chapter 3 – Revelation

A calm pool of water rested in the middle of the dark chamber. Pale, hairless men and women rested on their knees around the pool, staring into it with pure white, unseeing eyes. The dank room was musty and smelled of moss and incense. A flickering torch in a wall sconce just inside the heavy steel door provided the only light. Merek watched the surface of the pool as an image coalesced on it.

Grian, an apprentice of Merek's, also watched the scene with significant interest. "What are we seeing here Merek?" Grian stood several inches taller than his mentor, and wore the black robes of Grishtor, the god of Death. Silver thread adorned the edges of his robe and glittered in the dim light with every movement. Grian wore the hood of his robes down, contrary to customs, and kept himself well groomed and clean shaven.

"I'm unsure. The Scryes have been tasked with locating Krycin, and while this boy certainly looks like him, he doesn't have the same skill. Krycin's son perhaps?" The ancient wizard said.

"Should we retrieve him? It's obvious that he's one of them, regardless of who he is."

"Let me consult King Verand before we do anything. Go now, and fetch him. Tell him it is a matter of the utmost importance."

"Very well, Arch-Magus," Grian said, using the wizard's formal title, and turned to walk toward the door.

"Oh, and Grian?"

Grian turned back and looked in Merek's eyes. "Yes, Arch-Magus?"

"Keep this between us and the King. We don't need rumors and gossip of Lyecians distracting the people."

"Understood," said Grian as he turned and left the room. Merek looked back to the pool and continued to watch the images, his face filled with concern.

King Verand sat upon his throne before the court and listened to various advisers bicker among themselves. Matters of military size and strength, raising taxes, and border security were before the King. One scrawny councilor approached the throne, his hooked nose and beady eyes accentuated by a ridiculous artisan's hat colored bright purple. "Your Highness, our patrols have spotted increased Narshuk activity along the southern border in the Western Badlands. We must send more troops immediately to reinforce the border."

Another councilor, well-fed and wearing fine silks, shouted out in protest, "That's lunacy. There is no proof that these reports are accurate. And besides, where would the gold come from to equip these extra soldiers? We would have to increase taxes beyond a tolerable level. And if the reports prove to be false? The Narshuks have not been a threat in over a hundred years."

The first councilor gasped and turned on his heels to face the other. "Do you imply that you don't trust the reports from our own soldiers? Perhaps we should take the extra gold we need from your own coffers. That would more than make up for it."

At that point the court descended into bouts of bickering back and forth, each member of the court shouting louder than the previous until finally the King hammered his ceremonial rod down on the arm of his throne and shouted, "Silence!"

Those nearest the King hushed and took their seats, with the rest following suit once they heard that the King intended to address them. When all was quiet, King Verand spoke. "It is obvious to me that these reports should be confirmed before any drastic action is taken. The Narshuks have long been present along the southern border, and increasing military presence there might provoke them into an unnecessary conflict. Have a runner sent west to Caldoor and see if they can confirm these reports. When the runner returns and we have confirmation, then, and only then, will we send additional support to the southern border."

The sound of two hands clapping together, slowly and in measured beat, pierced the silence after the King's proclamation. Standing in the double doors of the throne room was the black-robed figure of Grian. "Well said, Sire, well said. And if that concludes court for today, and it pleases his Highness, Arch-Magus Merek most respectfully requests the King's presence," he paused, watching the faces of the indignant councilors, then smiled and continued, "in the basement."

Without waiting for a response, he turned and walked away.

The beady-eyed councilor stood and tried to speak, "I... but..."

"That's enough, councilor Shelmen. My decision is final, and this court is dismissed," said King Verand.

When the throne room cleared, the King got up and made his way to the basement where Merek waited for him. "What is it, Arch-Magus, that is so important you interrupted my court?"

"The Scryes have found a Lyecian, Sire," Merek said. Verand gave him a look of confusion, and so he added, "a Time Weaver. I believe it is Krycin's son, as the resemblance is uncanny." He motioned to the pool resting in the center of the room. As the King walked toward the edge, each step he took left a tiny ripple that rolled along the surface of the water.

"I wouldn't know Krycin if he stood before me," the King said, "but I trust your judgment. What do you advise we do?"

"There isn't much we can do. This image is from another world. The magic required to open a rift to this world has been banned by the Wizard High Council."

"Another world? Why would the High Council ban that magic?"

"The ban predates your time on the throne, and even your life. Many years ago, traveling by rift was common. It allowed us to get from place to place very quickly, but we didn't understand the magic behind that form of travel. Some of us researched the topic, and discovered how the magic worked: it would create a tunnel in the dimensional space between worlds. But when we learned that these tunnels didn't go away even after the rifts closed, we realized the error of our ways.

"The aether that surrounds our world is riddled with holes. Create too many holes and the space collapses, destroying our world in the process. With that discovery, the magic was banned. Only a select few now know the required spells, and if they *are* used, it must be done with extreme care."

"I see," said the King. "So we just watch this boy, and hope that he discovers our world and crosses over on his own? Won't he create the same kind of hole between worlds?"

"No, Sire. Time Weavers do not use dimensional rifts to travel between worlds. They simply cease to exist at one point, and appear at another. Such is the power of the goddess Lyecha. No wizard alive can control time the way they do. What I do know is that whoever this boy is, he is not a normal Time Weaver."

"Why do you say that, my friend?"

"Time Weavers normally have their powers at a very young age. This boy is well past his teens, and appears to be only just gaining his powers now. I have watched his world for some time, and while they appear to have some miraculous things, they do not wield magic the way we do. It's a dead world. For now, we can do nothing but wait, and watch."

"Very well, Merek. Keep a close eye on this boy, and report to me at once if anything happens." King Verand walked back toward the steel door, then called over his shoulder, "Have a word with your apprentice. Tell him the next time he interrupts my court in that fashion, there will be dire consequences."

"Indeed Sire, I shall relay the message. Thank you."

Grian made his way through the corridors of the castle as fast as he could, his black robes fluttering out behind him. *Finally, my chance has come,* he thought as he approached his personal chambers. He walked through the door, closed it behind him and took out a polished silver mirror with a brushed metal edge from under his mattress. Drawing upon the power of shadow, he spoke words of magic, "Spectras sentasa circumspicai."

In the center of the mirror a point of light appeared and grew to cover its entire surface. An image appeared in the light of a haggard old wolf-like face, its gray fur matted and dirty and one of its eyes cloudy with age. As it opened its mouth to speak, Grian could see some of its teeth missing, and what remained were black and decaying. "What do you want?" the creature asked.

"The Scryes have detected a Time Weaver in another world." Grian said.

"Excellent. Have you mastered the absorption spell?"

"Yes, Scrag, and I have also figured out the enchantments that bind the library door. The time for your revenge is upon us. Once we have the Time Weaver, nothing will be able to stop us. Just remember, when we take Findoor castle, I get the library, and I take the throne."

"Understood," Scrag said.

Grian waved a hand over the mirror and watched the image disperse. After placing the mirror under his mattress again, he left the room and walked to the lower levels of the castle where Merek's library was located. The great wooden door was traced with silver runes all around the edge, and barred with several physical locks. Behind the door resided all the accumulated knowledge of Findoor and its Arch-Magus. He looked over the door for a moment and then traced a finger along the runes. Calling upon the power of shadow, he whispered various syllables that deactivated the protections, then placed his hand flat against the door and spoke a single word, "Recludaperas."

Several ominous clicks echoed down the hallway as the locks disengaged. When he removed his hand from the door, it swung open and the earthen smell of old books flooded out. Inside the room rested row upon row of shelves, filled with books. Grian stepped in and walked down the aisles, looking for a particular book. Having been in the library with Merek several times before, he knew where he would find it.

At the very back of the library was a shelf full of ancient books. Some of the volumes were falling apart, their bindings long rotted away. There he found what he sought. A book bound with white leather, yellowed with age, stood out on the shelf. Gold lettering ran down the spine of the book in a language he didn't recognize. He pulled the book from the shelf and carried it over to a table.

Grian placed the book flat on the table and held his hand over it. Calling once again on the power of shadow, he whispered, "Hadra give me strength." The magical energy flowed slower this time, but filled him up just the same. He spoke the words to a powerful spell, "Decrustas comperasa epotai." When he finished the last syllable with perfect enunciation, a white light radiated from his hand and enveloped the book on the table. Like sugar in water, the book lost cohesion and melted away into the air. It streamed up into Grian's face as he inhaled, filling his lungs with the disintegrated book. The spell completed, and the book dispersed into his body, integrating the knowledge it contained into his mind.

He shuddered with the sensation, smiled and walked back to the same shelf. At the top of the shelf was a large unmarked black book. He pulled it from the shelf, but dropped it as soon as he saw the cover. Stretched across the book, and blackened with age, was the flesh of a human face, pulled so that its mouth was in a perpetual scream, and empty black eye holes stared out at him. *Well, at least I know I got the right book,* he thought, overcoming the shock and picking up the book. *With Gladius's spell book, I'll be unstoppable.*

He took the book over to the table and called upon the power of shadow once more, concentrating harder this time as the energy resisted. As he focused the power, he spoke the words to the spell and the book began to dissolve. He inhaled, and the stream of particles flowed into his mouth and nose.

He had almost finished consuming the book when a booming voice broke his concentration. The magical energy he harnessed burned inside him as his spell unwound. "Grian! What exactly do you think you're doing?"

Grian spun around, smoke rising from his eyes and ears. He swallowed back the pain as the last of the energy for his spell dissipated, cooking him alive. "Merek, you'll kill a wizard doing that some day."

"And I'll have no guilt in doing so, especially when said wizard is in my private library and stealing my books with forbidden magic. What is your purpose here?"

Shifting from one foot to the other, Grian stared at the floor looking for some lie that would avoid his instant death. "Master Merek, I was simply getting a head start on what will surely be our next task, retrieving the Time Weaver."

"I have advised the King against that action. However, the laws are clear: theft from the Arch-Magus, and by extension, the King, and practice in the forbidden dark arts is punishable by banishment."

"No!" Grian said, then took a step toward Merek, holding out a hand. Calling upon the power of death he summoned magical energy once again, the words of a deadly spell coming to his lips.

Merek's words came faster and his magic was stronger. "Relegatas." His gnarled old hand extended and a flash of bright white light flew toward Grian, striking him in the chest. The library melted away around him as the magic wrenched his body across a great distance. Trying to stop his spell would mean certain death for him, and so he continued to cast even as the library faded and a dark, rocky landscape appeared. His spell fired and struck a boulder before him, vaporizing it.

Taking a deep breath, Grian calmed himself. "No matter. I have what I need now. Scrag will be pleased, and we can send a Narshuk to retrieve that runt of a Time Weaver right away." He looked around, surveying the area. Grey jagged rocks spread out in every direction, and gravel rested under his feet. The sky was filled with dismal black clouds and what bit of vegetation could be seen clung to rock faces or sprouted from cracks, growing in whatever bit of soil it could find. Grian took a moment to assess his location. "Ha. The Badlands. Merek has no idea what a favor he's done me." A brief break in the clouds showed him the sun and told him what direction to turn. With a sigh, he began the long walk to Scrag's cave.

Chapter 4 - A Quiet Drive Home

On his way home from his Mom's house, Seth stopped for a red light. The intersection was familiar, although it now had pedestrian signals that counted down the changing of the lights. Cars passed back and forth in front of him as he stared at nothing, listening to the ticking of his turn signal. A quick left turn, one more block, and he would be home to get ready for his night on the town. As he waited, the slow steady countdown began.

Counters were added more for people driving than for pedestrians, to give them an indication of when the lights would turn yellow. *It's not like they'll stop for the yellow anyway*, Seth thought, *I don't know why people just don't slow down. Life would be better if people would learn to enjoy what they have, instead of rushing through it.*

He sighed and continued to watch the countdown. *I wonder why Sophie came back after all these years*, he thought. *Is she here for me? Dave didn't seem to have any trouble getting her to come for lunch, and she seemed pretty happy to come out tonight*, he thought as the counter hit zero and the opposing lights changed to yellow. He glanced up at the left turn lights and waited for them to turn on. When they did, he hit the accelerator and his car proceeded into the intersection. He was so lost in his own thoughts that he didn't notice the lights and sirens of the police cars coming from the right.

Halfway through his turn, Seth snapped out of his thoughts when a blue sedan sped into the intersection, coming right for him. In a split-second, the blue car smashed into his passenger side. The door crumpled and the impact jarred him hard enough to knock his head against the driver's side window. Glass exploded, horns blasted, sirens blared, and the screeching of tires could be heard for blocks.

The man driving the blue car wasn't wearing a seat belt, and thus flew forward with the impact, smashing through his windshield. Seth felt a splitting pain down the left side of his head, and then it all stopped.

Pain radiated through Seth's head as he opened his eyes and waited for his vision to clear. Pure silence met his ears. No sirens, shouts or screams. No shattering glass or bending steel. He lifted his head and looked at his steering wheel, then at the seat beside him where his laptop bag rested with his father's book inside. Something glittered in the air above the seat, but it took a moment for him to focus on it.

Tiny glass cubes reflected sunlight like raindrops frozen in the air. His passenger side window had exploded in, but the glass no longer moved. *What the,* he thought, turning his attention farther. The blue car that hit him remained attached to his. Its hood was crumpled up and the driver slid up it like a ramp. Nothing moved or breathed, except Seth.

He shook his head and flinched as pain flared up again. "Ow, damn it. This can't be possible."

Looking around a little further, he saw other people's reactions to the crash. Onlookers in other vehicles cringed and let out gasps of surprise, their expressions frozen on their faces. One of the police cruisers was about to crash into the back of the car that had hit him. The officer driving it held his hands up in a defensive position, bracing for the impact. The lights on the top still shed their blue and red light.

"What the hell is going on?" Seth tried his car door, and it opened, but the sound of the latch was muted. Before he got out of the car he grabbed his laptop bag from the passenger seat and slung it over his shoulder as he got up. It brushed against some of the glass shards, which moved when pushed, but stopped again with no momentum. Outside, he was met with overwhelming silence, the only sound being his own muffled footfalls.

Seth found it stuffy in the still air. Leaves dancing in the light breeze were suspended as if held up by wire. He struggled to breathe as a wave of panic washed over him. With his mind racing, he looked for some kind of movement and was drawn to the gas station on the corner. Forgetting about the accident, he ran for it.

Maybe people over here are okay.

As he approached the gas station, there were no signs of movement. A woman fumbling with her keys had dropped them. As

Seth ran past, he saw them suspended in mid-air. Her sudden exclamation was fixed on her face like an expression of pure terror. The sound of blood rushed through his ears as his heart pounded.

Seth's legs gave out from underneath him, the panic sapping his strength away, and he collapsed to the ground. "How could everything stop like this?" he said, noting that even his voice was muffled. "And why am I the only one still moving?" He struggled to regain control of himself, and through sheer force of will, brought himself to his feet. His legs wobbled beneath him, forcing him to steady himself on a nearby gas pump.

"Hello!" he shouted, looking around and listening for any reaction. There was no response. The only sound he heard was his own shallow breaths. He tried once more, "Hellllooo!"

Still nothing.

Come on man, get a grip, he thought, *You can't possibly be the only person on Earth that's not affected. Calm down and get a grip.*

Seth took a few minutes to stop and breathe, hearing every labored breath move in and out in the dead silence of the world around him. A calm came over his nerves and his heart settled to a dull thump. He looked around at the gas station and the accident in the intersection, taking in the utter stillness of it all, and felt very alone.

The silence was broken by a sudden humming sound that caught Seth off-guard. He looked around, but couldn't figure out where the sound was coming from. A nervous feeling in his gut grew to a twisting sensation.

He took several steps away from the gas pump and the humming sound grew louder. Unable to pinpoint where the sound was coming from, he walked back toward the intersection. It grew louder still, surrounding him like a blanket, threatening to smother him.

As he drew closer to the intersection, Seth ignored the sound. By the time he reached the corner it was loud enough to rattle his fillings and make his ears hurt. It reminded him of standing next to high tension power lines.

In the center of the intersection, the sound pulsed out in waves, and electrical arcs snapped and crackled in the air. A thin vertical line appeared with blue light seeping out of it, as though the sky itself split open. Seth watched in awe as the blue light flooded from the spreading tear, causing him to squint. The light flared up as bright as an arc welder and left spots in his vision. The smell of ozone filled the air as electricity lashed out and struck the pavement, leaving dark scorch marks anywhere it hit.

Adrenaline surged through his system causing his heart to pound faster than ever before. He watched as the tear grew to twenty feet tall and spread open five feet at the center. Electricity from the tear made the hair stand up on his arms. *Get away from here,* he thought, but his feet wouldn't move.

Go, you idiot!

Seth snapped out of his trance, blood rushing through his veins. He stepped away from the corner and backed into a post holding up a traffic light. Unable to take his eyes off the strange tear, he side-stepped around the post. Reminded of where he was, he continued to back up toward the gas station.

Almost paralyzed with fear and staring into the bright gash in the sky, he managed a few more steps back before it began emitting a deafening pulse. *Something's moving in there,* he thought as the center of the tear rippled.

Blue fire erupted from the tear and a strange black hand emerged from it. The hand had two large fingers and a thumb, each with a six inch claw, that tore into the side of the hole like the sky was made of fabric. Another three-fingered hand reached through on the other side and tore into it, hauling the monstrous creature through.

Jesus, what is that thing? Seth thought.

The creature's arms bulged with muscles and had the same black flesh, covered with mats of black fur. Seth guessed that it had a ten foot reach. Hauling itself further through the tear, he could see the thing's face now, its burning red eyes and slobbering, toothy mouth. Its features were canine, but looked nothing like any creature Seth knew. It let out a loud grunt and growl as it hauled itself out of the tear and onto the road with a loud meaty thud. Standing twelve feet tall, the creature was hunched over, with leather straps that crossed its torso. Its legs were massive and bent backwards much like a dog, with only its toes to keep its balance. Its teeth were long and sharp with elongated canines, and it looked around like it was hunting prey.

Seth froze with terror, even as his mind urged him to flee. He tried to move one leg, and managed a backwards step.

Stop staring at it and run, he thought, and listened to his head this time. As soon as he turned away from it, the terror abated and his body let go. Seth broke into a sprint through the gas station lot away from the creature. He could hear it growling and snarling behind him, though the sound muted as he ran away from the tear. A few monstrous thuds told him the thing was taking its first steps. Visions of the creature bearing down on him, catching his shoulder with those claws, and tearing into his flesh went through Seth's head. The vision only made him push himself harder, making his legs burn from the effort.

Nothing else moved around him as he ran. Even a couple out for a walk were frozen in time, the woman's face lit up with a smile that mocked him as he went by. He heard the snarling of the beast and a loud crash as it kicked a car out of its way. The car flipped up into the air and froze, having no momentum. Seeing the suspended car, the creature grabbed hold of it and smashed it down onto another that waited for the lights to change. Seth felt sorry for the unsuspecting people in the cars, crushed without even a chance to run, but the feelings didn't last long as the creature stalked after him.

Shit, it's chasing me. Why is it after me? What the hell did I do?

Seth ran past a narrow alley, then backtracked and ran down it. *Maybe if I stick to narrow places I can outrun it.*

He reached the end of the alley, stumbling over several garbage cans that had been left about. The sound the trash made was eerie and muted, tipping as far as his legs pushed it, and then stopping. Panicked and out of breath, he turned right and stumbled forward. The initial burst of adrenaline had worn off and his body cramped up.

There was a muted crushing sound behind him and he saw the building to his left shudder. The creature wedged itself into the narrow alley. It pressed forward, but as Seth suspected, it was slowed by a fair amount. Seth pressed forward, not taking his chances on slowing down too much.

I can't run forever, what am I going to do, he thought, panicked.

The passage exited to a residential area and once free of the alley's clutter, Seth broke into a new run, getting away from the end to hide his escape route. He moved slower now, his legs burning with the effort, but he managed to extend his lead on the creature. At the moment, nothing else mattered.

Don't stop. Whatever you do, don't stop.

Silence fell over the world except for Seth's own footfalls. He bolted across the street toward a narrow gap between houses and ducked into the space before it could see where he went.

A muffled crushing sound came from the street as the creature broke itself loose of the buildings. Seth could hear it plodding down the street. He pressed himself against the wall of the house and stopped. The creature made its way down the street taking slow measured steps, a contrast from its initial movements and unnatural speed. An odd, guttural sound came from it, "Grish'ta sna, kepic si narra".

The damn thing is talking, Seth thought, standing as still as possible. "Grish'ta sna, kepic si narra!" louder this time, more insistent.

It's calling me out, why does it want me? The creature's feet padding on the ground grew louder as it got closer, its toe claws clicking on the asphalt as it walked. The sound reminded Seth of how deadly the creature was.

It drew closer still and Seth found himself not breathing, trying to slow his heart. The terror and adrenaline had other plans however, making his heart beat faster and harder. He felt as if it might pound right through his chest.

An unearthly howl cut through the still air like a knife, louder than any creature on Earth could make. It carried on for what felt like hours to Seth and despite his fear, compelled him to confront the creature. His hands grasped the brick wall of the house in a death grip to keep him from walking out into the street. *What are you doing Seth, you must be insane!*

Another wave of fear and panic washed over him, the pounding of his heart now drowning out any sound the creature was making. He pressed himself harder against the wall wishing he could become one with it. *It's going to catch me. I can't run fast enough. What do I do? Think, Seth, think,* he berated himself. *If this thing can speak, then it's no normal animal. How do I fight that?*

A second howl ripped through the air, deafening Seth. The compulsion returned, stronger this time, and there was nothing left for him to do but face it. His fingers let go, his heart and breathing calmed, and he pulled away from the wall. He tried to will himself to return to his hiding spot, but couldn't. *Damn it,* he thought, then took a deep breath and walked out onto the street where the creature waited for him.

Chapter 5 - Defiance

King Verand sat in his private chambers at a small, hand-crafted wood table. His large comfortable chair was upholstered with fine silk. The rest of the room was furnished with lavish decorations: tapestries, thick rugs, comfortable bedding, and window dressings dyed rich colors. As he settled down for his evening meal a knock came at the door. He looked down at his dinner, steam rising from the meat. The aromas filled his senses and made his mouth water. He wanted nothing more than to ignore the knock, but instead called out, "Come in." With a sigh, he turned to see who dared disturb his evening meal.

A figure wearing a gold-trimmed gray robe drifted into the room. "Your Highness, my apologies for disturbing you." Merek lifted his head under the hood and looked into the King's eyes.

"This had better be good, my dinner is getting cold."

"I wouldn't bother you otherwise, but it seems we have a problem. My apprentice, Grian, broke into my private library and stole a very valuable, very powerful tome and attempted to steal a second, though I stopped him before he could. I was forced to banish him to the Badlands, but I fear that may have been a mistake." Merek's face was grave with concern.

"Tell me, my friend, what more bad news can you pile upon me tonight?"

"I had the castle guards perform a search of his bed chamber, and discovered a scrying mirror. One that was lost many years ago."

"Yes, get on with it." King Verand eyed his dinner, waiting for Merek to finish.

"During the Lyecian war a hundred years ago, this mirror had a twin. The Dark Lord used it to communicate with his Narshuk Commander. We have no reason to believe it is being used for any other purpose today."

"So, what was in the book he stole? What power have you sent him away with?"

"The first book held the spells used to open rifts. It gives him the power to not only travel where he pleases, but also to potentially open a rift to another world."

Verand sighed, then spoke once more, "And the other?"

"The spell book of the Dark Lord, Gladius. I prevented him from consuming that one in its entirety, but I have not yet assessed how much he got, or if any of it would be useful. Grian has taught himself forbidden magic. The consumption of books for personal gain is an abomination of the magical arts. We believe he's going after the Time Weaver."

Turning to his dinner, Verand cut a piece of meat, dipped it in gravy, and savored the bite before turning back to Merek. "So let me get this straight: Grian has stolen the means to retrieve the Time Weaver, possibly stolen some very powerful forbidden magics, and you promptly banished him to the one place he planned to be all along? Is there anything I missed?"

"No Highness. Except that I feel we should go against the wizard high-council, and attempt to retrieve the Time Weaver first. If Grian gains the powers of a Time Weaver, I fear that our nation, and possibly the world as we know it, could be in peril. It would be the Lyecian wars all over again, except this time we don't have Krycin to protect us. We must act fast, or we risk everything."

"And if we defy the High Council?"

"We risk far more if we don't."

"Answer my question, Merek. What are the consequences of defying the council?"

Merek looked out the window at the dimming light. "Death, to all involved in the decision, if the act is not justified. And there has seldom existed a good reason to act against them."

"Then we shall not. Send word to the council immediately. Inform them of Grian's crimes, and request approval to use a rift to retrieve the Time Weaver. We don't know yet if Grian has the means to strip the Time Weaver of his powers. Do what you can to stall Grian in his attempts, and handle this with the utmost discretion, Merek. I don't want the New Star Festival interrupted on account of this... inconvenience."

Lines creased Merek's face as his brow lowered. "Highness, you can't be serious. A delay in action could destroy us all. I have no reason to believe that Grian will wait, and he may already have opened a rift. We must act now, or risk more than our lives."

Verand slid back from his table and stood up to his full height, several inches taller than Merek. Looking down at the ancient wizard, he spoke with a firm tone, "Do not question my judgment, Merek. Not in my own room, and not in my own Kingdom. Had you done your job, you never would have let one such as Grian rise to the ranks that he did. Had you been wiser, you would have seen this betrayal long before it happened. No, Merek, I am done with your wisdom. You will do as I have asked, or you will face my wrath. Deal with this in the manner I have dictated, and leave me be. Do not bother me with this nonsense again."

"Very well, Sire. It shall be done." Merek turned and walked from the room.

Returning to his seat, King Verand went back to his meal.

The setting sun that night marked the eve of the New Star Festival in the Kingdom of Findoor. Held every year, the celebration heralded in the summer months, welcoming a new sun to bring prosperity during the growing season. The castle bustled with activity that would continue late into the night as citizens prepared decorations, set up market tents, and cooked vast quantities of food to serve to the people who would flock to the castle from miles around. Many who came to the castle sought entry into the great tournament of swords, which would bring glory and great reward to those who won. Not only would the winners garner the high regard of their peers, but tournament standings almost always mirrored officer ranks in the Findoor Militia.

One such warrior remained on the training grounds that evening. Clad in practice armor and wielding a longsword, the warrior faced off against a much larger opponent. They circled each other in the fighting pen when Merek approached. The larger opponent called to the smaller warrior, "You're going to hurt so bad after this, you'll miss the tournament recovering."

"You will have to catch me first. You are so slow, my grandmother could catch you," the smaller warrior said with a distinct and powerful female voice.

He stepped in a slow circle around her, keeping his back away from her. Looking for an opening in her defense, he tracked her movements and watched her sword hand. She lowered her sword for an instant as if it were too heavy to hold and he charged in for an attack. Feigning left, he hoped she would guard the wrong direction. She did just that, bracing for his strike on her right side. At the last moment, he pulled the other direction and made his swing, realizing too late that he fell into her trap. She ducked low and swung one of her long legs out in the other direction behind her. Momentum carried him into her leg, and she swept his feet out from underneath him. She regained her stance before he hit the ground.

A small crowd of onlookers cheered in approval. A few yelled jeers to the man who now lay sprawled on the ground. He scrambled to get himself rolled over and took to his knees. Rage filled him, but he was more angry with himself than her. Rather than move in on him while he was vulnerable, the smaller warrior held back and let him get to his feet.

He shook off the initial blow and readied for another strike. "You won't take me so easily a second time," he said, then charged in. His longsword flashed in the torchlight that took over for the setting sun. She parried his advance with ease and traded blows with him for a few moments, each trying to gain an advantage over the other. She dropped her guard for a split second when she saw Merek and he made his move. He rushed at her with his head down, determined to take her off her feet, even if he went with her.

She saw the incoming charge just in time to crouch low. Leaping straight up, she grabbed his arms and used them to carry herself over his head. She landed on her feet behind him and threw herself forward, still holding his arms. Leveraging her body weight and momentum, she pulled him backwards off his feet and propelled him up into the air. His weight dragged her forward and they landed on their stomachs, staring eye to eye and gasping for breath.

"Had enough?" He couldn't see the smile on her face, but could hear it in her voice.

"You've beaten me; if I continue, I dare say I may not make the tournament," and he raised his hand in resignation, laying his head down on the ground. A cheer rose from the spectators as she rose to her feet, and then held out a hand to help her opponent up.

She brushed off the dirt from the sparring grounds and approached Merek. As she crossed the practice pen, she pulled the helmet off that hid her identity. Underneath was a tangle of wild blond hair that spilled down her shoulders. One strand hung over the smooth skin of her high cheekbone and curled under her sharp jaw. Her deep gray eyes met Merek's and she gave him a polite bow. "Master Merek, to what do I owe the honor?"

"My dear Malia, you must come with me at once." His face was stern and serious and his voice hushed. Malia spent several years in the Findoor military against her father's wishes before deciding to take on an apprenticeship under Merek to become a Swordmage, a warrior proficient in the magical arts. Since then, she had never heard Merek use this tone with any student.

Trying to lighten his mood, she smiled and said, "Come now, Merek, you will have me out of practice to beat all these boys tomorrow."

He didn't smile back.

With a sigh, she placed her helmet on a nearby rack. "Very well then, give me a moment to remove my armor and clean up."

Merek shook his head and said, "There's no time for that. You must come immediately."

With her curiosity piqued, she let herself out of the sparring grounds. *It must be important if Merek is this insistent,* she thought. Merek never interrupted her practice or training in favor of his lessons, and with the tournament starting early the next morning, she needed all the practice she could get.

She followed Merek into the castle proper and expected to turn toward the magic training grounds. When Merek turned the other way, it surprised her. "Where are we going Merek?" she asked, staying close behind him.

"Patience, Malia. Hold your tongue, and follow me."

Merek was always calm and patient with his students. Taken aback by the sudden change in demeanor, she continued behind him in silence.

Leading her through the inner hallways of the castle, Merek walked down a flight of stairs into the lower levels. Below ground the only light was that of a few wall sconces that burned with a dim blue light. The air was heavy with moisture, but not musty as the hallways were well traveled. Occasional decorative shields and swords adorned the walls, but no tapestries or paintings. As they made their way through the dim passageway, they passed various solid wood doors that led to storage rooms, closets and servant chambers. Near the end of the hallway, Merek stopped at a door marked with silver runes. He traced a finger along the edge of the doorway speaking arcane incantations that made the runes glow. When he finished, the locks disengaged and the door swung open. Merek walked into the room, then turned back to Malia. With a much more gentle tone than before, he said, "Come in, please."

Inside were Merek's private chambers, filled with an array of shelves covered in books, trinkets and scrolls. He was not a neat person, but knew where to find any item at a whim. A table stood in the middle of the room with a crystal point in a stand resting on it. Malia couldn't place the herbal smell that filled the room, but it reminded her of the gardens her father kept around his house. That part of the castle was silent other than her steel boots against the stone floor. When she was inside the room, Merek spoke a word and the door closed.

"Have a seat, my dear," Merek said, pulling out a chair for her.

"Thank you, Master Merek," said Malia, sitting down. She watched as Merek took a seat across the table from her.

For a few awkward moments there was silence as Merek sat and stared at the table, as if he were pondering some great puzzle. "Malia, the matter I've to discuss with you tonight is of the utmost importance, and must be kept a secret between you and me. Can you abide by this?"

"Yes, Master, of course I can," she said, tilting her head in interest. A few tresses of her hair fell down in front of her face. She gave it a quick swipe of her hand to return it to its previous place.

"I will hold you honor-bound, then, to use the utmost discretion in the task I have for you. Earlier today, the Scryes detected the presence of a Lyecian in another world."

Malia's eyes lit up when she heard the name of the long lost race, born of their goddess of time, Lyecha. "You mean a Time Weaver?" she asked, using the common name for the race.

"Yes, a Time Weaver. We believe it is the son of Krycin, though we have not yet found Krycin himself. When he was discovered, my apprentice, Grian, was with me. It turns out that, without my knowledge, Grian has been studying forbidden magic and plotting against the Kingdom of Findoor. He has stolen the means to retrieve this Time Weaver, and..."

"He's going to use the Time Weaver's abilities to attack Findoor," Malia said, cutting her master off.

"Yes," Merek said. "With the ability to control time, Grian would be near unstoppable."

Malia thought long and hard about the problem, then looked up at Merek and said, "So why haven't we sent somebody to get the Time Weaver first?"

"King Verand has forbidden it. He fears the wrath of the Wizard High Council. Retrieving the Time Weaver would require us to open a rift, and we cannot afford to wait for their approval. Thus I come to you."

Confusion again washed over her face. "Master Merek, you know very well that I could not open a rift even if I wanted to. It is beyond my power."

Merek gave a hearty laugh. "No, of course not. And if you could, I would not ask such of you. What I do ask of you is just as important. We must retrieve the Time Weaver, tonight, before Grian has the chance. I will open the rift, one big enough for one person, one trip. Once you find the Time Weaver, you will have to convince him to bring you back here."

"Merek," she said, concern filling her voice, "why only one person?"

"Discretion is the key here. Opening a bigger rift would cause more damage than I am willing to do, and would attract the attention of the High Council. You are one of Findoor's finest warriors, and trained in the art of magic. That makes you my top candidate for this job."

"And what of the King's decree? Is this not treason?"

"I work in the best interest of the Kingdom, and the people within. I believe King Verand is wrong, and foolish for delaying this. Fortunately, it's a mistake I don't have to live with."

"So let me get this straight: you wish to send me to another world to abduct a Time Weaver from his home, in defiance of both the King and the Wizard High Council, and in the process commit an act of high treason. And on top of that, you ask me to do this in lieu of the New Star Tournament, an event I have trained months for, and in doing so, give up possibly my only chance to achieve the rank of Captain. Did I miss anything?"

"You know I love you like a daughter, Malia. I wouldn't ask this of just anyone, but I truly fear for our Kingdom. Grian will attempt to gain the Time Weaver for himself, and he will stop at nothing until he succeeds." Merek's voice was grave and filled with concern. His brow lowered and formed creases in his forehead. His eyes pleaded with Malia to accept the commission.

Malia thought about it for a few long minutes, weighing the options in her mind before finally speaking up, "All right, I accept. When do we begin?"

A smile spread over Merek's face. "Immediately."

"If I am to go anywhere, I must change out of this practice armor. It is awkward and clumsy."

"Go then, and be quick about it. Meet me in the magic training grounds in twenty minutes. If anyone asks, you are taking a late-night lesson with me and are to be undisturbed."

Malia stood up from the table and turned toward the door when she heard Merek speak one last time. "Thank you, Malia, you have no idea how important this task is."

"It is my duty, and my honor, to serve this Kingdom." She then turned and left the room.

Twenty minutes later, Merek waited in the training grounds for Malia. He just started to wonder if she was having second thoughts when she walked through the door and closed it behind her. She was shrouded in a large cloak with a deep hood, but outfitted with her full battle armor underneath. Polished steel interlocking plates covered her body, and a scale mail skirt hung around her waist. The chest plate was adorned with the Findoor crest - a crown with a sword through it - and any places that weren't covered by plates were protected with chain mail. The armor was specially designed for her as she was much smaller than the typical warrior in the Findoor army. At her waist hung a scabbard with a longsword.

Smiling at Merek, she dropped the cloak as she crossed the grounds to where he stood. "My apologies for running behind, Master Merek. It is difficult to get armor on by one's self, but I cared not to explain why I was preparing myself for battle."

Merek nodded in approval. "Very wise indeed. We haven't much time, but I have a gift for you."

"A gift? Merek, that is not necessary," she said, lowering her brows at the ancient wizard.

He rustled in his robes for a moment, then pulled out a longsword forged of black steel. "Take this, with my blessings. It was last wielded by the Dark Lord himself during the Lyecian war. It is a powerful artifact, but we cannot risk failure, and so I shall trust you with it. Keep it safe, wield it well."

Malia's eyes lit up at the sight of the long sword. "Master Merek, I was taught that this sword was lost at the end of the war. Are you not worried that Gladius tainted it with his evil?"

"Not at all. This sword's power predates Gladius by many hundreds of years. He stole it from Findoor when he turned. After Krycin defeated him, I found it on the battlefield, buried in the grass up to the hilt."

"And you've hidden it all this time? Merek, I do not deserve a treasure such as this."

"Nonsense child, you're a full fledged Swordmage. Take it, it's yours now. Do not fail us," Merek said, smiling.

Malia let her eyes drop to the sword once more, her fingers curling around the hilt. She lifted the sword and a warmth washed over her. The sword felt light compared to its size, and perfectly weighted. She took a few steps back to give herself room and swung it. Flames trailed behind it, leaving smoke hanging in the air. Turning to Merek, she said, "Thank you, Merek. I will not let you down."

"Come now, we must hurry, we're almost out of time. When you cross over you will be disoriented, but make haste. Grian, or one of his servants, may already be there. If he obtains the Time Weaver, I fear all will be lost."

Merek stepped into the center of the room, facing the back wall. He unrolled a scroll and began to chant, focusing his entire mind on this one task. The incantations rolled off Merek's tongue, smooth and melodic like a slow ballad. His spell built gradually, and increased in strength as he recited the words, his voice raising as he went. When he neared the end of the spell, he dropped the scroll to the ground and it withered and turned to ash as if it were on fire, yet no flames appeared. The remainder of the spell fell from his mouth as if he wasn't speaking it at all, his hands moving in gestures that seemed to visually mimic the words, and then he went quiet. Power blazed forth from his hands in a stream of liquid white light, pouring into a spot on the wall. A blaze erupted at the point where the energy was focused that shone with a blinding light.

The flow of energy tapered off, and stopped when the blaze glowed as bright as the sun. Merek looked over at Malia and motioned her to come closer. When she was beside him, he said, "The rift is prepared. Once I open it, I will only be able to hold it for a short time. Retrieve the Time Weaver, and use his powers to come home. If you fail, there won't be a world left for you to return to."

Malia nodded. "I understand. I will not fail you."

Speaking several more words, Merek raised his hands toward the light on the wall. He spread his hands and the light split open in a line down the center creating a gap in the fabric of space about six feet tall. Electrical arcs snapped and pulsed within the gap and Malia could see the blue aether that lay between worlds. From what she learned in Merek's classes, the aether should have been solid, but what she saw was tattered and shredded with holes.

So that's why these spells are banned, she thought, and watched Merek for his signal. He motioned with his hands as if to spread the gap wider still, and it responded in turn, widening enough for Malia to fit through it.

He turned to Malia, the strain of the spell visible on his face. "Go now, and may the gods be with you!"

Malia walked to far end of the room and turned to face the rift. Crouching, she set a foot against the wall, then sprang forward in a full sprint toward the rift. She reached the edge of the rift and leaped with all her might, springing into the air and letting her speed and momentum carry her into the rift. Her body flew like an arrow through the air and her aim was true, plunging her into the center of the rift. The moment her feet passed the edge of the rift, Merek let it go. The rift slammed shut behind her, and the stone wall shattered. Merek fell to the floor, unconscious.

Chapter 6 - Face-off

There were thirty feet between Seth and the middle of the road, but it felt like miles. He fought each step with all his will to keep from confronting the creature, but the compulsion drew him out despite his best effort. The scene played out in slow motion for him, one step after another bringing him out into the middle of the street to face the beast who chased him down.

The creature watched him step out from between the houses where he hid, but made no move. Seth reached the yellow line that divided the road and stopped. He turned to face the creature, looking into its red eyes. The two stared each other down for a long time, with Seth trying to build his courage to say anything at all. After a long pause, he said, "You want me? Come and get me, you son of a bitch."

"Ahh, Grish'ta sna! Ka narra si!" growled the creature as it bared its teeth into a smile that made Seth shudder. It moved first, and stood up to its full height, letting out another of its unearthly howls that shook the earth beneath him. Then it lowered its head and broke into a charge.

As the creature ran at him, Seth crouched down low to the ground. He didn't know why, but it was what his body wanted to do. The creature approached him like a speeding vehicle and he drew his fist back. A warmth surrounded his hand, and when the beast was only feet away, he closed his eyes and braced for the inevitable impact. At the last second, he drove his fist forward toward the creature's lowered head.

Heat exploded in Seth's fist, flames licking out and around his arm. As he drove it into the creature's head, the impact created a shock wave that spread out from the pair and shattered windows. Searing pain spread through his hand as he watched the beast come to a sudden stop, and then fall backwards, the flames igniting its fur.

Snarling with rage at the unexpected pain, it lashed out and grabbed at Seth with its long claws, snaring his leg and digging deep into the muscle tissue. Seth forgot about his hand as the claws sank deep into his calf and thigh, tearing at it and pulling him to the ground. Asphalt bit into his back, shredding his skin, as it dragged him across the pavement. The smell of the creature's pungent burning fur filled his nostrils as he tried to fight back, kicking at its hand with his other foot. Pain washed over him in waves as its claws dug deeper into his leg, ruining what remained of the muscles. He screamed, tears streaming from his eyes and down the sides of his face. Seth once broke his leg in a tree-climbing incident and had thought that was the worst pain imaginable until now.

Blood gushed from the wounds, covering the creature's hand and spilling onto the ground. The world faded from view for a moment as his eyes closed. He managed to maintain consciousness long enough to see his attacker standing over him, breathing into his face. The last thought that occurred to him before the world went black was, *why did the windows shatter?*

The flow of time is different in the space between worlds, and thus a trip that took mere moments felt like hours. Malia traveled through the conduit that Merek created in the aether and to the other side. The conduit collapsed in on itself as she flew through it, and pushed her to the other side.

A light up ahead gave her something to aim for, her only hope being that it was the right place to go. She knew that the ancients used to travel through rifts all the time, which brought her some comfort.

The light grew closer until she could see a rift in space the same as the one she jumped into. Even though she thought she was directing herself toward it, it was the conduit that pushed her. A few minutes later she could make out shapes through the rift, and then objects.

Without warning, the conduit ejected her out onto solid ground, making a great clatter as her body skidded over a paved surface. *The rift looked further away than that,* she thought. She picked herself up off the ground and cleared her head, turning around just in time to see the rift close.

The scene before her looked like chaos. Dozens of large metal boxes with people in them waited on what looked like smooth stone roads. *Those must be carriages, but there are no horses,* she thought. She came out of the rift at the corner where two of the paved roads met, and in the center of the intersection, two carriages had impacted, but they were still now. A short distance behind those two carriages was another, larger rift humming and snapping away. The blue aether inside the rift churned and whirled, captivating her for a moment. *Nothing is moving.*

She looked around again and realized nothing made a sound other than Grian's rift. People rode in the carriages, but they didn't move, nor did the carriages move. Considering the rift at the opposite end of the intersection, an alarm went up in her mind. *Grian has beat us here.* Malia looked around once more and saw the trail of destruction that led away from the roads.

Following the path of destruction, she walked around some overturned carriages. In the distance, she heard a long slow howl. *The gods help us, it is a Narshuk,* she thought, and broke into a run toward the sound.

She tracked the Narshuk to a narrow alley that it had forced itself down. After examining the destruction of the surrounding buildings, she was able gauge its size. With the walls crushed in and rubble strewn everywhere, her progress slowed, but she picked through it with relative ease. As she approached the end, she heard a second howl from the creature. A compulsion came over her to find the source of the sound which drove her forward even faster. *Narshuk magic,* she thought.

As she burst from the alley, a third and final howl echoed through the still air. Just down the street from where she stood, the creature readied its attack. A man stood facing him with dark brown hair and a slight build. *He looks like a money-changer, or a councilor of the King's court.* The Narshuk's magic made him battle-blind, not seeing anything beyond what he was focused on. He set himself for the Narshuk's attack as it charged. *He'll be torn to shreds,* she thought.

No sooner did the words enter her mind, then she saw the impact of the two. The man's hand connected with the Narshuk's head, but as he swung his arm toward the Narshuk, his fist burst into flames and the fire spread onto the Narshuk's head and ignited its fur. The shock wave created by the impact spread out and blew out any nearby windows. When they broke, they didn't remain still as she expected with the flow of time stopped. Instead, they exploded inwards, the glass clattering on floors. *Time is moving again,* she noted to herself.

The creature shook off the attack and moved in for the kill. Malia launched herself into a full run, her feet pounding the pavement. The Narshuk buried its claws in the man's leg and dragged him to the ground like a rag doll. Pulling him across the pavement, it dug its claws in deeper, the man's leg now gushing blood.

She drew her sword and prepared her own attack. A fiery red glow surrounded the blade, and with an unfamiliar fury, she ran toward the creature and set her blade for the impact. It was about to finish its opponent when its senses kicked in and it spun to meet her, seconds too late.

Malia wasn't a heavy woman, but she ran at a full charge, and with the magic of the sword enhancing her attack, she hit the Narshuk with all the power of a freight train. She buried her blade in the Narshuk's gut, knocking it backwards. The man's unconscious body tripped the Narshuk as it stumbled back, and it fell to the ground with a monstrous thud.

Without a second thought, Malia extracted the sword from the creature's gut. Chunks of meat stuck to the searing hot blade. It howled with pain and fury as she did this, lifting its head to see its attacker. Her blade crashed down in a powerful stroke and cleaved through the middle of its head, the two halves lolling back in separate directions. Its brain and blood ran out onto the street below them.

The Time Weaver! Her mind raced back to reality as she jumped down off the massive creature. The man lay on the ground, pinned under the creature's legs. *He certainly looks like Krycin, only younger.* Malia had seen paintings and tapestries depicting Krycin in his many battles alongside Merek. She jumped down off the creature and examined the man's wounds. Blood poured from his left leg. *I need to get him free of this beast.*

Backing up, she concentrated, focusing her entire mind on the task. Calling upon the power of fire, she spoke in a clear and powerful voice, "Incendras." The energy flowed with ease as she focused it into a single burst on the creature's side. A small explosion sent the creature flying. It landed several yards away with a meaty thud.

Turning back to the man lying on the ground, she was aware that onlookers were starting to gather around the site of the battle. A quick check told her that none of the people were armed and so she guessed them to be peasants. She refocused herself on the man lying on the ground bleeding to death. Calling upon the power of water, she again focused her mind and placed her hands over the largest of the wounds. Drawing energy to her, she spoke a word, "Restitas," and infused the energy into his leg with a warm blue glow. When the glow faded, many of the wounds were gone, leaving only traces of scars.

Malia looked around at the growing crowd and thought, *How am I to get home when the Time Weaver is unconscious?* She picked up her sword and cleared most of the gore from it before re-sheathing it. A sound in the distance caught her attention. Above the murmur of the small crowd around her, she heard a distant crackle and hum from the intersection she emerged in. *The Narshuk's rift. It is my only hope.*

A bag that had been slung over the Time Weaver's shoulder now rested beside him. *That's going to get in my way,* she thought. Removing it, she slung it over her shoulder and across her chest the way he carried it. She then hoisted the man's body onto her shoulders and began to walk back the way she had come. His body was heavy, but manageable. Some of the larger men in the crowd moved to block her path. One of them stepped up. "Hey! You can't just walk away with him. An ambulance is on its way, we've already called nine-one-one. Put him down."

She heard hesitation in his voice that told her he didn't want a fight. *These people are scared,* Malia thought. She didn't want to fight the unarmed peasants either. "Please, my lord, you don't understand. I must make haste, and this man must come with me. He will be well taken care of where I am going, but you must let me pass."

Her voice was strong and steady, insistent even, but not threatening. The self-elected leader of the group made another step forward. "I can't let you do that. Listen, the police and ambulance are almost here. He's hurt. We can't let you just leave without some kind of explanation."

Speaking again, firmer this time, Malia said, "See that thing over there?" She pointed to the corpse of the Narshuk. Various people had gathered around it; some were holding little boxes in their hands, pointing them at the creature. Occasionally the boxes would emit a flash of light. "There are more of those coming, and if I don't get to the rift soon, they will be here. I'm pretty sure you aren't equipped for battle against one of those. So either you step aside and let me pass, or I cut you down where you stand, for you have no idea of the forces that you are meddling with." She tossed it out as an empty threat, but hoped they were frightened enough to believe her. There was no doubt that more Narshuks would come if this one didn't return with its mark. Panic spread over the man's face.

"I... I... Alright. Where do you need to be? Move fast -- if the police see you, you'll have a real fight on your hands," he said, his voice wavering. He stepped aside and motioned others to do the same.

Malia turned her head as she passed, speaking over her shoulder, "Thank you my friend. I will not forget this." She continued down the road back toward the intersection where the rift remained open. It wasn't far, by the sound of it. Malia took the long way around the buildings, as the alley had collapsed in as soon as time started again, and came within view of the rift.

The intersection before her looked like total chaos. Carriages were crashed and smoking, people were screaming and crying everywhere. Still more looked at the rift with awe and terror in their eyes. She picked up her pace, struggling under the weight of the body she carried, and made her way toward the now wavering rift.

As she walked into the intersection, several excited people saw her and pointed their little boxes at her. She ignored them, having precious little time to get to the rift. It was now big enough to swallow half the intersection, and several of the carriages fell in.

She was halfway through the intersection when she heard a voice, strong and clear, call out behind her. "Put the body down and drop your weapons."

I don't have time for this, she thought, ignoring the voice and taking several more steps toward the rift.

"Ma'am, put the body down and drop your weapons." He was firmer this time, but she continued to walk. Malia could see the rift start to waver, the edges stretching and trembling.

Twenty more paces.

There was an ominous click behind her. She didn't know what the sound was, but something in her heart said she should stop. As she turned to face the source of the voice, she said "I know you are doing your job, but I must make haste. A delay now could cost even more lives."

A man stood aiming a metal weapon at her that looked like something the smithies of Findoor had toyed with from time to time.

This one, however, was much better crafted. He was dressed in a blue uniform and wore a belt with many objects attached to it. "I'm not going to tell you again, put the body down, and drop your weapons."

Malia considered her options. She could make a run for it, and risk him attacking her from behind where she was most vulnerable, or she could disarm the man with one of her combat spells. With a glance to her right, she saw the rift still holding, and decided to take the safer option. She called upon the power of fire as she lowered the Time Weaver's body to the ground. Standing back up, she held her hands out in front of her in a non-threatening manner.

A look of relief washed over her opponent's face when she did as he asked. "Now, lay the sword and any other weapons you may have on the ground and step away from the body."

Her eyes darted from the man in blue, to another beside him, and then back to the Time Weaver. She lowered her hands to the hilt of her sword as she summoned the last of the energy required for her spell. When her hands reached her weapon, she turned them palm out and in a calm steady voice, said, "Crucintas."

What happened next she would remember until the end of her days. She intended to disarm her opponent by heating the metal weapon to red hot levels, thus making him drop it. But when she let the spell loose, the weapon heated, then exploded with a flash, sending shards of metal in all directions. A searing pain shot through her knee as a projectile from the weapon struck it, making her fall to the ground. She let out a cry of pain as blood ran out of her leg and onto the ground, forming a small puddle.

The man holding the weapon lost his hand, as the explosion blew little pieces of it in every direction. His partner fell to the ground as a shard of metal from the weapon flew at him and buried itself just inside his skull. Malia didn't understand what had happened, but had little time to think about it.

She reached out, taking hold of the Time Weaver's arm, and hoisted him onto her back. Unable to walk, she crawled with him on her back toward the rift. A trail of blood on the pavement showed her progress. *Ten paces*, she thought.

As shock set in and the exertion drained her, she began to feel light headed. She had trouble focusing and the whole world faded in and out. Her progress slowed as she tried to clear her head. *Focus. Focus on your objective.* She thought the words that Merek had spoken to her so many times during her lessons. *Only a few more steps.*

Her body gave out at the edge of the rift and she collapsed with the Time Weaver on her back. She reached out with one hand and grabbed the edge of the rift. It was solid, not what she had expected, like grabbing the edge of a door frame, but it trembled as if any second it would close. With a strong grip and one last burst of strength, she pulled them both through.

All she could do was cling to the unconscious body as they tumbled through the aether between worlds. Pain ripped through her leg and she felt blood pool inside her armor. She hooked her fingers inside the Time Weaver's belt and hoped it would hold if she passed out. Then everything went black.

Chapter 7 - Witnesses

The sound of his military-issued cell phone startled General Mathers as he walked through his kitchen. He was supposed to be on leave for two weeks and spent much of the day packing for a family vacation. Luggage was piled up by the front door, and his three children ran around the living room singing jingles from the amusement park that was their destination. His wife sat at the kitchen table and stared at the phone like it was some kind of wild animal. "Ignore it, just this once," she said, her eyes pleading with him.

"I can't do that, darling," he said, picking up the phone. "This had better be good."

"General Mathers, sir," Captain Toby Smith's voice said on the other end. "You know I wouldn't call if it wasn't important, Sir. There's something you need to see."

"What is it Toby?" Mathers asked, having little patience for people who dance around bad news.

"Sir, we're getting strange reports in from Denton. Something about a tear in the sky, and some kind of wild creature found there, dead. I think you should come to the base sir, the local police have secured the creature." Toby's voice was very serious, almost scared.

How very unlike Toby, he thought.

"Alright Toby, I'll be there as soon as I can." He hung up, and moments later the General was ready to go. Mathers apologized to his wife, kissed her cheek, then left for the base.

Twenty minutes later, he pulled into the parking lot at the base and parked his SUV in a spot close to the offices. Looking around the lot, he saw very few empty spots and thought it odd that so many vehicles were there already. *Something is definitely going on here,* he thought as got out and walked toward the main office door, *so much for my vacation.* He sighed, and walked into the chaos.

As he walked through the office, people stopped what they were doing, stood up and gave him a salute, and then went back to their work. He looked around the room and found who he was looking for. Toby leaned over a large table covered with photos, maps and various other documents. He recognized the largest map, of the west end of Denton, but didn't get the chance to see anything else on the table before Toby stood up and saluted, blocking his view. "General Mathers, sir, we'll start the briefing as soon as you're ready."

Mathers nodded. "Then let's go. Consider this briefing started. If we get this over with quick, I may still make my plane."

An announcement went over the intercom calling all senior officers to the conference room. Toby led Mathers in and set up his presentation. Once all officers were present, Toby cleared his throat and began. "Hi everyone. My apologies to those called in from their holidays, but this matter is of the utmost importance, and has been deemed classified by the Pentagon. At seventeen hundred twenty-three hours today, traffic cameras at the intersection of Park and Henry, in the city of Denton, Iowa recorded a traffic accident. This would not normally catch our attention--traffic accidents happen every day--but in this case, the recording shows some unusual events."

Toby turned to a computer and clicked a few times, starting a video on a projector. As the video played, it showing a black sedan making a left turn through an intersection. When it turned, a blue car being chased by police ran a red light and struck the black car. The moment the blue car struck, there was a blip in the video, and then the door of the black car was open, and the driver was gone. The two vehicles smashed through the intersection, striking several more cars in the process. At the far end of the intersection, well away from the area of the crash, one vehicle was overturned on another, with most of the occupants crushed. The car underneath rolled into the intersection and was struck by more cars. On the right side of the screen, a blue light flickered and waved, and an ear piercing hum accompanied by loud crackles could be heard. There were a few minutes of chaos as some people helped those involved in the accident, and others pulled out phones and cameras to take pictures. The police on the scene tried to keep the situation under control, but the presence of the blue light had many people worked into a frenzy.

Several minutes later, a woman dressed in polished steel body armor walked toward the intersection with a laptop bag strapped to her, and a body slung over her shoulders in a fireman's carry. She looked like someone out of a renaissance festival with a large sword hanging from her waist. The woman walked toward the blue light and stopped only when one of the responding officers pulled his gun. She turned around, set the body on the ground, and stood up. Words were exchanged between her and the officer, and then she held up a hand, spoke a word, and the gun exploded. She collapsed to the ground, then took hold of the body, hauled it onto her back, and crawled into the blue light, which then disappeared.

At this point, Toby paused the video. "The man she took through the portal was the same man who drove the black sedan. One second he was in the car, about to be involved in what would likely have been a fatal accident, and the next second he was gone."

Mathers looked up at Toby, his expression calm. "How can we be certain that this footage isn't fabricated?"

"Sir, we've questioned all eye witnesses, who all report the same events. Also, the crowd who gathered around the creature gave similar statements. One second the street was calm, just like any other day, and then their windows are bursting, and the creature is brawling it out, first with him," he pointed to the man being carried, "and then with her. She made quick work of it. Whoever she is, she knows her way around a sword. And we can't even begin to figure out how she made the officer's gun explode. Forensics say every cartridge went off at once. Only one bullet was unaccounted for; we think it's what took her down."

"And what about this 'creature'? What creature are you talking about?" asked Mathers.

"Oh, that's the best part. We're calling it creature X. A transport vehicle should return with it soon. The woman in the armor took it down with the sword she carried. Sliced right through the creature's skull, right down the middle." Toby tapped a few more keys and brought up some new pictures. "It looks like it walked right off a movie set. Our first instinct was to find out if one of the major studios was doing some kind of publicity stunt, but it appears not. This is real. We believe this creature, and the woman in the armor, are from another universe."

Mathers raised an eyebrow at that prospect. "And the man she took with her? Who is he?"

"Seth Alkirk, sir. Works for Griffin Technologies, pays his taxes, obeys the law, not even so much as a parking ticket. We've tried to contact his mother, who also lives in town, but thus far have been unable to locate her. We're collecting DNA samples from his house as reference so that we can figure out whose blood is whose at the scene."

"Good work, Toby. Send any information you have on this incident to me, and keep me informed of any and all progress in this case. When the creature arrives, I want to see it. No doubt, videos of this will have already hit the Internet. We need to come up with a viable cover story for this. We don't need any wide-spread panic, and somebody will no doubt raise the doomsday alarm over it." With that, Mathers got up, left the conference room and went to his office.

Closing the door behind him, he thought, *Yup, it's gonna be a long night.*

Chapter 8 – A Long Rest

Merek slept the dreamless sleep of pure exhaustion. The spell he cast had to be perfect, and so he funneled all of his power and strength into it. A matron stationed next to his bed was instructed to inform King Verand the moment he awoke.

The New Star Festival began at sunrise that morning, on schedule, and Merek was supposed to speak at the opening festivities as he had done for many years. The entire Kingdom was saddened that he could not make one of his legendary inspirational speeches. Some even thought it an omen of ill times to come. Merek continued to sleep until just after lunch, when he finally stirred.

The matron saw his hand move and heard his groan as he rolled over. After summoning a runner to inform the King, she stood at Merek's side as he came to. His eyes fluttered open, his ancient lined face grimacing in the bright afternoon light.

"You'll kill yourself pulling stunts like that," the matron scolded. Merek managed a smile at the woman who acted so much like a mother, and yet was less than half his age. "But we're all glad you're alive. Gave us a good scare. If it hadn't been for the healers doing a late-night practice before the festival, you'd be dead." Merek began to prop himself up, but the matron objected. "Oh no, no no no. No you don't young man," she said with a wink and eased him back into bed. "I've already sent a runner for The King."

Merek couldn't bear to lie around, but he thought the old matron just might tie him down if he moved again. He could see the light shining in through the window. "My lady, would you know how long I slept? Did I miss the opening of the festival?"

The matron gave him a warm smile. "Don't you worry your head about such things. The only thing you need worry about is getting better." She continued about her work, fussing over the room and making sure things were tidy, until King Verand arrived.

It was no surprise when he did arrive. The commotion that the runners, guards, and various other members of his entourage made as he approached would have woken Merek out of the deepest sleep. But when they arrived at Merek's door, Verand turned and shooed them all away, insisting that he would not be long and that there would be plenty enough hours in the day to attend to all of their business.

He came through the door alone, leaving only a single runner outside the door in case they needed anything. He looked at the matron before saying anything to Merek. "My lady, you have done a fine job tending to Arch-Magus Merek," he said, using Merek's formal title, "but for now, I must beg that you take your leave. Return when the runner is sent for you, I have business to tend to with the Arch-Magus, and you needn't worry. I dare not over-stress him and cause you further work." The last he said with a smile. The old matron got a scowl on her face at the notion that they would be talking business, but left without argument.

Verand closed the door behind her and walked back over to Merek's bedside. Sitting on a nearby wood chair, he said, "Merek, you old fool, how are you feeling?"

Merek tried to prop himself up on his elbows, but his body protested. "Like I've been trampled by a herd of wild elk. But I will heal."

"What were you doing in the training grounds that late at night, and by yourself?"

"Doing something that you lacked the courage and resolve to do yourself," Merek said, his voice level and plain. "I've sent one of Findoor's finest young Swordmages, Malia Corsair, to retrieve the Time Weaver. The burden is not yours to bear, your conscience is clear. If somebody is to answer to the High Council, it shall be me."

"And answer you shall. When the High Council finishes with that beggar Grian, they will be coming here to deal with you. You have defied me for the last time, Merek."

The ancient wizard sat up in his bed and looked into Verand's eyes. "Indeed. If in my defiance, I have given this Kingdom a fighting chance, then so be it. I shall be more than willing to accept the consequences of my actions. At least I acted."

"How dare you speak to me in that fashion! I should have you chained up in the dungeon right now. If you weren't such a dear friend of my father's, I would have gotten rid of you after his death. It is for that reason alone that I endure your presence and the presence of those infernal Scryes."

"I speak to you as the child that you are. If I should be put to death, then I shall accept my fate, and know that I died having done everything I could to protect this Kingdom. Could you say the same? Could you say that you even tried to save your people? This world? To give them a fighting chance? Or would you die a bitter, lonely old coward, having no wife and no heir?" Merek finished his tirade, and collapsed back onto the bed.

Verand seethed, but remained silent. He stood up, turned, and stormed out of the room, slamming the door behind him.

Having exerted himself more than he planned during the exchange, Merek sighed and closed his eyes. "Pompous windbag."

Merek rested a few moments before he remembered the matron, who would be back in to nag him soon. He thought it might be enough time to accomplish what he needed and so focused his thoughts and reached out to the Scryes with his mind. His eyes turned white and his head dropped back on his pillow as he found them.

My friends, I have a task for you.

Yes master Merek, the voices of the Scryes returned in unison.

Watch for Malia and the Lyecian. Notify me if they re-enter this world.

There was silence for a moment inside his head as the Scryes contemplated the task. After a long pause, he heard, *Yes, master Merek.*

Thank you, friends. He broke off the connection. When he refocused his mind on the room, the nursemaid was just coming back in. He almost dreaded the verbal lashing he would have gotten for performing any kind of magic while still bedridden, but he knew this was important.

Feeling drained again, he rolled himself over and drifted back to sleep.

Chapter 9 - Lost and Found

Something tickled his nose, like a fly had landed there. Out of reflex, he swatted at it, and pain flared through his right hand like it was on fire. Seth gasped and tears filled his eyes, his peaceful sleep now over. He didn't yet have the courage to open his eyes but could feel that he rested on something soft, like feathery grass. The air smelled clean and clear, and sunlight warmed his skin. Were it not for his throbbing hand, he would have thought he was in heaven.

A female voice with a strange accent spoke. "Good morning."

The sound startled him enough to open his eyes, and once they adjusted to the light, what met them surprised him. Silhouetted against the rising run was a beautiful female form. Her body was thin and athletic, like the women he saw in figure skating competitions on television. Delicate features were framed by untamed blond hair that fell around her shoulders. Steel plates rested on the ground around her and she appeared to be tending to her own knee, tearing strips of fabric and making a bandage out of them. Half-buried by the armor plates was a familiar black bag.

After a few moments to clear his head, Seth spoke up, "Who are you?" Looking around to get his bearings he saw green pasture filled with feathery grass, dotted with occasional wildflowers. In the distance, trees broke up a skyline that was otherwise unblemished. Seth didn't spend a lot of time outdoors, but he knew most of the local plants where he lived. He examined some nearby plants and trees, and he didn't recognize any of them. "And where am I?"

The girl grimaced as she pulled a bandage tight against her knee. Then she looked at Seth and forced a smile. "My apologies. I would have liked to have introductions on better terms, but since we are both here now, my name is Malia Corsair and I am a Swordmage of the Findoor militia."

Seth had something in his head before she spoke, but when she lifted her head to look at him, it escaped him along with his breath. "I... who..." he said, trying to find the right words again. *My god, she's beautiful,* he thought, unable to break from her gaze.

Tired of waiting for him to reply, she interrupted. "You have been sleeping a long time, but I thought it best that I leave you be. We are safe here, at least for now."

She went back to wrapping her injury, leaving Seth alone to sort out his head. He looked down at his tattered pants and shifted them aside, not sure what to expect. Several long scar lines could be seen where wounds had healed. He looked back up at the girl and asked, "Am I dreaming?"

Lifting her head to face him again, she laughed, a hearty clear sound. "Nay, this is no dream."

"Am I dead?"

"Nay. What do you remember?"

It took a few minutes of thought for Seth to piece together his memory. "I was driving home, and I had a green light. Some jerk ran the red, and there were police cars." He lost himself in her eyes as he tried to remember more. "He T-boned me, and I hit my head... and then nothing."

A warm, almost pitying look came over Malia's face. "You remember nothing else? Your name? Where you are from?"

"Seth. My name is Seth Alkirk. And I'm from Denton, Iowa. Lived there my whole life." He paused and thought some more, his head still foggy. As he lifted his right hand to rub his temples, pain flared up through his arm, and reminded him of the injury.

Malia looked at Seth's hand and frowned. "I think it is broken. I am not yet powerful enough to mend bones, though I healed the rest of your injuries," she said, motioning to his leg.

He looked down at his leg again, then back at Malia. *Swordmage? Powerful? Healing? I'm not the only one who hit their head.*

The thoughts must have been apparent on his face because she spoke up once more, "No, I am not crazy. And neither are you. I was sent to retrieve you from your world, to ensure that you did not fall into the wrong hands. There is a very powerful wizard looking for you, and he will not stop until he finds you. Had I been moments later than I was, he would have you right now."

"What? Wait, stop. I'm a little lost. Wizard?" Confusion washed over Seth's face as he tried to put pieces together in his mind that just wouldn't fit. "My world? What's going on here?"

Trying to be patient with him, she started again, "I am a Swordmage from the Kingdom of Findoor. You may not recognize the name, because I live in a different world than you. I was sent to retrieve you, and protect you from a powerful wizard named Grian. Your hand is broken because you attacked a Narshuk, and I'm pretty sure you cracked its skull in the process."

"So, I was in a car accident, hit my head, and now I'm hallucinating. Good, I'm glad I got that sorted out," Seth said, his voice dripping with sarcasm.

Malia's brows lowered and her forehead creased. "I assure you Seth, this is no illusion. You are in danger, and we are both injured and in need of a healer." She looked Seth over and, still seeing the confusion on his face, continued, "You remember nothing?"

"Not a thing."

"Rest assured, I am here to protect you."

"Why me? What makes me so special? And why should I trust you?"

Her face drained of all emotion as she looked at Seth with a blank stare. "You really do not know?"

"No, I don't. I don't know why I'm here, or who you are, or where we are, and heaven knows what's going on, because I sure don't. And no, I don't know what makes me so special, so please, Malia, enlighten me." He thumped his hand down on the ground to emphasize his point, but the pain that lashed back at him reminded him of the broken bones. "God damn it," he said, blinking back more tears.

Malia let him be for a minute while she tied off her bandage on her knee. "I am going to need a splint for this. And I will not be able to get it myself. Can you handle a sword?"

Without warning, Seth launched into a tirade again, "Do I *look* like the kind of person that can handle a sword? I've never even touched a sword, or even been within ten feet of one."

Malia scowled at him, but then softened her expression to one of compassion. "Seth, I understand this is a lot for you to take in right now. The truth of the situation is, we are not going to be safe here for long. Eventually, Grian is going to find us, and come after us. We must be prepared, which means we must find a town with a temple where we can get our bones mended. If I wanted to kill you, or harm you in any way, I could have done it while you slept. I need you to trust me so that we can both make it to Findoor alive."

"I... I'm sorry. I didn't mean to unload on you like that. What can I do to help?"

"Thank you, Seth, and speak not of it again. There is no need to apologize." She looked down at her knee again and said, "I will need two strong, straight tree limbs the length of my leg to secure it, and another longer one to assist in walking. Take my sword and be quick about it. I fear we don't have much time."

Seth looked around and found the sword. He picked it up and withdrew it from its scabbard. It felt lighter than it looked for its size. Making his way to the nearby trees, he spotted several limbs that would work. Seth approached the first and hoisted the sword up over his head with his left hand. Swinging it down with all his strength, he braced for the impact, expecting it to embed part way into the branch. Instead, the blade flashed, and the sword cut clean through the limb and pulled Seth off his balance. He stumbled forward with his momentum and the branch came down on top of him.

From a distance, Malia watched the display and laughed. Seth managed to sort himself out and got the branch off his head, then dragged it back to her under his right arm, being careful not to bump his hand or use it. She continued to laugh when he dropped the branch at her feet.

"That's right, laugh it up." he said with a smile. He handed the sword back to her, making the mistake of passing it blade first.

Malia got her laughter under control, and then said with a smile, "Pardon my laughter, I do not mean to mock you. But Seth, in the future, when you pass a blade, do not pass it sharp side first."

Seth looked down and realized his mistake. Malia turned the sword around and began to remove the bark and twigs from the branch. After cleaning and trimming it, the Y-shape at one end made it ideal for a crutch. Seth watched her finish cleaning it, then took the sword and got two additional smaller branches, being sure not to make the same mistakes again. Malia cleaned those and used more strips of fabric to secure them to the back of her leg, forming a crude splint. Using the makeshift crutch, and help from Seth's good hand, she rose to her feet. She looked at Seth with the best smile she could muster through the pain of her wounded knee. "That should do it. You will have to carry the damaged pieces of my armor until we can get it, and my leg, fixed. Could you help me get the rest of my armor back on? I will guide you as to where and how they go on."

"Alright, I think I can manage that," Seth said, looking down at the pile of metal plates and straps. With Malia's help, they got most of her armor back on. The last pieces to go on were the chest and back plates, which were lying on the ground. Seth picked up both pieces and examined them, then dropped the chest plate again, his jaw hanging open.

Malia looked from Seth, to the armor plate, and then back to Seth again. "Is there something wrong?"

Unable to find the right words, Seth stood in silence for several minutes, looking down at the chest plate. On the front of it, was the symbol of a crown with a sword through it.

"Seth?" Malia asked, trying to get his attention away from her armor.

"I've seen that symbol before."

"Oh, that. That is the Findoor crest."

Seth looked around, as if trying to find something, then spotted his laptop bag lying in the grass where the armor sat. Kneeling down, he wrestled it open with his good hand and found what he was looking for. Inside the bag was his father's old leather-bound book with the steel locks still in place. "I've had this book all my life. My father used to read it to me at night before I went to sleep. It's the only thing I have left of him, and just..." he was about to say "this morning" but then realized he had no idea what day it was. "Well, just recently, I got it open for the first time."

Malia looked at the book with some interest and nodded. "It is a conditional lock. They are quite common, and usually require certain circumstances to be true before they will open."

Setting the book down on the ground, he traced his finger down the plate on its cover. An ominous click pierced the air and the band that held it closed let go. Opening the book revealed the front page for Malia to see. "This is the only place I've ever seen that symbol before," Seth said, "I had no idea what it meant or where it came from. Can you tell me anything about the rest of the symbols in the book?"

Malia lowered herself to the book using her crutch and flipped through several pages before looking back up at Seth. "The script in it is Lyecian, which confirms what Merek thought. You must be Krycin's son."

"No. Oh no," Seth said, "my father was a car salesman."

There was a short awkward silence before Malia spoke again, "Was? Did something happen to him?"

"He left when I was five. I don't remember much about him, or even why he left, and mom won't talk about it. She always gets upset when I try to bring it up. Thing is, I don't remember him, other than his name and what he did. I can't even remember his face. I'm not sure what makes Mom more upset: the fact that he left, or that she remembers as little as I do." Seth looked at the ground, sadness filling his voice, "I've tried so many times to learn about him, but nobody ever wants to talk about it but me. It's like he made everyone forget him, what he looked like, what he did, what he was like, nothing. Nobody knows anything, and it makes them all angry just to talk about it."

Malia rested a gentle hand on his shoulder. "I am sorry things worked out that way for you. If it is any comfort, I fear you might not be far from the truth. There are complex spells that one can cast in order to disappear, and Krycin was a very powerful Lyecian."

"My father's name wasn't Krycin. And what exactly is a Lyecian?"

Her face darkened as she thought about her words, and only spoke after a long pause. "Lyecians were a race who existed over a hundred years ago. They were born of the Goddess of Time, Lyecha, and could control the flow of time--slowing it down, speeding it up, and even stopping it entirely. We more commonly call them Time Weavers, but Merek insists on teaching us the old names for everything. A hundred years ago, there was a war that we call the Lyecian war. A powerful wizard named Gladius discovered a spell that could fracture a Time Weaver's soul and remove that part of them that gave them their powers. Many Lyecians died in that war, and Gladius became so powerful his dark army nearly wiped out our entire Kingdom.

"It was Krycin who rescued us. He defeated Gladius, and destroyed the Dark Lord's army. But in the resulting blast, he was lost. Nobody has seen him since. We thought Lyecians were extinct, until Merek found you."

Seth stared at the book on the ground and thought about her words, then looked up into her eyes. "Merek, Krycin, Gladius... Those are all names that Dad used in the stories he read to me. But there's no way I'm a Lyecian. I can't control time. I'm just an ordinary guy."

"That may be," Malia said, "but Merek is seldom ever wrong. Come, let us finish here and set out; we can talk about this more as we travel."

They finished putting her armor on, leaving the damaged leg and knee plates off. Then they gathered up their remaining belongings. Malia looked around at the landscape, trees and sky, then turned to Seth and said, "I believe we are in Caldoor, a neighboring Kingdom to the west of Findoor. Which means we should head east. I am unsure of how far into Caldoor we are, but we should seek out a town or village and find a temple. That way we can both be healed." With that, she turned and headed off toward the sun.

Seth and Malia walked for hours, slowed only at the beginning by Malia's hobbling on the make-shift crutch. It didn't take her long to get the hang of it though, after which she kept up with Seth, sometimes surpassing him when he started to get tired. They stopped for breaks every couple of hours, allowing Seth to catch his breath and Malia to check her wounds and ensure that infection wasn't setting in. The pastures they walked in were covered with the same feathery grass that extended out in every direction. The northern landscape was spotted with dense forests and to the south were hills and then in the far distance, jagged mountains. In the sky, Seth spotted several types of birds that looked like sparrows and starlings, but also others that he had never seen before. One such bird swooped down out of the sky to get a better look at the travelers. To Seth it looked a bit like a heron, only with bright blue feathers striped with black and white, and long blue and red tail feathers that it used to steer its flight. It squawked out a warning call at them and rose back into the sky.

After about five hours of walking, they found an old worn path that looked promising. "It looks like an old Merchant trail," Malia said. "We can follow this, and it should eventually lead us to civilization."

Walking on the path allowed them to increase their pace. After another two hours there was still no sign of civilization, and both companions were getting tired and hungry. During their walk, the landscape changed from large rolling hills and pastures to flatter, more forested land. Malia kept her eyes open for small game that she might be able to catch so that they could at least have something to eat, and at one point she veered off the path and found some berries she knew were safe to eat. Unfamiliar to Seth, Malia described them as stoutberries. They were black and sweet and reminded Seth of blueberries, but without the leathery blue skin. Not a satisfying meal, but enough to fight back the hunger for a little while.

When the sun began to set, Seth slowed his pace, turning his head and listening for something. Malia kept a close eye on him to ensure he didn't fall too far behind. After about ten minutes of this, Malia stopped and turned to face him. "What is it Seth? Is there something the matter?"

Seth nodded and said with some uncertainty in his voice, "I can't shake this feeling that we're being watched. Maybe even followed."

Her face darkened as she affirmed what Seth already felt. "Yes, we have been followed for the last hour. Though I am uncertain of who it is."

Malia's hand on her sword's hilt caught Seth's eye. As they stood in the middle of the path, she pressed a finger to her lips to indicate silence, listening for the slightest noise. After a number of minutes, she opened her mouth to speak, but was interrupted by the sharp twang of a bowstring.

Seeing it in slow motion, Seth watched Malia duck to the ground as an arrow flew from the woods to their left. It glided through the air toward him, moving slow enough for him to see the blue and white feathers used in the flight. When it got close enough, he plucked it from the air before it could strike him. Time resumed its normal flow once he grasped the arrow.

A look of pure shock came over Malia's face. "By the gods," she said, getting up and forgetting about who fired at them.

Seth opened his mouth to respond when laughter came from the trees--a male voice, crisp and hearty. Malia drew her sword at the sound and steadied herself on her crutch. "Show yourself," she said into the trees.

Without speaking, a figure deep in the forest hopped down from a low tree branch and strutted out of the grove. A man dressed all in black with a mask over his nose and eyes and a broad brimmed black hat topping his head approached the two companions. Dressed for travel, he wore long pants and leather boots, a light tunic, and a cloak that hung loose over his shoulders and a pack strapped to his back. Malia spotted a quiver of arrows strapped to his right thigh and a dagger in his left boot, but no other weapons. His lips curved up in a genuine smile, and as he walked, he slung his bow over his shoulder.

"Well met, good sir. Well met. You have bested me," he said, his voice ringing with the same crispness as his laugh. His tone was clear and practiced, like that of a singer, and there was no hesitation or fear in his words.

Malia placed herself between Seth and the stranger. By Malia's reckoning, his voice and swagger put him about the same age as Seth, though he stood just taller than Seth, and had a heavier build. "Well met indeed. I should cut you down where you stand. State your name and purpose, or I shall do just that."

Again he laughed. "Friends, do not take offense. Your man here seems to have things under control." He looked at the arrow still in Seth's hand, "and besides, if you cut me down, you'll never find what you're looking for."

Malia scoffed, "And what makes you so sure of what we seek?"

"Two people, wandering around on merchant paths, both injured? The answer seems obvious to me. You're looking for somewhere you can rest, find a healer, and eat a good meal. I bet you're both hungry."

His arrogance grated on Malia's nerves. "Okay, you have our attention. What do you want?"

"Why, to help of course," he said, smiling.

Both Seth and Malia looked at the arrow. "You have a strange way of showing it," Malia said, returning her gaze to the stranger.

He looked at the ground for a split second, and there was something almost sheepish about the way he did it. "Yes, that, well, I was aiming at a tree behind you. The intention was to give you warning, but apparently I'm not as good a shot as I thought." A smile spread across his face again as he said, "Good thing your friend's reflexes are as sharp as a razor, otherwise our conversation would be very different right now. May I?" He reached around Malia for the arrow, and Seth surrendered it to him. Sliding it into the quiver strapped to his leg. "Now, back to business. You have a need, and I believe I can satisfy that."

"Do you, now?" Malia asked with one eyebrow raised.

"I can escort you to the nearest village where you will find hot food, warm beds, and even a healer who can mend your bones. Six days' time, and you'll be rested and ready to take on the rest of the world." Smooth and charismatic, his voice grabbed their attention with his promise.

Malia approached him with caution. "And what price would you ask for your services?"

"Price? Why, I'm appalled that you think I seek money for my good will." He feigned indignation, raising a hand to the top of his mask near his forehead. "Oh, very well then, my price. Take me to Findoor with you, and vouch for my presence there."

"What makes you think we are going to Findoor?" Malia narrowed her eyes at the masked man. *Just how much does he know about us,* she thought.

He let out another laugh, one he did little to control. "Why, my dear, you wear the crest upon your armor. Where else would you be heading, but back home? And, if I might say, you have quite the journey ahead of you."

"Just how far into Caldoor are we?" she asked.

"It's eighteen days to the Findoor border, and another forty or so to the castle."

"By the gods," Malia said, taking a step back. "Perhaps having a guide would not be such a bad thing. We accept your offer, but first, what might we call you?"

"The name is Cedric, the traveling Bard, at your service," he said, making a dramatic bow. "And you, my lady?"

"Malia Corsair, Swordmage in the Findoor army, and this is Seth, a..." she thought a moment about how to describe Seth to Cedric, "...diplomat, from a far off land."

Cedric paused a moment, looking from Malia to Seth, then back again. "Diplomat huh? I've never seen a diplomat catch an arrow like that before. But that's fine, we'll go with that. It's a pleasure to meet you both. Now, we should be going, as night shall be falling soon."

He side-stepped his new companions and led the way down the path, guiding them as promised. Malia and Seth stayed close behind, Malia watching Cedric's every move.

When night fell, Cedric led them off the path to a small clearing in the woods. Several tree trunks rested in the center of the clearing, arranged around a central fire pit like benches. Ashes rested in the pit, remnants of other travelers now long gone. The smell of fragrant burnt hardwood lingered and mixed with wildflowers that grew along the edge of the clearing. Gathering up some fresh wood, Cedric arranged it in the pit, then held out a hand and said, "Incendras." A small fireball shot from his hand into the wood pile, setting it ablaze.

"Holy shit," Seth said, stunned, as the flames licked up the wood and consumed bark and twigs.

Surprised, Cedric turned to Seth. "Something the matter?"

Malia watched Cedric with suspicion while she rested on one of the logs, but said nothing. Seth looked from Cedric, to the now blazing fire, and then back to Cedric. "How... how did you light that? I mean, I was a Boy Scout, we learned all sorts of ways to start campfires, but you did that without friction, or flint, or matches."

"Where did you say you were from again? It's the most basic of spells."

"What do you mean spell? Like... magic?" he asked with a nervous laugh.

"Yes, magic." Cedric looked at Seth with curiosity, his voice level and patient.

Seth opened his mouth to say something again, but Malia cut him off. "Seth is from a distant land where magic is not performed. Perhaps you can teach him?"

Cedric turned his masked face toward Seth. "Certainly. I bet you'll pick it up in no time."

Standing up, Seth turned around and walked away from the fire. His face was pensive and his eyes darted from the ground, to the various flowers growing along the edge of the clearing, then to the sky that filled up with unfamiliar stars as the sun set. "I can't do this, Malia. I can't lie. I'm too confused and upset to maintain any kind of story you might make up. The truth is, Cedric, I don't know what I'm doing here at all. I don't even know where here is. And to be honest, the talk of magic has me thinking more and more that I hit my head pretty darn hard in that accident."

Malia flashed Seth an angry look and opened her mouth to say something, but Cedric cut her off. "Do not be angry with the poor fellow. It's obvious he is under some stress, and besides," he smirked at Seth, "I didn't believe your story anyway."

With a sigh, Malia softened her voice to a gentle, soothing tone. "Seth, come, sit by the fire, and I will try to answer all of your questions the best I can. But you must understand that only Merek will be able to help you find all of the answers you seek."

"I'm always up for a good story," Cedric said, getting as comfortable as he could on another log.

Hesitating at the edge of the clearing, Seth looked around one more time, then turned back to the pair at the fire. "Alright, I'll listen. It's not like I have a choice, right?"

"Thank you, Seth," Malia said. "I am part of the Findoor army, and the only female warrior. I worked for many years and fought hard to get where I am. Initially, I trained as a member of the infantry, taking on swordsmanship and hand-to-hand combat. When I mastered that, Merek took me in as a student and began training me as a Swordmage. A Swordmage is a warrior who is trained in both combat and magic skills, and it has taken me many years to learn what little magic I know. It was this reason that Merek chose me over others to come to your world. An understanding of magic gave me an advantage over other warriors.

"When Krycin defeated Gladius a hundred years ago, he disappeared. Being the last of the Time Weavers, we thought your kind was extinct. Nobody would have guessed that Krycin would take his unborn child to another world. Still, Merek never gave up hope that one day he would find Krycin, or another Time Weaver, and so he trained the Scryes to seek out the signature of a Time Weaver's powers. It was the Scryes who found you."

She went on to tell them about the situation with Merek and Grian, and how Grian betrayed the Kingdom. When she got to the part about how and when she first saw Seth, he perked up and showed particular interest, asking frequent questions, and receiving the best answers Malia could give. She explained what the creature was that attacked him, and who sent it, and how she got back to the rift before it closed. The only blanks she couldn't fill in were how they returned to Galadir, despite them being unconscious, and how long they remained that way before she came to. The discussion took them well into the night, and when she was done, they all laid down in the grass of the clearing to sleep.

As he was about to drift off, Seth spoke up one last time, "Thank you for saving my life, even if I don't remember all the details."

"It is my duty, Seth. I have no intention of failing."

Chapter 10 – Corruption

Grian watched his rift with anticipation. The hum and crackle of the huge hole in the aether filled the clearing where he worked, making many of the Narshuks around it nervous. Rocks and dust littered the dull gray ground, and solid stone walls surrounded them. This location was chosen for just that reason; the tall straight walls were laced with a metal that blocked any attempts to scry on him. Scrag stood beside him--the old gray Narshuk almost twice Grian's height--and tapped his toe claws against the ground, creating a rhythmic clicking sound. *Five years to master the absorption spell, and ten years enduring Merek's "lessons", and all this brute can do is tap his toes,* Grian thought.

The rift wavered and pulsed, like something was about to come through, and Grian smiled. "Here he comes boys, get ready. We don't know what this Time Weaver might do, or what power he possesses."

Narshuks in the clearing all looked to Grian, and then exchanged glances with each other. Most crouched, ready to pounce on the Time Weaver when their warrior brought him back through the rift.

Scrag crouched low and spoke in Grian's ear, trying to keep his voice down, "I still don't know why we could only send one warrior. Your magic is powerful, Grian. We could ready an army."

Turning to face the ancient creature, Grian found himself nose to nose with him. "Because, you imbecile, if we open a rift large enough to send an army through, we would risk shattering the boundaries of our plane. I want to rule this world, not destroy it. Your people have languished in the Badlands for far too long, and yet you survive on nothing but small game. Imagine how your people could thrive in the lush Findoor land? And once we take Findoor, then Caldoor. And after that, we move east. One nation after another will fall before us."

The edges of the rift quivered and shook, sending arcs of lightning out in every direction. Something floated toward them through the rift. Two man-sized figures tethered together, one wearing armor, approached the opening. "That's not a Narshuk coming through with him, be ready," Grian said, his brows lowering with the effort of keeping the rift open. When the pair were no more than twenty feet inside the rift, he realized they were both unconscious. His laughter filled the clearing, overtaking the sounds of the rift and echoing off the walls. "There will be no fight today, they sleep, like..." A sudden convulsion around the edges of the rift cut off his monologue. He struggled to keep it open long enough for the pair to come through, but nothing he did would stop the edges from caving in. The rift collapsed, a force railing against Grian's magic that took him by surprise. He dove at the rift, trying to take hold of the pair that were just inside now, but he was too late. It slammed shut, and his outstretched hand hit the solid wall. "No," he shouted from the ground. "No, no, no, no, no!"

He shook his head and cleared his thoughts as the fury welled up inside him. Getting up, he dusted off his black robes and turned back to Scrag. "What happened? Where – is – my - Time Weaver?" he said, his voice growing louder with each word.

Scrag shied away from the enraged wizard. "Grian," he said in his feral voice, "something closed the rift from within."

Grian lifted his eyes up to meet the Narshuk's blazing red eyes. "Find him. I don't care how, I don't care what it takes. We search to the ends of the multiverse if we have to, but find him!"

Nodding, Scrag backed away. "It will be done." Scrag skulked away from the clearing, muttering to himself in his own language, and made his way to his tent.

Grian was about to do the same when a commotion rose up from just outside the clearing. Howls of pain and sounds of combat drifted in. "Oh what now," he said turning to face the entrance. Blasts of magical energy sent waves through the area and raised the hair on the back of his neck. He watched and listened as the blasts got closer to him. Holding up his hands, he chanted several words, "Clypas custodiasa tuitai." A curtain of blue energy erupted from the ground in a semi-circle around him, reaching up into the sky above him, and then curving over his head and coming down the other side behind him. The edges sealed together creating a barrier around him. Just as his spell completed, seven wizards blasted their way into the clearing, each wearing different colored robes with hoods drawn over their heads, hiding their faces.

Leading the way was the black robe, representing Grishtor, the god of death, then a white robe, representing the god of life, Anam. After that was a gray-robed wizard for Hadra, the goddess of shadow. The red and blue robes came next, taking places to either side of the first three. They represented Ignith, the god of fire, and Philana, the goddess of water, respectively. Coming in last were the yellow and green robes, for Skeiron, the god of air, and Torenna, the goddess of earth. When they took their places at the ends of the line, the black robe stepped forward. "Grian, servant of Grishtor, you will surrender yourself to this council at once and disband any army you might have raised."

Grian let out a chuckle, and looked at the black robe. "This has happened once before, hasn't it?" He paused, and the black robe went to answer, but Grian cut him off. "Oh no, there's no need to answer. I can smell your fear. You come to me, blasting your way in here and speaking your words, but you're scared, because this is familiar. Do you remember when the council approached Gladius, over a hundred years ago? Seven members, just like today. Where is your eighth?"

"I do remember, Grian. As clear as if it happened yesterday. Do not make the same mistakes Gladius did. We will not show the same lenience that we once did." The black robe drew his hood back to expose his ancient face. Lines creased his age-spotted skin, and his white hair flowed long down his back like water over a waterfall.

"Oh come off it father. You know very well that without the eighth, without your precious Time Weaver, you are just a bunch of haggard old men making noise. The council is irrelevant, I will do this with or without your blessing. But know this, I will not tolerate your interference in my plans. If you insist on getting in my way, I will dispatch the lot of you."

The black robe, Grian's father, stepped forward. "You cannot win against all seven of us at once. Although we do not have a Time Weaver, you know this council is strong. Stand down now, and the only charge you face is opening a rift without authorization. Continue on this path, and the consequences of your actions will be much more dire."

"Don't you understand? I no longer owe allegiance to Grishtor for my magic. I call from all elements now." Grian grasped the edge of his black robes and tore them open, casting them to the ground before the High Council. Beneath his robes was a suit of black armor. Thin lines of all colors ran through the steel plates, like threads woven through fabric, and emblazoned on the chest plate was the symbol of a lily with a snake wrapped around the stem. All members of the council gasped.

"You dare don that symbol before this council. Very well, you leave us little choice, Grian. All who bear the mark of Gladius shall be offered no mercy." Grian's father lifted his hands above his head and swept them down, pushing forward like he pushed an invisible force. As he did this, he spoke, "Obitas nexasa mortai."

From his hands erupted a gout of black energy that flew toward Grian like a stream of tar. It slammed into the invisible shield surrounding Grian, oozing over and around it. Grian focused all his strength to maintain the shield, summoning the power of life to counter it. The shield glowed white-hot, burning up the sticky black energy and reflecting some back upon the caster. It hit his father, knocking him back and breaking the spell. The black matter, now laced with strands of white, ate through his father's robes and descended onto his flesh, searing through it and working its way into his body. It spread under his skin, eating at the muscles and spreading through his body leaving black lines over his skin. His screams of agony echoed through the clearing long after he could no longer make a sound, and he was left lying on the ground, his shallow breaths only just keeping him alive.

Grian laughed. "Is that all you've got, father? A member of the High Council, and all you can muster is one measly spell?" His eyes darkened as he stretched his arms and hands out to the side. "I'll show you the true meaning of power."

Stepping forward, Grian focused on all members of the council, drawing massive quantities of energy from every element at once. Each member also summoned their own power to try and defeat Grian. The council finished first, and as each spoke their words, blasts of energy of every color flew toward Grian. Fire and water, lightning and stone all struck the protective shell, creating cracks in it. Pure white holy energy pounded at these cracks and spread them wider, and the illusory powers of shadow threatened to unwind his sanity. All at once, Grian's shield gave out and crumbled. As it collapsed, he spoke the words to his spell, "Infuscas consceleratai."

The words echoed off the walls and pierced the ears of everyone in the room. A wave of energy spread out from Grian, corrupting all other magic. The council's spells turned on their casters, twisting the meaning of their words, and assaulting them with fire, water, earth, air, shadow and life. The screams of the council members pierced the air and echoed for miles around, inciting howls of glory from all Narshuks who heard them. The white robe fell first, his body succumbing to the massive assault. Red bloomed on his robe as blood burst through his skin, his body cooking from the inside out. His eyes exploded, spraying the ground before him with blood and other fluids, and smoke rose from the empty sockets as his brain roasted. The remaining five council members suffered a similar fate, filling the air with the grotesque smell of cooked flesh.

When the air cleared, Grian stepped over to his father, lying on the ground in a puddle of his own blood, his breaths growing quiet. "Grian, what have you done?" the old man said.

"Only what was required, father. This world will be mine. Won't you stand by my side? Tell me you're proud of me. Tell me that I've done well. Look at the power I wield, and tell me you would not seek this for yourself if you could."

The light faded in his father's eyes, and with his dying breath, he said, "You are a corruption of nature. I am ashamed." His head lolled to the side and his breathing stopped. Grian stood up and looked around at the Narshuks in the room. Many of them lay in heaps against the walls, scorched and still. He walked out of the clearing to find something alive, and came across a Narshuk waiting at the edge of the main camp.

"Gather their heads, and take them to the front gates of Findoor. Let them know what's become of their High Council," he said. He then stormed off to his own tent to rest.

Chapter 11 – Answers and Questions

General Mathers sat up all night, wading through pictures, reports and videos of what happened the previous day in the city of Denton. He tried to wrap his head around the event, and began to put the pieces together. Up on his cork board he pinned up several pictures of people or things involved in the event. A picture of Seth, and the girl in the armor, several pictures of places, and strings between all of them to show relationships. Facial recognition systems would not work on account of the helmet the girl wore, and their only positive lead in identifying her was a sample of her blood, which was still at the lab being run for DNA.

The creature was a whole other story. It was brought onto the base about an hour after Mathers got there. The local police took their time getting it there, and Mathers planned on having a word with the chief when he got the chance. The creature was placed in a cooling chamber under tight security, with only Mathers and his appointed scientists having access to it.

Mathers had never seen anything like it. Standing twelve feet tall, it would dwarf even the tallest man. Reports said the girl with the armor cleaved its head clean down the center with her sword. The thing reminded him of a werewolf from the classic horror films he used to watch, only much larger. He shivered just thinking about it again and pushed the pictures underneath some papers on his desk.

Around mid morning a careful, measured knock came at his door. *Well it's certainly not Toby. Must be one of the scientists,* he thought. "Come in," he said toward the door.

The door opened and a middle-aged balding man stepped into the general's office. He wore a white coat and glasses, and squinted at

Mathers before giving him a polite salute. "John MacPherson, sir, from science. Captain Smith sent me up to report to you. The DNA results are back on the girl from the intersection."

Mathers raised his eyebrows, surprised at how fast it could be run when a general told them to hurry. "Well? Do we have a positive ID on the girl yet? Or the creature?"

"Sir, the creature is a species previously unknown to science. It shares some common genes with wolves, but that's the closest thing I can find. Most of its DNA is unique to it." MacPherson didn't seem very interested in the creature's report, but instead flipped through some papers until he found the girl's results. "We have, however, found something interesting in the girl's DNA."

"Well, go on. What's so interesting about this girl?"

"She has 24 chromosome pairs," MacPherson said, as though Mathers should know exactly what he was talking about. The general looked confused, and so the scientist continued. "See, much of her DNA is human, like you and me. But normal humans have only twenty-three chromosome pairs that carry our genetic material. This girl has twenty-four. She has an extra pair, and we think we may have figured out why as well."

Mathers nodded at the scientist to show he was listening. "Go on."

"Sir, the girl's blood reacts to microwave radiation. Based on her DNA, we think her whole body does. It acts like a battery, storing and releasing the radiation in bursts. One of our samples exploded after being left next to a running microwave oven. The organic tissue can harness cosmic background radiation, a type of microwave radiation left over from the big bang. The implications of this are incredible, sir."

Mathers was now much more interested in this information. "What does this mean to us?"

The scientist flipped through some more papers. "Well, what it means is these people can harness energy out of nothing. Magic, as it were. That's how the girl made the officer's gun explode. She heated it up with a burst of microwave energy. If we could synthesize this property and turn it into some kind of gene therapy, the result would be a serum that, when injected, would give our soldiers the ability to harness energy the way they do. But that's not the best part, Sir."

"So what's the best part?"

"We analyzed Alkirk's DNA sir. We're not really sure what to make of it. It's infinitely more complex than a normal human's DNA." He flipped through more papers until he found some images captured from an electron microscope. "When we first tried to sequence his DNA, the sequencer wouldn't work. We tried five times, and got nothing back. So, one of the men on the team suggested we take a look at it using the electron microscope. What we saw was incredible. A normal human's DNA is a double helix pattern, made up of base pairs. Alkirk's DNA is a triple helix pattern, made up of base triples, and contains more complex information than ours."

Mathers thought about this, trying not to focus on the technical aspects of it. "So when we boil this down to basics, what you're saying is, Seth Alkirk is not human?"

"Yes sir, that's exactly what we're saying. I'm not sure where he came from, but nothing on earth can produce DNA like that. We're not even sure we can call it DNA. Seth is an evolution above humans. His genetic material resists mutation. Research into this could yield an end to all genetic diseases. Perhaps even an end to all viral infections. The possibilities are endless sir. It's a scientific and medical miracle."

A smile spread across the general's face. "Excellent work. I want you to start research on creating that serum you talked about right away. Report to Toby Smith on your progress; he will keep me updated. We'll hold onto the Alkirk research for now. Don't breathe a word of it to anybody, we don't need the media breathing down our necks any more than they already are."

MacPherson wrote down several notes as the General spoke, "Yes sir." With that, he turned and left the office.

Chapter 12 – Waking Up

When Seth woke up the next morning, it took him several minutes to orient himself. Deep down, he hoped he would wake up at home in his bed. There was a twang of disappointment that hit him as he looked around and saw the clearing, the trees, and the smoldering remains of the campfire. Once he was alert enough to get up, he reached out and laced his fingers together and stretched his arms. Sleeping on the ground left his muscles stiff, but he managed to get himself moving. Malia's voice started him out of his wake-up routine when she stared at him in disbelief. "Seth, your hand!"

He looked at his fingers, arm, then back at her. "What?"

"When we went to sleep you had a broken hand. How can you now stretch it like nothing happened?" she asked.

Seth held his right hand up and flexed his fingers. "I don't know."

Cedric sat up and turned his masked face toward the pair. "Regeneration? How odd and unlikely that an ability thought lost to our world, suddenly turns up here and now. Lyecians wielding water magic could do that, but there haven't been any Lyecians on Galadir in almost a hundred years. Not since the Lyecian war. Then again, now that I think back on my teachings, you do look an awful lot like Krycin, the hero of the war."

Staring at Cedric with a blank expression, Seth shrugged. "I have no idea what you're talking about. I mean, I recognize the names, but only from my father's stories, and those were just fairy tales."

"Fairy tales?" Cedric said, with some amusement, "I've heard Fairies tell quite good tales actually. Have you ever considered that your father's stories might have held more truth to them than he let on?"

Confused and stunned at the same time, Seth took a minute to decide what to say first. "No... no, they were just stories. He sold used cars, for god's sake. He worked hard, too hard from what little I can remember of him. Spent very little time at home. And when all was said and done, no matter how devoted he seemed, he left us all alone with no explanation. The only reason I even think of him anymore is because of this stupid book." He kicked the laptop bag that rested at his feet to emphasize his point.

Cedric stood up and walked over to the bag. "Is that what's in there. Might I see it? Would you mind?"

"No, go ahead. I don't even know why I'm still carrying it around with me."

Leaning down to open the bag, Cedric examined it, picked it up, turned it over in his hands, and passed it over to Seth. "Would you mind? I'm rather embarrassed to say that I can't find the clasp."

Seth reached over and took the bag, set it down, and pointed at the zipper-pull. "Pull that."

Cedric followed the simple instruction, then looked up at Seth with a broad smile. "Marvelous. I've never seen a closure like that before. What do you call it?"

"It's a zipper," Seth said with a smirk.

Malia let out a laugh of her own at the Bard's expense as he lifted the leather-bound book out of the bag. "Fascinating. I've seen a great many books in my time, enough to know a valuable one when I see it, and this, my friend, is priceless." Cedric ran a finger down the plate on the front of the book, then scoffed when it did nothing. "It's keyed as well. Can you open it?"

Reaching down, Seth ran his fingers over the plate in the same way as Cedric. There was a loud click from the lock and the band that held the book closed released. "Yeah, but I've had the book for twenty-five years and could never get it open until a few days ago."

"Indeed." Cedric opened the cover and saw the symbol on the first page, the crown with a sword through it. "Findoor," he said to himself, then turned the page. "High Lyecian script. Seth, whether you want to believe it or not, the evidence is here. I believe you are Krycin's son, and thus, that makes you a Lyecian as well. You might very well be the last Time Weaver in existence."

"No," Seth said, standing up and turning his back to the other two. "No, that's not it. I don't know what's going on, or what evidence you think you have, but I'm not a Time Weaver. I can't stop time, I can't cast spells or use magic, and my father was *not* Krycin.

Krycin is a character from a fairy tale, and so is Merek, and this," he motioned all around him, "this is just a really bad dream, a head injury from a car accident, and I'm going to wake up in a hospital, and everything is going to be okay. Back to life as normal, no more hocus pocus, or stories, or magic, or Time Weavers, or Galadir. Nothing." With that, he stormed away from the campsite and into the forest.

Cedric and Malia looked at each other, then at the spot at the forest edge where Seth had stomped the growth down. "Touchy," Cedric said.

"One of us should go after him. Would you mind? I am afraid I will not be able to keep up with him with my wounds," Malia said.

"Never fear, I'll have him back here in a twinkling."

With that, Cedric swept away in a flourish of cloak and passed into the forest. He moved as fast as his feet could carry him through the thick forest, following the trail that Seth left. Despite still being early morning, the forest was well-lit, which made following easier. Beams of light broke through the treetops and shone down on the undergrowth giving it the valuable light it craved, and the smell of fresh morning growth filled his senses. Birds chirped their happy morning songs and various ground foragers scrambled away as the masked Bard made his way after Seth.

It took only a few minutes of walking before Cedric could see a drop-off ahead. Seth stood at the edge looking out over the ravine. They faced south, and the forest continued at the bottom of the cliff, creating a lush green blanket that spread out before them. He slowed his pace as he approached the fragile man. *And now for some fancy footwork to convince him to come back,* he thought.

About ten feet from Seth, he spoke up, "It's beautiful, isn't it?"

Seth started and turned to face him, tear lines ran down his face. He wiped his cheeks with his wrist to try to hide the fact that he'd been crying. "Yeah, I guess," he said, turning back to the landscape.

Cedric walked up next to him. "I mean, I see this all the time, and it never fails to amaze me. But perhaps your world is a vast improvement over this." He didn't face Seth as he spoke, but kept his gaze fixed on the scenery.

"No, you're right. I've never seen something as beautiful as this. Where I live, all you can see are buildings, power lines, cars, and smog. They cut forests like this down to make way for farm land, or development projects. And the sky is never this clear. There are always contrails left in the sky from planes flying around, and light pollution at night from the city lights."

"It sounds positively splendid," Cedric said with mock enthusiasm.

"Really?"

Cedric flashed him a grin. "No, not really. I wouldn't trade this for anything. There's not enough gold in this world to make me leave it. I imagine you feel much the same about your home, and yet you were taken from it without even a choice. I don't blame you for being upset."

"It's not even that. It's just that this is all so far-fetched."

"I agree, Seth. We all have challenges to face in our lives, and I can tell that this is one of the biggest ones you've ever faced. But have faith in us and we shall not let you down."

Seth turned to face Cedric. "Really? Can you promise me that if I stick with you two, everything will be okay?"

"I'm certain Malia will do her utmost to protect you, and the lands from here to Findoor castle are pretty safe and well-traveled."

Returning his gaze to the forest, Seth thought for a long time, taking in the sights. After several more minutes, he said, "Alright, I'm sorry I ran off like that. I don't even know where I would go."

"Come on back to camp, I'll show you the spell I promised to teach you."

Seth hesitated, then turned and began walking back the way he came. "Sure, but keep in mind I've never done this before."

Cedric laughed as he followed. "Oh not to worry, I've never taught anyone before either."

The three companions sat around the smoldering remains of the fire from the night before. Cedric gathered up some fresh wood and set it up in the pit as small separate piles around the edge. Before he began, he looked up at Seth with a smirk. "Now be careful, we're playing with fire here. We don't want anyone getting burned."

Seth nodded, with a nervous look on his face.

"Right then. There are three steps to casting a spell. First, clear your mind of all stray thoughts and distractions. This is of particular importance, as this can cause you to miscast the spell, which can be rather detrimental. Whatever you do, don't skip this. Second, draw the energy to you to fuel the spell. This will be the most challenging step for you, as I don't think you'll even know what you're looking for. And finally, speak the words to focus the energy into the desired shape or form. In our case, we are focusing the energy into fire. You must pronounce the words with perfect inflection, or the spell will not come out right. Are you ready?"

"Yeah, I guess. Ready as I'll ever be," Seth said.

"Excellent. The spell we will cast is a single word. Like I said, simple. Incendras."

Seth echoed the word back to Cedric, "Incendras."

"Good. Don't forget it. Practice it a few more times if it makes you more comfortable. We're not in any rush."

"No, I think I'll manage. Incendras. Got it."

"Excellent. Now, you need to clear your mind of everything. Close your eyes, and focus only on my voice," Cedric said with a calm tone.

Seth obeyed, closing his eyes and listening for the sound of Cedric's voice.

"Forget about us. Forget about life, and troubles. Forget about your world and our world. None of it matters. Clear your mind of all your questions, all your troubles. Now think of a focus, something important to you that you can use to center yourself. Visualize it, see it, touch it, smell it. Let it drift out before you. Feel the world around you pressing in, and let it. Let the energy of the world fill you up, and direct that energy into your focus. Energize it, until it won't hold anymore, until it's bursting to let that power free. Then open your eyes, hold your hand out, point it palm up toward the camp fire, and speak the words."

Following the instructions, Seth cleared his mind until all was black before him. A calm washed over him, and he summoned into his thoughts the only constant in his life right now, his father's book. He saw the book before him, its metal reinforcements and leather bindings. The gentle smell of the old pages filled his senses as the book opened and the pages flipped, the black symbols filling page after page.

The world around him pressed in, and he allowed it, pulling the energy in and focusing it in the book. As he did, the symbols lit up with gold light that glittered as the pages continued to turn. Once the flow started into the book, Seth found the energy moved easily, like a river flowing through him, and into it. The image of the book grew brighter as it now pulled at the energy, as if it hungered for it, and Seth was the only supply. He thought he had control, but when he attempted to finish the spell, to open his eyes and speak the word, nothing came to him. The word was gone, and his body wouldn't respond. Still, the book in his mind's eye consumed the power from the world around him, pulling faster, trying to take even more through Seth than he was able to give. It pulled at his thoughts, his very essence, and still was not sated.

The more power it consumed, the more it wanted until finally the flow was like a torrent racing through Seth, and the book shone like a sun before him. The pages continued to flip, and when they got to the end, they would turn over and flip the other direction. A nagging feeling came over Seth, a compulsion to read, and so he read from the book, upside down, from the back to the front.

Unlike before, he found he could read it, and the stories held within. He remembered it all from his youth, the stories of Merek and Krycin and their travels through the world. The stories of Findoor and its fine warriors and unbeatable army. And at the end of the book, the Dark Lord Gladius, and his bid to annihilate Findoor that was thwarted by Krycin. When he got to the final battle, he saw the word, and it burned through his head.

Incendras.

Seth opened his eyes and turned his palm out toward the wood in the fire pit. With a glorious display of fire and heat, all the energy he took in erupted from his hand and blasted down onto the wood in the pit. The wave of hot air from it spread out in a circle and billowed up to the tops of the trees. He thought the stream of fire would never end, but then the symbols in the book in his mind faded to black, and the image of the book dispersed.

The flames sputtered out, and Seth was left sitting at the side of the pit with Malia and Cedric staring at him, open mouthed. When the smoke cleared from the pit, all that remained was ash.

"By the gods," Malia said, still staring at him.

Seth looked up at his companions like nothing had happened. "What?"

Cedric walked over to him and knelt down to look in his eyes. "'What?' You nearly incinerated us, and half the forest, without speaking a word."

Seth returned a blank stare. "Oh," he said, "sorry. All I saw was my father's book." His gaze shifted down to the smoking ashes in the fire pit. "I did that?"

"Indeed, you did. And I believe this settles it. Whether you want to believe it or not Seth, it doesn't change who or what you are. You are a Time Weaver, and might very well be the last of your kind. There is no other race, nor other person who can manipulate that much power with just a thought. What I don't understand is how you can be your age without knowing what you are. A Time Weaver's powers normally manifest around their coming of age." Cedric shook his head and said, "This isn't right. There is somebody we must go and see. Let us be off and visit that town, and then we shall pay a visit to an old friend of mine."

Malia opened her mouth to object, but Cedric raised his hand and cut her off.

"I insist. It shall not hinder our journey to Findoor, and if anything, may actually speed it along. I swear to you, we shall be parading through the front gates of Findoor castle in no time."

The three companions packed their things up and set out on the merchant trails once again. It took six more days to reach their destination. Malia's knee no longer bothered her unless she put direct pressure on it. The trails were easy to navigate and the weather was warm and sunny for the duration. Seth did not attempt any further magic along the way, at the insistence of the others, and remained quiet and reserved. Most of the time he was lost in his own thoughts, or watching the scenery go by. Occasionally he was distracted by some plant or animal at the edge of the trail, and Cedric took the time to explain what they were and how they could be used, and the general history of the subject, proving himself to be an infinite well of information. By the time they reached the small town, both Seth and Malia felt more comfortable with the Bard's presence.

Walking into the town, Seth could see an inn and tavern, what passed for a blacksmith, and several other shops and stores. Surrounding the main commercial area were many small houses, and at the center of it all was a tall building with ornate stone walls and a peaked roof. On the double doors of the largest building was a symbol that looked like two S shapes turned sideways, like waves, with a spot under the right side of the bottom wave. All around them, children played and men and women worked, doing all the things that Seth took for granted. Women scrubbed the washing against washboards in large tubs, wrangled children who ran about laughing and playing games, swept front porches, and any other number of domestic tasks. Men hammered steel at the smith's, chopped wood, skinned and butchered animals, and tended the fields in the surrounding farmlands.

Cedric walked out in front of them, turned, and bowed. "As promised, all you could ever need for tired feet and empty stomachs, the merchant town of Ely. Now, if you don't mind, I shall find myself a room and retire for the night." With a smile, and a flourish, he turned and walked off toward the inn, his mask flashing in the remaining sunlight of the day.

Seth turned to Malia and asked, "So where do we find a doctor in this place? We need to get that knee fixed up."

He was met with a confused gaze. "Doctor? I am unsure what a doctor is, but there is a temple to Philana right there. We should be able to find a healer inside," Malia motioned toward the tall building at the center of the courtyard, "though it will not be free." She took out a small pouch that she carried at her waist and rustled through it. There was a jingle, like coins hitting together, and then she pulled out a small handful of copper.

He reached over to take one, asking Malia, "Do you mind?"

"Not at all."

Seth took a coin and examined it. It was discolored and worn, but the stampings were still visible and easy to make out. On one side was a lily wrapped in vines, and the other side had a crown with a sword through it. He looked up at Malia and smiled. "It's amazing how similar our worlds can be, and yet so different." He reached into his pocket and pulled out some change. The coins were much smaller than Malia's, a selection of pennies, nickels, dimes and quarters. She examined them with genuine interest, then smiled back at him.

"Those won't do you any good here though," she said as she turned to make her way to the temple.

Seth followed, putting the coins back in his pocket. As they walked up to the door of the temple, he asked, "Who is Philana anyway?"

She stopped and turned to face him. "She is the goddess of Water, element of life. Her priests will be able to mend my bones."

"More magic then?"

"Yes. Pay attention, it may come in handy. If you are anything with water magic like you are with fire, you'll be able to heal even the most critical of wounds. But I doubt it," she said, giving him a somber look.

"Doubt it? Why?"

"Because most people can only wield magic from one element, sometimes two. The gods are careful in their choices. The two most powerful wizards in history could only wield seven of the eight elements. Time Weavers often have two, but only because you are the sole keepers of time. Only children of Lyecha can wield that element." She looked at the door when she finished and reached for the handle. "Come, we should get on with this. Night will fall soon."

Seth followed Malia into the temple. The inside of the temple was more ornate than the outside. Rows of pews ran up each side of the room creating a central aisle that led to a platform at the other end. The outer walls were covered with large detailed tapestries showing incredible storms, tidal waves and whirlpools on one side, and calm rivers, waterfalls and oceans on the other. The moment Malia stepped through the doors, she used a crutch to lower herself to the floor, bowed her head, and mumbled a prayer. At the far end of the room on the platform, a man dressed in blue robes also knelt in prayer. Hearing people enter the temple, he stood up and turned toward them. His voice rang out across the room, sounding as if he were standing before them, "Come in, my friends, all are welcome."

Malia used her crutch to lift herself up, refusing help from Seth. With much reverence, she spoke, "Elder, forgive our intrusion. I am in need of aid, if you would give it."

The elder nodded, his face calm and wearing a slight smile. "Nonsense, child. Come, let us see the wound, and pray that our goddess wills it done." He led her up the center aisle to the altar at the front of the room. "Lie down."

Malia laid down on the altar and let the elder remove the splint and bandages. Though there were no open wounds under the bandages, having been healed by her own magic, her knee was various shades of black, blue and purple.

The healer placed his hands over the wound, without touching it, and closed his eyes. A blue glow encompassed his hands. He spoke a single word, "Restitas."

The soft blue light streamed from his hands and surrounded her knee. An audible crack echoed through the room and Malia screamed with pain as the bones set. A moment later there was a tiny clink as something metallic fell and landed on the altar. The glow flared up and lit the room like daylight, before it died down and disappeared.

Malia breathed a sigh of relief as the elder stood up and offered her a hand. She stood up and applied weight to her knee and found it now supported her. Turning to the elder, she reached into her pouch and pulled out some coins but he stopped her and said, "There is no need for payment. Our goddess grants these miracles so that we might all fulfill a purpose. Your purpose has yet to come."

Malia bowed low. "I am in your debt, elder."

The elder turned to face Seth and lowered his voice, "My child, I sense that your friend is lost, or out of place. Physically and spiritually. Help him find his way."

Malia smiled at him and nodded. "Yes, elder, I will. Thank you again." She bowed once more and walked back to Seth. "Let us find the smithy so that I can get my armor repaired, and then we can get a good meal."

"Sounds good," Seth said, following close behind her as she led the way out of the temple.

The rest of the night passed without event. They paid a visit to the local blacksmith, and haggled a good price to get Malia's armor repaired, and they bought some chain armor for Seth. Malia insisted that Seth carry at least a short sword "just in case" and promised to teach him how to use it when they had time.

Getting a room at the local inn gave them a place to sleep and the tavern below provided a hearty meal. Seth wasn't sure what he was eating, even though Malia named most of it. A stew with chunks of gamy-tasting meat, some kind of root vegetable that was a cross between potato and carrot, and a host of other morsels, followed by some of the most mouth-watering desserts he'd ever tasted.

At the end of the night, after food, lodging, weapons, armor, and some new clothes for Seth, Malia had only a few coppers left. The room they got at the inn had only one bed, which Seth insisted Malia take. He slept in a chair that felt comfortable, but by the morning, he was stiff and sore.

Neither of them dreamed.

Chapter 13 – Found and Lost

Merek slept a long natural sleep after speaking with the Scryes. Rebuilding his magical reserves after he had drained himself took time. He awoke to a shout in his head that jarred him out of his dreams. *The Time Weaver, he is found!*

He clutched his head, unprepared for such an intrusion on his mind. *Easy friends, you shout,* he responded to the Scryes. They never invaded his mind like that, even though their minds were bonded by magic. The Scryes had always respected Merek's individuality before that day.

The Time Weaver, he comes! They eased a small amount after Merek's reprimand, but they remained excited.

My friends, this is splendid news, where is he? And what of Malia?

In the setting sun, with a gleam of hope at his side. Merek smiled at their cryptic response, glad to hear that Malia made it back alive with her charge, and surmised from their response that they were somewhere to the west.

Easy friends. Thank you. Your task is done. Merek severed the connection to them and opened his eyes. Remembering where he was, he sat up and saw the matron still there doting over him.

"Oh, you're awake again, dear," she said as Merek swung his legs out of bed to place his feet on the floor, his joints protesting as he did so.

"Yes, mum, and the better for it too. I am fine now, you may take your leave," Merek said in a matter-of-fact way. "And fetch me a runner on your way out. I must confer with the King at his earliest convenience. It is a matter of great importance."

The matron walked out the door, muttering to herself about bossy old wizards as she left. Merek smiled to himself and stood up to get himself back into his gray robes. Once dressed, he left the room, making sure to close the door behind him.

Outside, the runner sent by the matron waited for instructions. Merek approached him and said, "Go and inform the King that I am well, and request an audience at the earliest possible convenience. It is a matter of great urgency."

"Yes, Magus," the runner said. He then turned, and walked away as quickly as was polite, breaking into a run at the end of the hall. Merek made his way to the upper levels of the castle, to the throne room where he would meet with the King. By the time Merek arrived, Verand's court had already gathered and were seated.

"What news is this I hear?" Verand asked as Merek entered the room.

"I have news of the Time Weaver, Sire. Malia was successful in her bid to retrieve him, but I'm afraid we know nothing more than that at this time. The Scryes inform me that he is currently located to the west, though I know not how far. He is under our protection." Merek paused for breath, and Verand broke in.

"Well then. This would be the second order of good news for you today. We received a delivery this morning, carried by Narshuk. We had archers posted at the gates dispatch the beast." He motioned to a large sack resting on the floor before his throne. The bag was made of a coarse burlap, the kind that root vegetables would be stored in, and was stained with large patches of dried blood. Several small insects buzzed around the bag, and the faint smell of rot hung in the air. Turning to a sickly looking servant standing next to the bag, Verand said, "Show the Arch-Magus what he has brought down upon us."

The servant twisted his face up in an expression of disgust as he removed the hemp rope that held the bag closed. He upturned it, dumping its contents on the floor. Seven large objects tumbled out of the bag, one of which rolled across the floor and came to a rest at Merek's feet. Heads, shorn from their bodies, rested on the red carpet between Merek and the King. The one at Merek's feet had a small swatch of black fabric stuffed in its mouth, its eyes frozen open in an expression of horror. The skin was starting to dry, but the brains that yet remained in them were rotting and oozing out, and maggots squirmed through them, frantically trying to get out of the air and back into the nourishing dead meat. "By the gods," Merek said, backing up a step.

"Yes, Merek, all seven of them. So I gather you shall have no fear of retribution from the High Council for your indiscretion." Verand laughed, but it came out more like a cackle that raised the hair on the back of Merek's neck. "Rejoice, Merek. We've retrieved the Time Weaver, and you shall not face death for it. Good news all around, is it not?" His voice increased in volume as he spoke to overcome the murmuring of the court, who were just coming out of their own state of shock at seeing the gruesome display.

Merek shook his head, his eyes filled with fear and sorrow. "His own father. Grian's soul is more tarnished than I thought." He turned his gaze to Verand, who sat on his throne with a smug expression on his face. "And you, your Highness, should be ashamed of yourself."

"For what? Speaking the truth? It was your apprentice who did this, and it was your teachings that led him to it. And we shan't forget where he obtained the magics in order to accomplish this task. I am not blind, Merek. I can see what you're doing here."

Rage filled the ancient wizard as Verand spoke. He stood up to his full height, his eyes fierce. "You dare to accuse me of such treachery? While our enemy gathers his armies at our borders, and strips our defenses, you would place the blame on the one person who sought to remedy the situation? What did you do to prevent this? Did you consult your court? Talk it over with advisers? Sit in your throne while the enemy consorted with one of our own, who was only placed beneath me at the request of the council themselves? At the request of his father, whose head now lies at my feet?

"No, your Highness, this is no fault of mine, but the simple scheming of one touched by a darkness so foul it consumes his very soul, and an ignorant King who refuses to see the truth right in front of him. But there is hope still." Merek's voice took on a calm, level tone.

Verand shook his head and scoffed. "And what hope is that, Merek? To defend against a phantom army? Grian is but one man. We have an entire army. The Time Weaver will be safe in our keeping, and should that vagrant apprentice of yours show his face in Findoor again, he shall suffer a wrath like no man has ever known."

"Verand, listen to reason. Deploy our armies to the southern borders; confront the enemy before they set foot on our land. The Narshuks yet remain disorganized and scattered, we can stop this madness now. Grian will come for the boy, and he will not stop until he takes him."

Verand's face darkened as he stood up. "You dare speak to me like that? In my own court? I should have you hanged for treason. We have no evidence that the Kingdom is in any real danger. Just a scare tactic from a fool who thinks he can bully the greatest Kingdom Galadir has ever known. Take your friends," he waved his hand out toward the heads scattered about the carpet, "and get out of my court. Leave the business of running the Kingdom to the real men, and go back to your Scryes."

Merek looked about the court to each of the councilors. "Surely there must be one man in this room with some sense? Can you not see the danger? These seven men were the most powerful wizards on Galadir. You can see with your own eyes what Grian has done. If he is allowed to summon up an army of Narshuks, it will be the Lyecian war all over again. Except this time, there will be no savior, only death and destruction as Grian sweeps across the land." He paused, looking for any sign that a councilor would side with him. Each one turned to face their King.

Defeated, Merek turned to walk from the chamber. As he reached the door, Verand called after him, "Take your friends with you."

Turning to face the King once more, Merek said, "Clean up your own mess."

He then turned, and stormed out of the throne room, letting the doors slam behind him. The sound echoed down the corridors, and was heard throughout most of the castle.

Chapter 14 – Cracking the Code

General Mathers sat in a bunker, watching as various scientists set up equipment around a young man sitting on a stool. An old M1A2 Abrams tank was parked on the field in front of him. The summer sun beat down on the roof of the bunker, making it stifling hot inside. Heat rising off the dusty ground outside could be seen as waves dancing in the air. Sweat poured off all of the officers present, making the still air smell like a locker room after a football game.

Mathers looked over at Toby next to him and scoffed. "Are you sure this serum works?"

"Yes, sir. You won't be disappointed."

"We'll see about that. If he's as good as you say he is, we will be putting it into mass production immediately."

They watched and waited as the final preparations were made, and then the lead scientist came back into the bunker. He saluted the general as he approached. "Sir, we're ready to begin the demonstration."

Mathers gave him a nod. "Go on then, don't keep me waiting."

"Yes sir." He turned and walked back out to the field and stood beside the soldier. He said a word or two to the man, and then pointed at the tank.

A voice came over the speaker in the bunker. "Specter Project, Firing one in three, two." The speaker went dead, but nothing happened. The soldier stood up off the stool and lowered his hands, palm down, to his sides. Closing his eyes, he remained still for a moment, then lifted his hands, put them together, and pointed them toward the tank.

From the palms of his hands came a stream of fire that blasted into the side of the tank, blowing a hole through it in seconds and coming out the other side. Everything the flames touched melted and oozed. The air around it shimmered with the intense heat, and smoke now billowed up from the wrecked tank. Moments later the tank collapsed in on itself, melted from within.

Mathers had seen many a weapons demonstration during his command. Most of them were either too complex or heavy to be used in the field, or just plain didn't work. He wasn't ready for what he saw before him and bellowed in surprise, "Jesus Christ!" He stared in disbelief at the destructive force the soldier could produce. Smoke rising from the wreckage of the tank carried with it a brimstone smell mixed with burnt oil and electronics.

Toby gestured to a scientist to get his attention and said, "Go and get some fans to clear the field, and turn the ventilation up full blast." The scientist nodded and hurried off to accomplish his tasks. He then turned back to Mathers. "Sir, we had some trouble coming up with something that would work with only the girl's DNA. Turns out they aren't as similar to humans as we thought. But when we added Alkirk's DNA to the mix, the results were, as you can see, staggering. We haven't unlocked all the secrets of this powerful serum, but we know that he can produce superheated plasma, and can heat up and ignite flammable objects with a thought."

Mathers looked at Toby, getting over his awe. The soldier who performed the demonstration was visibly tired now, and was resting on the stool. "So he needs no weapon. We just put him in some armor, and send him out to the field to..."

Interrupting the general, Toby said, "Uh, no sir. No armor. We tried that. It works by harnessing microwave energy from the surrounding area, and focusing it into some desired effect. Put him in armor, and it disrupts the flow of radiation. Also, his cellular structure can only handle so much energy. A blast like the one he just did will leave him fatigued for hours. If he uses it too much, it would tear him apart."

Mathers nodded. "Good work Toby. This project is seeing greater results than I ever imagined. My report will be issued to the Pentagon later today, and I will be recommending that we go to full production as soon as possible." He thought for a moment. "How often does it need to be administered? The serum I mean."

"Once, sir. The effects are permanent. We are altering the subject's DNA, which is no easy task. To undo it could kill him."

"Have the science team work on a way to neutralize the effects. If one of these soldiers goes AWOL, who knows how much damage they could cause."

"Yes, sir."

"Toby, this is the biggest discovery this world has seen since the invention of the atomic bomb. Make sure this project remains classified."

It was a quiet day in New Orleans that same afternoon. Many people stayed in their houses or shops, preferring to huddle in the air conditioning rather than brave the hot sun. Sundown would bring cool night air, with neon lights and drunks and prostitutes walking the streets. But one man wasn't waiting for the sun to go down. Dressed up in a black suit, with a black dress shirt, jacket, and broad brimmed hat, the well-groomed man walked up the street with confidence, his black leather boots clicking on the sidewalk as he went. Long black hair rested down the middle of his back, brushed straight and tied into a ponytail. His face was that of a middle-aged man, but free of wrinkles and blemishes, and despite spending most of his time outdoors, remained pale. A trimmed mustache and beard decorated his face below deep black eyes that sent shivers down the spines of those who looked into them. *Twenty-five years I've waited for this,* he thought as he strolled along, looking for something.

He passed by shops and taverns, not giving them a second glance, instead focusing his gaze on the road. Several cars drove by, and he walked several city blocks before he stopped, a broad smile spreading over his face. *Perfect.*

Coming up the street was a black Cadillac. It was a classic; elegant and polished to a fine shine. The man who drove it was an overweight politician or lawyer by the looks of him, who paid no attention to anything but that which was right in front of him.

The Man in Black turned on his heels and walked out onto the street to stand before the moving vehicle. Facing the car and its occupant, he held out a hand, palm facing out, and said in a smooth, melodic southern voice, "Stop." The driver paid no attention to what was in front of him, but his body obeyed the command and hit the brakes, stopping the car just short of hitting him.

"Get out of the way, asshole," the driver said, blasting his horn at the Man in Black.

He met the driver's gaze, locking eyes with him. "Now, is that any way to speak to a stranger?" Taking a step to the side, he again gave a command, "Come on out here and talk to me."

"Are you kidding me? I'm not gonna come out there. Get the hell out of my way before I-" his words were cut off as he realized he was again moving without meaning to. He reached for the door handle, pulled it and pushed open the door. "What the..." he said as he stepped out of the car.

The Man in Black walked toward him with slow, purposeful steps until he stood face-to-face with the driver. Leaning into him, he whispered in the driver's ear, "Walk until your feet bleed." His soft voice turned the aggressive man docile, sending a wave of calm over him as he turned and began to walk down the street away from his car. When he was out of sight, the Man in Black smiled to himself, got in the car, and drove away. *Now,* he thought, *to find the Lyecian.*

Chapter 15 – In Pursuit

Grian watched out over the plateau below him, the dark and rocky landscape of the Badlands looking like a wasteland. The sky was perpetually gray here, and it rained often, leaving the gathering Narshuk army wet and reeking of damp fur and sweat. Each hour the mass of creatures grew, all seeking to exact their own revenge on the civilized world for dooming them to live in the harsh wilderness. A cool wind blew from the west that gave Grian chills. He looked up in the sky and saw storm clouds approaching. As he was watching the deep black clouds swirl and churn in the sky, Scrag approached him from behind. Grian turned to face the ancient creature; it peered at him with its beady eyes and snorted. "Must you be so utterly disgusting?" asked Grian.

Scrag ignored the insult. "Grian, I have located the Time Weaver." The common tongue was difficult for Narshuks to speak, and so many syllables were drawn out, and some were missed as his mouth was incapable of producing the sound, yet Grian got the gist of what he was saying most of the time.

Grian brightened up at the news. "Well? Don't just stand there drooling. Out with it, where is he?"

Scrag snuffled and scowled at Grian. "He is in the western region of Caldoor accompanied by a Findoor Swordmage."

"So, the old man beat me to him then. What are they doing in Caldoor? Hiding?"

"I do not know. It appears that is where they re-entered our world. The Time Weaver must have closed our rift, and opened another in Caldoor."

Grian turned away from the growing army and trudged back to his command tent, while Scrag followed close behind. Inside the tent were tables filled with maps of the Badlands, Findoor, Caldoor, and many other places at the farther reaches of the world. A lantern hanging at the peak of the tent provided enough light to read by. Though it was mid-morning, the dense cloud cover made the Badlands feel like they were clothed in perpetual darkness. The only other furnishings in the room were a cot to sleep on, and a rack of weapons near the entrance.

He walked over to a map of Caldoor and flattened it out, placing weights at each corner, then looked at Scrag. "Show me where he is."

Scrag hobbled up to the map, hunched over so that he would not damage the tent. Placing a single claw on the map, he growled out a few unintelligible words and the map came to life. In the northeastern corner of the map was a dot that moved eastward at a slow, steady pace. Scrag lifted his claw and stabbed it down onto the dot, and an image appeared on the map. A man, wearing new clothes and a chain shirt, walked alongside a fully armored Findoor warrior. Another man, ahead of the other two, wore all black, with a mask over his face.

"This man, this..." he paused for a moment, trying to think of the right word, "pathetic excuse for a man, can control the flow of magical energy? Is a master of space and time?"

"Yes, Grian. Do not underestimate him," Scrag said, staring into the image. The Time Weaver stopped and looked around, exchanging words with his companions. He then looked up and stared back at them. Letting out a whimper, Scrag lifted his claw from the map and the image dispersed.

"He could see us?" Grian asked.

Scrag nodded, but didn't say a word.

"So, he's mastered shadow. That, combined with time, makes a formidable opponent. Send only our best, Scrag. I want him alive."

"Yes, Grian. I shall send the Elite."

"Excellent. Keep me updated on your progress, and once you have captured the runt, bring him to me. He will complete my work and give me access to time. All eight elements in the palm of my hand." A dark smile spread over Grian's face.

Scrag left Grian's tent in a foul mood. *Human swine*, he thought, *treating me like a common slave. Once I have the Time Weaver, I can do*

away with that worthless piece of human filth who leads us, and raise the Dark Lord.

Scrag made his way to the camp of the Elites to give them their instructions. The Elites had splintered off into their own camp away from the others. They considered themselves above the rest and so would not share a camp. Scrag didn't care about their politics; all he cared about was getting the job done.

He approached the edge of their camp and announced himself. Despite their animal appearance, the Narshuks followed a complex system of etiquette that could cost one their life for even a simple breach. Scrag waited for an invitation into the camp, and then proceeded, bowing low as he did.

A rather large Elite met him just outside of their common area, where they did most of their training. Scrag lowered his head to the Elite in a show of respect, which was returned in kind by the Elite. It spoke in the Narshuk tongue, "Master Scrag, you have orders?"

"You are to gather the Elites. There is a human you must recover and return to me, alive."

The Elite returned what would pass for a nod. "Just one human? Is he guarded?"

"He is guarded by a single female soldier and a Bard. It is imperative that the human not be harmed. Fetch him, and return him to me." Scrag spoke very matter-of-fact with the Elite.

"And what of the female?" the Elite inquired.

"Do with her as you please; she is unimportant. I will transport you to their location. They are currently located at the northeast corner of Caldoor, and time is of the essence."

"Very well, Master Scrag."

He turned and stalked away toward the training grounds to alert the others. Scrag followed and waited at the grounds for the rest to arrive.

Twenty minutes later, the Elite gathered in a large circle around Scrag. The one who met him at the edge of the camp approached. "We are all accounted for."

Scrag looked around at the circle of hulking monsters before him, then reached into his satchel for a small crystal pendant. As he handed it to the beast he told them all, "I will transport you to Caldoor. When you have the prisoner, crush this crystal and you will be returned to me. The man is to be unharmed."

There was a pause, and a final bark of approval from the group, then Scrag let out a long keening howl as he drew magical energy to him. Focusing it through an amulet that hung around his neck, he sent a wave of light out around him that encompassed the group. When the wave dissipated, the Elites were gone.

Returning to the plateau, Grian looked out at the army below him. Thousands of Narshuks gathered under his command, ready to wreak havoc on the world that had forgotten them. He cleared his throat, and then raised his voice as loud as he could make it. "Friends, victory is upon us. Too long have you been oppressed, forced to live in the Badlands, struggling for a meager existence. Today, we begin our march north and fulfill a destiny that began a hundred years ago. Together, we will complete what the Dark Lord Gladius started, and you will live in the light. One by one, each nation of Galadir will accept you, or crumble under the thunder of your feet." A mighty roar rose up from the army below him as each beast howled out an enthusiastic battle cry. It took several minutes for the crowd to settle before Grian could speak again. "Follow me to your new homes, awaiting you in the lush green lands of Findoor. Follow me to a war to end all wars, one that will leave the armies of men in ruins. Follow me to victory!" He turned on his heels and led the way out, getting on his warhorse and riding north. The bulk of the army followed, heading toward the Findoor borders. A few of the younger, smaller Narshuks stayed back to pack up command tents and follow in their wake.

The thunder of the Narshuk army could be heard for many miles around as they charged north into Findoor lands.

Chapter 16 – On the Road Again

Malia and Seth woke up with the first light of day. Early morning sunshine lit up the room like it was on fire, and the smell of fresh baked bread, sizzling meat, and a pungent but pleasant drink that reminded him of coffee, filled the air. They both felt refreshed after a good night's sleep, though Seth's neck was sore from sleeping in the chair.

Malia ate a light breakfast and went out to pick up her armor plates, trying them on to make sure they fit after being repaired. She thanked the smithy who bid her good travels as she left to join Seth.

They found Cedric in the center of the town, sitting on a little stone wall and playing a lute for a small gathering of villagers, who all tipped him a copper when he finished. Standing up, he gave a deep bow and thanked the crowd, then joined the rest of his companions. "Are we all rested up? Ready to go? You're looking better Malia; I presume you paid the temple a visit then?"

Malia smiled and swung her left leg in the air to show that it was fine. "Yes, Cedric, our Lady Philana was quite generous."

"Right then. Off to see an old friend of mine, and then we shall make our way to the Findoor border. Three days' travel, then another seven," Cedric said, leading the way out of town and across the Caldoor country side.

Trying to be chivalrous, Seth offered to allow Malia to go next, but she shook her head. "Nay, Seth. I am still sworn to protect you from harm, and that is difficult to do if I cannot see you."

Accepting her logic, he walked after Cedric and let her take the rear. He followed at a good pace at first, but Cedric walked much faster now. It didn't take long before he was falling behind, and Cedric was forced to stop and wait for them to catch up.

"Come now, Seth, we'll be an extra day at this pace," Cedric said with a smile.

"I'm a software developer, I don't get out much," Seth said, out of breath.

"Software? I'm not familiar with that term. Would you tell me about it, and of your world? I'm curious," Cedric said, baiting him into a conversation to keep his mind off the walk.

"Yeah, software, it's basically a list of instructions that tell a computer--a machine--what to do. In my world, machines are used for everything. There are even whole buildings full of machines that make other machines."

"So do you do anything for yourselves?"

"Well, sure we do. Mostly we use machines to make our lives better. Many of the most dangerous jobs that used to be done by humans are now done by machines. It's saved countless lives. But perhaps machines have made many people lazy." With a sheepish look he added, "Myself included."

Cedric laughed at that. "Yes, but never fear my friend. We'll have you worked into shape in no time."

Seth scoffed, "Yeah, right. Honestly, I've been meaning to get back into shape for a long time, and being able to get outside like this is nice for once."

"Are you married? Courting?" He asked, trying to make more conversation, and noticing that Seth's pace was now increasing.

"No, I mean, courting? Well, I suppose you could call it that. I had a date arranged with an old girlfriend the night before I came here, but I guess that fell through." He smiled, trying to hide the disappointment in his voice.

"Ahh, the one that got away. So how about you, Malia? Any man at home waiting for you?" Cedric asked, calling louder over his shoulder so she could hear.

"Nay, unless you count my father, not that it should be of any concern to you."

"A beautiful woman like you, and no lovesick young men chasing after you? I must admit, Findoor is not what it used to be. There was a time when no woman was allowed to take up arms."

"Indeed, you are right. But I fought hard for my placement in the army, and Merek helped a lot. Still, I train twice as hard to prove myself, and though our King would prefer I remained at home and take a fine young man to wed and to bed, my heart belongs to my Kingdom." She became aware that the conversation turned on her, but didn't mind. The goal was to keep Seth's mind off the walk, and so she continued, "Seth, I am considering teaching you some lessons on combat. My commander is fond of the saying 'an untrained ally is more dangerous than a trained opponent'. I think it may be referring to heavy weapons and siege machines, but it applies to this situation as well. After seeing how you handled my sword when we met, you could use the lessons."

Surprised at the sudden turn in the conversation, Seth said, "You're going to train me with a sword? You really are brave, aren't you." He flashed a grin over his shoulder at her.

"I am sure you will do well after some instruction."

Seth looked around him at the countryside and pulled in a big breath of fresh air. "You don't get air this clean in my world. Not unless you're in some remote tropical location. And there's so much green everywhere."

"There was green in your world, I remember seeing it," Malia said. "But you are right, there were many paved roads as well. Is your whole world like that?"

"Well, no, but a lot of it. I don't live in a big city though. There are cities in my world that are nothing but miles and miles of tall buildings that we call skyscrapers. Those cities have very little green space in them." Seth thought about New York City, one of the biggest cities he had ever visited; he remembered it as all steel and concrete, the only green space being Central Park, right in the middle of the massive city.

"It sounds like a marvel to see. Perhaps someday I will get to see it. We have no such cities here. Our biggest cities are built around castles, like Findoor Castle, and only serve as a center for trade. Most people live and work on farms, like my father." There was sad note to Malia's voice as she finished. Seth guessed it was because she missed her father.

Their conversation continued as they walked. The companions stopped once, when they decided to rest for a midday meal. Most of their talk revolved around the differences between their worlds, what they each did for a living, and Seth at one point asked why Cedric wears the mask all the time. "'Tis the mark of my trade. We Bards enjoy many luxuries in cities far and wide, and are generally considered to be hubs of knowledge and secrets. In return, we become faceless, retaining nothing of our previous life but our names."

"That seems like a lonely existence," Seth said.

"At times, it can be. But then there are upsides as well. I gain particular favor from my goddess Hadra, and have certain... skills, unique only to Bards."

They carried on after their break, and picked up their pace to try to make up time they lost that morning. Seth's feet were getting sore but he didn't complain, as he carried very little compared to Malia, who seemed unaffected by the long march across the land. It was mid-afternoon when something caught Seth's eye in the sky, and he stopped for a moment to see what it was. His sudden stop alerted Malia, who asked, "Seth, what is it?"

Seth didn't move, but he did respond. "I see something, like looking into a pond, or rather, out of a pond." He peered at the spot in the sky, but could only make out a wavering blur of a figure.

Cedric stopped and turned to face his companions. "Is there somebody there, Seth?"

"I... I don't know. It's hard to make out what it is. It's like we're underwater, and looking up at the surface at something watching us from above."

The masked Bard walked over to Seth and stood behind him. Putting his hands on his shoulders, he said, "Focus, Seth. Don't force it. Relax and clear your mind."

The soothing voice in his ear allowed Seth to clear out his mind. Once he did, the power flowed like a river to him, and the image cleared. Through the window in the sky, Seth could see a horrifying creature that looked like an old gray mangy wolf with one cloudy eye and broken teeth. It panted as it stared down at him, looking like a werewolf ready to bite into him. "Jesus Christ!" Seth shouted, turning his head away from it and dropping to his knees. All at once the memories flooded back to him.

In his mind he could see the intersection where his accident happened. The blue car barreled through the red light and slammed into the side of his car. Seth hit his head, and the impact would have carried his car into the light post, but then it happened. Time stopped. And then the tear opened, and the creature who came through chased him. All the lost memories from that day came back, making his head pound.

Seth cried out, grabbing the sides of his head. The world swam around him and a wave of nausea hit him, causing him to vomit on the side of the path. When the retching subsided, he looked up to see Malia kneeling beside him. "I remember it all. Everything you described before, it all came back. And that thing that I saw in the sky, it's another one, like what attacked me before," Seth said once he got his breath back.

"Are you okay? Can you travel? If what you say is true, then we must hurry as it means Grian has found us."

"Yeah, just give me a minute and I'll be fine. What was that?"

Cedric approached the pair and smiled down at them. "That, my friend, was a miracle." He offered Seth a hand, which he took and hauled himself to his feet. Being pulled up by Cedric, he realized the Bard was stronger than he looked.

"A miracle? Why?"

Malia rose to her feet as well and said, "Do you remember how I told you that most people can only wield one element?"

"Yes, I remember," Seth said, looking at her with keen interest.

"And Time Weavers typically only wield two. But you have thus far demonstrated four elements. As a Lyecian, we know you can control time. You wielded fire when you hit the Narshuk in your world, and when you cast the blaze back at the camp. Then water, when you healed your hand. But now, you wield shadow. You were able to detect Grian's scrying, which is shadow magic."

He returned her words with a blank stare. "I don't understand, what does this mean?"

Cedric cut in this time, "What it means is that you are far more powerful than any of us imagined. To wield four elements is extremely rare, and to do so without words, without a focus, is tremendous. But, enough about you. We must go, for if what you say is true, we should be seeking cover to avoid any more of your friends."

Seth nodded. "Right, let's go then."

Cedric turned and took off ahead of them at a full run. Seth moved slower, as he was still recovering, but managed to keep Cedric within sight. Malia had no trouble keeping up with Seth, running behind him and never letting him leave her field of vision.

Several miles down the road, Cedric disappeared from view into a patch of trees off to the left of the path. The pair followed the Bard into the forest, but couldn't keep up with him through the dense foliage. About twenty feet into the forest, Malia called for Seth to stop and dropped down to her knees. "Come Seth, get down."

Seth complied, squatting down next to her. In a whisper he said, "What now?"

She looked into his eyes and put a finger over her lips to hush him. As she did, Seth noticed for the first time how deep her eyes were. He forgot where he was, and saw only her face. Her jaw was set and her lips pursed to keep the sound of her breathing down. When she turned her head away to listen to the edge of the forest, it exposed her long, thin neck, with her blond hair tied up in a small piece of leather to keep it out of her face while they traveled.

Moments later, the sky rippled over the road creating a high-pitched keening sound that pierced the air. At the center of the ripples a small beam of light shot straight down into the ground. The light stretched and pushed out, forming a curtain that spread into a circle. The pitch of the sound changed as the circle widened, lowering into a dull pulse. As the curtain of light spread out, it thinned and Seth could see various monstrous forms appear behind it. *We're in trouble,* Seth thought, counting twelve hulking beasts who looked like heavily armed giant werewolves.

The light around them faded and the one closest to them sniffed the air, growled, and turned to face them. Seth remained motionless and held his breath, not knowing what to expect next. Another sniff, and the creature let out a blood curdling howl that hurt Seth's ears. He'd heard one like this before, the first time he encountered one of the beasts, and expected to feel the same compulsion as before, but none came.

Malia stood up before him and began walking toward the edge of the forest before Seth could figure out what was going on. *Shit, they have her,* he thought, scrambling to his feet. She stepped out into the clearing and drew her sword, the blade coming to life in a wave of flames. Seth walked up behind her and moved to her right, his heart pounding in his chest. Turning to face her he said, "You ready for this?"

As she began a charge toward the closest one, she called back to him, "Ready or not, I do not have a choice."

Seth watched with horror as the creature facing her broke into a charge and bounded across the road toward her, intent on tearing her to shreds. As they approached each other, Malia dove to the ground into a roll, ducking beneath its claws just in time. She came out of her roll inside the creature's reach and slammed her flaming sword into its gut with both hands. Her weight wasn't enough to break its charge, but as her hand left the hilt of her sword, she fell back to the ground and uttered a single word. Without warning, the blade in the creature's gut burst into flames, tearing the creature in half and sending blood and meat flying in every direction. With one smooth movement, Malia got to her feet and ran for her blade as another creature began its charge toward her.

Seth froze on the field, watching the horror before him. Blood and gore splattered across the grass and through the air and made him sick to his stomach again, though there was nothing left to vomit up. Two of the massive beasts turned to face him as he stared, mouth open and in a trance. One led the other as they made a move toward him, growling and snarling with satisfaction that they might claim their prize, despite having lost one already.

Without warning, Seth remembered the image of his father's book in his mind, and felt the magical energy flowing to him. *Incendras*, he thought, the word triggering a violent release of energy before him as he held his hands up. Flames burst forth from him and encompassed the two creatures, burning their hair off and searing their flesh. They dropped to the ground with a horrid mix of barks and yelps. The putrid smell of burning hair wafted up from them into Seth's nose, and this time he did turn away and vomit, dropping to the ground, retching out what bile remained.

With Seth on the ground, another of the creatures took advantage of the situation and charged forward. The sounds of battle deafened Seth as he heard Malia's battle cries mixed with the growls and howls of the Narshuks. As the third creature approached Seth at a run and opened its mouth to scoop him up in its powerful jaw, a hush fell over the field. Seth lifted his head at the sudden silence and jumped back away from the creatures open mouth, frozen before him.

Everything was still and quiet. Time had stopped. Not even the whisper of a slow breeze could be heard, as the air itself didn't move. The creatures all stood like horrific statues waiting to come to life and devour their prey. Getting up, Seth walked to the middle of the road and looked around one more time before everything started moving again.

The creature who lunged at Seth crashed to the ground with several audible snaps as its head bent in an unnatural way, and its weight carried it forward. It rolled and collapsed to the ground, dead with a broken neck.

It took a moment for Seth to realize what was going on, but once he got his bearings, he ran for the woods where he could find cover.

Two more of the creatures pursued, but didn't make it to the trees before the music started.

Above all the excitement of the battle, above all the sounds of combat, the snarling, and Malia's battle cries, there was music being played. Some kind of string instrument that was playing a soft, soothing tune. As the song played, a voice could be heard accompanying the music.

Sleep my child, at last sweet dreams,
The world is yours and mine to keep,
Turn down the lights and prep the sheets,
Sleep my child, at last sweet dreams.

Rise my moon, the stars are out,
Crickets chirp their song out loud,
Children rest in beds so warm,
Rise my moon, the stars are out.

Speak wise owl, the night is young,
Mice are running from their homes,
Soon the sun will rise anew,
Speak wise owl, the night is young.

Each verse rang out in the midday air. It sounded calm and relaxing, like a lullaby. So distracted by the music, Seth didn't notice his surroundings. Verse after verse, the music soothed all who could hear it. The Narshuks all stopped and lay down. Malia did the same, the calm, soothing words overtaking her and ushering in a deep sleep.

When each person and creature was still, the verses stopped, but the music continued. Seth followed the sound to its source, high up in a tree in the forest. Cedric sat on a tree branch playing his lute and grinning down at Seth. The notes continued from his lute even as he slid from his resting place at the top of the tree and stepped from branch to branch. With a hop, he made it to the ground, never missing a note.

"Friends of yours?" he asked with a smirk.

Seth took a second to clear his head, then looked around at the carnage that littered the field. "I was beginning to think you abandoned us."

"Shh," he said, lifting a finger to his lips and stopping his music. "Of course not, but I felt them coming, and needed time to prepare my spell."

"We should go, now," Seth said, turning toward the road.

"Indeed. Let's gather up Malia and make ourselves scarce, lest our friends here wake up and make us into lunch." Cedric walked over to Malia and placed a hand over her mouth, then shook her awake. Her deep gray eyes fluttered open. The excitement and adrenaline of the battle persisted in her mind even after she slept, and so she struggled against Cedric's grip. Her hands felt around for her sword and she kicked the ground, trying to get up. Cedric moved his face into her field of vision and said in a quiet, soothing tone, "Shh. You are safe, calm now." Malia settled when she recognized his face, but said nothing. When Cedric was confident she wasn't going to scream, he removed his hand. "Come now, we must make haste."

The three of them left the area without a sound and made their way back down the road. With Cedric leading the way, they traveled for several miles until he veered off the path to the left and into the brush. The other two companions weren't sure where he was going or why, but several seconds later he popped his head back out and said, "Well? Are you coming?"

Seth and Malia looked at each other before they shrugged and followed after him.

Cedric led them down a small path and through another grove of trees. This one was larger and denser than the one Seth and Malia had tried to hide in. The old overgrown path twisted and turned through the forest as Cedric pushed forward. After about twenty minutes of walking, they emerged into a clearing in the middle of the forest. Cedric strolled into it and sat down on the ground.

The other two joined him; they sat in a small circle, facing each other. After a moment of rest, Cedric piped up, "The beasts will be out for several hours if they are undisturbed. Night will be falling soon, but I'm thinking we should continue through it to press our advantage. My old friend lives but two days' travel from here, and then we shall turn ourselves east toward Findoor."

At this point, Malia spoke up, "You have yet to tell us of this friend of yours."

Cedric smiled at her. "He is an ancient friend, from the time of the Lyecians. If we are lucky, he will give us a ride, and our journey to Findoor castle shall be expedited. It's not my intention to be secretive, but a visit with this particular friend is quite the experience, and I wouldn't want to ruin the surprise."

Malia raised an eyebrow at him. "Indeed."

Shaking his head, Seth said, "No, I'm not sure I can handle any more surprises. I'm so scared I'm shaking. I've puked my guts out so bad I'm not sure there's anything left to come out, and I just killed something for the first time in my life. I'm tired, sore, and I just want to go home."

Cedric opened his mouth to say something, but Malia shook her head to silence him. Then she turned to Seth and said, "We have no choice, Seth. We must continue or get caught and face death. I know how hard this must be for you-"

"No you don't," Seth shouted, cutting her off. "You have no idea what this is like! You two have lived this your entire lives. The magic, and the monsters, and wizards. There's no such thing in my world. Fairy tales, Hollywood movies, nothing more. You live and breathe this, train for it, and you both seem to have some kind of inkling of whats going on. Me? I'm just along for the ride, because without you, I'd be dead, or worse. So no, you have no idea what I'm going through!"

"I... I'm sorry Seth. I hadn't thought of it that way," Malia said with an apologetic tone. "When we reach the safety of Findoor castle, then we will have time to go through everything with you, and perhaps Merek can help you find the answers you seek. It is rumored that Merek is so old, he even fought with your father a hundred years ago during the Lyecian war. Maybe he can even tell you a thing or two about Krycin."

Cedric spoke up, cutting into their conversation, "I'd love to sit here all night and talk, but the Narshuks will be waking up shortly, and they aren't likely to be happy. We should make haste for the north, and save our discussion for later." He got up and stretched his legs, then led the way out of the clearing into the forest again.

Seth and Malia followed Cedric through a twisting maze of faint paths that led through the forest. It was several hours before they came out the other side onto a vast plain. With the sun setting, the plain loomed before them, but all was quiet except for some song birds singing their last tunes before going to sleep for the night. Cedric stopped and turned to face the other two companions. "We will have to move quickly across this plain. Even if the Narshuks pick up our scent, with their bulk it will take them many hours to traverse the forest. Once they reach this plain, however, they will catch up fast. On the other side of this plain, there is a vast swampland we must pass, and then up a mountain. Are you all ready?"

Both Seth and Malia nodded, and before they could say anything further, Cedric was off, running as fast as he could without burning himself out. The other two followed close behind him. As they began their run across the plain, the distant sound of a wolf howl echoed through the still night air.

Chapter 17 - The Man in Black

In the early morning hours, Toby arrived for work just as the first rays of sunshine were peeking over the horizon. The parking lot held the usual array of vehicles, most of which were large trucks or SUVs, and the air was crisp and cool for a summer day. Near the front entrance to the office area of the compound, parked across two handicap spaces, was a big black classic Cadillac. Toby looked at it and shook his head. "Hmph. Asshole," he said, walking past it and making a mental note to contact security to have the car removed.

Entering the office area, he made his way to the elevators, answering several friendly greetings as he went. He pressed the button to go down, and thought to himself as he stood waiting for the car to come. *Now that we have a working formula, we need to figure out how to harness other types of energy,* he thought, organizing his tasks for the day. *Don said he might be on to something. I'll have to check and see how he made out.*

A bell chimed, startling Toby out of his thoughts, and the doors slid open. The elevator carried him deep beneath the compound. When it reached his floor, he stepped out, then walked to his office. Upon opening his office door, he saw a man sitting in his chair with his feet up on the desk. From his cowboy boots and dress pants to the shirt, jacket and tie he wore, everything was a deep black. Even the broad-brimmed hat that he wore, tilted forward to cover his face, was black. Toby reached for his sidearm and drew it, aiming it at the man. "If you move a muscle, you're a dead man," he said, his other hand reaching for his cell phone.

The Man in Black lifted his head and looked straight into Toby's eyes. A chill ran over him, as if the temperature dropped ten degrees in that instant. Toby stared into the black murky pools that were the man's eyes, forgetting his gun, phone, and what he was going to do with them. "You were saying?" the Man in Black said, with a calm, smooth southern accent that both soothed him and grated on every nerve in his body at the same time. He felt the words bore into his head and infect his system, traveling through his body to his heart, his lungs, his brain. System by system, the words took control like a parasite in his body.

When Toby managed to break his gaze, the Man in Black waved a hand, and Toby's gun flew out of his grip and across the room. It clattered against the wall and fell to the floor. Toby looked first at the gun, then back to the Man in Black and said, "Alright, you have my attention. Who are you, and what do you want?"

The Man in Black lowered his head again, the brim of his hat covering his intense eyes. Relief washed over Toby until the man spoke again. "The name's Cy Cooper," he said, swinging his legs down and sitting up straight in the chair. "You have something I want. Now where is he?"

"I don't know what you mean," said Toby. Cy's voice continued to reverberate through his body, shaking his nerves and making him want to cry out. At the same time, he could feel his body surrendering to the strange man before him.

"The Time Weaver. Where is he?" His southern voice grew impatient, making Toby's ears hurt. The corner of Cy's mouth raised in the suggestion of a smile as he looked at Toby's feet.

"Time Weaver? I have no idea what you're talking about," Toby said.

Cy stood up, the vague smile disappearing from his lips. "Come now, boy, we both know you're not fooling anyone. Drop the facade and come clean. Thirty years ago, I was marooned here on this gods-forsaken world, robbed of my powers, and left to die. All that time I've searched for him, for the one who keeps the doors to the other world closed, and I want him. I want to go home. And just the other day, I felt him, right here in this compound. So you either tell me where he is, or I'll kill you, and tear this compound apart brick by brick until I find him myself." As Cy talked, he took measured steps around Toby's desk. He was taller than Toby thought, but didn't have a large build. In fact, Toby observed, Cy looked pretty gaunt; starved, even. But his voice, the calm measured tones and perfect pitch, was a pleasure and a pain to listen to, as it pleased his ears, but invaded his body and mind.

"I honestly don't know what you mean; I wish I did," said Toby. Fear built up in his gut as Cy stepped closer, and his heart began to pound faster. He wanted to turn and run, but couldn't make his body respond. A thought occurred to Toby, *He's talking about Alkirk, he must be.* "Are you talking about Seth Alkirk?"

"Is that what he's going by now? No matter what his name is. Seth, Krycin... the point is, he trapped me here. And I want to go home."

"Seth isn't here. Never was. I don't think he's even in our dimension anymore. I'm sorry, but I can't help you."

Cy walked closer until he was almost nose-to-nose with Toby. "Don't fuck with me boy, I know what I felt. Whether it is Seth, or somebody else, there is a Time Weaver here. I felt his magic, I felt time stand still." As he spoke, he lifted his head revealing his eyes again and locked Toby in his gaze. The darkness in his eyes enveloped Toby with despair and loathing and fear.

Panic overcame Toby, and he spouted out, "I don't know of any Time Weaver here, but there is one who uses magic. He's just a test subject, and lives here on the base under observation. We made a serum that could give anyone the same powers that Seth has."

Lowering his head again, Cy broke his gaze with Toby. "A serum, you say? Take me there, to where you keep this serum. And no tricks, or you'll be dead before you hit the floor. Understand?"

"Yes, right this way." Toby couldn't see any weapons on Cy, but had no doubt that he could do what he said. He turned around and led Cy out of the office and back to the elevators, where they caught a ride down one floor. Stepping out of the elevator, they found themselves in a vast lab filled with chemistry equipment, machines and computers. Scientists in white jackets walked here and there and the sounds of printers and hums of cooling fans made a white noise that was almost deafening. Cy urged Toby on, "Come now, boy. Let's get what we came for."

Nodding, Toby led him through the maze of workstations to a vault door at the other end of the room. His heart raced as he took out his ID badge and swiped it through the security console, and the light on the console turned from red to green. A latch hummed and clicked as the vault door unlocked, and Toby pulled it open. Inside the vault was a vast array of projects, all numbered and cataloged. Leading the way in, Toby walked up to a fridge, filled with labeled vials, that sat against the back wall. He opened the fridge and perused the vials until he found the one marked SPECTER in large bold letters. The vial was filled with a black liquid that blocked all light coming through it. Turning to face Cy, Toby offered him the vial. "Here. That's all we have right now. It's hard to synthesize, so production is slow and expensive. This will be our latest trial."

Cy snatched the vial from him, turned, and stormed out of the vault without another word. Toby ran after him, surprised at how fast Cy could move given his relative build. Catching up to him, Toby could hear him muttering something in a language he didn't understand. "Sir, what are you planning to do with that?"

Coming to a dead stop, Cy turned to face Toby. "Why, I plan to use it of course."

"Then you'll need help. It can't be administered alone. It has to be injected directly into the spinal fluid."

A silent rage built up in Cy that reflected in his pure black eyes. The surface was calm, but underneath the facade, a tempest was blowing. Cy's gaze burned into Toby's head, the torrent of emotions flooding through some unseen exchange between them. And then there was a sudden calm. "Then you will help me, or I will have no further use for you."

Toby nodded, "Alright. Come with me, there's a private lab where we can work." Without waiting for a response, Toby turned away from Cy and led him to a nearby hallway with several doors on each side. Picking the first door, Toby opened it and flicked the lights on. The room was pure white, sterile, and fully stocked with test equipment, medical equipment, fridge, burners, and many other items that might be required during an experiment. Toby walked inside and opened a drawer. After a moment of searching through boxes, he withdrew a syringe in an individual package and opened it. Turning to face Cy, he held out his hand. "Give me the serum, and take a seat. When I do the injection, it's going to hurt, a lot. But I'll need you to keep as still as you can, or I could damage your spinal cord."

Placing the vial in Toby's hand, Cy sat down in a nearby chair. Toby pulled the cap off the needle and punctured the top of the vial. Turning it over, he pulled the plunger back on the syringe, filling it to just above the 5cc mark. He then tapped it a couple times to knock any air to the top and pushed it out, making sure he had exactly 5cc's. Looking down at Cy he said, "You ready?"

"Boy, I've been ready for the last thirty years." The wicked smile that spread across his face made it look almost skeletal.

Cy removed his hat revealing his short, clean-cut black hair in anticipation of the needle that would pierce the back of his neck. *Thirty years in this infernal world, and finally I will be free,* he thought as he waited.

A second voice spoke up inside his mind, a deeper, darker voice. *And once we're back on Galadir, you will take me to Scrag, if he is still alive. Vengeance will be ours my friend.*

Yes, my Lord. Vengeance will be ours.

A searing pain ripped through the back of his neck, like somebody stabbed him with a knife. The sensation started cold, as Toby pushed the plunger down on the syringe, but as his spinal column over-filled with the fluid, it turned into a burning pain and raged down his back and up into his head. He let out a gasp and clenched his hands down on the arms of the air. The serum began its work, restructuring his body's DNA. Fire coursed through his veins and lit up every nerve as every cell in his body was sent a message to mutate into something new. His heart rate and breathing sped up to a tremendous level and he collapsed out of the chair into a fit of convulsions. Somehow the chair disappeared as Cy tried to arrest control of his body. Several minutes later, and with much effort, his heart slowed down and the pain eased in his body. He lifted his head and looked at Toby with is murky black eyes. Catching his breath he said, "Thanks, boy. You have no idea what you've done here today."

Toby backed away a step to let Cy get to his feet. Cy extended a hand up to him as if he needed help getting up, but as Toby took it, Cy pulled him to the ground. "I have no further use for you, but you'll make a fine meal."

Before Toby could get another breath to say something, Cy squeezed his hand, focusing magical energy into him. A white glow spread over Toby's body that flowed like liquid into Cy's hand. The words that were meant as a reply faded into a dull gasp as the air escaped his dying lungs. His heart shut down, and his vision faded. The white energy completed its trip into Cy's body, and left Toby lying on the ground with a vacant, dead stare of horror.

My Lord, a soul to sustain you, he thought.

The dark voice again chimed in, *Very good. Now let us return to Galadir and reap our rewards.*

Yes, my Lord.

Cy stood up, turned and walked out of the room. Making his way back to the surface, not one person seemed to notice him. Even the security guards walked by without questioning the strange Man in Black who carried no security badge.

In the parking lot outside the office building, Cy found a clearing and positioned himself at the center. He was about to begin a spell, when the dark voice in his head again interceded, *Make sure this rift doesn't close. Ever. When I am finished with Galadir, I will have no further need of either world. Let them crumble into the aether.*

It shall be done, he thought. Cy called upon the power of time and death to fuel his spell. Standing in the parking lot, he held his hands out before him. As the power built up inside him, his hands glowed with a white light and his eyes closed. He focused on his home land, the grassy Kingdom of Findoor, picturing the rolling hills and tall trees in his mind. He saw the Findoor banner flying high on a pole at the tallest peak of the castle, the gold symbol of the crown with a sword through it shining in the sunlight. Fluffy white clouds drifted in a blue sky, and no power lines marred the view.

When his eyes opened, the energy poured out of his hands and blasted a spot in front of him, rippling the fabric of space and time and tearing it open. The energy stream from his hands continued as sparks flew from the tear and it widened into a circle. The blue aether between worlds swirled and churned as the spell blasted a hole through it, and when the spell reached the other side, it ruptured the fabric of space there, and formed a permanent bond between the worlds, creating a shock wave out from it.

With a thunderous boom, the spell ended, and Cy dropped his hands to his sides.

The shock wave from the portal rippled out beyond the army complex and traveled throughout the country. The ground shuddered and shook like a great earthquake, rattling houses and setting off car alarms. It traveled across the world, and then continued to ripple out into space, picking up more speed. Worlds across the entire universe felt the shock wave, like a ripple in time itself.

King Verand sat in his throne room watching as several councilors squabbled over tax rates for various regions of the Kingdom. He grew tired of the same old arguments and was about to call it a day when the shock wave hit. The entire castle shook on its foundations and startled all of the councilors. He opened his mouth to say something, when the doors to the throne room burst open.

Merek charged through the doors, yelling at a runner to go and see what happened, and then turned to face the King. Surprised by the sudden chain of events, King Verand bellowed about the commotion, "Order in my court!"

The gathering of councilors shrank away from him and silenced. Merek, on the other hand, kept walking right up to the King. Verand opened his mouth to say something, but Merek beat him to it. "Whatever you think you need to say can wait until I've said my piece."

Turning to face the crowd in the court room, Merek cleared his throat and began, "Early this morning, a massive Narshuk army burst across the southern Findoor border. Easily ten thousand strong, they decimated the entire southern army, and are now on their way here."

Gasps sounded out throughout the chamber as the news sunk in. Even Verand was shaken by the news, the lines around his eyes extending as he lowered his head in thought. After a few moments, he looked back up at Merek. "How many died? What are our losses in this attack?"

"Total, Sire. They slaughtered every man, woman and child in their path. Whole villages are being wiped off the face of the world. Our stationed troops there fought bravely, but were no match for an army of that magnitude. Had I not been keeping an eye on the border with the Scryes, we wouldn't even know about it now."

"But there were over a thousand troops stationed down there. By the gods, Merek, I've been a fool. What do we do?"

"We send out a call to arms. Every available soldier to the Losteron Plains. We can still mount a defense, but we must act now."

Verand nodded and motioned for a runner. "Send out the runner hawks immediately. Every soldier is to report to the Losteron Plains. We go to war."

The runner took off as fast as he could go. As he sped out of the room, another arrived, out of breath. Merek recognized the boy as the runner he sent to check out what made the castle shake.

"Sire, Arch-Magus Merek, a rift has opened just outside of our south walls. A single man came through it and walked toward the south, but the rift hasn't closed."

Merek turned to face the King. "It seems we have more to worry about than just Grian."

Scrag followed on foot behind Grian, who rode a glorious black warhorse. News of the Elites' failure to catch the Time Weaver disappointed him, but time yet remained, and Scrag instructed them to track the maggot and capture him as quickly as possible. Scrag was lost in his own thoughts when the shock wave hit, jarring him back to reality. Grian looked over at him from the top of his stallion. "What the hell was that?"

A grumble went through the Narshuk army as Scrag looked toward Grian. "How should I know?" he asked in his strange snarled common.

Grian smiled down at the hunched over Narshuk. "It's a sign Scrag, today will be a good day for us, and the Narshuk people. In several days we will reach the Losteron Plains, and then it will be smooth sailing from then on."

Scrag nodded and trudged on beside him.

Cy stepped forward through the portal that pulsed and flared in front of him. As he did, he took a deep breath of the fresh clean air flowing through. On the other side were the same rolling hills he envisioned, with Castle Findoor standing in the background. "Home at last," he said as he surveyed the area.

Scrag is south of here, meet up with him, the dark voice said in his head.

Yes, my Lord, he thought. Turning to the south, he walked, ignoring the shouts of people now looking on at the portal resting at the top of the hill.

Chapter 18 - Into the Swamp

Seth and his companions ran as fast as they could across the open plain, heading for the line of trees off in the distance. Cedric began to lose his momentum first, his cloak that flew out behind him at a run now hung limp at his back as he slowed to a jog. Malia and Seth caught up to him minutes from the edge of the swamp they would have to cross. The trees were not what Seth expected, and were nothing like the forest they just left.

The forest behind them had lush foliage, bright green trees and smelled of sweet flowers that covered the forest floor. Though the swamp loomed up ahead of them, they could already smell the damp must of decaying wood. The trees were twisted and dull, and a mist hung in the air just off the ground. Seth wrinkled his nose at the smell; it reminded him of an old wet basement.

They all slowed to a walk and approached the swamp with caution. Cedric was in the lead, and stopped them at the edge of the swamp, the ground soft under their feet. The swamp was home to a whole host of wildlife that didn't live on the plains or in the forests he had traveled through so far. Clouds of gnats drifted here and there in the air, and various other flying insects had to be batted out of his face as they approached to check out the creatures who encroached on their domain. Cedric pointed out things to beware of as they walked: a deep puddle here, a sinkhole there. The ground was wet and spongy. Seth's shoes weren't waterproof, and were soon saturated with water. The mist that drifted over the surface of the ground swirled and churned as they walked. It wasn't thick enough to hide the ground, but could still be seen dancing around their feet as they disturbed it.

Several times as they walked, Seth felt like they were being watched, only to find some small furry creature examining them from a tree branch or a hole in the ground. The creatures were small, about the size of a squirrel, but more feline in shape and stature. A bird swooped down out of a distant tree and nabbed one of the poor things, carrying it away while it squealed, only stopping when the bird squeezed its talons around the creature, puncturing its lungs.

After a number of hours of walking through the muck and moss of the swamp, the companions stopped in a raised clearing that was dry enough to set up camp. The sun had long since set, and the swamp was dark enough that it was becoming treacherous to navigate.

Setting up camp took very little time, as each companion didn't have much in the way of baggage. Cedric used his bow and hunted down something to eat. Malia used her magic to cook it without lighting a fire.

As the night set in, various insects came out of hiding, many of them carrying a phosphorescent glow. Seth sat up and watched the tiny specks of green and yellow and orange dance in the dark, almost mesmerized by it.

Malia watched Seth; the look of wonder on his face made him look rather charming and innocent in the fading light. Breaking the sudden silence she asked, "Do you not have glow flies in your world?"

Seth started, not expecting the sudden voice. Smiling he turned to face Malia. "Well, we have something like them, but they only flash in the twilight. We call them fireflies."

Cedric broke in at that moment with a smirk. "Hate to be a spoilsport, but we must decide who is going to stand watch and on what shifts."

Both of them turned to face Cedric, but it was Seth who spoke up first. "I'll take first watch. I couldn't sleep just now even if I wanted to. You guys get some rest."

Malia agreed and lay down on the soft moss to get some sleep. Cedric also lay down, using his cloak as a pillow. Seth's watch passed with only a few howls heard off in the distance as the moon rose. When he was later relieved, and managed to get himself settled, he fell into another dreamless sleep.

Seth snapped awake in the morning. The night's chill had caused the mist to settle on everything, and left the companions damp and uncomfortable. Both Cedric and Malia were up already, with Cedric in the process of performing some kind of ritual on a waterskin. Seth's sudden movement broke his concentration and the magical energy he harnessed snapped back at him with a small burst that knocked him on his back.

Seth looked around, panicked, as if he wasn't sure where he was, and Malia ran to his side. "Seth, is everything okay?" she said, with genuine concern. She got down on her knees beside him, placing one hand on his shoulder for comfort. It was obvious that something startled him.

Seth's eyes focused on Malia. "Yeah, sorry, I'll never get used to waking up in strange places." He looked over at Cedric, who was just getting up off the ground. "What happened to you?"

Cedric got to his feet and brushed himself off. "Well, I was trying to purify water. But now you've witnessed what happens when you disturb a spell while it is being cast." He shot Seth a wry smile from under his mask. "Come, we must make haste or the angry horde of Narshuks will catch us. The swamp will only hide our scent for so long."

Cedric went back to his ritual, this time finishing it. Lifting the waterskin off the ground, he offered it to Seth. "Here, it would never do for us to escape the dim-witted beasts only to have us collapse of thirst. Drink, and then we can go."

Seth wasn't sure about it at first, but found that after the previous day's excitement, he was quite thirsty. He hadn't noticed until the water was offered to him. He took a sip of the cool clear water and found it quite refreshing. The water he was used to came through a city plumbing system, and often tasted like the chemicals they used to treat it, or the pipes that it flowed through. This water was pure, tasted of nothing, and quenched his thirst. When he was done, he passed it on to Malia, who also drank deeply from the skin.

Cedric took it last, and hung it from his belt when he was done. The companions finished getting ready, and headed out into the damp swamp land again.

Grian and the Narshuk army marched onto the Losteron Plains early in the morning. As they crested the last hill before the plains, they spotted a vast army at the other end. Scoffing at the gathering of Findoor troops, Grian turned to Scrag. "It seems they've decided to come to the fight after all."

Scrag let out a strange choking growl that might have passed for a laugh. "Yes, and it's about time, the troops are getting hungry."

Hoisting a banner high into the air, Grian signaled to the Narshuks to ready their charge. The black banner fluttered in the light morning breeze. A lily with a viper wrapped around the stem was embroidered in silver and gleamed in the sunlight. "Ready," Grian shouted, his voice echoing across the lines of vicious creatures.

Like a wave, the Narshuks lowered their heads and set themselves to charge.

"Attack! Kill them all, let no man survive to rise up against us! Claim your new home from those who oppressed you. Show all the nations of Galadir that the Narshuks are a force to be reckoned with!"

Chapter 19 – The Battle of Losteron Plains

The Findoor commander watched the flood of Narshuks wash over the plains, trampling the grass and knocking over trees. "Archers, ready," he shouted and lifted a flag with a bow embroidered on it. Waiting until the leading edge of the Narshuks was within range, he dropped the flag. "*Fire!*"

A cloud of arrows flew out over the battlefield, arcing high in the sky. With well-trained precision, each archer nocked another arrow and readied it. The arrows rained out of the sky on the Narshuks, some of them flying true and striking the beasts through the top of the head or through the eye socket and causing them to fall and trip up others. The remaining arrows caused only minor wounds or fell to the ground without harm.

The commander again raised the archer flag, then dropped it. "*Fire!*"

Another cloud of arrows flew. More Narshuks fell, getting trampled by those continuing their advance. The losses didn't seem to faze them as they ran. The fallen were mere obstacles to be dodged around, or jumped over. Still they swarmed across the plains.

The Narshuks were much larger than the Findoor warriors, and so a thousand could look like four thousand, and four thousand could look like fifteen thousand. The commander was trying to gauge his chances of winning this battle, but couldn't get an accurate count of just how many there were.

The archers readied another volley of arrows, waiting for the order to fire again. The command put up a different flag, one with a torch on it. "Wizards, ready!"

Throughout the front line of soldiers, many cloaked figures emerged, all chanting, ready to cast their spells. The commander waited for the hush to fall over the army, to tell him that their words were spoken, and then he dropped the flag. *"Fire!"*

The Narshuk line was a mere hundred yards away when the Findoor line erupted with bursts of flame rushing forth in a wave toward them. The fire flowed like a tsunami over the battlefield leaving the ground bare and scorched. The wizards on the front line focused on maintaining the wave of fire, the magical energy crackling across the line.

The wave of fire hit the Narshuk line, blasting the leading edge back and breaking their charge. Screams of fury from the Narshuks could be heard as they were burned alive in the intense heat. Smells of burnt meat flooded out onto the battlefield, with the fallen Narshuks still burning even after they were dead. One by one, the wizards in the Findoor line exhausted themselves and retreated, leaving first small holes in the wave of flame, then larger ones.

When the smoke cleared, the Narshuk line stopped where they were, many hundreds of them on the ground in charred and smoking heaps. Still more howled with rage, running around and rolling on the ground, trying to put out the flames that threatened to consume them. The rest of the Narshuks waited for the chaos to settle, and then began their advance again, marching this time instead of charging.

Having little time to survey the field, the Findoor commander prepared his next order. The Narshuk line remained tight and strong despite the losses, and they could hear the snarls of the creatures and see the vicious teeth and claws they would use to rip the Findoor army to shreds. As he looked around, the commander found what he was looking for. A man among the beasts, riding atop a great black stallion. Next to the stallion marched a Narshuk who was gray rather than black and looked much older than the rest. Ancient even.

He pointed out the pair to his lieutenants and told them to get some archers trained on those two. Instructions received from Merek himself dictated that they were to find Grian, and kill him if possible. Once the order was given, various arrows flew toward Grian.

As if he expected it, he looked up and watched the arrows fly. Grian didn't seem concerned about the arrows that were about to rain down on him. A moment later, and the commander knew why, as the arrows glanced off an invisible field surrounding him.

The Narshuks continued their march, ignoring the smoking hulks as well as those who were burning to death. With fifty yards between the Narshuks and the Findoor army, and still thousands of the beasts approaching them, the commander raised a flag with a sword on it. "Infantry, ready!"

The ranks of foot soldiers drew their weapons all at once. The ring of steel drowned out the stomps and snarls of the Narshuks. Had it been a human army they faced, it would have struck fear in their hearts. The Narshuks were undaunted by it.

The commander dropped the flag and called out, "ATTACK!"

A flood of soldiers poured forth at full charge, their steel armor flashing in the afternoon sun. Booted feet pounded scorched earth, swords and shields rattled, and the two armies clashed with a roar that echoed for miles around.

The commander held back the cavalry, positioned to either end of the main force, waiting for a chance to close around the Narshuks in a pincer maneuver and wipe them out. What he hadn't expected was how much fury the Narshuks fought with. For every Narshuk who fell, five Findoor soldiers went down, their bodies rended in half. Blood drenched the soil of the plains as the Findoor infantry was depleted.

The rising sun reflected off the glistening battlefield, flooding it with an eerie red glow. Many of the foot soldiers began to tire, while the Narshuks continued to fight relentlessly.

In a bid to save what remained of the Findoor army, the Commander called in the cavalry from both sides of the battlefield. The hooves pounded the ground and the elevated soldiers were able to get better strikes at the Narshuks' vulnerable heads. A wave of Narshuks fell as the cavalry crossed the field, giving the infantry a break in the battle. The commander bellowed, "Infantry, fall back!"

The cavalry fought back the Narshuk line long enough to allow the infantry to fall back. The commander began shouting orders for a retreat, signaling a small group of cloaked figures who sat at the back behind the rest of the troops. They spread out across the back of the line and began chanting. As they did, the Narshuks pushed back the Findoor lines.

Once by one the cloaked figures finished their spells, and gouts of blue energy erupted from them, spreading out like giant umbrellas over the waiting Findoor army. The energy flickered and crackled as more Findoor soldiers scrambled to get under the dome.

The old gray Narshuk held up a staff and swung it out in a wide arc, firing a bolt of black plasma at the dome over the commander. The bolt struck with a crash causing the dome to waver and collapse. The energy from the barrier spell fed back into the cloaked wizard casting it. He convulsed as the energy spread through his body, frying his flesh from the inside out. Screaming from the sudden wave of pain, his skin blistered and split, and his muscles spasmed. His eyes exploded out as his brain superheated in his skull, and then he fell to the ground, smoke rising from his empty eye sockets.

Panicked, the commander shouted for another wizard to take his place, but the Narshuk army closed in on him and his soldiers. Before the Narshuks could reach them, he raised one final flag, the Findoor standard, signaling the rest of the army to leave.

One by one the umbrellas of blue energy disappeared, the soldiers under them gone, leaving only trampled grass where they once stood.

A panicked wizard worked at the center of the commander's group trying to summon the energy to perform the transport spell, but the Narshuks were already slaughtering the remaining solders around him. The commander drew his weapon and fought off the Narshuks as well as he could, but it was no use. There was, at his best guess, two hundred soldiers left on the field. The rest of the army had been transported to the safety of Findoor castle.

The wizard at the center of the group began to gather the energy required for his spell, but could not concentrate through the shouts of the men around him, the snarls of the Narshuks, and the smell of the roasted wizard at his feet. He lost his focus and the magical energy recoiled into him, knocking him unconscious.

Minutes later, despite a valiant fight, the remaining Findoor soldiers fell, with the commander being one of the last to die. He swung his blade with expert precision, slicing through creature after creature, his men falling around him to Narshuk teeth and claws. He struck one of the monsters in the throat and sliced its neck open, causing blood to gush out. The Narshuk fell back to the ground groping at its neck, a gurgling sound coming from it as blood filled its lungs. A second lost a leg in one swing and fell over, giving the commander a chance to bury his sword in its chest. He was trying to wrestle his sword free when a third Narshuk swung out with its razor-sharp claws and buried them in his gut. In one swift maneuver, the Narshuk pulled free of the commander's torso, dragging much of his liver, stomach and intestines with it.

The commander fell to his knees still holding his sword, now supported by it. His blood and guts poured from his torso as his body gave out, and he collapsed on top of the Narshuk he had just killed. The last thing he saw was Narshuks everywhere devouring the soldiers of the Findoor army, and then everything went black.

Chapter 20 - The Portal

General Mathers sat in his office shuffling through the Specter serum paperwork. The President was asking questions and he now worked on coming up with plausible explanations for the funding he received. The goal was to justify the funding without revealing the true nature of the projects they were working on at the base. The Secretary of Defense approved the funding, and they were written a blank check for the projects, but it was on the condition that they had to keep it ultra-classified. The only other project of this magnitude in existence was Area 51, and General Mathers had no idea what they were doing there.

He finished up the report and was getting ready to send it off when his phone rang. The display showed it was a call from the lab on the lowest level. Answering it he said, "Mathers here."

The voice on the other end wasn't the one he expected. Rather than Toby's voice telling him they had some breakthrough with the serum, it was some lab rat. "General Mathers, Sir, our security has been breached."

The General sat up straight and his brows lowered into a scowl. "What do you mean our security has been breached?"

"Sir, the latest test run of the Specter serum has been stolen from the vault," the lab rat said on the other end.

"God damn it, why am I not hearing this news from Toby? He's in charge down there."

"Sir, because Captain Smith is dead."

Cy Cooper walked for three days, never tiring, never taking breaks. The rolling hills of the Findoor country side stretched out in every direction, spotted with trees and shrubs. He passed several small villages and hamlets on his way, pausing there to get water and food that he ate and drank while he walked. Even the setting sun did not deter Cy, and his steady pace carried him through the night.

When the sun broke over the horizon on the third day, Cy could smell something burning, like a steak left over a fire to char. Small streams of smoke rose in the distance. *The Narshuk army*, the dark voice in his head said.

Another half hour later, the smell of burning meat grew to an almost unbearable level, until he crested over the last hill before the smoke plumes. On the other side the view was horrific. The ground was scorched in a long swath through the plains below. Thousands of Narshuks milled about, some devouring raw meat off bones, others carrying bodies to pyres that burned the dead. Blood soaked the ground, creating a gruesome slippery muck. Swords, shields and various other debris were scattered all over the field, and the smell of meat, rot, and blood all mixed together churned his stomach.

Glorious! Cy thought, and walked straight into the chaos.

The Narshuks ignored him at first, but as he ventured deeper into the encampment, the occasional creature approached him. When they looked into his eyes, they stopped, and bowed before him.

A command tent stood at the center of the camp, set up on one of the few dry spots left in the plains. Cy headed straight for it. A buzz of activity surrounded the tent, but as he approached, the creatures moved away from the tent and hushed, finding somewhere else to be, or something else to do. Walking straight into the tent without warning or invitation, Cy wiped the gore from his black boots on the grass.

Inside was a mess of maps scattered about a large table. A human stood at the table with another Narshuk. The human snapped his head up and looked at Cy, a surprised expression on his face. The Narshuk looked up as well, but after looking him over, returned to his maps. After a second to regain his composure, the human in the tent said, "Who are you? And what are you doing in my tent? Make it good, as you will not get a second chance."

Cy walked up to the table without fear, his eyes meeting the human's eyes, capturing him there. Without warning, the temperature in the tent dropped ten degrees. In a voice that sounded like a thousand tormented souls screaming in unison, the Man in Black said, "The question is not who am I. The question is: who are you, and what are you doing with my army?"

A look of sheer terror washed over Grian's face. He had watched Narshuks kill and eviscerate their enemies, had peered into some of the darkest parts of the world. As a former follower of Grishtor, he had seen terrors that would send a normal man screaming, that would haunt their worst nightmares for the rest of their lives. Grian had never felt terror the way he felt it now. His face went pale and he backed up a step, but couldn't find the words to respond. He was being challenged, and all he wanted to do was run away and claw his eyes out to get the vision of that man's face out of his head.

At that moment, it was Scrag who spoke up in his drawn out accent, "Welcome back, betrayer."

The air cleared, and the temperature returned to normal as Cy looked at Scrag. His southern drawl returned. "Good to see you, Scrag. A real pleasure." Looking at Grian, who still appeared uncertain, he extended a hand to the wizard. "The name's Cy Cooper. Good to meet you."

Attempting to regain his composure, Grian shook his hand. The color returned to his face when Cy turned to leave and said over his shoulder, "See ya 'round, Grian."

General Mathers hung up on the lab rat. He'd heard enough. *It's time to take control of the Specter project before things get out of hand.* He pushed away from his desk and went to get up when a shock wave hit the office building, rattling windows and knocking small items off his shelves. Startled, Mathers said, "God damn it, now what?"

A blinding flash of light coming from the parking lot outside his window answered the question before he had the chance to talk to anyone. Pulling at the blinds, he looked out at the portal pulsing and arcing in the parking lot. A man dressed all in black was walking through it.

Mathers bolted out of his office, shouting orders at whoever would listen. "Get a science team up here right away, and an armed squad. Did anyone see who that man was? I need the video surveillance from the last six hours for the entire complex, delivered to my office twenty minutes ago!" He ran for the door and burst outside to the parking lot, running toward the portal with his weapon drawn. By the time he got within twenty feet of the gaping hole in space, the Man in Black was long gone.

The edges of the hole rippled and arced with electricity, sending sparks tumbling to the ground. Through the hole, Mathers could see another world, with green rolling hills covered with a strange feathery grass. Small trees and shrubs dotted the landscape, and a great walled castle city rested in the background. As he stood and admired the hole, the first of the science team arrived. Mathers broke his gaze from the portal and looked at the man. "How do we shut it down? How do we close it?"

The man in the lab coat looked from Mathers, to the portal, and then back again. "I... I don't know. I've never seen anything like it before."

Chapter 21 - Morganateltheranthumagus

The swamp was damp and humid that morning, more so than the previous day, as the companions trudged their way through it. There were fewer dry spots as they got closer to the mountain and they found themselves walking in mucky water that went as high as their knees. There was still no sign of the Narshuks who followed them, but the howls they heard the previous night told them that the creatures were narrowing the gap between them. Sometime around midday, the first drops of rain began to fall through the trees.

At one point Seth tried to make conversation, but his words were lost in the constant white noise. He sighed and resumed in silence through the most unpleasant place he had ever walked. The rain fell harder the closer they got to the mountain until they were forced to hold hands to avoid losing each other in the downpour.

Seth had never seen rain fall like this before, but could tell by the way they walked that there were fewer trees here, and the ground was starting to get more solid. Their journey straightened out, and Cedric's almost uncanny sense of direction got them to the foot of the mountain. The weather cleared up as they climbed through the foothills and the sun broke through the clouds.

"Oh thank god," Seth said as the sun's beams cut through the clouds like a razor. "I'm not sure how much more of that rain I could take."

Malia removed her helmet at some point through the rain, and her hair was drenched down the back of her armor, water still running off of it. When it was wet, her blond hair reached almost to the base of her back, but the curly wave it had when it dried made it seem shorter. She smiled back at Seth as she led the way up the side of the mountain. "I would have to agree with you. The sound of that horrid rain on my helmet was absolutely deafening, and I'm going to take hours to dry in this armor."

Seth shifted his gaze to the bag slung over his shoulder. "Hang on a second, I want to make sure my father's book is okay."

The companions stopped while Seth placed his bag on the ground and opened it. Expecting to see the bag half-filled with water, he was surprised to find the inside bone dry. He looked up at Malia and said, "I can't believe it. It's dry."

She nodded back to him. "As I would expect. If it is as priceless as Cedric claims, and I have no doubt that it is, then it likely has enchantments on it to keep it safe and dry."

"Oh," said Seth, with a dumbfounded expression on his face. "Alright, let's go then."

A clear path zigzagged up the side of the mountain to a dark cave entrance. Seth guessed that if they walked at a good pace it would take them another two hours to reach it. Soaking wet from the rain, the three companions started up the mountain.

It was a smooth walk to begin with, the path being well worn into the dirt of the foothills. It didn't take long before the packed dirt started to break up and the path became rocky. It was clumsy to walk on, and Malia and Cedric helped Seth keep his balance more than once.

The path went straight up the sunny side of the mountain for about thirty minutes and turned at a small plateau. By that time, the sunshine had dried both Seth and Cedric, and they were able to enjoy the view off the side of the mountain. The landscape around was like nothing Seth had ever seen, with the twisted trees and mist of the swamp surrounding the base of the mountain, and then further out a wide skirt of rambling plains. The landscape was unmarred by human inventions and took Seth's breath away. He stopped for a few minutes, just to admire it, and said in passing to his companions, "I've never seen anything so beautiful."

Cedric nodded. "It is quite a stunning view, isn't it?"

"In my world, there's nothing like this. Everywhere you go, there's houses, or skyscrapers, or power lines, or something else that breaks up the landscape. This," sweeping his arm out across the horizon, "this is absolutely breathtaking."

A hand came down and rested on Seth's shoulder, startling him out of his fascination. He turned to see Malia standing behind him. "I hate to interfere, but we really must keep moving. The Narshuks are not going to care how beautiful it is out there. They only want you, Seth." She pointed to a spot about halfway through the swamp where the trees looked like they were shifting slightly. "There they are, charging through the forest on our tail. It will not take them long to finish crossing the swamp."

Seth let out a sigh and turned, continuing up the side of the mountain. By the time they reached the mouth of the cave, the path was steep and treacherous. Rocks gave way at every step, and the surface was loose and hard to get a proper foothold. The path all but disappeared in the loose terrain, so they walked in a relatively straight line toward the cave entrance.

At one point Cedric slipped and started to fall, but Malia and Seth managed to catch him and help him regain his footing. The companions reached the cave entrance as the Narshuks emerged from the swamp below them. Cedric pointed out the creatures just before ducking inside the cave. Seth and Malia followed him close behind.

Darkness enveloped the companions as they walked into the musty cave. There was a very distinct silence within the cave that made their footsteps echo, and the usual clinking of Malia's armor sounded much louder. They spent ten minutes navigating the twisting tunnels, walking deeper into the mountain, when they saw a faint blue glow ahead of them.

Seth whispered to the others, "What's that?" The blue light was cool but not harsh, and seemed out of place in such a cave. If anything, Seth expected to see the warm glow of firelight, but after the last few days, nothing much surprised him.

Cedric responded, being more familiar with the area. "That, my friend, is our destination at last."

A feeling of relief welled up inside Seth as they turned the corner. Before them was a shimmering wall of blue energy that looked like somebody had drawn a curtain across the tunnel. *Two weeks ago I would have been running for my life from this,* Seth thought with a smile.

He stopped just short of the curtain of energy and waited for his companions to catch up, then turned to face them. "So now what?"

A smile came over Cedric's face. "After you, our fearless leader." The jovial Bard's taunt didn't bother Seth as he turned around and pressed through the energy curtain. The places where he touched it seemed to grow brighter, and it felt to him like pushing through a wall of jelly, but the resistance did not prevent him from passing through in any way.

When Seth was all the way through, Malia tried next. She walked up to the curtain and placed a hand against it to push through, but the curtain pushed back. She pushed harder, and the resistance increased. A scowl came over her face and she turned to face the masked Bard. "What is going on Cedric? Why can I not follow him?"

Cedric smirked. "I apologize, my dear; I haven't been entirely truthful with you. Only a Time Weaver may enter."

Seth didn't notice his companions staying behind. The sight before him was dazzling. The walls and floors were made of glittering blue crystal, smooth but faceted, giving the cave a delicate, almost fragile feel. Seth walked through the long corridor, drawn in by something deep inside the cave. The crystal let off a faint blue-white glow that lit his way. Moments later he emerged from the corridor into a large room, also made of crystal.

The room was large enough to hold a small group of people, with the far end of the room opening into a great cavern. Seth walked to the edge of the opening and looked out into the cavern. It was pitch black, lacking the glow that the crystal held around him. No bottom could be seen in the larger cavern, and no other walls. A slight rush of warm air rose out of the cavern and drifted up to an invisible ceiling. From within the cavern there came a slow *whoosh, whoosh* sound that filled the crystal room. A rumble traveled up through the inner cavern that shook the ground he stood on, and reminded him of a large dog growling, only much louder and much deeper.

From the growl came a low guttural voice. "Who disturbs my rest?" The voice carried all around him and shook him to the bone, rattling his teeth. The intensity of the voice made his ears hurt and reminded him of the bass line in the dance music he used to listen to in clubs when he was younger. No words came to him and so he just stood at the ledge until the voice came again. "Who disturbs my rest? I can feel you there, answer me." The voice was louder this time, and fueled by impatience.

Somehow Seth found his voice and managed to scratch out, "Seth, Seth Alkirk."

The booming voice came once more, "Well Seth, Seth Alkirk, I trust you have a good reason for waking me?" The intensity of the voice eased up some and made it tolerable for Seth. He tried to make out what was at the bottom of the cavern as his eyes adjusted to the dim light, but he still could not make out a bottom. There was a great rush of air that came up out of the abyss as he stood at the edge and said nothing. He was reminded that a question had been posed, and he still had not answered.

"I'm sorry for the intrusion, Cedric the Bard brought me here. He said you were a friend of his, that you could help us."

"A friend? Of sorts. As far as help goes, state your case, Time Weaver." the voice boomed back.

Caught off-guard by the stranger's apparent knowledge of what he was, all Seth could muster was, "Time Weaver?"

"Yes, Time Weaver. You look like a human, but you do not smell like one."

"I am human. I mean, I thought I was. That's sort of the reason I'm here. I'm not really sure what's going on anymore. Two weeks ago, I had a good, normal life. Now I've been taken from my home, escorted across wilderness in a foreign land, chased and attacked by monsters, and apparently I can now use magic, though I don't know how."

There was a long pause before the voice spoke again, but when it did, it was much more soothing. "So you are from the dead world then?"

"Dead world?"

"Yes, I believe you call it Earth? It is dead to us; my kind can no longer exist there. We can barely exist here, and I may very well be the last." There was a note of sadness to his voice, which disappeared with his next words. "And magic you say? What elements can you wield?"

"I... well... Fire, Water and Shadow. And I guess Time."

"Impressive. Your father could only wield two."

"My father?" Seth asked, confused about yet another reference to his missing father. "Just who are you anyway? And how do you know who my father was?"

There was movement in the wide cavern before Seth. He felt it more than he saw it at first, but then the illusion of blackness of the cavern melted away revealing a glittering cavern filled with treasures beyond his wildest dreams. The walls were made of crystal similar to the room he stood in, but the floor was covered with a hoard of gold coins, gemstones and jewelry. They seemed like mountains as he looked down on them. Resting on top of the largest of the golden hills was a great gold dragon, glittering brighter than all the treasure in the world. He was looking at the side of the dragon's head, its massive eye piercing through him. It unfolded its wings and stretched them to their full breadth, reaching from one end of the cavern to the other. He estimated at least sixty feet per wing, but it was hard to tell before it refolded its wings down onto its back.

It spoke again, "My name is Morganateltheranthumagus, but if you are fond of a shorter name, you may call me Morganath. And I once flew with your father."

⤜

Malia turned to face Cedric. "Not entirely truthful? What do you mean, not entirely truthful? What part of this quest have you been not truthful about?"

Cedric shied away from the fuming warrior. He knew this moment would come, but had not prepared himself for it. "Malia, my dear, Seth must learn to control his powers. And this is just the... thing... to teach him."

Malia stood tall, her fingers wrapped around the hilt of her sword. She was not one to give in to emotions like anger, but she allowed herself this one concession. "Cedric, what's in there? You said we were going to see a friend of yours, and now I find out that you've misled us?"

"Well, he's not exactly a friend. More an acquaintance. A friend of a friend... of a friend. Either way, Seth is in good hands, and when he emerges, I assure you, he will most certainly not be the same person who went in."

Malia opened her mouth to berate Cedric, but stopped when the sounds of the Narshuks echoed down the hallway. Instead of giving him a tongue lashing, she said, "And what do we do if they make it here before Seth is done?"

Cedric shrugged, then with a smile said, "We fight."

⤜

Seth turned back and watched as the great gold dragon stepped down off the mounds of gold and navigated them like they were solid ground with practiced precision. He had a hard time believing that something so massive could be so graceful, and yet, it was before his eyes. Every step Morganath took was thought out, measured and executed with a precision that astounded him.

Morganath lowered his head toward the ledge, his great eye staring at Seth. "Krycin," he said, his booming voice trailing off into a memory. "You resemble your father."

Not sure whether to scream and run, or stand his ground, Seth moved back a step from the edge. "Yeah, so I've heard. But I still don't know why everybody believes this. Whether I look like Krycin or not, my father was a car salesman named John Alkirk. He abandoned me and my mother when I was five. There was nothing heroic about that."

A strange sound came from Morganath's throat; it might have been a laugh, but Seth wasn't sure. "Your father was a Time Weaver, and his name was Krycin. But I don't blame him for wanting to hide the truth from you," said the dragon as it positioned its head down in front of the ledge. "Climb on."

"Climb on? Are you insane?"

"If your friends are still waiting outside, they are in grave danger. Narshuks approach my lair, and with or without you, I intend to exterminate them," Morganath said, moving so that the gap between himself and the ledge closed.

Seth reluctantly placed a foot on Morganath's head, then hoisted himself up on the back of the dragon's neck. "Hold on tight, young Seth. I don't imagine you've ever ridden on dragonback before." Morganath's skin was smooth and covered with fine scales. Seth ran his hand down the golden hide and found a hold on one of the many spines protruding from the dragon's crest.

With one leg to each side of the dragon's neck, Seth called up to him, "Alright, I'm ready." He couldn't quite understand why he wasn't nervous about flying on the dragon's back. He had flown in planes a number of times in his life and was always fighting a lump in his throat when the plane took off. But now it felt like a natural place to be, like he belonged there.

Morganath stepped away from the ledge, giving Seth a much better view of the inside of the dragon's lair. The light coming from a large hole in the far end of the lair made the gold glitter and shine as it shook loose from its piles and tumbled down the slopes. Seth could see many of these piles distributed around the lair, and not a single spot on the floor was visible through the treasure. Morganath's muscular legs flexed and propelled them into the air as he stretched out his wings and swept them down in one smooth motion. Before Seth could figure out what was happening, they were aloft in one of the smoothest takeoffs he ever felt. Even the giant airliners from his home could not match it.

As Morganath pumped his wings up and down, they rose into the air and toward the hole in the mountain where the sun shone in.

Seth squinted as they emerged, holding on tight to the spines so that he wouldn't fall from the dragon's back. With one last kick off the edge of the mountain they were aloft in open air and out in the sunshine, Morganath glittering like a beacon in the sky.

Malia scowled at Cedric. "Why did you not just tell us that to begin with? Why the pretense?"

"Because, my dear, there was no way that you would ever agree to something that was going to cause a delay in your journey. I've dealt with enough headstrong warriors to know that once you get an idea in your head, it takes beating it with a ten-pound hammer to get it back out again. But offer you a way to get there faster, now we're talking. Manipulative? Yes, but effective in accomplishing my task."

"Did your task happen to include getting us killed?" The question was more rhetorical than anything. There was a scuffle just outside the cave entrance and the Narshuk's growls and snarls echoed off the cave walls. Malia drew her sword, prepared to fight to the death if she had to. One of the creatures rounded the bend that led out of the cave and stood facing the two companions. Its fur was muddy and matted, and it was still wet from the swamp rains that seemed to continue even in the sunlight. A foul odor drifted in ahead of the creature that smelled like swamp scum mixed with wet dog. The thing's panting and growling echoed all around the two companions and seemed to penetrate their skin.

The Narshuk let out a long slow howl when it spotted its target at the end of the tunnel and alerted the other creatures. Its shoulders just cleared the rock walls, and it stooped to avoid the ceiling, but Malia suspected that it would be just as dangerous as it was in the clearing. Long sharp claws clicked against the rock floor as it lowered its head, readying for a charge. Malia focused on her blade and the steel blazed to life in a curtain of flames.

A few tense moments passed while Malia and the beast stared each other down. Its heavy breaths filled the air with a stench that almost made Malia retch, but she stood tall and strong facing the much larger creature. It made the first move, ducking its head down and running at her. Malia watched its movements and waited, not wanting to give up too much too soon in the fight. The Narshuk launched at her, putting its entire bulk into one massive leap. Malia ducked to the side at the last second and swung up with her sword, tearing into the monster's hide and setting it on fire. Cedric

144

crouched off to the side, not equipped to battle hand-to-hand with a creature of this magnitude.

Malia worked her way around the Narshuk to get between it and Cedric while it writhed on the floor, howling with rage and trying to put out the flames that would otherwise consume it. Malia lashed out a second time and grazed the creature's arm, leaving a wide gash that filled with blood. Another howl told her that the wound she had inflicted was deeper than it appeared. It got to its feet, battling off other advances from Malia with one hand and taking many smaller wounds in the process. Blood gushed from its wounds, soaking its fur and pooling on the floor. Still it advanced with another attack at Malia. She swung back aiming to kill, but the Narshuk caught her blade mid-swing with its free hand. Her blade cut deep into the palm of its hand, and it countered with its own attack, its razor-sharp claws bearing down on Malia.

Malia held tight to her sword and used it to swing her body away from the beast. Its claws caught her chest-plate and tore several wide gouges through the steel, leaving Malia with minor flesh wounds. Her sword flared with heat and flames, the creature's hand sizzling against it causing the smell of its burning hair and flesh to fill the air.

Cedric readied his bow and fired several shots down the hall to keep the other Narshuks at bay. They snarled in protest to this, but one well-aimed shot struck one of them in the eye and drove into its brain. It slumped to the floor, prompting the rest of them to back off.

The Narshuk fighting Malia pushed at her sword and drove her back against the wall, pinning Cedric into the corner. It lifted its good hand again, meaning to kill her this time.

Morganath pumped his wings and maneuvered himself in front of the cave opening, the first of the Narshuks taking notice of the dragon hovering in the air behind them. Morganath's shadow blotted out the sun over them and caused some of them to panic. "Stop time," he called over his shoulder at Seth.

It took Seth by surprise. "What do you mean, stop time? I can't!"

"You must. Your friends may already be dead, but if they aren't, the only chance they have is if you stop time. Clear your mind and focus on what you want." Morganath spoke like this was something he had witnessed many times before, but the experience was still new to Seth.

Thinking about what he had been through the last two weeks, the glass falling in the restaurant, when time stopped in Denton at the intersection, when Cedric shot the arrow, and the attack of the Narshuks after that. On each occasion time either slowed down or stopped; it hadn't occurred to him that it was his doing.

Morganath drew closer to the cave entrance as some of the Narshuks prepared attacks against him. The band of Narshuks below howled with rage at the dragon. In turn, Morganath inhaled, filling his lungs to capacity, and let out a roar of his own that deafened Seth and broke his focus on what he was doing. "Clear your mind Seth, don't think about doing it, just do it," he called back to Seth as the Narshuks loosed arrows at them.

Think of nothing, he thought, *clear your mind.* He closed his eyes and let the sensations of the world fall away. The arrows that were flying through the air slowed, Morganath's beating heart calmed, then stopped. Seth could hear nothing, feel nothing. No air rushed past his face, there were no growls or snarls, no battle cries. The flow of time obeyed his command, and stopped.

Seth opened his eyes. A gout of flame flowed from the dragon's mouth, aimed at the Narshuks below. Arrows intended for both dragon and rider hung in the air, unmoving. Clouds in the sky sat like wads of cotton on a great blue table. *Now what?* Seth thought as he looked down at the ground at least a hundred feet below. Morganath's tail came the closest to the ground, and so Seth climbed down, using the dragon's spines to support himself. When he got to the end of the tail he could see the ground only twenty feet below him. He lowered himself down as far as he could so that his feet were no more than fifteen feet from the ground, and then let go.

Seth braced for the impact, but was surprised when he drifted down on a sudden but powerful air current instead. The solid ground touched his feet and he was able to steady himself on the steep slope that led up to the cave entrance. Picking his way to the top where the Narshuks crowded the cave entrance, he weaved his way through them and into the cave. The lupine creatures stood like statues, terrible snarling expressions on their faces. They seemed to be holding back from the bend in the tunnel where Seth had left his friends. There was one creature lying on the ground with an arrow through its eye. Blood and fluid oozed out onto the thing's face as it lay dead.

Rounding the bend in the tunnel, Seth spotted one of the Narshuks poised to make a killing blow at Malia. Malia cringed away from it, her armor already torn open across her chest. Several arrows hung in the air as he walked toward his companions; fired from Cedric's bow, they kept the rest of the Narshuks at bay while the other two fought.

Seth approached his companions and laid a hand on each of their shoulders. With a thought, time restarted for them. Malia finished a startled yell that had frozen in her throat. She felt the hand on her shoulder and turned toward it after she reassured herself that the Narshuk wasn't going to move. Surprise filled her face at the sight of Seth. Cedric stood up, a grin across his face. He brushed off his clothing and adjusted the mask on his face. "Well then, I knew you could do it!" Cedric said before Seth could speak.

"Yes, come on, we have to go," Seth replied as he offered a hand to Malia.

She hesitated, her heart still pounding in her ears. "Yes. Just one moment. I have a score to settle here." She pulled her sword free from the Narshuk's grip as Seth and Cedric backed away. In one fluid motion, she swung up at the frozen creature and sliced through its throat. Without a second thought she followed the other two companions out of the cave.

Morganath exhaled a stream of flames intended to kill the small group who fired on him and his rider. The fiery breath came like a fountain from a volcanic geyser that seared through the Narshuks' fur and flesh. Their screams let him know that he hit his mark. The arrows flying through the air toward him bounced off his golden hide without a scratch on the interlocking scales that protected him. As the creatures below him burned, he became aware of the weight absent from his neck. Seth was gone.

The massive dragon looked around below him, his great wings pumping to keep him aloft and in place. Movement caught his eye on the side of the mountain. Three figures raced down the slope away from the cave. Morganath's keen eyes focused in on the figures and he recognized one of them as Seth. Turning his head back to the cave, he blasted a stream of fire into the opening, flowing like a liquid and scorching everything in its path. Screams of pain and rage echoed from the cave that captured the attention of the three companions. Moments later the cave was silent.

Morganath swooped through the air and found a clearing near the bottom of the mountain where he could land. The companions reached him just as he touched down on the rocky surface. The weight of the massive dragon cracked the stone under his feet, snuffing the life out of any small plants that dared to grow in such an inhospitable environment.

Seth reached him first, stopping and turning to wait for the others. Cedric followed close behind him, not bothered by the giant golden dragon who now blocked their path. Malia came last, her steps slowing as she drew closer to the majestic beast.

Smiling as she approached, Seth introduced the dragon. "Malia, Cedric, this is Morganath. Morganath, meet my friends, Malia and Cedric."

Looking up in awe, Malia said, "Never in my life have I seen a dragon. You are so large, so beautiful. My name is Malia Corsair, a Swordmage from Findoor. It is an honor to stand in your presence." She performed the best curtsy she could in full armor.

Morganath turned his head to look at Malia. "Indeed, as it is a pleasure to meet you." Turning his gaze toward the masked figure standing next to Seth he said, "And you are Cedric the Bard, I presume?"

Cedric made a deep embellished bow toward him. "It is a pleasure, I assure you." He stood up and turned toward Seth. "I trust you found what you needed in there?"

"Well, sort of. But not really. I think I have more questions now than answers," Seth said, shifting his gaze to the ground and shuffling his feet.

The massive dragon shifted its gaze back to Seth. "If it is answers you seek, I shall give them where I can. What is your next destination?"

"We are heading for Findoor castle, to see Arch-Magus Merek, and to provide protection for Seth," Malia said, cutting into the conversation.

"Then climb up, and hold on tight. I shall fly you there, and provide what answers I can. It is three days' flight from here. If we leave now, we can make some distance before nightfall." Morganath lowered his neck and shoulder to allow the companions to climb on.

As he climbed up, Seth said with a smile, "Please, don't use the word 'fall' when talking about flying."

All the companions had a good laugh, Cedric most of all. Even Morganath rumbled an approval. Malia climbed up behind Seth and wrapped her arms around his torso to keep from falling. Her armor dug in at a few spots, but Seth found unexpected comfort in the contact. Cedric was last, looping his fingers in the leather straps of Malia's armor.

Morganath waited until Seth gave the all clear, and then launched himself into the air. With a powerful stroke of his wings he was up and in flight. The companions were jarred back during the takeoff and Seth felt Malia wrap her arms tighter around his waist. Morganath circled a number of times to gain altitude, then turned away from the sun and began the long journey to Findoor.

Pain and rage coursed through the Narshuk. Its wounds gushed blood, causing its vision to blur. Its target vanished, throwing its balance off in mid-attack and causing it to tumble forward into the blue curtain of energy that protected the lair, and then onto the ground. Gasping for breath, it felt the slash across its throat. It made an effort to get up, but every movement made the blood rush out faster.

The rest of the Narshuks advanced after their targets disappeared. The largest of them approached the one lying on the ground. It bled out into a growing pool, its fur matted and scorched. The large one looked down at it, and said in its guttural language, "You disgust me." It raised its foot and brought it down on the wounded Narshuk's head, crushing it with a single blow. Brains and blood sprayed out all sides, and the creature's body twitched the last of its life out.

A commotion at the entrance of the cave drew the attention of the largest Narshuk. Howls of approval turned to panic and rage as a flood of fire poured into the cave, flowing like a deadly liquid. It faced the imminent danger and snarled with rage at the coming wave. The flames hit the creature with enough force to knock it back against the energy curtain, crushing it. Fur and skin burned away, exposing the muscles beneath. The pain only lasted a brief second as all the nerves charred. All the other Narshuks fell to the dragon's breath, with the commander howling through the attack. When the flames pulled away, the burnt and broken creature slumped to the ground without a sound. But even as the companions prepared and took their leave, this last remaining Narshuk crawled his way to the entrance of the cave through the ashes of his monstrous companions, fleshless and gasping for breath.

Chapter 22 - Festering

Merek and King Verand stood in the war room looking over the enchanted maps of the battlefield. They watched as the Narshuk army earned a victory against their troops on the Losteron Plains. "My gods, Merek, how can we face such an enemy," Verand said while watching the Narshuks celebrate their victory. "Our forces are devastated." Deep lines creased the King's face, the stress of the war already taking its toll on him. They failed to hold back the tide of Narshuks flooding in from the Badlands, and soon the vicious army would march on Findoor Castle.

"We must lock down the castle, Sire. It is our only choice. Allow the troops to remain out front of the city and set up camp. We will begin our preparations for defense immediately."

Verand looked forlorn at this prospect. "And let Grian march to our front gates?" He looked up at Merek with a darkness in his eyes that chilled Merek to the core. "No, I will not allow that. We must launch a counter-offensive; now, while they aren't expecting it."

"Verand, you know as well as I do that doing so would be as good as condemning the whole Kingdom to death. We have time before the army reaches us, and Malia yet comes with the Time Weaver. There is still hope, but we must conserve what energy we have and make it count. If you wish, I will notify the city and what remains of the army right away."

"No, Merek; I'll go myself and tell them the news. It is my responsibility."

Merek nodded. "As you wish, Sire." He turned to walk away, but as he did, The King spoke one last time.

"Merek," he paused for a long while, trying to find the right words. "I am sorry for the words I spoke to you. I understand now how right you were, and why my father valued your counsel."

The old Arch-Magus thought for a moment, then came back with a response the King hadn't expected. "Sire, not even a Time Weaver could go back and change things now. Do not mourn for what is done that could have been done differently."

"You're right of course, old man. I'll go now, and hopefully spirits can be lifted, and bodies mended before the tide rolls in. How long do we have, Merek, before they reach us?"

Merek thought carefully for a moment. "Four days, maybe five. Grian's army is strong, but they have suffered casualties. It will take them time to regroup and resume their march. I shall have the Scryes keep an eye on the situation and update me as they approach. We will not be caught unawares."

"Very well. Thank you, Merek. Meet me here again this time tomorrow," the King said as he opened the door for Merek, who nodded in response.

The two men went their separate ways. Merek descended to the Scryes to see if they had any news and to give them their next instructions. Verand approached the waiting army in the field before the castle. Runners were dispatched to summon every available healer and to inform the kitchens to prepare for additional people as the city would soon be evacuated.

The King stepped out of the city walls and into a scene of utter chaos. Miles of fields were now covered with the Findoor army. As far as the eye could see there were armored men milling about, helping the wounded and setting up tents. Some healers had already arrived and were tending to the worst of the wounded. Random smatterings of sloped canvas roofs, poles and ropes made the field look more like a refugee camp than an army.

Walking among the troops, Verand was trailed by an entourage of runners, pages and bureaucrats all looking for him to do or say something. He looked over the scene surrounding him, then turned back to the men and women who followed him. "Don't chatter at me like a bunch of gulls. Go, make yourself useful. Get bandages, supplies, food, anything you can carry or do that will help our brave men. We have four days to prepare. Let's not waste them, for our enemies will not wait for us to be ready." He turned back to the masses of men who occupied the fields and spoke a few words of magic, a simple spell that he learned many years before. When he cleared his voice to speak, it amplified and carried all the way to the edges of the army so that they could hear him as clear as if he were beside them. "We have lived a time of peace and prosperity, a time of light. Now that darkness descends upon us, it is more important than ever that we stand together. Rest now, and recover from your hard-fought battle. Enjoy some time with your families, and above all else, maintain hope that light will somehow shine on us again."

The companions traveled as far as they dared into the night on the dragon's back. Seth urged Morganath to land after Malia had nodded off with her arms still wrapped around his waist. The gentle up-and down motion of the dragon's flight was soothing, and had almost lulled Seth to sleep as well.

The sky was clear that night, and they were out of the forested lands again, flying over great plains spotted with rivers and small lakes. Foreign stars lit up the sky, creating strange constellations. A thin crescent moon hung high in the sky, but it was much larger than the one Seth was used to. The dim light it shed let them set up camp. Cedric helped Seth ease Malia down off the dragon's back; she was now in such a deep sleep that even transferring her to the ground did not wake her. She seemed peaceful, and so they left her and approached Morganath.

"You said you once flew with my father. When?" Seth said as he sat down close to the massive dragon.

Morganath laid his head down on the ground like a cat preparing to sleep, his chin flat against the ground. His slow, measured breathing was directed away from the two companions who sat near him. "It was many years ago when I last saw your father, or any Time Weaver. Had it not been for your friend the Bard, I might never have seen another." There was a distant note to Morganath's voice that sounded almost haunting. "Dragons and Time Weavers have always been companions. There are few who live as long as we. I spent many years with your father before the war, but when Gladius began his attacks, your mother and father were the first to lead the charge against him."

"Wait, my mother?" Seth interrupted, "She knew as well? God damn it! Why didn't anybody tell me? Why was I left in the dark for so many years? My whole life is a lie, and I'm just supposed to be okay with this?"

Cedric had an amused smirk on his face, having kept quiet so far, he felt it was now the time to speak up. "Seth, your life hasn't been a lie. You have lived your life as a human, and from what I can see, you lived well. But make no mistake, you are, and always have been a Time Weaver. Nothing can change who you are."

A sudden calm came over Seth, though he couldn't think why. Many questions still circled in his mind, but the urgency for answers had eased. "Thanks, Cedric, but that doesn't tell me what happened to my father."

Morganath shifted to get comfortable and made the ground tremble with his weight. Turning his head so that the two men were visible to him he said, "Your father destroyed Gladius, but nobody is really sure what happened to him after that. Time Weavers are extremely difficult to kill. Gladius discovered a method to rob a Time Weaver of Lyecha's gift, which he used to wipe out many of your people. Your mother was pregnant with you when her powers were taken, and she would have died by Gladius's hand but for your father. His actions on that day saved many lives. Nobody knew what your father did with you and your mother. All he would say was that you were hidden, and safe. But he was a changed man after that day, and when he battled Gladius on the Findoor fields, he was a mere shell of his former self. Only your father knows what truly happened the day he and Gladius disappeared from the world."

Tears welled up in Seth's eyes. "Alright, I've had enough. I need to get some sleep, and I can't bear to hear about him anymore. I'm not sure I want to know now. I can barely remember his face, and it was so many years ago. The only reminder I have left of him is this book." He motioned to the laptop bag still slung over his shoulder. "And even this only contains a bunch of stories he once read to me."

Cedric gave a slight nod. "It's getting late, we should all get some sleep."

The great dragon huffed out a breath that knocked down the grass before him. "I have no need of sleep. I will keep watch. Sleep well, young ones."

It was still early summer, but when the companions awoke in the morning, a cool rain was starting to fall. Seth woke up first from his dreamless rest. Not long after that, Cedric and Malia woke. The flesh wounds on Malia's chest looked superficial, but redness spread out around them in lines. Cedric helped her remove her chest plate and tended to her as well as he could. The scratches ran from her collar on the right, diagonally down to just above her left breast. "You'll need a new shirt to travel," Cedric said, taking out a black silk top from his pack and handing it to her. "Here, take this one."

"Thank you Cedric," Malia said as she took the shirt from him. She turned her back to the two men and shed the tattered old shirt, letting it flutter to the ground. Cedric turned away from her to give her some privacy, but Seth was caught off guard. Her skin was smooth and pale, but marred with occasional scars from past battles. Her muscles rippled as she lifted the new shirt over her head. Her raised arms accentuated her smooth hourglass figure. She turned slightly as she stretched, and the soft curve of her breast made Seth catch his breath. The black silk slid down over her body and covered up her well-built, yet very feminine torso. She turned back to them in time to see Seth turn his head away, trying to hide that he was staring. She stepped past him, but could not hide her smirk. "Okay, boys, let us go now before the rain gets too heavy."

Morganath grunted approval as the three climbed back onto his neck and got comfortable. As he took to the air, the rain picked up and pelted them with cold heavy drops that pierced their clothing. Seth could feel Malia shivering, her arms around his waist again, her body pressed into his for warmth. The rain lasted only as long as it took Morganath to rise above the clouds and take to a steady flight. After that, the only challenge was the changing air currents that threatened to blow them off the dragon's back if they lost their grip.

A few hours later they soared over open country again as the rain clouds below them cleared. The land stretched out below them for endless miles and the sun was reaching up toward its apex. Green fields and lush forests covered the rolling hills of the countryside. Far to their right, Seth could see jagged mountains scarring the perfect skyline; lines of smoke rose up from various places in the mountains and despite the full sun, the whole range seemed dark.

Pointing at the mountain range he called back to Malia, "What's that?"

She squinted as she looked into the distance. "That's the Badlands. Where the Narshuks thrive, and not much else."

"So Humans, Time Weavers, Dragons, Narshuks... are there any other intelligent races I should know about? Dwarves? Elves?" He cracked a bit of a joke, remembering some of the races from the fantasy books he read in high school.

"Dorbs? Elbs? I know not of such races. I have heard that far to the east there is a race of wild tree dwellers, the Ardans, who live in an island rain forest. And Merek once told me of a black-skinned race of giants who shared the Badlands with the Narshuks, though they have not been seen in many years."

Malia leaned in close to Seth when she spoke to keep from yelling over the howling wind. Seth found himself wanting to continue the conversation, just so that he could feel the warmth of her body against his, her breath against his ear. "Your world is so different from mine."

"Yes, in many ways. I would love to see more of your world, with its great buildings, and horseless carriages. The wonders I saw in only the brief time I was there."

"It's not all it's cracked up to be. I'd much rather be here, I think."

"Well, you are lucky then. There is nobody, other than Merek, who can train you on the use of your powers. Though, once you are trained, you will be able to travel between worlds at will."

"Really? You mean I could send myself home?"

"Time Weavers have many talents, most of which revolve around your control of magical energy. It was once thought that Time Weavers were second only to gods, though Gladius showed us differently."

"But I can't control my powers yet. At least, not very well."

She smiled and shook her head. "Always doubting. Seth, you must open your mind. You can stop time. Merek is one of the most powerful wizards who ever lived, and even he cannot stop time. And yet you can do it with a thought. Time Weavers are said to be able to control massive quantities of magic. Students of magic in this world study for years to be able to cast their first spells. Wizards like Merek have devoted their lives to studying magic. I myself can only cast very minor spells. And yet you are able to do it naturally."

"This is all so strange and new to me. Where I grew up, magic was something you only saw in movies or on TV. I'm just not sure if I can handle this."

"Merek shall teach you. Do not worry, Seth, when we arrive at Findoor castle, all will be made clear." Malia looked away from Seth and out to the land stretched out below them. There was a village below them where children ran out of their houses to see the dragon flying by. Many of them ran through the streets waving and yelling up at the dragon and companions. "Seth, can you tell Morganath to land here? It is approaching midday, and we have yet to eat a decent meal."

"Yeah, sure. I'm starved." Seth let the topic of magic drop. He didn't really want to think about it. He let Morganath know that they wanted to eat, and moments later they were circling down to land in a field outside the little town.

Cedric piped up from the back just before they touched down, "My friends, why are we stopping?"

Malia turned back to him. "Are you hungry?"

"Famished. I wondered when we might stop to eat. Here's hoping they have something good cooking." Cedric flashed a smile from under his mask as they braced for the imminent landing.

Children in the town were already running out into the field to see the great gold dragon, with their mothers following close behind them to keep them out of trouble. Morganath folded his wings to his back and lowered his head to allow the companions to dismount. Malia rubbed at her chest and winced. The children flooded past them as they walked away from the dragon and toward the town. Cedric flashed a grin to the women running after the children. "It's alright, my dears, he won't harm them."

A big burly man walked from the edge of the town, far behind the ladies. His confident stride told the companions that he was in charge. Cedric stepped forward to represent them. "Greetings my friend. Pardon us for dropping down on your fair town like this. We are on a journey to Findoor and are in need of nourishment."

The man approaching them was large, but not fat. His broad shoulders and muscled arms spoke of a life of hard work in the fields surrounding the town. His hair was black with just the beginnings of silver streaks in it, and he wore a full beard with pride. A callused hand stretched out to Cedric as he came to a stop, and with a smile he said, "Welcome, friends. Come, enjoy our hospitality. We don't see many dragons around here these days; he's an impressive looking beast." Morganath, who was still within earshot, gave a low rumbling scoff and shuddered from snout to tail at the man's assertion, but said nothing. "The name's Erith Porter, and this, our little town, is Sampson."

Cedric took Erith's outstretched hand to give it a shake, and was taken by a vice-like grip that brought tears to his eyes. He did his best to keep his composure while the big man grinned down at him. "Pleasure to meet you, Erith." Cedric seized his hand back from the man before his bones gave out, trying to be as polite as he could. "My name is Cedric, and this is Seth and Malia. If you would be so kind as to show us the tavern, we'll be no trouble at all and on our way in no time."

Erith nodded and gave them another of his broad grins. "Right this way, friends." He led the companions to a small building at the center of town where, even at midday, flickering light flooded through the windows and doors.

The tavern looked like an old-fashioned Western saloon. Everywhere he looked there was wood: creaking floor boards, old worn wood chairs, large tables where the townsfolk would gather for food and drink, and a long bar that stretched across one wall. Small lanterns hung from the rafters, shedding light on the room. The smell of old booze and smoke hung in the air along with the food that cooked in the kitchen.

The companions pulled up chairs at a table. An overweight barmaid came lumbering out and took their orders. Malia rubbed her chest again, wincing at the pain radiating out from her wounds. Seth saw the gesture and grew concerned. "Those scratches are getting worse aren't they?"

"'Tis nothing Seth, a bit of infection; it will clear up."

"Clear up, my ass. Let me see it."

Malia pulled down shirt to the tip of the first scratch at her collar bone and peeled back the dressings that Cedric had placed over it. Red lines of infection spread out around the scratch like worms under her skin. The center of the scratch had turned black and was filled with yellow oozing pus that smelled of decaying flesh. Seth gasped and turned away, repulsed by the wound. Cedric leaned in and took a closer look. "We must find a healer for this immediately, Malia. It seems the Narshuk you fought may have won the battle after all."

She pulled the bandage out further so that she could see. "By the gods, what's happening to me?"

With a forlorn expression Cedric said, "The blasted creature was diseased. If we don't treat you soon, your flesh will continue to rot away. This particular disease moves quickly, so time is of the essence. You two eat. I shall go and hopefully return soon with a healer." He leapt from his seat and ran from the tavern as fast as he could.

Seth turned back to face Malia and looked at the wound that was growing more putrid with every passing second. The color left Malia's face and she stared at nothing. When the barmaid returned, her mouth dropped open in shock and the plates she carried fell from her hands. Seth saw it in slow motion and nabbed them in midair with what appeared to be lightning reflexes. "Blessed Anam!" said the barmaid.

Her voice brought Malia out of her daze and she covered the wound with the now sodden dressing. "Oh, my apologies, you need not worry yourself with this," she said to the barmaid.

"Need not worry? My dear, you're rotting alive! Come now, there's a bed out back you can lie down on, I'll get some fresh water and clean dressings for that wound and summon a healer."

Malia tried to object but the old barmaid was already leading her away. Seth followed her and said, "Our friend has already gone to find a healer, thank you."

The barmaid led them into a back room, where an old cot had been set up. The darkened room smelled of sweat and dry preserves. Shelves full of jars and bags of grain lined the room, with the cot against one wall. "Go on missy, lie down and rest. As for you," turning to Seth, "come and help an ol' maid carry water."

Seth did as he was asked, following behind her as she fetched items and handed them to him to carry: a decanter of fresh water, some clean wash clothes, clean towels and a few other small items that the barmaid carried herself. They returned to the back room and found Malia asleep on the cot, her face white as new fallen snow. The maid turned to Seth and said, "Now you wait outside a moment while I make her decent." Seth waited outside the makeshift door while she removed Malia's shirt and covered her with a blanket. When she summoned him back in, she used a wash cloth to blot away pus from the wounds and rinse them clean with water. He watched for a long time as the barmaid wiped away as much of the infection as she could, removing small pieces of rotting flesh in the process. The wounds that started as small scratches were now three large gashes across her chest and were continuing to fester even as the barmaid worked to clean them up. The flesh around them turned black with decay and Malia's entire chest flared with red now. Still, a deep sleep spared her much of the pain.

Twenty minutes passed before Cedric returned with the town's healer. Her ancient face surrounded by gray straw-like hair accentuated her stooped hobbling figure. She walked with a short staff that looked like the only thing keeping her from tumbling forward. Seth motioned for them to come to the back room. "She's back here, sleeping now. She looks like hell."

The old healer shuffled toward Seth. "Yes, thank you boy. I will do what I can." She disappeared behind the curtain and a few moments later the barmaid emerged from the room.

She approached Seth and Cedric who waited at their table picking away at their food. "She's in good hands now, but I'll be honest with you boys. In all my years working in this traveler's town, not once have I ever seen a wound like that. Not once. And I've seen a good many, I'll have you know."

Chapter 23 - The Rundown

Grian's army of Narshuks marched toward Findoor over the next day. When they set up camp that night, Grian's command tent was the first to go up. Standing over maps as usual and going over battle plans with Scrag, Grian said, "We cannot underestimate Merek. He is no Time Weaver, but he will not go down quietly either."

"No, we discovered this once before."

"And what of the Time Weaver? I'm growing impatient waiting for you to deliver him. We can't count on an easy victory at Findoor castle, but with the Time Weaver's powers, they will all bow at my feet. And Merek's library will be yours."

Scrag sneered, showing his yellowed broken teeth in his large snout. "Yes, Grian, the boy will be yours."

Grian was about to launch into a tirade at him, but was defused by a sudden commotion outside his tent. Growls and snarls in the rough Narshuk language carried into the tent. Grian slammed his fist down on the maps, frustrated with the distraction. He walked to the entrance of the tent and stepped outside, shouting in his powerful voice, "May the gods strike down the one who started this. What is going on out here? And it better be good."

Scrag followed close behind Grian and translated for him, knowing the creatures would have trouble understanding Grian's common. "Speak, imbeciles, or face death."

The larger of the two Narshuks stood to its full height and stared Scrag down. "This doesn't concern you, Human puppet."

Scrag's nostrils flared at the insult. He was old and stooped, but his movements were still fast. His hand lashed out at the creature standing over him, latching onto its throat and digging his claws in.

The creature's blood flowed, and as Scrag spoke words of power, the creature struggled against his grip. Drawing magical energy in, he focused it into the creature's throat. Its eyes flared with flames and it screamed with rage and pain as Scrag released his grip on the creature and let it fall. Howls of approval erupted from those in the front that spread throughout the entire camp. The Narshuk who insulted Scrag twitched and writhed on the ground, its eyes smoldering until its head finally collapsed in, consumed by the fire inside of it.

Scrag turned toward the other Narshuk in the disturbance. "What is this about, that you would cause so much trouble outside Grian's tent?"

The other Narshuk kept his distance from Scrag. "The Elite has returned. We disagreed on what should be done with him."

"The Elite? Only one returned?"

"Yes, Scrag, only one, and he is barely alive. It was my opinion that he should be put out of his misery."

A slight growl was the only warning this Narshuk got before Scrag swung his claws out and tore his throat out in one smooth stroke. He stood gasping through his trachea and clutching at the gaping hole left in his neck for one very long moment before collapsing from the shock and blood loss.

Scrag relayed the news to Grian, who scoffed at the two dead Narshuks now at his feet. "Does anybody else wish to deliver any bad news tonight?"

He was met with a strained silence.

Turning to face several of the beasts standing to his right, Scrag said, "Clean this trash up before it starts to stink. Where is the Elite?"

Scrag got directions from one of the Narshuks who looked on--now all too willing to offer his assistance--and then led Grian to where the Elite lay on the ground. The creature looked half dead when they reached it. Grian didn't recognize it as a Narshuk at all. Almost all of the creature's fur was burnt off leaving mottled pink and black skin that wept from the great many burns that covered the creature. One of the thing's eyes was sealed shut by the flames that torched it and a faint wheezing came from its snout. It smelled of burnt hair and flesh that nauseated Grian the moment he stepped within range of it. Backing off, he turned to Scrag and said, "Take care of this thing and report to me when you're done. By the looks of it, I'm not going to like this."

Grian walked away as fast as he could without losing face and left Scrag standing beside the dying creature. Scrag stooped down beside it and looked into its one good eye. "What happened? Where is the Time Weaver? One runt of a boy could not possibly do all this. Where are the rest?"

The creature's eye rolled back in its socket and it convulsed for a moment on the ground. When it subsided, it turned back to face Scrag. "Dead."

"Dead? What do you mean dead? It's one man! How can they all be dead?"

The creatures voice was nothing but a whine. It tried to say something that Scrag assumed were more excuses, but he made out two words that struck fear into even his heart. "Dragon fire."

Scrag got up and looked out at all the others who gathered around. "Walk away. There will be no mercy killing for this one. He will suffer the full wrath of the damage he has sustained, and any who attempt to help him on his way will suffer the same fate. Leave him, he does not exist."

Those Narshuks who gathered around did not hesitate, turning and walking away to go back to their business. Scrag stormed away from the Elite, furious at the loss. Heading toward the command tent and not looking forward to explaining the situation to Grian, he was interrupted by the velvet southern voice of Cy. "Having a problem?"

Scrag stopped and would have slain him had he been any other person, but instead spat out the response, "The boy is proving troublesome." In his anger, his words came out in the Narshuk tongue.

"Indeed. He may be but a boy, but he is a Time Weaver." Cy's voice was soothing, enveloping. Scrag was angry and distracted, but caught himself before he was drawn in by the intoxicating spell.

"He knows little of his powers."

"That may be so, but remember who you're dealing with here. I was once one of them. Their instincts are powerful, even if their conscious mind is unaware of it. And if he has befriended a dragon, well..." Cy lowered his head so that his hat covered his face. "...then that poses a much bigger problem, doesn't it?"

Scrag let out a great sigh, frustration grating on his nerves. "What do we do?"

"Let me retrieve him."

Turning to face Cy for the first time during their exchange Scrag said, "We cannot risk your life. It is much too important."

With a broad smile Cy said, "I didn't know you cared. Look, this one is strong. Quite possibly the most powerful who ever lived. Certainly more so than Krycin if he is allowed to reach his full potential. And I think you'll agree that my guest and I can handle him as he is right now."

"If that is what you believe, then go. Grian can manage the army for now," Scrag said, looking around to ensure there were no eavesdroppers.

"Indeed." His one-word response reverberated through Scrag's head long after he walked away. When he realized Cy was gone he stood before the command tent and damned himself for falling for Cy's mind tricks.

The sun was just past its peak before the healer emerged from the back room where Malia lay; her face was grim, sending an unspoken message that the companions knew before she said a word. "I'm sorry, boys, I've done all I can. I can heal her wounds, but the accursed disease rages on. It's beyond my ability to cure anything of this nature."

Tears welled up in Seth's eyes. Nothing prepared him for that news. "There must be something you can do, some treatment! You can't just let her die!"

Cedric put a hand on Seth's shoulder and gave it a squeeze. The old healer hobbled over to Seth. "I'm sorry, son, I can do nothing more for her. She's in the hands of the gods now."

Seth stood up, shaken, and walked toward the back room. Just before he entered the room he heard the healer's voice one last time, "I'll warn you, she doesn't look good. Make your peace, as I don't expect her to live through the night."

"Thank you," Seth said with a disturbing calm to his voice. The air in the back room was still and smelled of the incense and herbs the healer had used during her attempts to stop the disease. In among the aromatic smells, the subtle scent of death lingered in the air. Malia lay on the cot, white sheets pulled over her body, her hair pulled to one side. Even then, a few blond strands remained defiant and curled around her face. Her skin was pale and mottled with dark spots that looked like bruises. Some of those spots came to the surface and ruptured into weeping wounds filled with pus as the disease devoured her from the inside out.

Seth fell to his knees at her bedside, tears flowing from his eyes. He whispered to her sleeping form, "Why did it have to be you?" He lay his head down on her torso and listened to her slow, weak breaths and her faltering heartbeat. "You're too strong for this. You can't die."

He rested his head on her for a long time, praying that she would pull through. When a chill came over him, he lifted his head and looked around. He wasn't sure if he fell asleep, or if he just didn't notice, but Malia's heart had stopped, as well as her breathing. "No, this isn't right," he said, his quiet voice faltering with the grief welling up inside of him. "You're not supposed to die." The air felt stuffy and still, making it hard to breathe.

A moment later and Seth realized that no sounds came from the dining area. The tavern was dead silent. He looked around at the back room and noticed that the few flies that were flocking toward the smell of death hung suspended in the air, unmoving. *Time has stopped again,* he thought, *but I didn't do this. I'm sure of it this time.*

He stood up and walked toward the curtain that separated him from the main room. Pushing it aside he walked out into the tavern. When he let go, the curtain remained where it was rather than falling back into place. It caught Seth's attention for a second before he turned away.

Surveying the main room was like looking at a photograph. Cedric had taken out his lute and was playing something for a small group of patrons, perhaps a slow sad ballad, while he waited for Seth. The barmaid behind the counter was pouring a mug of ale for a customer waiting on a stool. The liquid was frozen in place, like a waterfall in deep winter. Various patrons seated at the bar were having conversations among themselves, some of them townsfolk and some travelers just passing through. The silence of the frozen image got to Seth, making his skin crawl. He was about to cross the room toward the door when a noise caught his attention.

Outside the batwing doors of the tavern, a pair of booted feet taking slow, measured steps made muted clicking sounds as they hit the wood floorboards. Seth froze, realizing that time had not resumed yet. The doors swung open and a dark figure stood in the doorway. He was a tall, thin man with a thin face wearing black dress pants and a black button-up shirt. Around his neck was a black tie and a black suit jacket rested on his shoulders. Topping his head was a broad rimmed black hat that covered thick black hair. He walked with an unnatural confidence until he saw Seth. Their eyes met and the man stopped dead. "Krycin?" he said, sounding unsure of himself. He thought for a second, but before Seth could say a word, he continued in his smooth southern voice, "No, not Krycin. Not hardly. Krycin was older than you, stronger, he demanded respect with his very appearance. But you are the spitting image of him, I do say. Then you must be Krycin's boy."

There was an allure about the man's voice that Seth couldn't place. Whether it was the southern drawl, or just the elegant way every syllable was pronounced, he couldn't say. But he felt like it was more than that. The man's words were drawing him in, bringing a comfort that would be a drug if he let it take him. Seth resisted it and found his own voice. "So I've been told. The name's Seth. And you are?"

"A remnant of the past, a sliver of your imagination. You're not supposed to exist, boy." The man's voice changed as he spoke, there was a hint of another voice there, something that felt familiar and alien at the same time. It was many voices, all at once. The air chilled in the room as the man spoke, "I killed you." His deep black eyes shifted down to the bag slung over Seth's shoulder. His voice returned to the southern accent. "And what have we here? Well, I came for you, but it seems that I have found so much more. Come, boy. Come with me now. Leave this place behind you and discover your destiny." He walked toward Seth and extended a hand.

Seth hesitated. *Something is wrong here,* he thought. Looking around the tavern, he saw that time remained frozen. Turning back to the Man in Black, he said, "I... I can't. There is somebody who needs me, and I won't leave her now."

The Man in Black opened his mouth as if to speak, then closed it. He took only one step more before erupting into an unexpected tirade, his southern accent escaping him. "You think these people care about you? You think it matters if they live or die? You will fight for them, knowing that they use you for your talents? Don't be foolish, Seth. I will show you a reality without limits, without boundaries. We can go anywhere, do anything. We could be gods among these mortals, and yet you would pollute yourself? Lower yourself to these... these ingrates?"

Seth reeled from the verbal assault, and still through it, the man's voice pulled at him, trying to draw him into its trap. The Man in Black took another step forward, narrowing the gap between them to

166

a few paces. With a sigh, he returned to his former composure. "If you don't come willingly, boy, I'm going to have to take you by force. We wouldn't want to cause a disturbance in this..." He looked around and smirked. "...*fine* establishment."

"I'm sorry," Seth said, standing his ground against the Man in Black. "I can't leave my friends."

"Have it your way." The words dripped from his mouth as he spread his arms wide. His black suit, boots and hat erupted with an almost living darkness that shrouded his entire form. Swirls of black smoke trailed his every move as he walked toward Seth and reached out to grab him. Putting his hands up in front of him to block, Seth closed his eyes and flinched away from the man. He grabbed Seth's arms, the blackness digging deep into his flesh like knifes. His arms drained of all color, and pain seared down them. Seth cried out and dropped to his knees.

"Do you see now what you have chosen? A lifetime of pain and suffering. Come with me, Seth. It doesn't have to be like this." The Man in Black dug his fingers deeper into Seth's arms. Black lines slithered down them underneath the flesh. Seth tried to pull away, but the Man in Black only held on tighter. "Go on, Seth, struggle and fight, yell and scream if you think it will help. I thought you would be a powerful man, but so far all I see is a boy."

Seth slumped down, letting his head hang down, his chin pressed against his chest. The figure shrouded in black standing over him let out an inhuman laugh. He was ready to give in when a voice inside his head spoke to him, *fight back.*

Tears streaming down his cheeks, the pain at an almost unbearable level. *I don't know how,* he thought back to the voice.

Don't think about it, do it.

Clear your mind and focus. Morganath's words reverberated through his head. He tried to clear his mind of the fog of pain that was taking over. The black tendrils that worked their way up his arms slowed, the pain eased.

The Man in Black looked surprised, but not discouraged. "That's it boy, find your strength. Embrace the rage that you know is inside you."

Clear your mind and focus. Seth heard the words repeated in his head and he pushed back at the Man in Black, managing to get up off one knee, placing his foot flat on the floor. The fog in his mind cleared as the pain receded from his arms.

Another laugh escaped the Man in Black, streamers of black flitted away from him as he struggled to maintain his control of the situation. "You've got it now, boy. Find the killer inside of you. Become what your father never could."

The spark did light inside Seth, his mind cleared and he drew the power that he sought. Energy flooded to him like a tidal wave, and he grabbed the Man in Black's arms, focusing the stream of energy into those two points. Flames ignited under his hands, searing through the jacket that covered the man's arms, then through the flesh itself. An unexpected cry of fear and rage escaped him as the flames tore through muscle and sinew, and finally through the bone itself severing both of his arms at the elbow.

Seth stood to his full height and shook the severed hands away as the Man in Black staggered back. Shock and disbelief spread over his face as he looked at the stumps of his arms that now remained. A sickening smile full of malice spread over the man's face as the black cloud covering him dissipated. "I knew you had it in you, boy."

A shudder ran through him as new bones grew out the ends of his arms, fresh muscle, veins, nerves and skin reaching out to cover them. Within seconds the Man in Black had two complete arms again, though there was a scar that ringed each arm where they were severed. "Your powers really are amazing, boy. Now, let's see what you can really do." He laced his fingers together and turned his palms toward Seth, stretching his arms out.

Seth's hands were still smoking, but he no longer felt pain. He looked up into his opponent's eyes and said, "Get out, before you really get hurt."

"Me? Oh, no no no. See, this is how this is going to go. You're going to come with me, and quietly, or I'm going to start killing the people in this little hole in the wall. Now I don't know who you've been traveling with, but I'm sure I'll get someone important to you eventually. Understand, boy?"

Seth's eyes flared with an inner light as he pulled back his fist and let it loose at the Man in Black. Flames flared up around it as he struck him full force in the chest and sent him flying back toward the door, smoke trailing him as his suit smoldered. He hit the door frame with a crash and fell to the floor like a rag doll. "Stop calling me boy," Seth said.

Several seconds went by before Seth realized that time was moving again. Patrons sat in their seats eating and drinking, Cedric played a haunting little tune on his lute, and the barmaid behind the counter finished pouring the ale. The smells were what snapped Seth out of his daze. The smell of fresh cooked food filled his nose and lungs, making him remember how hungry he was. Then he thought of Malia in the back room, suffering.

Cedric stopped playing mid-song when he saw Seth appear across the room. "Seth, what..." Cedric began, but was interrupted by a groan that came from the doorway of the tavern.

The Man in Black lifted his head, then pushed himself up off the floor. "That's a nice trick." He got himself to his feet and faced Seth again, his torso was blackened and burnt, a large hole in his suit exposing what should have been flesh underneath. But bone and muscle and other internal tissues could be seen through the hole as it re-grew and closed up. In seconds the gaping wound in his chest was closed, leaving another scar in its place. "Now look here. You're starting to bother me, boy."

Cedric's gaze darted back and forth between the two men standing off in the tavern. He watched as the Man in Black cupped his hand and a sphere of black energy appeared in his palm. The ball swirled and pulsed with a life of its own and when he threw the ball at Seth with an unnatural speed, a trail of black smoke followed it. Seth tried to duck, but the ball flew too fast and struck him full force. It exploded into a series of black tendrils, that wrapped around him, some of them plunging into his flesh, some working their way down to the floor. When they reached it, they attached themselves there, pulling Seth down. He cried out as pain flashed through his whole body. It felt like something reached into his soul and was pulling it to the ground, corrupting it with darkness. He dropped to his knees once more.

Cedric had his bow out in a flash with an arrow nocked and ready to fire. The Man in Black stepped toward Seth and Cedric loosed the arrow. It flew without error, but the Man in Black raised a hand and batted the arrow out of the air like it was a fly, and then continued on his course.

More of the black tendrils wrapped around Seth and reached for the ground, constricting around him and plunging deeper into his body. Seth fought it, but couldn't overcome their strength. The Man in Black stood next to him and reached down, patting Seth's head, "Now be a good boy, and come with me." He took the strap of the bag that Seth carried with him and removed it from Seth's shoulder. "Oh, and I'll take that."

Cedric nocked another arrow and loosed it at the Man in Black, who again batted it away. "Fight it Seth, stand up, don't give in!" he said from across the room.

"I think he's all out of fight. You're good, boy, but you're not that good." The Man in Black lifted a fist, ready to strike Seth down. "And now, you'll be coming with me."

He was just about to strike Seth unconscious when a movement caught his attention. There was a feminine grunt, and then a black long sword flew end-over-end through the air. As it flew, it burst into flames. The blade plunged into the man's chest, running him through. A figure stood tall in the doorway to the back room, bandages wrapping her torso, blond hair tumbling over her shoulders and down her back. "Like hell he will," she said.

"Oh blast it all," the Man in Black said as he stepped back, the sword burning him up from the inside out. "This isn't the end."

He disappeared, leaving the sword hanging in thin air for a second before it fell to the ground with a loud clatter. There was a popping sound as air rushed into the spot that he occupied.

Malia took one more step, then collapsed to the ground next to Seth. The black tendrils dispersed and Seth rolled his head over to face Malia. Staring into her deep gray eyes he said, "Thanks." She managed a slight smile before consciousness left her again.

Cedric ran to the pair and helped Seth up. "Are you okay, Seth? Who was that?"

"Yes, I'll be fine," he said as he pulled away from Cedric's helping hands and rushed to Malia's side. "I'm not sure who he was, but he knew my father. He was sent by Grian I think."

"Of that I have no doubt. It seems they are getting more desperate." He reached down to help Seth, who was struggling with Malia's body, trying to get her back to the bed in the back room. Seth put his arms under hers and lifted one side of her, and Cedric took her feet. They gently laid her back onto the cot and pulled the sheets over her to keep her warm.

Seth turned to face Cedric. "I think I understand now. I can fix this."

Cedric looked over Malia's face and arms; bruises covered her, and many of them had opened into sores that were devouring her. "If you can do something, now is the time. I have my doubts that she will last an hour at this rate."

Seth got down on his knees next to the bed and spread his hands over her torso. *Clear your mind and focus,* the words repeated in his head. He cleared his mind, thought of nothing, and willed the power to come to him. A few patrons gathered outside the room now and tried to see in, one of whom was the concerned healer. They watched in awe as Seth's hands glowed with first blue energy, and then white, that flowed down into Malia's body. The energy spread out into her torso and made its way throughout her body. Seth drew more power, focusing his thoughts on both water and life, to heal the wounds and to destroy the infection. The light glowed brighter still, blinding those who looked on, and when it dispersed, Malia's eyes fluttered open. All of the bruises that covered her skin faded, and the color returned to her skin. The sores were gone, as well as the wounds on her chest.

"Seth," Malia said in a weak voice, "I thought you would die."

Seth pushed several locks of hair out of her face and smiled down at her. "I thought you were going to die too. We have to leave as soon as possible."

Cedric nodded in agreement and sent the barmaid to fetch some food for Malia, shooing all the others out of the back room in the process. People were in awe of what Seth had done, and even the healer was dumbstruck. She was about to walk out of the room when she turned back to Seth. "If you were able to do that, and I don't rightly know how you did, but if you could, why didn't you to begin with?"

Seth smiled and said, "Because I didn't know I could."

Chapter 24 - Betrayal

The ground shook as the massive Narshuk army advanced toward its target. The afternoon sun was hot that day, and it beat down upon Scrag's shoulders, making him sweat. When they reached a small river, they didn't bother trying to find a bridge; many of the Narshuks jumped right into the rushing water and drank. They stopped here while they refilled their water reserves and rested a while. Grian insisted that they be no more than an hour before they began walking again. Scrag was growing concerned that Cy had not returned since the previous night. When he told Grian that he had sent Cy away to retrieve the Time Weaver, all Grian had to say was, "Good riddance."

Scrag rested on his own when they stopped, preferring the shade that his small tent provided to the hot sun. They were just about to pack up and file out again when a commotion outside drew Scrag's attention. He stepped out of his tent into the sunshine and saw the problem. Several Narshuks stood in a circle near the banks of the river. In the middle of them was a dark figure slumped on the ground.

Scrag walked toward the group and they parted to let him in. The figure in the center of them was crouched over something. He recognized the figure as Cy, but his elegant suit was in tatters. Lifting his head to look up at Scrag, Cy said with a smile, "Tonight we raise the Dark Lord."

A murmur of growls and grunts spread through the crowd around them at the mention of the long dead warlord. Scrag lowered his head to Cy's level and said in common, "Are you mad? We do not have the right spells."

Cy laughed and held up the old leather-bound book. Scrag looked at it with curiosity, then took it from Cy and tried to open it. The cover and lock would not budge.

"What good is this to us? It is wizard-locked."

"Yes, wizard-locked, and tuned not to a specific person, but a specific race." Cy stood up to his full height and stretched out his arms, the scars much more obvious in the afternoon sun. With a nod his tattered suit took on a life of its own, threads extending and weaving themselves together to form new fabric, buttons appearing where appropriate, popping up and opening like a blooming flower. In seconds he was clothed in his usual elegant wares. "There, much better. The boy's got spirit, I'll give him that."

"Time Weavers?" Scrag asked, ignoring the rest of what Cy had to say.

"Indeed." Cy reached over to the book and ran his hand over the lock. It whirred to life and made an audible *click* as it unlocked. Scrag flipped the cover open and looked at the first few pages. "This is useless to me. I cannot read high Lyecian. Nobody can anymore."

"On the contrary," Cy said as he reached for the book. Turning the book over in his hands he flipped to the last page and placed a hand over the page. Speaking a word, the pages rippled and then changed, each one splitting in two and attaching to its neighbor. An arcane script now filled the pages. Cy flipped through several more pages to ensure the rest would show, and then handed the book back to Scrag. "The text in the book is heavily protected, designed to keep out those it was not intended for. You must know how to decode the knowledge contained within the book."

"How do you know this? And how is this important to us?"

"I know this, because I helped design the book. And inside are all the spells needed to raise the Dark Lord. The boy carried it. I don't think there is any doubt that he's Krycin's son. He's the spitting image of him."

"So we have all the pieces then? We don't need Findoor or the old fool Merek. You are right then, we stop the army, and raise the Dark Lord tonight. I'll take care of the rat that's been leading the army." A sneer came over Scrag's face. He could dispose of Grian and bring back the rightful ruler of the Narshuk army, and then present to his master the Time Weaver book that would unleash the full majesty of the Dark Lord's power.

Cy's face spread in a wicked grin as he looked up at Scrag. "Don't kill him. I have a much better idea, something much more befitting of a rat like him."

Grian was packing up his maps when Scrag barged up to his table. He started and dropped the map he was rolling up, then watched dumbfounded as the map unfurled itself and spread across the table again. "The gods damn you, Scrag," he said, scrambling to get the map rolled back up. Scrag was a smaller Narshuk than most, but still towered over Grian.

Scrag struggled with the common tongue to relay his message. "Grian, you must come immediately. The Time Weaver has arrived."

Grian's eyes lit up at the news. "Well it's about time somebody got something right around here. We will strip him of his powers and take Lyecha's gift for our own, and then nothing will stand in our way. After we take Findoor, the other kingdoms will fall easily."

Scrag almost laughed, but coughed to cover it up. He then turned and walked toward the river where a large congregation of Narshuks were milling about. When they spotted Grian, they parted, allowing him to walk to the center of the congregation where a figure lay in a heap on the ground. Grian stood tall over it. "So, runt, we've finally caught you. I'm going to enjoy this immensely."

Grian focused his mind and called upon the power of life and death. He held out a hand, palm to the ground and began to chant the ancient words of power. The magic flowed to him and electrified him, creating a black haze around him. A globe of darkness appeared underneath his outstretched hand and began to grow, clinging to his palm. As the words poured forth from his mouth, the figure on the ground began to move, and a sound came from it that Grian wasn't prepared for.

Laughter. A hearty, smooth laughter. The figure rose from the ground, causing Grian to pause in his spell casting, but only for a split second. When he felt the magical energy push back at him, he continued for fear that it might destroy him. His chanting continued as the figure stood to full height and he saw its face. The black globe began to pulse and tendrils reached out for the figure, but Grian's shock at who stood before him caused him to stumble again, this time leaving him unable to recover. The magical energies lashed back at him, hitting him like a wave hitting the shore. Grian felt it burn him up from the inside out, causing him to cry out. His skin blistered from the heat and smoke rose from his mouth and ears.

The laughter continued. "Now, Grian, you didn't *really* expect that to work, did you?" The smooth southern voice of Cy greeted him.

Grian collapsed to his knees, his whole body now smoking from the energy, but his heart still beating. "You!" was all he could muster.

"Yes, me. I'm surprised you didn't realize before now. A true testament to how arrogant and ignorant you are." A chill washed over the area as Cy drew up to his full height, his eyes filled with black, and his voice came down on Grian like a thousand swords biting through his flesh. "And now fool, you'll lament the day you felt yourself worthy of my army."

Reaching a hand down, Cy placed it on Grian's head, his palm on his forehead, fingers extending into his hair. Black fire erupted around his hand searing into Grian's flesh, a mark that would never fade. Grian shuddered and fell to the ground, letting out a scream that was heard throughout all the ranks of the Narshuks and beyond.

Cy's velvet southern voice returned. "Now, see? That's better. Kneel before your army. Watch as we raise the Dark Lord, and witness a new era, as he succeeds at a task that you failed utterly to complete."

Grian lay in a heap on the ground, unable to move for the burning in his body as the last of the magical energy faded away.

Raising his voice loud enough to carry across the entire army, Cy said, "Tomorrow this will be a new world, one that will see Findoor in the iron grip of the Narshuk race, and one that will have our Dark Lord as master of not only this world, but all worlds!"

A cheer roared over the army of Narshuks, their howls carrying for miles around.

176

Chapter 25 – Homecoming

The Scryes' pool shimmered in the darkness of the damp cave, a lantern hanging from a hook on the far wall the only source of light in the room. The Scryes surrounded the pool, focused on their task at hand. Merek stood outside their circle as they worked silent magic to discover the nature of the portal that breached the boundaries between worlds.

Designed to invade, it shall not close, The Scryes said inside Merek's head. *To the dead world it leads.*

Merek spoke his replies out loud, "It shall not close? What does that mean? Can we undo the damage?"

What is done by a Time Weaver, must be undone by one.

"A Time Weaver did this? The young one? Or another?" Merek's face wrinkled in a scowl.

Another. The Betrayer.

"Cy? But he's dead, I saw the Dark Lord slay him after he betrayed Krycin. How could he have done something like this?"

Once appeared perished, twice imprisoned. He returns, and brings with him doom.

"So all these years, Cy has been imprisoned. Clever indeed. What of this doom? What could Cy do to make things worse?"

The Dark Lord returns. Their last words echoed through his mind and sent chills down his spine. Merek left no further instructions for the Scryes. Panic overcame him and he bolted from the dark basement chamber.

King Verand watched his maps in the war chamber as usual, but lines of concern marred his face as he looked from one map to another. His focus on the maps was so intent that when Merek burst into the room, he nearly jumped out of his skin. "By the gods, Merek, you'll be the death of me."

Merek stopped at the other side of the table, looking down at the maps and then up into Verand's eyes. "Sire, we have a bigger problem than just the Narshuk army. We must call a summit of the world leaders. The Dark Lord returns."

A feeling came over The King at that moment, like thousands of tiny bugs crawling over his skin, making him visibly shudder. "Merek, how can this be? Gladius was defeated over a century ago."

"I am uncertain, Sire. The Scryes gave me few details, but there is a Time Weaver involved, and not the one who we've been trying to find."

"Another Time Weaver? I shall contact the leaders of the other nations at once," The King said, then motioned to the enchanted maps before him. "What do you make of this Merek? The Narshuk army has stopped their advance."

Merek watched the maps with keen interest. "How long have they been there?"

"Since before high noon. Could this be the confirmation we need that they are indeed doing what your Scryes advised?"

"I believe so, my friend. If they do succeed in raising Gladius, then our entire world is in peril. Gladius was nothing short of insane the last time he attacked Findoor. Had it not been for Krycin, we would have fallen, and the rest of the world would have followed shortly after. We must get Malia back here with the Time Weaver as quickly as possible. He may be our only hope." Merek's face was grave. He wished he had better news for the already stressed King.

The companions took no time getting back to Morganath so that they could continue their journey. The sun was well past the midday mark when they approached him. Morganath turned his huge head to watch their approach and grumbled a greeting to them. "I thought you'd never return."

Seth was the first to get a word in, though Cedric looked like he was about to make a smart comment back at the massive dragon.

"Sorry 'bout that Morganath. We were tied up, but everything is fine now. Let's go, we've got no time to lose."

Morganath gave a sniff as they approached. "Is everything okay?"

"Yeah, everything's just perfect." He flashed a knowing smile at Malia, who smiled back as he climbed up onto Morganath's neck. "Nothing I can't handle."

Seth reached down and offered a hand to Malia to help her up and then Cedric followed. Malia wrapped her arms around Seth's waist again and held on tight. A few of the townsfolk, and many of their children rushed out to see them off, waving and yelling goodbyes and fare-thee-wells.

Morganath leapt into the air, and with one massive down-stroke of his wings, was off and flying. The companions held tight until the dragon's body stabilized. Seth watched as the countryside spread out before him, lush and green, and littered with trees that reached for the heavens to taste the sunlight. Shadows began to extend as the Sun made its way toward the horizon. The air was clear and fresh and filled Seth's lungs as he took in a deep breath.

When they reached Morganath's cruising altitude, Cedric pointed up ahead of them and yelled, "Up there is the Findoor border, the Algorn Canyon. We're lucky, there are few bridges that cross it. It won't be long before we're seeing the Findoor standard flying high above the castle."

The ground ahead of them stretched out in a great grassy plain. At the center of the plain, running from north to south was a great gash in the earth that stretched as far as their eyes could see. When they were directly above the canyon, Seth made out a great river running along the bottom of it.

Malia laughed. "I look forward to it. Never have I seen Findoor castle from the sky. It will be a sight to keep with my fondest memories."

The companions flew for some time before another word was spoken. When the silence was finally broken, it was Morganath who spoke. "Seth, I spot a small contingent of soldiers below us. They are flying a Findoor standard."

Seth thought about this for a moment before speaking to Malia. "There's Findoor soldiers below us. Should we greet them?"

"Nay, it is likely a border patrol. How long until we reach Findoor castle?"

Seth relayed the question to Morganath, who responded only after some deep thought. "Another day and a half if I remain at this pace. Shall we land to make camp for the night?"

The prospect of sleep appealed to him, but Seth wanted to get to the castle as fast as they could. "No, press on."

Without a word, Morganath beat his wings faster and the wind increased. Malia pulled in close to Seth, holding on tight. When the sun set and the stars were out and shining bright in the sky, they set down on a small plateau and made camp. In the morning they were off again, flying across the Findoor countryside. Morganath again got Seth's attention. "Seth, if you slow time, we can make it to Findoor castle by late afternoon."

"I can do that?" Seth asked.

"Krycin used to do it all the time. Remember what I taught you."

Seth cleared his mind and focused, willing the flow of time to obey his command. The wind eased even though their pace remained the same, but the air became thicker as time slowed. Seth kept time steady for Morganath and his companions. Smiling to himself, he thought of what it might look like from the ground, a farmer looking up in the sky in the afternoon and seeing a great gold dragon rocketing through the air at an unnatural pace.

Soldiers camping outside the Findoor castle walls were the first to see the figure shining in the sky off in the distance. The sun lowering on the horizon made the object shimmer and glow as it moved toward them. An alarm was raised and archers were readied on top of the castle walls. King Verand and Merek watched as the object drew closer. A commander at the front lines called out orders. "Ready arrows, hold your fire, on my command."

Merek whispered words of power, concentrating as magical energy flowed to him to power his spell. The spell manifested itself in Merek's eyes, causing them to take on a pale white glow.

"What do you see Merek, should we be alarmed?" asked Verand after giving Merek a moment to look at the object through his spell.

"I think not, Sire. It's a dragon, one who I personally know, and there are three people riding on his back." The dragon's scales glittered like fine jewels in the late afternoon sun. Sitting at the front was a man, ordinary looking with dark brown hair. Behind him was a girl whose wild blond hair flew in the wind, untamed. And then a third figure behind her, wearing a mask and a black cloak. "Sire, it's

Malia, and she returns with the Time Weaver. Come, we must greet them."

Verand thought about it for a few seconds, then nodded to Merek. "You go on ahead. I'm tired, and must check on the state of the Narshuk army. I shall meet them in the morning after a good night's sleep."

The response caught Merek off-guard, but he obeyed. "Yes, Sire." He paused for a moment in deep thought, then asked, "Are you well, Sire?"

A long sigh escaped from Verand, his face lined with worry and stress. Dark circles drooped under his eyes and he looked much older that night than he actually was. "No, Merek, but I will survive. I worry for my people, and all the people of the world. I have read only stories of the Dark Lord Gladius, but if he is even half as ruthless and cruel as he is in the stories, then we are in very big trouble."

"Ahh. Go, sleep my friend. Tomorrow is a brand new day, and we have the Time Weaver on our side now."

"Perhaps you're right Merek. Good night, old man. Take good care of our guests." The King turned and walked away without waiting for a response. Merek knew there was still something troubling him, but didn't want to pry. Still, he couldn't shake the feeling that something was terribly wrong with Verand. Never before had he seen the kind of sadness the King had in his eyes now.

After Verand left, Merek gathered up his things and rushed out to meet the companions.

Morganath watched the top of the castle as he approached. His keen eyes spotted the archers on the battlements training their bows at him. "Should I land at a distance?" he asked, slowing his pace.

"No Morganath, I'll hold off any attacks. They'll stop once they know it's us, right Malia?" Seth said, craning his head around to look in her deep gray eyes.

"I doubt they will even fire on us unless we make a hostile move, but one can never be too careful." She smiled at Seth and held on tight as they began their final spiral to land in the field in front of the castle. Malia looked down at the castle, its many gray stone spires reaching into the sky, the walls thick and partially covered with moss and flowering vines. The field in front of the castle was covered with people, many of whom wore armor and carried weapons. A small city of tents was erected out in a field that once donned grain. At the top of a hill just outside the city walls was the portal, pulsing and arcing, growing larger with each passing hour. "Seth, the entire Findoor army is gathered outside the castle. And look there," she pointed to the portal, "a rift is open, I wonder why?"

They circled down, surveying the state of the castle and the people milling around it. When the soldiers out front of the castle realized they were going to land, a clearing large enough for the massive dragon was made. Morganath's wings beat against the air as it set down in the clearing and settled onto the ground. An important looking soldier, likely a commander, stepped toward the dragon's neck and hailed the companions. "Friends, welcome to Findoor."

Cedric was the first to swing his legs to one side of Morganath's neck and slide down. His movements were limber and agile, landing almost without a sound. He stood to his full height, then offered an exaggerated bow to the commander. "Well met my friend. We are in need of a hot meal, and warm bed, and many hours of sleep. And I do believe my friends here have business with the King."

"Well met indeed, and you are?" the commander asked.

"Forgive me, I am Cedric, a traveling Bard, at your service." Cedric stood to his full height, which was only slightly taller than the commander. His mask covered the upper half of his face, something that even Seth and Malia had not seen him remove. Before the commander could say anything further, Malia swung her long legs over Morganath's neck and slid down to land beside Cedric.

"Malia Corsair, Swordmage in the Findoor army. This is my traveling companion, Seth Alkirk." She left off his occupation and homeland on purpose, having no real idea how to explain it.

Seth was more careful getting down from Morganath than his companions were. He offered a hand to the commander, who shook it and asked, "Who's in charge of you three?"

The companions looked at each other, smiled, shrugged, and looked back at the commander. Before any of them could respond, there was a commotion at the castle gate.

An old man ran from the gates toward the companions, as fast as his ancient legs could carry him. Many who saw him could not believe their eyes. He was winded when he reached the companions standing in the field beside the dragon. Malia saw the old man run out onto the field and forgot her manners, breaking from the conversation and running to him. "Merek!" she called out as she ran, and threw her arms around him in a warm embrace. "How I have missed your face." She beamed and she took Merek's hand, leading him back to the rest of the companions.

"My gods, it is you," Merek said as he approached Seth.

Seth turned to look at the old wizard who approached him. It took Seth a minute to regain what he had been saying before addressing the wizard. He offered a quick bow and said, "Yes, it's me. And you must be Merek."

"You look just like your father," said the old man, who then walked into Morganath's view. "And Morganateltheranthumagus, it has been a long time. How are you, old friend?"

The dragon rumbled, "It has been many years, hasn't it? I am well, though I worry about your boy there. He has much to learn."

"Yes, yes indeed. I shall be taking care of that. Keep yourself well my friend, it is a shame we do not have longer to speak and catch up, but we have important things to discuss."

"Come see me later. I have no intentions of leaving just yet." Morganath lay his head down on the ground and closed his eyes.

Seth looked at the old wizard. "Important business? We can start with why I'm here to begin with, and perhaps where exactly I am, and then we can go from there."

"Oh, never you mind our business. We will discuss that later. Come, all of you. Let us have a hearty meal and a long rest. The sun will set soon, and you must be famished." Merek turned to face Cedric for the first time. "And you are?"

Cedric stepped forward as Malia introduced him. "Merek, this is Cedric, a traveling Bard. He has been an invaluable guide in our travels."

"Arch-Magus Merek, it is truly an honor to meet you." Cedric bowed low in a show of respect. "It is not often I make it this far east, as most of my travels keep me in Caldoor."

Merek nodded his head to acknowledge the strange Bard. "Indeed, you are quite out of your way." Seth started to say something, but Merek cut him off before he could. "No, no, save that talk for later. For now, come inside the castle and get cleaned up. The evening meal will be served soon in the banquet hall, so you will all eat well. Only then will we talk business."

Merek turned and led them back into the city that surrounded the castle. As they made their way through the city, Seth looked around, taking in all the sights and sounds. There were smithies, working hard creating weapons and armor and doing repairs where required. Stables were busy caring for horses, brushing them down, feeding and shoeing them. Taverns were filled with soldiers drinking and laughing and discussing battles both won and lost. This interested Malia, distracting her as they walked by a few standing on the veranda of a tavern. Many women ran around doing errands and taking care of children who played and laughed in the streets. The town was foreign in every way to Seth, and made him think about his own hometown, where nobody talked on the streets anymore, and everyone minded their own business.

People talked here, and all who saw the Arch-Magus leading the three through the city whispered it to others. Seth noticed the reactions, though he pretended not to. By the time they reached the gates to the castle proper, there was a buzz spreading its way across the whole town. It wasn't often that somebody important came to the town, and "they must be important if the Arch-Magus is escorting them," said one old maid to another.

Entering the castle was like stepping into a different world. Preparations were being made for a siege, and many of the people in the castle were too focused on their work and the challenges that lay ahead to pay attention to the visitors. The banquet hall bustled with activity. Servants ran around setting plates in front of hungry guests, runners conveyed messages to the kitchen about what needed to be cooked, and people of all shapes and sizes sat at row upon row of tables, eating and talking and laughing. Malia said to Seth as they walked through to the head table. "It's not always like this, but there are many more people here now due to the army being here."

They were treated to one of the finest meals Seth had ever eaten, despite many of the dishes being foreign to him. His hunger was greater than his sense of adventure, and so he opted to try a bit of everything.

When the meal was done, Merek discussed their journey with them and Malia was informed of the conditions in the Kingdom and why the army was outside the city gates. After several hours of conversation, the sun was long set and all of them were tired. Merek called an adjournment to their meeting, as the rest were too polite or too interested in the discussion.

"My friends, this day has left me weary, but hopeful for the future. These are dark times for Findoor. I shall retire for the night, and may morning bring new light to us all." Merek stood up from his seat. "Seth, Cedric, I shall have quarters prepared for you. Malia can show you around. Get some sleep and we will talk more tomorrow."

After Merek left, it was Seth who spoke next. "Wow. You never realize how tired you are until somebody else mentions it." He yawned and rubbed his eyes.

Malia also yawned. "Indeed Seth. It has been a long couple of weeks. Come, we'll have another busy day tomorrow." She called for servants to prepare two guest rooms in advance and then showed them around the important places in the castle while they waited for the rooms to be made up. When a runner tracked them down to inform them that their rooms were ready, Seth seemed surprised.

"Is that all they do? Run around and deliver messages?" Seth asked.

"Yes Seth, they are runners. It's their job. If you have a message to send, you give it to a runner, and they will deliver it. It's quite efficient actually," Malia replied.

"Where I grew up, all we do is text someone. I don't imagine they get paid much," he said, not really thinking about what he was saying.

Malia stopped in her tracks and chuckled. "Seth, they don't get paid at all. They are provided a room within the castle, meals, clothing, and an important job to do. It's an honor to become a runner. As it is an honor to be offered a job anywhere within the castle."

Seth thought about this for a while, then smiled as he looked up at Malia again. "I hadn't thought of it that way. We're taught at a very young age to value objects rather than the work we do. It's always 'work hard, get a good, high-paying job, be successful', know what I mean? I've never seen success defined in any other way."

The strong steady voice of Cedric piped up from behind them as they walked. "We all define success a little differently here. Many do still get paid, but do not measure their success based on that. I measure success based on my story-telling ability, Malia here measures success based on her prowess and magic. Morganath measures his success based on age."

"Morganath? But he has mountains of treasure; if he doesn't base his success on that, then why keep it?" Seth asked.

"Dragons hoard, it's what they do. It's also why there are so few dragons left in the world. They were hunted, almost to extinction, by greedy souls who forgot the wisdom and power of the dragons and could only think of the glittering shiny gold. Morganath may very well be the last of his species, for I have not seen another in a great many years."

The companions arrived at the first room prepared for them. "You can take this one Cedric," Seth said, "and thank you for your insight. I guess I still have a lot to learn, huh?"

Both Cedric and Malia laughed at this, Seth only smiled. "You will learn a great many things tomorrow my friend. Good night." Cedric gave the two a bow, and then retreated into the room.

Malia looked at Seth with a smile. "Come, we're nearly to your room as well." The two walked the rest of the way to Seth's room in silence. When they arrived, Malia pointed at the door. "Here we are. I do hope you find it to your liking. If you need anything at all, simply send a runner for it, or summon me and I can help."

Seth turned to face Malia and ended up almost nose-to-nose with her, her deep gray eyes looking almost black in the dim light of the hallway. He could feel her breath on his skin, her smooth complexion and pink lips looking more attractive than ever before. He took her hands and backed up a step, looking down. After a long pause he looked back up at her and said, "Thank you Malia, for everything." He turned and pulled away from her, reaching for his door when she stopped him, not letting go of his hand.

"Seth," she paused, an inner conflict apparent on her face. "I thank you as well. Had it not been for you, I would have died. It is the closest I have ever come to death, and it reminded me just how much I have to live for. I have been given a second chance, and for that I shall be forever grateful." She took a step toward him and kissed his cheek, her warm lips pressing against his unshaven face. "Sleep well, Seth, for our adventures are not yet over."

Seth's face flushed at the touch of her lips, he could feel it burning in his face. He wanted to turn his head, to press his lips on hers. His heart leapt and pounded in his chest, making him a little dizzy. Instead he backed away, and escaped into his room to sleep for the night. He flashed Malia one last smile before closing the door and listened to her footsteps echo through the hallway as she walked away.

King Verand sat on the edge of his four-poster canopy bed with a hand-woven wool rug under his feet. His personal quarters had its own fireplace where servants kept the fire burning. Tapestries hung from the walls of his room, some depicting past kings, and some displayed the more interesting places in the Kingdom. A small desk sat against the far wall. Paper, ink and a quill, along with the royal seal, a candle, and some sealing wax, occupied the surface of it.

He lifted his head out of his deep thought and looked at the entourage of servants, runners and various other staff who followed him around. Standing up, he spoke loud enough for them all to hear, "Leave me. I wish to be undisturbed for the remainder of the night."

His staff obeyed and left the room without question. The weight of the situation in the Kingdom crashed down on him, and though the advance of the Narshuk army was paused, he had little hope of it staying that way.

He got up and walked over to the desk. Sitting down, he began to write on the sheet of paper:

> *My good friend Merek,*
>
> *I have led the Kingdom to ruin, I fear, for the Narshuks stand at our door. With no wife, and no heir, I leave nothing behind me but a lazy leadership and poor decisions. I leave the Kingdom to your rule until such a time as a new, more acceptable King has been chosen.*
>
> *May the gods forgive me for my failures, and have mercy on me for my lack of strength to get me through this.*
>
> *Eternally yours,*

He signed his full name at the bottom and folded the letter in thirds, then dripped wax over the edge of the letter and stamped it with the royal seal. Just above the seal, he wrote a single word, *Merek,* and placed the letter at the center of the desk.

Walking back to his bed, a tear fell from his eye, rolled down his cheek and fell to the floor. He sat down on his bed and pulled his legs up with him, getting comfortable against the mounds of cushions and pillows at the head of the bed. He pulled the luxurious sheets and blankets over him and then took a vial out of his pocket. The contents of the vial swirled with black and blue streaks, a little something he was saving in case he was captured, but he now felt trapped in his own castle with no escape. *This will be my escape.*

Removing the lid of the vial he brought it to his lips and said, "May the gods have mercy on us all." He tipped the vial and poured it into his mouth, over his tongue and down his throat. The moment it hit his tongue it burned and his body wanted to take the vial away, but he fought the urge and finished off every drop.

He felt it sear down his esophagus and into his stomach. It made him retch, but he fought the urge to vomit and won. The effects were instant and devastating, spreading through his gut and making his abdominal muscles spasm. Racked with pain, he fell back against the pillows. Liquid fire coursed through his system, turning his veins black as they carried the poison to his heart. It sent his heart into violent spasms which infected his system even faster.

A strangled gurgle escaped his lips as black lines formed on the surface of his skin all over his body. Foam bubbled up out of his lungs and into his mouth as he gasped for air. One by one his systems failed. He lost bowel and bladder control as the larger muscles in his body spasmed. Darkness enveloped him as the pain subsided, his arms and legs settling on the bed, his eyes open, but unseeing. Black tears ran from his eyes, streaking his face, and then he breathed no more.

Chapter 26 - The Dark Lord

Scrag walked over to the slumped body of Grian and picked him up by the back of his robes. Walking over to the edge of the river, he heaved the limp body into the flowing water and watched it float away. Twilight faded to total darkness as he returned to Cy and a circle of high ranking Narshuks.

Cy stood at the center of the circle and outstretched his hands. "Tonight, we witness the rebirth of the Dark Lord Gladius. Too long he has remained trapped, his body long dead and decayed, his soul woven with mine. Tonight, we see the rise of the Narshuks as the dominant race in Findoor, and soon, the entire world. But it doesn't end there. Already a permanent portal to another world awaits. Led by Gladius, we shall rule all the worlds!"

The Narshuk army broke out in an uproar. Excited howls and barks could be heard for miles as they celebrated the coming of their leader. Scrag took the Lyecian book from Cy and held it before him. Reading from the book, he began to chant the words of power. He drew in energy from the world around him and focused it on Cy. His words ran together and a hush fell over the crowd as a beam of energy shot from him, into Cy's chest.

Cy mimicked Scrag's chanting and his body lit up with white light. Earth gathered at his feet, rising into the air before him. Fire bound the earth together into the shape of a human body. Water restored flesh and bone, muscle and sinew to the creation. Air restored breath to its lungs.

Still, he and Scrag continued chanting, faster each second that went by. The torrent of energy flowing into Cy almost overwhelmed him. Death ripped his soul from his body in a burst of energy that spun in the air. Shadow split the two souls, one returning to Cy, and the other floating over to the waiting body. Life restored both souls to their respective bodies.

The energy that flowed from Scrag to Cy dispersed, and both went silent in anticipation. All was quiet for several minutes as they watched the naked form standing before Cy, and then its eyes fluttered open and it let out a gasp as it drew its first full breath.

Cy dropped to his knees before the figure, bowing his head. "My lord," he said in reverence. Scrag and the rest of the Narshuk army followed suit, row by row of the beasts dropping to the ground to show their allegiance to their one true master.

Stretching out his arms, Gladius summoned the gray magic of shadow. With a few words, streamers of energy wrapped around his body forming black plate armor that covered his naked form. He looked down at Cy and said, "We move out tonight."

Scrag and Cy spoke as one. "Yes, master."

Gladius approached Cy and motioned for him to rise. "I must have that last Lyecian boy. Whether he knows it or not, he is the key. Go now, and do not return without him."

Rising to his feet, but keeping his head bowed, Cy said, "Yes, Master Gladius." He took a step back, and turned to walk away, heading North for Findoor castle where he now sensed Seth's presence.

Turning to look out at the massive army that surrounded him, Gladius spoke in a powerful booming voice that echoed across the land, "We move out, *tonight!*"

Chapter 27 – A New Day Dawning

Seth was the first to rise the next day. He gave up on sleep after the fourth nightmare and went wandering around the castle. Very few people were up that early, as it was before first light crept over the horizon. The occasional servant or nurse he passed in the halls bade him good morn and went on with their work without a second glance. Seth couldn't see what was good about it. *Everyone expects me to be some kind of hero,* he thought as he walked, *but what if I don't want to be a hero? Even after seeing what I can do, and experiencing it, is this really real? Have I lost my mind?* He made his way to the battlements where he could watch the sun rise.

The first rays of sunlight shot over the horizon in a dazzling array that half-blinded Seth. Despite the sprawling city before him, and the army on the outlying fields, he was still able to enjoy the view of this strange new world. He sat on the edge of the battlements watching the darkness turn to light, the grays turn to reds, oranges, yellows, and finally shades of green as full sun came up. When Merek came to find him, it was those few servants and nurses who issued their pleasant greetings that were able to direct him up to the battlements where Seth still sat.

Merek approached Seth, watching him watch the world come to life for a new day. Seth heard the old wizard's shuffling steps and turned to see who it was. "Oh, it's you. Good morning," he said turning back to watch the people of the city. Merck saw a sadness in Seth's eyes that wasn't there the night before.

"Good morn to you Seth. What brings you to the battlements so early in the day?"

Seth sighed. "I'm not really sure, to be honest. I needed somewhere to be alone. Things have happened so fast. I just don't really know what to think anymore. Two weeks ago I was just plain old Seth Alkirk, a boring senior programmer from Denton Iowa, with an interesting best friend and a boring life. And here I am at the top of a castle on who knows what planet, with no real idea why I'm here or what people are expecting from me. My life made sense before, but now, not so much."

Choosing his words with care, Merek replied, "Seth, I remember when your father sat on that very same spot. It was many years ago, and I was a much younger man back then. Findoor fought a terrible war against Gladius, and your father's people, your people, paid a tremendous price. Many of them stood against Gladius, some of them got away with only their powers stripped. Many more died at his hand. Your father was one of the last, and fought the hardest."

Seth turned to face Merek. "I remember that story. It was one of my favorites that my father told me. Malia called it the Lyecian War. Why was Gladius killing my people? What was he after?"

"Legends tell of a gatekeeper, The Traveler, who can open the path to the world of the gods. One man, blessed by all gods. The realm of the gods exists outside the flow of time, something even Time Weavers are bound to. Because while you can manipulate it by speeding it up or slowing it down, you cannot travel outside of it.

"Normal men and women cannot carry Lyecha's blessing to wield the power of time. Only Time Weavers can do that. And so, one blessed by all the gods had to be a Time Weaver. Gladius figured that out, and began killing them, one by one. When only Krycin remained, we thought he was the one. But Krycin could only wield the time and life elements, not all eight."

Seth looked up at Merek. "I can use six."

"By the gods, boy! Six?"

"Yeah. Time obviously, and fire. I used water to heal my broken hand, and air to slow my fall. When Malia was dying, I used life to cure her disease, and shadow showed me Grian's attempt to spy on us."

"You are indeed very powerful then. I sent Malia to rescue you and to bring you back here so that I could protect you. Grian wants your powers. I think he believes that you can grant him Lyecha's blessing, but he is wrong. Gladius? He won't stop at Findoor. He won't stop at my world, or your world. He will consume as many worlds as it takes for him to find what he seeks."

"Teach me. Show me how to use and control these powers I have. Help me help you defeat our enemies."

Merek nodded. "Come. Follow me and I shall teach you all that I can. We will work together so that your father's effort all those years ago might not be in vain."

Seth's spirits lifted as he followed Merek through the halls of the castle. The day's activities were just starting for most people in the castle, even though Seth had been up for several hours already. Merek led Seth to a special chamber near the training grounds. Inside the room were seven pedestals, each with a symbol on them. The first was a dot with a curve around it like a candle flame, and the second Seth remembered from the temple door, the dot with waves washing over it. The third was a dot with two arcs that looked like rolling hills, and the fourth, a dot surrounded by swirls. Looking at Merek, he pointed to each one. "Fire, water, earth and air, right?"

"That's right my boy."

Turning back to the pedestals, he examined the last three. One had a dot with two arcs around it that made it look like an eye, the second was a dot surrounded by two arcs, and then a circle around it all. The last pedestal was a dot with two half circles around it, one above, and one below. "Shadow, life and death?"

With a light laugh Merek said, "You learn quickly."

"And where is time?"

"Ah, we don't include time in the test. You see, one either is, or is not, Lyecian. It must be in your lineage. There has never been a human blessed by Lyecha."

"Test? What are you testing me for?"

"Each person is different. When I take on a new student of magic, they must subject themselves to this test which detects which blessings you carry, and to what degree you can use them. Place your hand over each, and the symbol will light up if you can indeed use it. The intensity of the glow tells me to what degree. Once you have done that, I can decide how to best go about teaching you."

"Alright, I'll give it a try." He walked over to the first pedestal and stood behind it. A nervous feeling crept up out of his stomach, but he swallowed his fear and placed his hand over the platform. There was no waiting involved as the symbol burst to life with a bright red glow. Moving to the second, he placed his hand over it, and the symbol of Philana lit up bright blue.

Merek nodded, and with a smile said, "Fire and Water we already knew."

Continuing down the line, Seth placed his hand over each pedestal, lighting them up one by one. When he reached the last, he hesitated. "Merek, what does this mean?"

"Well, thus far it means you wield only seven of eight elements. If you can wield death, then it is that much more imperative that we keep you safe. Go on, we shan't know unless you try."

Seth stared at the last pedestal, marked with the symbol of death. It was a long time before he worked up the courage to even say anything. "Death. I don't want to wield death."

Walking over to Seth, Merek laid a hand on his shoulder to comfort him. "My boy, death isn't all evil. It's a natural part of life. Any element can be used for good or for evil. Do not fear it. Embrace it as your destiny."

"I guess you're right. I've just never thought of it that way." He turned to face the pedestal and lifted his hand. "Here goes nothing, right?"

Merek nodded. Seth moved his hand toward the pedestal, his heart raced and his stomach churned. His hand shook as he moved it forward. *Come on, Seth, you can do this,* he thought, and pushed his hand the rest of the way.

A long moment passed, as both men stood and stared at the pedestal. When Merek was satisfied with what he saw, he turned and walked away, motioning Seth to follow. Seth stared at the symbol, a bit shocked at what he saw. "So? What does it mean, Merek?"

The ancient wizard stopped and turned back to him. "It means you're a wizard who can wield seven elements. Now come, and I shall teach you how to use them."

Seth followed him out of the room, but turned back one last time. The pedestal with the symbol of death on it remained dark. Despite not wanting his powers to begin with, he found himself almost disappointed.

Seth followed Merek out to a training area designed for students learning to cast spells for the first time. The walls were made of solid gray stone and there was no roof. The dirt floor was packed sand, and scorch marks decorated the entire room.

Merek stopped in the center of the area, turned, and without warning flung a dagger toward Seth. It flew from his hand, turning end-over-end in the air. Seth spotted it, floating through the air like a video playing in slow motion. He leaned to the side as it approached and it flew past, smacking the wall hard behind him and clattering to the ground.

Stunned, Seth looked back at Merek and managed to stammer out, "You just... you..."

"Lesson number one, trust your instincts. Your powers will win you the battle, but your instincts will save your life."

Seth stared at the dagger on the ground. It took him a moment to realize that Merek was even talking. "You just tried to kill me. What the hell?"

Merek laughed. "You're fine, and you've learned a lesson from it. It's no accident that you can dodge attacks like that. Time Weavers have a finely tuned instinct for self-preservation. It's only when you ignore those instincts, or are unable to act on them, that you'll get hurt. Now come, there are other lessons to learn, and precious little time to learn them."

Seth picked up the dagger and handed it back to Merek, who returned it to his robes. He gave Seth another pat on the shoulder and then proceeded to work with him through each of the elements, describing what they do and how to use them. Seth remained focused on the lessons; by the end of the day he was casting powerful spells which would have taken an average student weeks to learn.

"By the gods, boy, I've never seen somebody learn magic so quickly. Of course, in the time of the Lyecians, the process of learning to control your powers was much more gradual. Typically a Time Weaver would begin their training in their adolescent years. It's curious that your powers didn't show up until you were older. It's almost as if they were suppressed, but that can't be possible."

Giving Merek a curious glance between spells, Seth said, "Why is that?"

"Because a Time Weaver's powers can only be suppressed by the possessor. Which is to say, the only person who could suppress your powers, is you."

Merek opened his mouth to continue explaining the situation to Seth when a runner came to the training grounds, out of breath. He stopped at the entrance, calming himself before he said anything. "Arch-Magus Merek, you must come to the King's chamber at once. It is of the utmost importance." Before Merek could say a word, the runner turned and left.

"Well. Shall we go and find out what this is about?" Merek asked as he got up and walked toward the door.

Seth followed him. "Yeah, I could use a distraction."

The two men made their way through the castle as fast as they could. They arrived at the King's chamber minutes later where a large group gathered around the entrance. Merek pushed his way through the troubled group. "Make way, stand aside."

He entered the room to see the King's closest advisers standing around his bed; some of them wept, some stood with their heads bowed in respect. Merek walked with careful measured steps toward the bed and gasped when he saw the King's face. Black lines covered his skin, and his blue lips drew no breath. He lay still in the quiet chamber, no life left to even attempt to bring back. Merek spotted the letter on the desk, still sealed. Seth remained in the doorway until Merek picked up the letter, turned, and spoke to the room. "Everybody must leave this room at once."

Seth stepped into the room and to the side to allow them to leave. With a wave of his hand, Merek slammed the door after the last person left, leaving only himself, Seth, and the dead King in the room. He slid a single finger under the edge of the letter and broke the seal, then unfolded the letter, and read it. "Seth, these are dark times for Findoor. To take your own life is to die in utter disgrace. His body will not be given the proper respect that it deserves for leading us through many years of peace. As there is no heir, there will be a power struggle, but no man can claim royal ascent until either they have passed the King's trials, or the council unanimously agrees on a successor. And during a time of war as we are in now, the King's trials will be impossible to achieve."

The smell of death lingered in the air, making Seth uncomfortable. "Merek," he said, "who is going to run the Kingdom then?"

Merek looked up at Seth with tears welling up in his eyes. "That's a good question my boy. A very good question indeed."

Chapter 28 – The Dead World

Merek announced the King's suicide that night. Nobody held remorse for the King, now dubbed a coward in the face of the Kingdom's most treacherous peril in many years. Instead, a ball was planned for the next night to celebrate Seth's arrival.

In Merek's study, the old wizard told Seth, "My boy, we must get you fitted for the ball. If these people are going to recognize you as their hero, you're going to have to look the part." A smile creased the old man's face.

"I know, Merek, but I don't feel like a hero. How can I possibly stand against an army of that size by myself? And I still can't fully control my powers."

"By yourself? Who said anything about you facing them by yourself?" Merek let out a dry chuckle. "So very much like your father you are. He carried the weight of the entire war on his shoulders. He blamed himself for the war, even though there was nothing anybody could have done. But enough of that, we have work to get done. Tomorrow is a celebration!" With that, Merek stood up, and walked toward the door of his study. "Come now, boy."

Seth followed him through the corridors of the castle and out into the city surrounding it. A few minutes later, they stood outside of a shop with a sign hanging over the door. Painted on the sign was a spool of thread with a needle struck through it. The face of the store was white-washed and highlighted with a pale blue. Planters hung below each window, filled to overflowing with colorful flowers, many of which Seth did not recognize. The shop held a simple elegance that he admired as compared to stores in his home town.

Merek opened the front door and motioned for Seth to follow him in. Inside the shop was a wide array of fabrics and designs. Wire models stood at various spots in the shop showing off the latest fashions in formal wear. Light streaming in through the front windows highlighted the bright colors that seemed to be the trend among the nobles and those who could afford such luxuries. Merek walked to the counter at the other end of the room to speak with the keeper. "My friend, I need a suit for this young man here. Money is no object, but I require it for the ball tomorrow."

The keeper looked up from his work and scoffed. "It takes days to put a proper formal suit together."

The old wizard reached into his robes and pulled out a small bag tied off with a draw-string. He tossed it onto the counter before him, a distinct jingle echoing through the room. "That should cover the clothes, and if you succeed, I'll double it."

Standing up from his work, the keeper walked over to the counter and pulled the pouch open to look inside. His eyes grew wide at the sight of the gold coins within it. "D...double, you said?"

"Yes, you heard me right."

"Right away, sir. Come, we will have to work fast." The keeper walked out from behind the counter and offered a hand to Merek. "You have my word--I shall have the suit ready by tonight. I'll send a runner for you when it is complete. Do turn the sign on your way out. Thank you." His words came out so fast Merek struggled to understand him.

"Thank you, my friend," he said before turning to Seth. "Do as he asks, you will be in tip-top shape in no time."

Seth smiled at him as he walked toward the door and called out, "I will, Merek. Thanks."

Merek returned to the war room where Findoor's Generals tracked the Narshuk army. He spread out the map on the large table and spoke an incantation on it, energy spreading forth from his fingertips out onto the map. It sprang to life, scanning the distance between where they were and the last known position of the Narshuk army. The map stopped at the half-way point, showing a horde of Narshuks approaching. At the head of the army walked a hulking figure in black armor. He reached out with his mind to the Scryes. *My friends, awaken.*

Yes master, the many voices of the Scryes spoke in unison.

Who now leads the Narshuk army?

The Dark Lord, Gladius. There was a note of fear in their voices.

How long do we have?

Not tomorrow, midday the next.

Merek thought about this for a moment, *Thank you my friends.* He severed the connection with the Scryes and went back to the map.

He's after Seth, Merek thought, trying to sort through what was going on, *but he doesn't know that Seth isn't the Traveler. But if not, then who?* He dismissed the enchantment on the map and ran from the room as fast as his old legs could take him, searching for the one person he had not yet spoken to on the subject: Cedric.

Cedric sat in the great room on the stage where he would play the next night for the ball. Streamers and colored lanterns hung from the rafters, shedding light on the dance floor. Tables lined each side of the room with many hundreds of seats, all with full table settings for the feast to be served before the festivities began. The air was filled with the chatter of runners and servants, and even a few soldiers who volunteered to help out for the occasion. Cedric strummed his lute, practicing for a long night of good food and good music.

Despite the hectic pace of everybody involved with the ball, peace settled over them. A sly smile on Cedric's face held the only indication of his involvement. That was until Merek burst through the doors and interrupted him.

The doors slammed into the walls on either side, and it startled Cedric so much that he missed his mark on the lute, catching on a string and breaking it with a loud *twang*. He almost uttered a curse, but held his tongue when he realized that every eye in the room was focused on him. Instead he muttered, "Sorry," and reached into his pack for a new string.

Cedric watched Merek's approach as he stormed across the great room toward him, his expert hands taking control of replacing the broken string. "Good afternoon, Arch-Magus Merek. Something I can do for you? I've an excellent selection of tunes lined up for tomorrow's ball. Or perhaps a story?"

Merek raised an eyebrow to the fast-talking Bard, but did not look amused. "A story, yes. Tell me a story about a Time Weaver. He came from another world with a warrior, and met up with a Bard."

"Why yes, I know this one, what a wonderful story. But how does it end?"

"That has yet to be seen. What do you know of the Time Weaver? What do you know of Seth?"

"Not much, I'm afraid. I know he grew up in the dead world without his father. Such a shame. And there was something curious about him. For a Time Weaver, he was old to be getting his first taste of power."

"Yes, much too old. His powers were suppressed."

"Right; as I said, curious," Cedric said, working at getting the string wound back up on his lute.

"What do you know of the Traveler?"

Cedric paused in his task and looked up at Merek with a serious expression. "Nothing I care to discuss in the company of others."

"Come then, for this is of the utmost importance."

Merek led him to his private chambers, where they sat at the table in the center of the room. Looking at Cedric he said, "Now, talk."

"Yes, well, The Traveler. Gifted by all the gods, the Crossroads shall open by his command. Though in my circles, 'gifted by all the gods' is subject to some interpretation. Many believe that it is the one person with the ability to wield all elements. But others think that the gods' gifts could take other forms. For instance, our god of life, Anam, could grant a second chance and restore one to life."

"Indeed, the gods' gifts take many forms. Not all of them magical," Merek said. "So what of our boy, Seth? Is there anything he has received, or that has happened to him that could be interpreted, unquestionably, as a gift from one of our gods?"

"Not that I know of. I understand he is very talented, wielding numerous elements..."

"Seven."

"Seven? By the gods, he's at least as powerful as Gladius once was. Which element is missing?"

"The gift of Grishtor, god of death."

"Indeed, and not a gift given lightly by that god. His gifts can also be difficult to interpret. Some don't believe them gifts at all."

"I believe our boy Seth is the Traveler, though he has been through the test and found to only wield seven of the eight gods' powers. I think Grishtor's gift came in another form. Why did you refer to Seth's world as 'The Dead World'?"

"Well, you see, many of the stories I get are second- and third-hand. This particular one comes through a friend of a friend of a friend. The dead world is referred to as such by dragons, as they were no longer able to tolerate living there. At one time, many of them lived there and thrived, but as the population of man grew, the magic in the world disappeared, and they could no longer sustain themselves. They left, along with the old gods of that world, and moved on, dubbing it the dead world, as it was a magic dead-zone. It's my understanding that Time Weavers once used the world as a prison, to lock criminals away so they could do no harm to others. Even Krycin is said to have sent the betrayer there."

"Could Grishtor himself suppress a Time Weaver's powers?"

"That, my ancient friend, I do not know. But how that could be considered a gift is beyond me."

"The Dark Lord Gladius has returned and recovered control of his army. We don't know what has become of Grian, though I suspect he is now dead. The Narshuk army will arrive not tomorrow, but mid the next day if they maintain their current speed. And I believe Gladius is after Seth."

A look of shock and terror passed over Cedric's face. "Returned, but how?"

"I'm unsure. The spells to perform that type of miracle were locked up many years ago, and sent away with Krycin."

Cedric's face went pale, even under the mask Merek could tell he was in shock.

"What is it, Cedric?"

"The book. It was marked with the Findoor crest, and contained High Lyecian script. Seth carried it with him into this world, but it was taken by the man who attacked us, the Man in Black."

"We are fools then; while we thought we had this situation under control, it seems we have played right into the Dark Lord's hands. Go now, and tell no one of this. We have enough to deal with right now without causing a panic."

"Indeed. I shall return to my practice, and breathe not a word of it." Cedric stood up from the table and turned to leave. Before he walked out the door, he turned back to Merek and said, "I hope you have a plan, my friend."

Chapter 29 – The Betrayer

It took several hours for the tailor to fit Seth with a suit for the ball, but when he finished, even Seth was happy with the results. The pants and jacket were made of the finest black silks and fit better than anything Seth had ever worn. There was a sheen to the silk that reflected a slight blue color and made it appear to glow with an inner light. The jacket had a long tail that flowed down to knee length and was adorned with silver buttons and buckles. "None of that polished steel rubbish for you my boy!" the tailor said while sewing them in place.

Underneath the jacket was a white tunic with more silver buttons. The collar was loose fitting at Seth's request, and the original ruffle on the sleeves was taken in. "The fashions of the King's court dictate the style of many of my garments," the tailor said.

"I have no interest in looking like a noble of the King's court," Seth responded.

The tailor nodded and did as Seth asked, and was pleased with the result.

The boots Seth wore were polished to a mirror-like shine with a pointed toe and silver thread patterns sewn into the leather. Despite being more rugged than Seth was used to, they were comfortable. "Comfort is of paramount importance if you are to dance at the ball tomorrow," the tailor said after Seth commented on them.

"Dance at the ball? Oh, well, I don't really know how to dance," Seth said.

"Have you never been to a ball before? My goodness boy, where have you lived all your life?"

"In a far away land," said Seth with a smile.

"Aye. Well, in any case, I think you are ready to go. You'll be popular with the ladies tonight," he said with a wink.

As if on cue, the front door to the shop opened, and Merek walked in. "By the gods, Seth, you look dashing," he said as he crossed the room.

"Thanks again, Merek. You really didn't have to do this, you know."

"Nonsense, I'll not have you dressed in rags for such an occasion. Come now, we have more practice before the festivities tomorrow, and I would like you to learn some swordsmanship." Turning to the tailor, he reached into his pockets and retrieved another bag, similar to the first, and handed it to him. "My thanks to you for doing such a fine job, and on such short notice too. Splendid work, simply splendid."

The tailor accepted the pouch without question. "If there is anything you need, just drop by my shop here, we'll get you all fixed up."

"Indeed," Merek said, then turned and headed toward the door. Before heading out to the castle again he checked to be sure that Seth was following.

Seth gave the tailor his thanks as well and followed close behind Merek.

The following night, the great room bustled with activity as residents of the town and castle alike dressed in their finest attire, mingled and discussed mundane things like the lovely weather they've been having, and how the cattle were looking so early in the season. Many made their way to seats at tables around the perimeter of the room. At the front of the room, laid out before the stage was a long table reserved for royalty, high ranking nobles, and honored guests. On this night, Merek took the King's seat, and invited Seth to sit beside him. Cedric was also there, and various other nobles that Seth was introduced to.

As Seth looked around the room, disappointment filled his heart. Nowhere could he see Malia in the vast crowd of people. Merek saw the look on his face and put a hand on his shoulder. "Don't worry my boy, I'm sure she'll be here."

"Hmm?" Seth broke out of his daze. "Oh, thanks Merek."

As the remainder of the people took their seats, Merek stood before the congregation and cleared his voice. "Welcome, friends. Runners and nurses, pages and squires, servants, farmers, smithies, bakers, and bartenders. All people of all faiths, all occupations, and every social standing. On this night, we are equals. We dine at the same tables, and consume food from the same platters. And though our Kingdom has flourished in a time of peace, war comes, and it makes no mind of whether we are ready for it or not. The Kingdom of Findoor will remain strong and proud against those who would see us wiped out. We will not lay down and die. And again, at our time of greatest need, we find an ally. A Time Weaver, our honored guest, Seth Alkirk. And though tomorrow brings war, Findoor shall carry on, the greatest nation this world has ever known!"

A cheer roared up from the crowd of people filling the room. As Merek sat back down, trays of food were brought out to fill the tables, starting with soups and breads. There were vegetables and fruits, and meats of all kinds, common and exotic. The smells that filled the air drove Seth's hunger more than anything else, and he ate healthy portions of all the foods presented to him. When at last the desserts came around, Seth was still looking around. "Merek," he asked, "where is Malia? Shouldn't she have been here by now?"

Merek leaned over to Seth. "I would have thought she would be here. However, I'm sure she will arrive before the night is done."

"I hope so." Seth sat back in his chair and watched as the young men in the crowd lined up in rows around the center tables. All of them dressed in their finest, trying to impress the girls who walked past the lines. Two by two they paired off and took a position for the first dance of the night. The food and tables were cleared from the dance floor, and Cedric stood up and joined the small band on the stage. Up until then the music was background noise, drowned out by the murmur of the crowd in the hall. As Cedric took the stage, all eyes turned toward him, and he strummed the first notes of the opening song of the night. His voice rang out clear and true. The couples on the dance floor glided through the room, dresses whirling and bodies swaying as everyone enjoyed the celebration.

Seth sat at the head table beside Merek and watched, but would not get up to dance even when asked by several attractive young women. Merek turned to him and said, "You're not going to sit there and sulk through the entire ball are you?"

"No, I was just hoping Malia would be here, that's all."

As the song ended, there was a commotion at the large double doors of the hall.

Cedric stopped playing and stared, his mouth dropping open. The couples out on the dance floor all stopped as well and turned their attention to the door. Seth stood up from his chair so that he could see what the fuss was about.

Standing just inside the door was Malia, dressed in the most elegant gown Seth had ever seen. It glittered in the lantern light of the great room, a pale blue adorned with white braids. The gown hugged her figure and highlighted her feminine curves. The straps were simple, showing off her shoulders, and she wore long pale blue gloves that covered her arms just past her elbow. Her wild blonde hair was tied up in braids that cascaded down her back. A silver tiara topped her head, and her pale complexion was set off by a mild blush on her cheeks. Her gown spread out below her waist just enough to accent her hips and ended at ankle length, revealing silver slippers on her feet.

Seth caught his breath. Had it not been for Cedric starting a new song, he might have stood there all night, just staring at her. When the music began to play again, a slower song this time, he walked around the table and toward her. Malia spotted him as well and smiled, taking a few steps in his direction.

The crowd on the dance floor parted creating an aisle for the two to walk in. For Seth, nothing else existed but Malia. His steps echoed through the room, the quiet music complementing their approach. Cedric's voice rang out with the first words of the song, but they were background noise to Seth. He reached Malia and stopped, staring into her deep gray eyes. "Sorry I'm late," she said with a smile that lit up the room.

Seth took her hand and kissed the back of it, then pulled her in close to him, wrapping one arm around her waist, the other holding her hand. "I'm glad you came. You look beautiful."

Malia blushed, following Seth's lead, moving across the dance floor and ignoring everything else in the room. The crowd stood watching the pair.

Merek watched them dance with a smile on his face. Even he could see that they were in love. He was about to get up and retire for the night when something tugged at his subconscious. He opened up his mind to see what it was, and it pushed through. Two words in the unmistakable voices of the Scryes, *The Betrayer.*

He tried to respond, but something blocked it, like a thick fog in his mind. He worked harder to sift through and contact the Scryes, and when he managed to reach them, he didn't expect what he got from them. *The Betrayer, he comes!*

Before he could act, a dark figure appeared at the doorway. Standing tall in a fine black suit and a broad rimmed hat, he thrust his hands forward, dark energy crackling in a beam toward Seth and Malia. The blast hit them both, sending them flying in opposite directions into the crowd. His southern drawl called out above the crowd, above the music. "I've got a score to settle with you two."

Seth was up in an instant, shaking off the blast that left his suit smoldering. He walked out into the aisle and faced Cy. "This is between you and me. Leave her out of it," Seth said taking a step forward. Merek was already chanting the words to a spell behind him.

"Have it your way, boy." Another stream of dark energy burst forth from his hands, but this time Seth's instincts kicked in. Time slowed, the energy arc approached him, and he dodged to the right, avoiding a direct hit. The blast continued on behind Seth and hit the table where he and Merek sat for dinner. The table exploded in a shower of splinters, spraying up and around Merek, but the wizard continued his chanting.

Seth thought back to his lessons and how to use magic, but couldn't clear his mind fast enough.

Cy walked toward him. "Perhaps an introduction is in order. If I'm going to deliver you to the Dark Lord, you should at least know my name."

"I told you before, I'm not going anywhere with you," Seth said, still struggling with his focus.

As Cy approached him at the center of the room, Merek completed his spell. White light flooded the room in a blinding flash. When it faded, all of the people in the room were gone, including Malia. Only Seth, Cy and Merek remained. Cy looked past Seth to fix his gaze on Merek. "What an interesting trick. I've got an even better one," he said with a sneer.

He began to draw energy to him. Merek tried to speak, to warn Seth to get away from him, but Cy was fast and finished his spell before the words could come out. An energy field appeared around Cy and Seth, enveloping them into a blue shimmering globe. Merek cast another spell, but the effect reflected off the barrier, leaving a scorch mark in the high ceiling of the ball room. Cy turned his attention to Seth now that Merek could no longer interfere. "Now, boy, I will restate my offer. Come with me willingly, serve the Dark Lord, and live forever. Or I will take you by force, level this entire castle and kill every last soul in it, including your little girlfriend."

Seth looked at Cy, trying to clear his head, but still the fear clouded his mind and he couldn't make the magic come. Cy took advantage of the pause. "I can make this all go away. I can make your dreams come true. All you need to do is take my hand and leave here with me. Whaddya say, boy?" He whispered, but it was clear in the quiet ball room, the only sound was the hum of the globe surrounding them.

"Okay," Seth said, holding his hands out to Cy, "I'll go. But nobody else gets hurt."

"Seth, no!" Merek cried from the other end of the room.

"Too late, old man. The boy's made his choice. And what a choice he has made." Cy smiled and took hold of Seth's arms. He called power to him that Seth could feel rushing in, and it reminded him of a story he was once told...

> ...Krycin called upon the power of his people, the element of time and space. He drew the energy not from the world around him, but from Gladius, using the sword as a conduit. A torrent of magical energy poured from Gladius, robbing him of his strength and of all the power taken from Krycin's people.

The magic was there, held back like a dam. Seth's mind cleared, and he lifted his head to stare into his opponent's eyes. As their eyes locked, the dam broke, and Seth pulled the magical energy through him, robbing Cy of his spell. Seth's eyes lit up with a fiery red light that flowed out before him and reflected off Cy's face. Seconds later, Cy was drained. He tried to pull away, but Seth held on, his hands heating up and bursting into flames.

Cy faltered, a look of horror coming over his face. "No," he managed to get out, as his confidence faded.

"Yes," Seth said with a smile. He released Cy's arms and made a fist with his right hand. He threw his first punch at Cy, hitting him in the gut, the flames searing away his clothes and leaving a large burn in the middle of his torso. Cy flew back against the energy barrier that surrounded them, gasping for breath. Seth didn't wait for him to recover, but approached him and threw another punch with his other hand. This time his left hand connected with Cy's face, the flames searing through Cy's flesh, tearing through his cheek and leaving his teeth exposed on one side of his face.

The barrier surrounding them faltered as Cy began to waver, but held. He tried to take a swing back, but Seth caught his hand mid-air, then returned the shot, hitting Cy again in the stomach, this time burning through a fair amount of his skin, exposing muscles and tendons underneath. Cy let out a cry and dropped to his knees. "You'll regret this boy. The Dark Lord will never stop. Never give up. Gladius has already beaten death once. Even if you defeat him this time, he will be back again, and again, and again."

Seth looked down at him with his burning eyes. "Then so be it." Unleashing the remaining energy coursing through his body, a red-orange bolt of energy fired from his hands, striking Cy square in the chest. The energy wrapped around him, consuming first his clothes, then his skin, muscles, bones and internal organs. His screams echoed through the ballroom even after the last of his body, now nothing but ash, settled on the floor. Seth lowered his arms and breathed a sigh of relief.

A figure appeared in the doorway of the ballroom, her gown scorched from the initial hit she took, Malia struggled to catch her breath. "Oh thank the gods, you are unharmed," she managed to get out between breaths.

Seth turned his head toward her voice, saw the state of her gown, and called upon the power of earth and water to mend both Malia and the gown. Burnt threads extended and wove back together. Reddened skin faded and healed. In seconds both Malia and her gown were as beautiful as the first moment he saw her walk through the ball room doors. He walked toward her with slow measured steps, his eyes never leaving hers. As he approached her, he held out his hands, took hers within his, and pulled her into a warm embrace. Their lips touched, pressing together in a long, slow kiss.

Chapter 30 - Battle Plans

Grian opened his eyes to a wide blue sky above him. Cold and wet, he found himself shivering despite the warm morning air. Lifting his head, his vision blurred causing him to blink a few times. His feet dangled in the stream that trickled by, but he lacked the strength to lift them out. *Where am I,* he thought, looking around to get his bearings. *That piece of trash is going to pay.*

Summoning all of his strength, he dragged his feet out of the water and got himself up onto dry land. *They'll all pay,* he thought as he located the sun. It remained on the horizon, just rising for the day. When he looked at the bright orb in the sky, pain lashed through his skull. With a gasp he closed his eyes and clutched his head. "Damn it."

Reaching out, he grasped the power of water and called forth the power to heal his wounds. The splitting pain in his head subsided and his body calmed and stopped shivering. Once he was better able to focus, the power of fire warmed him and his armor and dried him off in minutes instead of the hours it would normally take.

With his physical needs taken care of, he stood up and looked around. Grassy fields stretched out to the east, and a thick forest to the west. Several miles to the north, there was a small hamlet with stone houses and small streamers of smoke rising from chimneys. *I need a horse,* he thought, and walked toward the town.

Twenty minutes later he strolled up to the stable at the edge of town. A burly man walked out to meet him. "Greetings friend, what can we do for you?"

Ignoring the formalities, Grian spoke in a harsh tone, "I need a fast horse, and the fastest route to Findoor Castle."

"In a hurry huh? Well, we got ol' Champ over there, he's the fastest we've had round these parts in a long while. But he'll cost ya, as he's good breeding stock. As for Findoor castle, head north about twenty miles and you'll reach a merchant road. Follow that and you'll get there. That's as direct a route as any."

With a nod Grian offered a handshake, which the man grasped with a strong shake. Grian looked up into his eyes and spoke, "Obitas nexasa mortai."

The man gasped as magical energy flowed into his body and removed his soul. With a violent convulsion, he surged backwards and fell. He was dead before he hit the ground.

Bypassing the body, Grian walked into the stable and saddled up the dark brown stallion. Leading it out of the building to the edge of town, he took one last look behind him. Somebody noticed the dead body on the ground and shouted at him. Ignoring the outcry, he rode away to the sound of the alarm being raised.

Tension increased the following morning as everybody worked hard to prepare for the impending siege. Soldiers outside worked through the night to reinforce the outer walls of the city and to prepare themselves for battle. Townsfolk inside the walls spent the day moving supplies into the castle proper and gathering their things to move inside. Merek gave instructions to have the city evacuated that morning when he discovered that it could be as early as mid-afternoon when the Narshuk army would arrive. It was the commotion outside that woke Seth up that morning from a short rest after a long night of dancing.

Opening his eyes, the bright morning sun streamed into his room, lighting up the room that looked so dreary and dark before. Dust swirled in a light breeze that blew in through the open window, looking like tiny specks of fire dancing in the rays of light. The air was fresh and clear, and smelled of bread and fried meats that made his mouth water, reminding him of mornings living with his mother as a teenager; she always made sure there was a hearty breakfast on the table when he woke up. He could feel Malia's head on his chest, her golden curls draped over his torso, her strong, lithe body pressed against his. "Please tell me I'm not dreaming," he said in a whisper.

"You are not dreaming." She lifted her head and propped it up on one hand, staring into his eyes with a dreamy smile on her face.

"Good. Because if I am, I never want to wake up." He lifted his head, his lips met hers and they kissed once more.

After Cy's attack on the ball was resolved, the townsfolk returned on Merek's reassurance that it was safe, and there would be no further interruptions. Seth and Malia resumed their dance, taking the dance floor alone to a slow tune that reminded Seth of some of the great love songs from his world. After their first dance, there was another but the rest of the guests joined in, filling the ball room with swirling, graceful couples dancing the night away. There was drink as well, of which both Seth and Malia had plenty. And at some point they ended up in Seth's room, laughing and teasing like school children. There was little sleep had that night, but Seth felt refreshed.

"You are more charming than I originally thought. Or were you simply attempting to have your way with me?" Malia said with a playful smile.

Returning a crooked smile of his own, Seth replied, "Who, me? Trying to have my way with you? I'm offended!" They both burst into laughter.

"Oh yes! I know all about you boys. Always trying to get us girls out of our skirts." Malia climbed up onto Seth, straddling his legs and leaning her naked body down over his, her nose just touching the tip of his. "Yes, only one thing on your mind."

Seth wrapped his arms around her body, and in one smooth motion, rolled them both over so that he was above her. There was another fit of laughter from them both, followed by another long, slow kiss. "Well then, if that's the case, perhaps I'll just have you put your clothes back on and march right back to your room," he said, teasing.

Malia wrapped her strong arms and legs around his body, clinging to him, holding him down. "Oh no you don't. I shan't have you leading me on like this, only to leave me wanting. You want to have your way with me, then have it." The hungry look in her eyes told Seth that she had more than just lighthearted play on her mind. Seth tried to feign indifference, but her grin, and the fingers she trailed along his shoulder, sent a wave of heat through him that stopped any teasing he might have attempted. He buried his face in her hair and kissed her neck, and with a shift of his hips, he obliged her.

As passion gave way to quietude, Malia was the first to speak. "There is much to be done today."

"I know. I wish I could stop time forever, and run away with you, far away from all of this." They lay together, her head on his shoulder, his arm around her. Malia propped herself up and looked into his eyes. She gave him a warm smile, sighed, and looked away.

"Yes, as do I. But we both have responsibilities. And these are my people. My family."

"I know. I've been welcomed into your world, with open arms, and open hearts. And I still sometimes doubt my own powers, or even how real this situation is, but I know that this is now my home too. A home worth fighting for."

"A home worth dying for," Malia added as she sat up on the side of the bed. Seth watched her as she reached for her undergarments and the gown that was dropped to the floor the night before.

"I'll do it for you. Merek wants me to take on Gladius. He believes that I can stop him. And maybe he's right, but I had trouble with Cy. I'm not sure I can defeat Gladius by myself, but I would try, for you."

"You must believe in yourself Seth. You wield more power now than many of the most powerful wizards alive combined. And you have learned to use it in such a short time. It's taken me most of my adult life to learn what small amount of magic I can use. You must understand how truly remarkable that is." She looked down at Seth, her eyes holding a sincerity that Seth had never seen in anyone from his world. Perhaps it was love. Perhaps a misplaced confidence. But it reassured him, whatever it was.

"Thank you. You'll never understand how much that means to me."

"I already do, my love. I already do. Come now, we must get up and get moving." Her words spurred him into action, and he got up and dressed in no time. He took a quick look in the polished steel mirror on his wall, fixed his hair and splashed some water in his face. Holding the door for Malia, they attempted to make a discreet exit from his room.

As Seth closed the door behind him, he said, "I have to talk to Merek this morning and find out what the plan is. You should get proper clothes on, and then meet me up there."

"Indeed. This gown is hardly suitable for combat," Malia said with a smile. "I shall see you at Merek's, and then we will talk war."

With one final kiss, Malia went off to her quarters to get changed, and Seth made his way to Merek's chamber.

It took longer than he expected to get to Merek's room as he was still getting used to navigating the large castle. When he did arrive, he was about to knock on the door when it swung open, leaving his fist in the air. "Come in, Seth. Come in," the old wizard said from within.

"Good morning Merek. How are you this morning?"

"Not bad my boy. Not bad at all for an old man. But there is much to do, and little time to do it. Our commanders await us in the war room, we must make haste."

"Oh. Malia-" Seth began, but was cut off.

"I have sent a runner to notify Malia of the meeting. We can hardly discuss our plans without our general, now can we?"

"General?" Panic made his heart jump in his chest. He expected her to have a safe position behind the walls of the castle. To be well protected during the Narshuk attacks. The news that she would be at the front lines, the general commanding the entire Findoor army, sent a surge of terror through him. "When did she become general?"

"Oh, she didn't tell you? She volunteered after the King took his own life. The King held that role himself, refusing to appoint somebody with that responsibility. I suspect she wanted to be by your side." Merek looked Seth in the eye and gave him a wink.

"I - no, she -" Seth stammered.

"Relax, my boy. I would no sooner put her into danger than would you. But she has proven herself capable, and I don't believe there is any way you could stop her, no matter how much you or I want to. She is a strong woman, and a born leader."

Seth heaved a sigh in resignation. "Yes, I know. And I've seen her fight. She's good. Probably one of the best. But that won't stop me from worrying about her."

Merek smiled as he walked around the table to Seth. Patting him on the back, he said, "Love will do such things, my boy. But you will both be all the stronger for your love. Come now, we have a war to plan."

"Alright, let's go." Seth walked out, heading toward the upper levels of the castle where the war room was located. Friendly smiles and nods from the residents of the castle left him feeling even more at home. When they arrived at the war room, the commanders were already present and waiting, but Malia was not yet there.

"Good Morning, commanders," Merek said, "We will wait for General Corsair before we proceed. She will be along shortly."

As if on cue, Malia walked through the door, outfitted in her full battle armor. The steel plates fitted her slender form and reflected the bright light of the room making her look like she glowed as she entered. Her wild blonde hair fell down her back, pushed up out of her eyes and tied back with a ribbon. She carried her helmet under one arm, and a bundle of maps under the other. Seth flashed her a smile which was returned without hesitation. "Good morn, gentlemen. Let us get these plans worked out quickly so we can all enjoy a hearty breakfast. It is set to be a long day for Findoor, and I do not want our commanders going to battle on an empty stomach."

A chorus of voices rang out "Here, here!" as she arranged the maps on the table.

"Gladius's army is a raging animal coming in our direction. But there is one thing I do know," Malia began, "if you cut off the head of the animal, it dies a swift death. Seth, that will be for you and Morganath to accomplish. You are the only one powerful enough to take on Gladius. Merek, we must have strategically placed healers out on the field. If our troops are to stand against Narshuks, we will require healing as we battle. We cannot wait until the battle is done this time. How many wizards do we have that can wield earth? I have a special task for them."

Merek raised an eyebrow toward her. "Oh?"

"Yes. We are going to raise a wall of stone. Split our army in half, and have them flank the battlefield out of sight. When the Narshuk army approaches, allow them to reach the outer walls, then raise the wall of stone behind them. We can catch them in a pincer attack with nowhere to run. Once they are herded into a tight group, we can focus our magical attacks on a small area to do the most damage."

Words of approval came from all participants in the room except for Seth. His focus rested somewhere past Malia, appearing to be in deep thought. When he focused back on Malia, she was about to speak again, but he cut her off. "And where will you be?"

The various commanders all looked to each other with curiosity, each one shrugging to the other, then returned their gazes to Malia, whose face was now stern. "I will be leading the charge from the front gate. At your side. If we leave no troops at the gate, they will get suspicious and halt their charge. I want several companies of volunteers to join me at the gates to lead the initial defense against them. It will be dangerous, but necessary for the good of the Kingdom."

A shadow passed over Seth's face as he turned his gaze down to the maps. Lines drawn out showed the positioning of troops, enemies, spells, and the wall that would be raised. He realized that those leading the charge at the gates would not only face the leading edge of the Narshuk army, but also would be caught in the area that was to be bombarded with spells once the wall and the rest of the troops were in position. After thinking about this in silence while the rest of them talked over the remaining plans, he spoke up, interrupting the discussion, and leaving them all a bit confused. "That's suicide."

Malia's gaze shot to Seth, a scowl on her face. "I beg your pardon?"

"Your plan, that's suicide for both you, and the volunteer soldiers. There has to be a better way."

"Do you have any suggestions?"

Seth looked into Malia's eyes and gave her a grin. "I just might."

Chapter 31 - Onslaught

Seth and Merek stood upon the battlements, surveying the land before them. The sun shone through a clear blue sky that afternoon, creating a warm glow over the now empty city. A cool gentle breeze blew over them from the west, trying to take Merek's long white hair along for the ride. The last of the citizens could be heard gathering their things and evacuating into the castle from the surrounding city. The walls of the city were constructed of thick stone and had never been penetrated by an attacking army, but Merek took no chances with the people of the Kingdom. "Are you ready for this?" asked Merek, turning to face Seth.

Seth flashed Merek an uncertain smile. "Do I have a choice?"

The kindness Seth saw in the old wizard's eyes took him off guard. "There is always a choice, my boy. The challenge in life is knowing what the right choice is. What's right is not always easy, and what's easy is not always right."

Looking out on the distant hill where the Narshuk army would crest, Seth breathed a sigh. "You're right, Merek, as usual."

"Make no mistake, Seth, it is sometimes a curse. There are times I am right when I wish I were wrong."

A nervous laugh escaped Seth. "If only I could be wise enough some day to have that problem."

Rumbling in the distance caught their attention and brought them back to the impending battle. The last stragglers below them made their way into the castle, and shouts from various commanders drifted up to them. Soldiers took their positions and portcullises slammed shut, locking down the castle. A golden figure drifted through the sky, riding warm air currents above the castle; it caught

Seth's eye as he looked up. "Do you think there will be enough room for Morganath to land up here?"

"I'm sure he will manage." Merek was about to say more, but footsteps behind them caught their attention. Both men turned to see Malia approaching them.

"Arch-Magus Merek, everyone is in position, are you ready?" She asked.

"Yes, we are prepared to cast the spell on your mark. It will be difficult to maintain the illusion, especially one so large and complex, but we will try."

"The Narshuk army is minutes away. Our scouts report that Gladius is leading the charge. Seth, are you sure this will work?" Malia turned to face him, love and concern apparent on her face.

After a few moments of contemplation, he replied, "I'm not sure about anything anymore, besides us." He reached out and took her hands as a great shadow passed over them. Morganath began one last descending circle before the gold dragon landed on the battlements, not resting his entire weight on them until he was sure they would support him.

Malia blushed at his admission. "That is very sweet of you, my love. Just, promise me you will use caution when battling Gladius."

"I will." He leaned in and gave her one last slow kiss before turning to walk toward Morganath. He was halfway there when he heard Malia's voice one last time.

"Seth?" she said, pausing to be sure she had his attention. "Destroy him. Utterly destroy Gladius."

Seth nodded and turned back to the gold dragon waiting for him.

"Ready for a battle?"

Morganath's booming voice responded, "I've been ready for this all three thousand years of my life. Climb on."

Seth hauled himself up onto Morganath's neck, and took hold of two spines to stabilize himself. With a great leap, and a stroke of his wings, Morganath launched into the air. Seth felt like he had swallowed a stone. "Get as high as you can. We'll come at them from the east, swoop in and drive them forward with your breath," Seth shouted over the wind ripping through his hair. Morganath altered his course and pumped his wings even harder to get higher still. When they reached their position, he settled into a glide and circled, giving Seth a good view of the coming army. To the south of Findoor castle was a swarm of black dots moving north over the fields. Seth remembered as a child walking outside to see a swarm of ants moving along the edge of a sidewalk. It fascinated him how the ants always managed to find their way, even though they looked like chaos. The swarm of Narshuks reminded him of those ants, moving over the countryside.

At the head of the swarm ran a large dark figure, leading the Narshuks to battle. Seth focused on the figure, assuming it to be Gladius. As the figure ran, it did not dodge around trees or alter his course. If something was in his way, he would wave a hand, and a boulder would fly in one direction, while a tree exploded into a cloud of splinters in the other. Seth leaned in close to Morganath's head. "He's very powerful, isn't he?"

Morganath took a second to respond, and when he did, the answer was short, almost terse, "Yes."

"Can we win this?"

"If the gods are with us, yes."

"And if they aren't?"

"Then may the gods have mercy on us all."

Neither of them spoke again for the next minute. Gladius and his army stormed forward, approaching the crest of the final hill before they reached Findoor castle. Seth watched for the signal as Morganath steadied himself to a hover in the air. There was a flash of light just inside the main gate of the castle, and then a curtain of energy spread across the front of it. Blue light shimmered from it for a moment before it disappeared, taking the castle with it. A smile spread across Seth's face as the rest of the castle disappeared from sight. What remained appeared to be a plain empty field, just another stretch to cross for the Narshuk army.

"That's our sign, Morganath. Let's go," Seth called to the dragon.

The Dark Lord Gladius charged forward, magic fueling his super-human speed, as he reached the last hill before Findoor castle. His army thundered behind him, but they mattered not to him. His focus was on acquiring the Time Weaver. He shouted out, drawing magic to fuel his booming voice projecting it across his army, "Charge forward and destroy your enemies, tear the castle down brick by brick if you have to. No man walks away!"

Thousands of Narshuks behind him all let out earth-shaking howls that drowned out the rumbling of their feet. It fueled Gladius's charge further, and propelled him over the crest of the hill. When he came within view of where the castle should have been, he stopped dead.

Before him lay an empty field. The grass swayed in the breeze, and the rays of the sun gave the scene an emerald glow. "No!" he screamed, fury filling his voice. "Where is it, it must be here!"

Many of the Narshuks continued their charge on what should have been the castle. None realized there was a problem until they passed where Gladius stood. He looked around, the thunder stolen from the Narshuk charge. From the east, a golden light approached the tail end of the Narshuk army. As it descended on them, a massive gout of flame burst forth from it, pouring down on the Narshuks caught at the back of the line. Gladius focused on the light, and realized what it was only too late. Panic flooded through the Narshuk army as hundreds were caught in the stream of flames pouring down on them. Instead of a well organized charge, Gladius's army descended into a panicked mob, trying to flee the dragon's breath. They ran down the hill past Gladius, who stood his ground.

The dragon finished its run at the back of the line, leaving a scorched path in the grass riddled with dead Narshuk bodies. The smell of burnt meat filled the air as smoke drifted up the hill toward Gladius. Panicked Narshuks ran from the dragon, tripping and trampling each other as he came about for another pass.

Gladius spoke up with his amplified voice, "No. No. No!" He realized all too quickly that his words, no matter how loud, now fell on deaf ears. The dragon began its second run across the back of the Narshuk line, blasting flames in a long swath that spurred even more Narshuks into a frenzy to get away from it. All bloodlust drained from the vicious army. Gladius lifted a hand, spoke a few words and sent a bolt of energy flying at the golden dragon. The black bolt crackled in the air toward its target, but when it was about to impact the flying beast, it reflected and flew back toward Gladius, who had to dive to avoid getting hit with his own spell.

He looked again, this time closer at the dragon, and saw what he suspected. A man sat astride the dragon's neck, holding the dragons spines and shouting orders to it. *That must be the Time Weaver,* he thought. *Nobody else could have turned my spell like that.* A smile spread across his face, and he began to chant ancient words of power that could be felt as well as heard when he spoke them. Calling upon the power of earth, the ground shook as he drew energy to him, his hands glowing red. Before him, a split formed in the grass that spread out into a spiderweb of cracks. Some of the Narshuks tripped on them and were trampled in the stampede. The center of the web sunk down and crumbled away, creating a hole in the earth. Seeing this only made Gladius chant faster and louder as he drew more power to him. A large clawed hand reached up from the hole and grabbed the side, sinking its talons into the grass. A second one reached up and grabbed the other side, crushing several Narshuks in the process. Black smoke and ash rose up from the hole as Gladius shouted louder still, his booming voice echoing across the land. "Arise my pet, arise and take me to the sky. Together we shall take down this Time Weaver, and together we shall rule all!"

The creature in the hole lifted its giant grotesque head from the pit, hauling its massive body out. Its feet pounded the ground, crushing Narshuks into pulp. Its head was the height of three Narshuks, with great black horns and red flesh that smoked and smoldered in the clear afternoon air. Its bovine features might have had it mistaken for a giant bull if not for the clawed hands the resembled the front limbs of a dragon. Folded to its back was a pair of black feathered wings that it stretched out to their full width as soon as it was able to. Spines ran down the creature's back that shook and shivered as it stretched its muscles, creating a rattling sound that made even the Narshuks cower away from it. Its back legs came to rest on the ground with a long tail dragging behind it. The end of the tail was adorned with a large spiked ball that looked like it was made of pure bone. It let out a tremendous roar that carried across the battlefield.

Gladius was about to climb up onto the creature's back when he saw ripples in the sky where the castle should have been. The first of the Narshuks came to a stop and were now being crushed between the stampede and an invisible wall of some kind. *Clever, Merek, but it has only bought you time,* Gladius thought.

As if in response to his thoughts, the ground shook once more. The illusion hiding the castle dropped, and a chorus of voices could be heard chanting from the top of the walls. The castle loomed over him, the voices bore down on him, and he could feel the magical energy in the air. In a long line at the back of his army, cracks formed in the ground.

Thunder rolled from one end of the battlefield to the other as a massive wall of granite rose from the ground and trapped the Narshuk army between it and the castle. More panicked howls rose from the Narshuks as they realized their predicament. They had nowhere to run. Gladius nodded. *Well played Merek, but that won't save your Time Weaver.*

Gladius mounted the creature before him, and took to the air.

Malia waited with the east flank of the Findoor army, watching the hill and waiting for the coming army. Merek, aided by many of his most promising students of shadow, wove a great illusion spell over the castle to hide it and the two flanks of the army from sight. When the spell was complete, the army could see a shimmering wall of energy before them that distorted the battlefield. From the outside, the castle appeared to have vanished.

After a few moments of tense silence from the Findoor army, and listening to the Dark Lord's Narshuks rumble across the land toward them, Malia turned to her troops and addressed them. "If this works, the Narshuks will be like rats in a cage. They will have nowhere to run, and may fight a fiercer battle as a result. Today we make our last stand, and thus I expect that each and every one of you will fight with all your being and continue until the last beat of your heart.

"The Narshuks stand taller than us, and faster, and stronger, but for all their strength and speed, they are lacking one thing--the heart of Findoor. Never before has Findoor castle fallen to invasion. Never before has a threat against the Kingdom succeeded in extinguishing our pride, our spirit, or our soul." A cheer rose up from the army that drowned out the sounds of the Narshuks now pounding down the hill. Malia could see Morganath making his second run with Seth across the back of them. The sight of the huge dragon put the invaders into a panic. *By the gods, it is working,* she thought, watching the scene unfold before her.

Her smile was short-lived though, as the ground shook beneath her feet. She looked up to the castle walls where Merek was now positioned, and he looked back to her as if reading her mind. He gave her a visible shrug to let her know that it wasn't him, and she turned her attention back to the battlefield where Gladius stood. He was casting a powerful summoning spell, that much she could make out, but what he summoned she did not know. The beast that climbed out of the gaping hole in the ground surprised all of the soldiers. *The Tordrake,* she thought. Fear and concern overwhelmed Malia as she realized what Gladius intended to do. Her gaze drifted from the beast now standing before Gladius, to the shimmering gold dragon in the sky. *I hope Seth is ready for this,* she thought, longing to have him by her side.

Her attention was drawn back to the army of creatures before her now, the first of which were hitting the castle walls and getting crushed by the following stampede. The panic-frenzied Narshuks were disorganized; some were injured from being trampled, but many more were fine, and very angry. Malia raised a hand to Merek, giving him the signal to start the next spell, the one that would trap the Narshuks like the dogs they were. The chanting rose up over the voices around her, and over the commotion and howls of the Narshuks. Hundreds of wizards, lined up on the walls, all chanted in unison, drawing magical power to them and forcing it down into the ground to do their bidding. The ground rumbled again, but this time she knew it was Findoor's wizards who caused it. Cracks formed in the ground in a long line at the back of the Narshuk army, and the earth shook. Malia and many of the other soldiers in her companies struggled to maintain their footings.

The illusion that made them invisible dispersed, the shimmering cloak of magic fading as the long solid granite wall lifted out of the ground. The Narshuks turned and saw the wall. Some tried to scale the wall, others clamored on top of their neighbors to get higher, in hopes of reaching the top. Still more turned to either side of the trench they were now forced into and saw the waiting Findoor army.

Malia gave the order to attack, waving a green flag to signal the other end to do the same. A well-formed rank of Findoor soldiers filled the end of the trench and advanced on the Narshuks, who now had the demeanor of cornered dogs. Howls and snarls sounded from their front lines. Even as she advanced on them, she watched the sky for the last pass of Morganath that would wipe out a tremendous number of the Narshuk army.

The golden dragon positioned itself at the far end of the trench and began its run, flames bursting forth from its mouth like liquid flowing from a waterfall. It pounded down on the Narshuk army, setting them on fire, burning them alive. Malia was about to let out a victory cry when something very large, and very fast slammed into the side of the dragon and cut short its killing run. Panic washed over her as both beasts vanished from the sky. She forced herself to concentrate on her own command as the Narshuk army organized itself in the face of a pincer attack. Thinking fast, Malia gave the signal to the wizards on the wall to begin their assault on the trapped Narshuks, hoping to recover the upper hand in the battle. As the first spells completed and fire rained down on the Narshuks once again, Malia gave the order to attack at both ends.

Chapter 32 – The Traveler

Riding on the back of Morganath, Seth watched the carnage play out on the ground beneath them. Narshuks burned by the hundreds, ignited by dragon-breath, creating a haze of black smoke over the battlefield. The smell of grasses mingling with burnt meat wafted up from the field and filled his lungs, making him cough. Cries of rage and indignant howls rose from the confused and panicked army below them. As Morganath finished his second pass across the back of the army, Seth finally spoke up, "Enough. They're running scared, there's no need for this now. We'll wait till they're trapped by the wall, crowd them in, and finish the job."

"Very well," said Morganath, who pulled up and away from the Narshuk army. He soared away from the battlefield, circling the castle to get a better angle at the developing battle below them.

"When the stone wall goes up, we must finish off as many of the Narshuks as we can before they can get organized. I'll try to intensify your breath when we make our run," Seth said. "We will let Gladius come to us."

Morganath gave an approving grunt and continued to circle high up in the sky. It wasn't long before the wall rose from the ground and trapped most of the Narshuks in its embrace. "Now?" asked Morganath, before taking any action.

"Yes, now!"

The massive dragon folded his wings back and pointed his body into a dive. Seth held on with all his might to keep from being swept off by the rushing wind. The ground, and the Narshuk army, grew as the pair fell from the sky. Before they hit the ground, Morganath extended his wings to slow his descent and let out a mighty roar that shook the ground and deafened those nearest him. With his roar came a gout of flames, flowing like liquid from his mouth and spreading across the ground and through the Narshuks like a wave.

Seth drew in power and focused it on the flames, causing them to grow larger, flow faster, and burn hotter. The screams of the Narshuk's echoed through his mind as he poured the magical energy into the dragon's breath.

Again wafts of black smoke rose from the ground and filled Seth's lungs, making them burn. The sounds of the battle grew distant, slower, and his vision clouded over like he was in a dream. It took only a second to realize he was the one slowing time again, as an instinct. *Danger,* he thought, but too late.

The rest of the world around him came to a stop--creatures, soldiers, wizards, the wind, everything stood in eerie silence for a split second. He only had time to free Morganath from the frozen time stream before the Tordrake slammed into the dragon's side, causing him to abandon his breath weapon in favor of keeping himself aloft. Morganath pumped his wings with frantic precision to keep from crashing into the castle wall or falling to the ground.

Seth held onto the spines as best he could. "Shit!" he cursed as Morganath drew dangerously close to the castle wall. He spun his head around to see what attacked them in time to see the great bull head coming at them again. "Fly, Morganath. Fly with all your strength!"

Again the magic flowed to Seth as he called upon the power of air. A warm wind blew up underneath them and provided lift as Morganath worked his wings as hard and fast as he could to avoid taking another hit. Crimson blood spilled down Morganath's side where the Tordrake's horns had punctured his thick golden hide.

One last downstroke of his wings lifted him up at the last second and the Tordrake slammed into the castle wall below them, sending a shower of crushed stone into the air to hang above the city. Morganath flew higher to get himself up and away from the castle. With Seth still driving the winds behind them, the pair soared into the sky, leaving the Tordrake to recover beneath them. Seconds later, it was back in the sky and chasing them.

The wind rushed past Seth's ears, making it impossible to hear anything as they rose high into the sky. The only sound other than the wind he could hear was a chanting sound that seemed to carry through the air no matter how much wind there was. Seth didn't have to look back to know they were being chased. He focused his efforts on drawing magical energy to heal Morganath's wounds. Calling on the power of water, the golden dragon hide glowed blue, and the wounds closed and healed over. The chanting behind him increased in tempo, and he could see dark clouds rolling in from every direction. Lightning flashed through the sky, lighting up the landscape. Morganath was forced to dodge and weave through the sky to avoid being hit by the lightning, which grew in frequency and intensity the higher they got.

"We must turn and fight," Seth said as the first drops of rain pelted his face.

"Yes, I was just thinking that," the great dragon retorted.

"On my mark, we will turn and hit him with everything we have. Ready?"

"I have never been readier!"

Seth turned his head to look behind them at the Tordrake. The rain struck it and sizzled off the beast as steam, creating an ominous trail of cloud behind it. Seth could feel the water from the rain just starting to soak through his clothing. His eyes made contact with the Dark Lord's eyes, sending a shiver up his back. Had he not been holding the spines so tight, his hands would be shaking too.

No words were spoken in that instant, but Seth could see the hatred in the Dark Lord's eyes. There was no fear, no remorse. No doubt or pain. Only pure malice and the desire for power. As the distance narrowed between the two rivals, Seth readied himself for the battle of his life.

Drawing the power of light and life into him, he focused it into a weapon. Releasing one of the spines, he held out his hand and a sword of pure light appeared in his grip, glowing like daylight. He continued to channel energy into the sword, and from the hilt of the sword a mist spread down his arm and over his shoulder. It continued down his torso and traveled over his remaining extremities. As the mist solidified, it changed into crystal plates that covered his body. On the chest plate of the armor appeared four crescents that spread out around a central spot in a swirl, the symbol of Lyecha, goddess of time. He turned back to Morganath when his armor was complete. "Now!"

With a violent jerk, the dragon reeled in the air, tucked his wings back and dove at the Tordrake, letting out a tremendous roar as he did so. The two beasts clashed in the air in a flurry of teeth, claws and wings. Morganath sank his long sharp teeth into the Tordrake's neck, his claws into its flanks, latching the two together in a downward spiral. Seth added his own attack, plunging the sword of light into the Tordrake's shoulder. The creature let out a snarl of pain and shuddered, trying to shake the dragon off. Morganath dug his claws in deeper, blood now flowing from the wounds like the rain that drenched them.

A sound coming from the back of the creature caught Seth's attention. He looked up in time to see Gladius fire a black bolt of energy at him, blasting his chest and causing him to lose his grip on both the sword and the dragon. He flew back into open air and began to fall. To his surprise, Gladius leapt after him, leaving their mounts to their own battle. Seth focused more magic into his armor, creating a light that beamed off him making him look like a falling star in the driving rain. Gladius shielded his eyes, but did not stop his approach. He slammed into Seth and knocked the wind from him.

Seth gasped for breath as the pair fell, now in complete freefall.

A shout rose above the howling wind and driving rain. "You're mine now, Time Weaver!"

He pushed against the Dark Lord, wrestling with his iron grip. A flash of light went past his peripheral vision and he remembered the sword. "Not if I can help it." Extending his hand, he called the sword to him. It flew toward them with lightning precision and landed with the hilt in Seth's hand. Swinging it down, Gladius released his grip to avoid being decapitated. Instead, the tip of the sword grazed his cheek leaving a red line that bled down his face.

"You'll pay for that, boy." Using magic to direct his flight, he propelled himself toward Seth, the ground growing closer by the second. Seth realized their peril as they descended through the storm and hauled back on his sword again, waiting for the Dark Lord to come into range. He lashed out with a wild swing, but missed his mark. The sword glanced off Gladius's armor and left Seth open for attack. Gladius smashed his spiked fist into Seth's side, piercing his armor and crushing bone. "And now, you become mine. The traveler, my way into the realm of the gods," Gladius said. Words spilled from his mouth, ancient words that sent black ribbons of energy flowing toward Seth. Sticking to him, they invaded his body and his mind, threatening to take over.

Fight back, Seth heard in his head, a strong, valiant voice.

His face washed over with despair as he responded to the voice, *I can't. He's too strong.*

Gladius paused, the energy ribbons suspended between them, tethering them together. "What? This isn't what you had planned?

You thought you could defeat me? You're nothing but a runt. Weak, pitiful, hopeless, mindless. You never stood a chance."

The pain still scorched through him as he tried to respond, but all that came out was a single word, "No!"

"No? That's all you've got?" A hysterical laugh erupted from Gladius, sending chills through Seth. But he fought back.

The driving rain around them began to slow, as did their descent. Seth struggled against the bond now between them, linking them through the tether of black energy that hung in the air.

Gladius got his composure and said, "I don't know how Krycin pulled it off, but I'm glad I didn't kill you, boy. This is far too much fun." He focused again and spoke more words, the tendrils of energy surging into Seth's body.

Seth also reached for something, but it wasn't a weapon. His hands closed around the black energy tether that held them together. Drawing power into his body, he focused it into that tether, turning it into silvery threads that eased his pain, and reinforced the bond between them. A look of shock came over the Dark Lord's face.

"No... How?" he stammered as Seth began to pull the tether, reversing the flow of energy.

"How?" Seth finally said, now getting stronger. The rain was now mere drops suspended in the air, wanting to fall, but being held back by time itself. "Simple. I have the power of all the gods."

With a thrust of his hand, Seth used the power of earth to shatter the Dark Lord's armor, watching as the shards rained into the abyss below them. He called upon the power of air to push them back up into the sky, calling down a burst of lightning that struck Gladius in the chest, electrifying the air around them and drawing a scream of rage from the stunned wizard. A ball of fire welled up in Seth's hand, and he threw it toward Gladius, striking him again and consuming his flesh.

A strangled scream came from Gladius, terror washing over his face as one-by-one Seth called upon the elements and struck him down. Rain drops rushed toward Gladius and filled his mouth and nose, flowing down into his lungs and drowning him. His eyes opened wide as he burst into fits of coughing, still hanging in the air.

"How does it feel to be helpless?" Seth said. "To bow down before somebody stronger than you, and know that you're about to meet your maker? You want to go to the realm of the gods? Fine, I'll send you there, and you can settle up with them."

Raising his fist he drew the power of life, and slammed his glowing fist into the Dark Lord's chest, sending him flying back. The power of shadow caught him, the darkness enveloping him and lifting him back to Seth.

Gladius tried to swing a fist at Seth, but found his arm caught in mid-swing. Seth grabbed his other arm and held them firm. The rain began again, as did their free-fall. "No... you can't!" Gladius said, now sounding more like a groveling slave than a fierce warrior.

A smile spread over Seth's face. "Yes, I can." Their bodies raced toward the ground as Seth held Gladius by the arms and braced a knee on his chest.

"But... no..." stammered Gladius.

"I will punish you for your crimes and serve out justice. Vengeance for everything you have done. All you have harmed. I will take your life, as you once took my people."

The action was so sudden Gladius had no chance to react. They plummeted to the ground, and as they did, Seth hauled Gladius's body between him and the ground. The impact was like a meteor hit, an explosion around them of dirt, mud, and rock. Seth felt bones snap beneath his knee. The Dark Lord's chest caved in under Seth's weight and the force of the impact, blood spraying from his mouth as his heart exploded from the pressure.

Seth hauled back with his hand and called a dark power he hadn't felt before. *Take his soul, a* voice spoke in his head, *and bring it to us.* The voice made Seth shudder, but he felt the energy well up inside him and he plunged his hand down, phasing through Gladius's body and grabbing hold of the energy within. He pulled back and removed the dark orb of life force from him.

With the dark sphere firmly in hand, Seth fell backwards. He expected to hit the ground, exhausted, but instead continued to fall, as if there was a bottomless canyon behind him.

...wake up.

The feminine voice spoke to him. There was a distance to it that made it sound like it was over a bad phone connection. A warmth surrounded Seth--sunlight. He opened his eyes and was blinded by bright light until his eyes adjusted. The room was familiar, but he hadn't seen it in a while. His room. His bed.

"Wake up, Seth." The feminine voice repeated, clearer this time as the sleep fog left his mind.

Was it all a dream? He thought, trying to get his bearings. His room was the same as when he left, the nightstand next to his bed, serving as a table for an alarm clock, and this morning, apparently his breakfast. The smell of bacon and eggs wafted up and filled his lungs. He turned his head toward the voice. Standing a few feet from his bed was a woman, average height, thin, long brunette hair that looked like it hadn't been brushed yet. *Of course, it's morning.* She wore one of his t-shirts that covered her torso and hung just to the top of her thigh. His eyes traveled down to her legs, thin and fit. The kind of legs one would see on a model, but she wasn't.

Sophie?

"Come on sleepy head, was I *that* rough on you last night?" she said with a smile, a playful twinkle in her eyes. "I made you breakfast. It was the least I could do after the night we had."

Confusion filled his head as he looked at his hand that had held the black orb, but found it empty. *It couldn't have been a dream.* He lifted his gaze to Sophie and faked a smile. "Thanks."

"Eat up, you'll feel better after some breakfast. And drink some water, it'll help with the hangover." She gave him another grin, turned, and walked out of his room.

Seth looked back to the breakfast that was prepared for him, and the big glass of water next to it. *Was that there before?* He shook his head, and then regretted it as the splitting headache took over his foreground thoughts. *A hangover? So I blacked out because I drank too much?*

He picked up the glass and drank the whole thing in one go. The cool water did seem to soothe the pounding in his head, and helped to clear the fog that clouded his mind. *It seemed so real.* Picking up the plate of food, he ate and enjoyed his breakfast. The food invigorated him, giving him the drive to get up out of bed. Walking around the room, he picked up various articles of clothing and sorted them out on his bed into his and hers piles. *Man... why did I have to black out?* He got dressed and went to leave the room, taking Sophie's clothes with him, but something caught his eye. On his bookshelf, where his father's old leather-bound book should have been, there was an empty hole.

He shook his head and walked out into his living room. Sophie sat on his couch, her long legs folded under her, his shirt pulled down so as to make her at least somewhat decent. The television was on and showing some news broadcast he didn't care about. She looked over to him, saw the clothes he carried and gave him a cheeky smile. "What, you kickin' me out already?"

"No, not at all." He dropped the clothes down on the other end of the couch. "I'm a little hazy about last night..."

"You mean you don't remember?" She took on a mock angry tone, but couldn't keep it up, and instead broke out into a laugh. "Well with the amount you had to drink, I'm not surprised. Here," she got up from the couch and began walking toward him, her perfect features and smooth skin captivating his attention. "let me remind you of how the night ended."

She approached and wrapped her arms around him. As she did this, he looked into her eyes. She stared back at him with eyes like jet that drew him in. She leaned in to him, her breath warm on his skin, the smell of her now faded perfume filling his senses. *Something's not right.* His heart pounded as her lips brushed his, her hands touched his body. *Her eyes. Sophie's eyes were blue.*

The intersection, the accident, that was real. The memories came back, a trickle at first.

Something attacked me, and I was knocked out. He pulled away from Sophie, leaving her stumbling forward.

"What the hell, Seth?" she yelled after she caught her balance.

"This isn't right."

"What's not right? You and me? You certainly thought it was right last night. Right enough to fuck me. Oh wait, you don't remember that, do you?"

"No, I didn't forget. I didn't black out. It didn't happen. You're not real." His voice raise a little with each sentence.

"Not real? What the fuck kind of drugs are you on?"

"Your eyes, they're the wrong color. And where is my father's book?" He was shouting now, nose to nose with the not-quite Sophie before him.

She began to laugh, an eerie haunting laugh that sounded like a thousand voices, all at once, all laughing at him. Putting her hands on Seth's chest, she shoved with inhuman strength sending Seth flying. His back impacted the wall behind him, leaving a large dent, and then he slumped to the ground. "Did you really think you could defeat me?" the distorted voice said as she stepped toward Seth. "I could have given you everything. A life, a wife, anything your heart desired. You would never have any worries. Nothing but happiness for the rest of your days. And you would throw it away?"

234

The impostor's face distorted, warping into a combination of many at once. Seth lifted his head, his back aching from the impact. "It's not real. I can't live a lie like that."

The impostor laughed again, its hideous bone-chilling laugh. "Nobody will ever know. We can wipe your memories clean, you can start again. Come now Seth, all your dreams come true. Fame, riches, women beyond your wildest dreams, every pleasure and whim fulfilled. And we ask but one thing, one simple little thing."

"What?" Seth asked.

"The soul of the fallen. We want the soul."

Chapter 33 – In the Heat of Battle

The battlefield descended into chaos after Seth and Morganath disappeared. Malia led the charge against the Narshuks, cutting a large number of them down before they could begin to get organized. Part of the city wall exploded an instant after the charge began, and then the rain started to fall.

The sky clouded over, and the first drops began as Malia slashed through the throat of another beast. After only a few seconds, the drizzle turned to downpour, and the downpour to a torrent.

She turned to her nearest lieutenant and signaled him to approach. "We must fall back. We can scarcely see our enemy, let alone fight them."

"Aye, General Corsair, we'll lose more than one in the mud alone," said the lieutenant, then held a hand high in the air, and with a word, fired a flare into the air that would signal the troops to retreat.

Malia held the front, battling off what Narshuks she could while her troops returned to their rendezvous point. Her blade burst into flames that evaporated the rain drops before they touched the weapon. Three Narshuks approached her, but slowed when they saw the flames. The leading one hesitated for only a split second before continuing its advance on her.

Malia was ready for the creature's charge, and calculated her strategy before it reached her. She held her ground as the beast ran at her, and at the last second, dropped to her back, and thrust the sword up into the creature's gut. The blade sank deep into its flesh, cutting through tissue and bone like it was made of jelly, the heat cauterizing the wound as it traveled through the Narshuk. Its guts spilled out in a messy heap onto the ground through the gash the sword left behind. The creature continued a few more feet, its momentum carrying it, and then it collapsed into a quivering pile.

The ground was slippery beneath her from the rain and mud, making it difficult to regain her footing. She managed to sit up before the next creature arrived. She drew in power and spoke, "Scintillas." Her spell erupted from her fingers in a flash of light and sparks into the creatures face. A howl of pain and surprise escaped the creature as it tried to clear the sparks from its smoldering face. Malia took this distraction to regain her feet and then lashed out at the creature with a long swing of her sword. The blade connected with the creature's left arm, severing it at the elbow, and then continued through into its chest.

Despite the serious wound, the blade struck too low to hit the Narshuk's heart, and instead wedged between two lower ribs. The surrounding muscle cooked like meat on a skewer. Another, louder howl left her opponent's mouth as it took a swing back at her. Malia held tight to the hilt of her sword and was dragged along the ground as it twisted its body. Its swing struck wide and glanced off of her armor.

In a single swift movement, Malia jumped, planted one foot on her opponent's chest, heaved the sword free and swung it back at the creature. It connected with its head, slicing through its snout, the front of its face, and its eyes. The Narshuk's flesh and bone sloughed off, leaving blood pouring from the wound, and brain matter exposed where a portion of its skull was cleaved. A sound that was half gurgle, half scream escaped from the beast as Malia once again hit the ground with a splash into the growing mud puddle beneath them. The creature's remaining arm brought its hand up to meet its gushing face, burying its claws into the soft tissue inside its head. A convulsion ran through the creature like a wave and it collapsed forward, landing on top of Malia.

When the creature landed, she felt a distinct crack in her chest as the weight of the Narshuk pressed on her armor plates, breaking a rib. Pain ripped through her body as she lay, pinned to the ground. Her best efforts couldn't move the creature that was on top of her. She could hear the remaining creatures descending on her location, ready to take their prize. The body on top her began to lift off, relieving the pressure on her chest and taking away the pain. Hairy clawed feet rested on the ground next to her, and long claws dug into the body being lifted.

Before the body was clear of her, there was a blinding flash of light above her, and the Narshuk who was lifting the dead body was replaced by a smoking cloud of dust that blew away as the dead body fell back down on top of her. There was another snap in her chest. She screamed as pain flared through her torso. In front of her the clawed feet remained, bloody smoking stumps where legs were once attached. Several more flashes went off around her, but her focus was on the pain searing through her chest.

She made one last attempt to push the massive creature off of her, but could barely manage a nudge before the pain in her ribs became unbearable. An involuntary cry came from her when she tried, and her vision blacked out for a second. Each labored breath became more difficult than the last as swelling in her chest pressed against her lungs and the weight of the Narshuk crushed her.

Merek watched as Malia battled the Narshuks alone to let the rest of the soldiers retreat. Six of the beasts faced off against her, and he was about to go to her aid when a flash of light in the distance distracted him. Plummeting from the sky were two bodies locked in battle, shining with a white light that made them appear like falling stars. The bodies hit the ground with an explosion that shook the walls he stood on and sent up a cloud of dust and dirt around them, forming a deep crater in the ground. One of the bodies stood up, a black orb in its hand, then fell backwards and disappeared.

He turned his attention back to Malia's battle with the Narshuks just in time to see one of the hulking beasts fall down on top of her.

"Keep fighting," he said to a commander who stood by his side, "There is something I must attend to."

"Yes, Master Merek," the commander said to Merek's back as he fled the city walls.

Merek shot out of the front gates, blasting Narshuks with powerful magic as warriors closed the gates behind him. He ran with an unnatural speed for a man his age, attempting to reach Malia before she was crushed to death. Another Narshuk bore down on her pinned body, but before it could attack, Merek spoke a single word, "Decrustas."

The creature stopped, frozen where it stood, then exploded into dust. The remaining creatures backed away from Merek, and were shot down by archers who waited on the city wall for a clear shot.

Merek approached with caution, not sure what to make of the scene. "Malia?" he asked with a gentle tone, as he skirted the creature and saw the mass of her blonde hair flowing out from underneath the Narshuk.

He paused, horrified that she had perished on the field, when a gasp came from under the creature. Summoning what remaining power he could, he spoke with a level, even tone, "Levitas seriosa metai." The beast rose up into the air and relieved the pressure from her chest. Merek gave the floating creature a shove and it drifted away, coming to rest when it hit the city wall.

"Malia, by the gods, are you okay?"

He dropped down to his knees beside her, listening to her ragged breaths, but no response came.

Seth watched the impostor as the illusion melted away, revealing a plain white space. No walls, or doors, or windows; just plain white, as far as he could see. The orb was in his hand again, and he kept a tight grip on it. "Who are you?" He took a step forward to get a better look at the constantly changing face.

"You don't know me. You don't even believe in me. The only reason I granted you my gift was because this soul is important to me. Now hand it over, and you shall have your reward."

Surprise and realization washed over Seth's face. "Grishtor. You're Grishtor, the god of death, aren't you?"

There was a high pitched laugh of a child behind him. He turned, but all he saw was a glimpse of a figure standing behind him. "Answer me!" he shouted. Another laugh responded, but this time it was a low pitched cackle that sent shivers through him. "Come on you coward! Show yourself or you'll never have this soul."

The laughter behind him finally settled on a familiar voice. A smooth southern voice that was unmistakable. "Come now Seth, can't you see what I'm doing here?" Cy moved around Seth so that he faced him. "The power of the gods is not always as balanced as your friend Merek would have you believe. See, right now, the god of light and life has the upper hand. We're simply trying to... level the playing field."

"How?" Seth asked, confused at Cy's presence. "I killed you. How can you be here?"

"Gladius once killed you, and yet here you are. What is death but a new beginning."

"Where are the gods? What did you do with them?" Seth asked, his voice trembling with anger.

Grishtor spoke up behind him, "Never mind them, traveler. Give me that soul."

Seth stared at the black orb in his hand and recalled something Malia said before the battle began. *Destroy him. Utterly destroy Gladius.* He returned his gaze to Grishtor, and then Cy. "No. I won't."

"Have it your way, boy." Cy said, walking toward Seth.

Deep inside Findoor castle, standing in a dark room that only a few people in the Kingdom know of, and lit only by the phosphorescent moss that grows on the wall, Cedric watched the battle rage through the Scryes' pool.

"Here I am, stuck in the basement, while everybody else gets to have all the fun." His mock indignation fell on deaf ears as the Scryes sat silent and stared with their blank eyes into the pool. He sighed and looked around for somewhere to sit. "Not much for hospitality around here either, are they?"

Finding nowhere to sit down, he resigned himself to standing and watching the action in the pool again. The pool provided a reasonably clear vision of the events of the battle, right up until Malia was knocked down. Then the pool began to get hazy. "What's this? Come now, quit slacking and let me see what's happening," Cedric said to the emotionless Scryes.

The vision didn't clear, but he did manage to see some brief images. Malia fell under a Narshuk and Merek joined the fray. Then there was a flash of light that filled the entire chamber. Cedric squinted at the blinding light, which seemed brighter to his dark-adjusted eyes. Then as quickly as it appeared, the light disappeared again, leaving the entire pool dark. He looked around the room at the Scryes. "Oh come now, your job's not finished yet."

No sooner did his words come out, then the first of the Scryes slumped forward, its head splashing face first into the dark water of the pool. Each of the Scryes followed suit, their bodies going limp and tipping forward. One after the other hit the water with a splash that echoed in the subterranean chamber. Fear came over Cedric's face as he watched the last tip forward. He stared at the pool, speechless, for a long time. Ripples on the surface of the pool reflected and overlapped each other, creating crisscross patterns in the water. He stood and watched it, stunned, until the ripples calmed and the water was smooth again.

"Oh, this isn't good. Not good at all. Somehow," said the masked Bard, "I don't think this is how things were supposed to go. I can't see outside and something has obviously gone wrong. How am I to coordinate magical attacks from here?"

His hand closed on the latch of the door. There was a loud click as he turned the handle and the door opened. He stepped out of the room to silence, and drew his bow from his shoulder as a precaution. With an arrow at the ready, he proceeded up the stairs.

Cedric's footsteps were the only sounds in the castle now. An eerie silence filled the stone walls and made the whole trip up to the main floor unnerving. It was only when he saw the first runner in the hall did he realize why the castle was so quiet. He leaned over the body of the runner and placed his fingers on its neck. "Dead. By the gods, what's happened?"

Servants, runners, citizens, all were dead as he walked through the castle toward the front gates. "This almost certainly wasn't part of Merek's plan. Something is dreadfully wrong."

The main entrance to the castle was covered by two great oak doors that could not be opened by a single man. The bars that held the doors would stand up against the largest battering rams, and the steel bands that reinforced the door guaranteed that even fire would take a good long time to burn the door down. "Drat it all," Cedric said, forgetting that the doors would be closed for the battle. "Now what? There must be a way out of here." He looked around the area, trying to ignore the bodies of the Findoor people lying on the ground all around him. Soldiers in full plate armor lay in heaps of steel without a single mark on them. "They didn't even draw their swords. What killed them?" Cedric finally spotted some rope slung over the shoulder of one of the soldiers. "Ahh! Fortune favors the prepared."

Reaching down, he worked the rope off of the soldier's body. "Sorry, old chap, but I do believe I need this more than you now." He walked over to the front gates and placed the rope at the base of the doors. Taking a few steps back, he set his bow on the ground and dropped his lute down off his shoulder and into his hands. Playing a melody that rang out in the quiet air of the castle, he began to sing an upbeat work song often sung by men doing hard labor. As he broke into the first chorus, the end of the rope began to twitch and quiver with an unnatural movement. It snaked up the door and wrapped around the large wood shaft that acted as a bar for the door. The end tied around the bar while the other end of the rope wound its way up to the top of the door and ran itself through an eyelet at the top of the door. Cedric continued to sing through the song as the rope heaved up on the bar. It took three pulls of the rope before the bar finally clattered to the stone floor of the castle. Cedric stopped his song, and shouted out with a smile behind his mask, "Well done! Well done indeed." The moment his song stopped, the rope fell to the ground.

With the bar removed, Cedric found the large door swung easily on its well-maintained hinges. Once the door was open, he returned to his bow, retrieved it from the floor, and walked out into the empty city that surrounded Findoor castle.

Chapter 34 - Subversion

Grian moved at a full gallop on his acquired horse across the plains and hills that made up the Findoor landscape. Following the merchant trail made for an easy ride there. It was late afternoon when he crested over the last hill heading toward Findoor Castle. He stopped to let the horse breathe and surveyed the area to come up with a plan.

Before him lay the castle and surrounding city. A granite wall raised in front of the city gates hid a major skirmish that he could hear even from that distance over the driving rain. Snarls and howls mixed with the shouts of the Findoor soldiers. Spells rained down on the Narshuk army from the city walls where wizards were stationed. Off to his far right, at the top of a hill overlooking the area, a bright blue light flashed and pulsed. He turned to see what it was and found himself looking through a great hole into another world.

Grian turned his dark eyes back to the city just in time to see the portal flash with a blinding light out of the corner of his eye. He covered his eyes to shield them from the light. When it died down, he dropped his arm, and all was quiet except the pelting of the rain.

Grian turned to the castle and was unable to contain the sly grin that spread over his face. "At last, Merek, your secrets will be mine. No guards, no wards, nothing to stop me. Your library is mine."

He made his way down the hill and to the other side of the wall. Before rounding the corner, he turned long enough to catch lights flashing between two men on the battlefield, then proceeded toward the main gates to the city. On the other side of the wall, the grass was drenched with the blood of Narshuks as well as Findoor soldiers. Bodies lay littered over the ground as they dropped where they fought. He picked his way through the bodies, stepping between limbs and trying not to disturb them. *After all,* he thought, *all the more to serve me later.*

He reached the front gates and paused, looking up at the solid wood doors that were secured from the other side. Whispering words of power, he drew in magical energy to fuel an ancient spell, one that he had stolen from the Dark Lord's spell book. The magic coursed through him, down his arms and flowed out his hands, crackling and sparking as it formed a black ball between his hands. When he summoned enough power, he spoke, "Infuscas consceleratai."

Grian unleashed the black ball at the front gates. It hit them with a *splat* and stuck to the gates like tar. It spread out on the gates and seeped into the wood, turning it gray and rotting it. Seconds later, the substance covered over half the gate, and holes formed in the wood. He waited only a few more seconds before walking toward the gate and giving it a push with his hand. What was left of the gate crumbled into dust, flitting away on the summer breeze.

With a smile, Grian stepped through the gate and walked into the city.

Cedric's footsteps echoed through the quiet city as he walked toward the front gates. He kept his bow at the ready, with an arrow nocked just in case. *The whole city looks dead, but hey, you never know what you'll find out here,* he thought as he passed the tavern he knew to be the halfway mark. Getting closer to the gates, he realized that his were not the only footsteps to be heard. A second, lighter pair could be heard, and they grew louder with every step. "By the gods, there *is* somebody alive," he said out loud without thinking. On the path ahead of him walked a figure wearing black armor with a cloak that covered most of his features. What he could make out were the dark eyes of a familiar face, though he could not recall from where he had seen it. As a precaution, he drew his arrow back and prepared to loose it if required. "Whoever it is had better be friendly, or they won't know what hit them."

The figure on the roadway saw him as well, lifting his right hand, palm-up, and his left hand back, palm facing out in an offensive gesture commonly used by battle wizards. Cedric wasn't going to wait for the figure to blast him with attack magic, and so he presented first, stepping into the middle of the road with an arrow trained on the figure's heart. "Halt where you stand. In the name of the Kingdom of Findoor, identify yourself."

The figure let out a chuckle at the masked Bard, then in an icy cold voice, spoke back, "Identify myself? You're the one wearing a mask."

"Don't be a fool. I have an arrow trained on your heart. I need only let loose the string and you're a dead man. Now identify yourself."

"I'm the new ruler of Findoor. Bow down to your master, or be found guilty of treason and face the consequences." A crackle of energy appeared in the palm of the man's hand, black in the center, but fringed with blues and purples. It hissed and churned as it grew to the size of a small melon before it stopped.

"The King of Findoor is dead, and no successor has yet been named. You, sir, are an impostor. An opportunistic poser. You have no business being here. Now leave, or I will drop you where you stand."

A tense moment passed between the two men that felt like an eternity to Cedric. His heart pounded in his ears and his right hand began to strain from the effort of keeping the bowstring pulled. As if the man facing him sensed his condition, he spoke a word and the ball of energy in his hand launched toward Cedric. He let the arrow fly, but didn't see where it landed as everything around him went black. An unnatural darkness erupted from the ball as it slammed into his body. He looked around and tried to get his bearings, but the hit left him in a daze, confused about which direction he faced. He could hear the sounds of his mark escaping, but couldn't locate in which direction he ran. Rather than running blind, Cedric knelt down on one knee and began to sing, drawing energy into himself to try to counter the darkness that pressed in around him.

Grian let loose his spell, watching the ball of darkness fly toward the masked man. He knew the arrow was coming, and so leaned off to his right to avoid the killing shot. The arrow flew true, but his heart was no longer in the path of the arrow, and instead it plowed through his left arm, coming clean out the other side. Searing pain erupted in his arm making any further spell casting impossible for the time being, but at the same time, the ball hit its target, and the magical darkness erupted from the ball, covering the area and disorienting its target. Despite the pain, he moved through the city and got away from the masked man.

The darkness was still present when he reached the gates of the castle, which were now left open. He entered the castle and made his way straight to Merek's library. *By the time he gets himself sorted out, it will already be too late,* he thought, chuckling to himself. The pain in his arm was easing up now, and he was able to focus his mind enough to cast another spell. The door to Merek's library was locked, as always, but Grian knew how to get by those locks without triggering the traps. He cast another spell that sent a spark into the wall at the bottom right corner of the door. The spark turned into a tiny white-hot flame that began burning its way up the wall, across the top of the door, and down the other side. When it was complete, Grian gave the door a push, and the entire door, frame and all, fell in unhindered.

The musty smell of the ancient library escaped and filled Grian's senses, causing him to take a deep breath. He drank in the odor and taste of the books within. "I love the sweet smell of success." A wide grin spread across his face as he walked into the library and pulled a tome off the shelf. He took it over to a bench and cast a spell, "Decrustas comperasa epotai."

As he chanted the ancient words of the spell, the book dissolved on the bench, and rose into the air. It swirled in the air for a moment while the spell came to completion. Grian inhaled the small cloud before him. Holding his breath, he reveled in the knowledge that transferred from the dissolved book, into his mind. "Knowledge never tasted so good."

His eyes grew darker as he smiled and reached for another nearby book, repeating the same process. After only a few minutes, he consumed the better part of a book shelf and was drunk on the power that he had discovered. "This Kingdom is mine at last."

Chapter 35 – The Crossroads

Cy ran toward Seth and swung a fist. Expecting to be able to dodge it as time slowed, Seth made no move to avoid it. But time wouldn't obey his command, and the punch landed hard again the left side of his face, rattling his jaw and sending him flying back. Landing on his back, he only just maintained his grip on the black orb. Pain flared through his face as the swelling began.

A hideous laugh escaped from Grishtor's mouth. "Your 'gifts' don't work here, boy. Tell you what: you give me that soul, or I'll take all of the souls for myself. All that will remain are my followers, and then I'll be the only god left."

Fear washed over Seth's face. "You can't. You wouldn't."

"I can, and I will. Just watch."

The twisted form of Grishtor raised a hand and a rift opened. Through the rift Seth could see the Findoor battlefield below. A flash of light washed over the field and every person, every creature fell over, dead. A host of tiny lights rushed through the rift and assembled into a single large orb in Grishtor's hand.

"No..." Seth said, tears falling from his eyes.

"It's very simple; give me that soul, or I take the rest. Every soul in that pathetic little world."

Seth looked from Grishtor, to Cy, and then back to the rift. Cy walked over to Seth and reached down, offering a hand to help him up. "Come now boy; help us, and yourself, out here. It's one soul, or millions."

"Alright," Seth said, reaching for Cy's hand. He kept the black orb gripped in his right hand. As their hands met, Seth moved quickly, using Cy's weight to hoist himself up off the ground and sling-shot himself at Grishtor. As magical energy rushed in through the rift Grian opened, Seth took hold of it as he flew through the air and with a thought, he stopped time. He crashed into Grishtor's torso, sending him flying back through the rift. Both figures fell through the sky as time started again.

"No!" Grishtor screamed as they fell toward the battlefield, struggling against Seth's grip. "You don't understand what you've done. Send me back!"

The wind whipped past as the ground rushed up to meet them. "Return them," Seth said, holding tighter to the mortal form of the god.

A sly look washed over Grishtor's face. "If you kill me, you'll take my place. Are you prepared to do that? Are you prepared to become the god of death?"

Seconds before they struck the grassy plain below, Seth slowed time again, both their bodies hanging in the air. He loosened his grip and pushed away from Grishtor. "No. No I'm not. And I don't want to kill you. But I won't play your little game either. I'm going to return you to the realm of the gods, to face the others, and show them what you tried to do. And I'm going to destroy this soul. Utterly destroy it."

Before Grishtor could object, time began again. Instead of hitting the ground, the two forms struck a door that appeared below them. A plain wooden door in a plain wooden door frame, positioned flat on the ground below them. The wood door gave way under their weight and momentum, but the orb of souls Grishtor clutched did not follow, and instead released back into the world they came from. When both were through the doorway, it slammed shut, and disappeared.

Darkness. His eyes were open, but there was no light. *Where am I?* he thought as he tried to move. Seth could feel the smooth orb in his hand, like a glass ball. He squeezed it, trying to shatter it, but it wouldn't give. *What am I supposed to do?*

A voice echoed in Seth's head. A calm, comforting voice. *Destroy him. Utterly destroy Gladius.*

I don't know how, Seth thought.

The answer is there, in your memories, the voice reassured him.

In my memories? But there are so many. He thought of one in particular, the intersection where he had his first encounter with a

Narshuk. A single frame locked in time when the claws of the Narshuk came through the rift and pulled the hulking beast through. The scene appeared before him, banishing the darkness. The cars frozen in the intersection, the great rift lit up blue, and the black clawed hands that pulled the creature through. He shuddered at the thought of it.

More scenes flashed before him as he searched through past experiences, but still nothing. *How do I know when I've found it?*

You'll know, the serene voice answered.

He sat down on a chair in the latest scene, the tavern where he met Cy for the first time. Energy hung in the air in this scene as Cy tried to subdue the memory-Seth, and that Seth fought back, burning Cy's arms off. It was a memory, but he could feel the heat from the flames that seared through Cy's arms, and smell the burning flesh, like barbecued pork. A chill ran through him that caused him to shiver in his seat.

He stood back up and changed the scene, going back further. It was the morning of his birthday, when he first took the book off his shelf. His father's book stood out in his mind. *What about the book?* he thought. Then moved back farther looking for more clues. Previous days, months and years flashed before his eyes.

As he approached his childhood, he saw glimpses of a man, obscured from his memories, a blur and nothing more. *Father.* He went back until he came to the very first memories of his life. Buried deep in his subconscious, these were memories his mind had stored, but had not shown him as he got older. Things like his first steps, and first birthday. He continued going through them until he came down to one in particular. The very first memory his subconscious stored. It wouldn't have caught his eye but for the rolling green hills in the background. No power lines marred the scenery, no planes flew through the sky. It was green, as far as the eye could see, and in the distance, black jagged mountains that looked like rotten teeth. *Findoor, and the Badlands.* Seth stopped and watched this scene play out before him. The green stretched out before him, but there was nothing below. Nothing but air, and a faint hint of gold scales. *Morganath. So it's true then? This is home?*

He could feel the cool breeze blow past his face, and the gentle up and down motion of the dragon-flight. It soothed him, settled him. There were voices, but he couldn't see the people they belonged to. The memory only retained what his senses could perceive as a baby.

But the voices, those were familiar. A female voice, and a male voice, with a smooth southern accent.

> *"And just what do you plan to do with him?"* The smooth southern voice asked.
>
> *"Take him to the dead world, just like Krycin said."*
>
> *"You think your boy will be safe there? The Dark Lord isn't really dead you know. All Krycin did was destroy his body."*
>
> *"He's never led us astray. He knows what he's doing."*
>
> *"If that's what you want to believe, I won't stand in your way. But if he comes hunting for you,"* There was a pause as he considered his words carefully, *"Gladius that is, don't think that Krycin will be able to get you out of a bind a second time."*
>
> *"He knows what he's doing Cy. He's seen the future."*

At hearing the name, Seth froze. Cy. A pain ripped through his mind. *God damn it, help me out here. What am I looking for?*

The answer is there, in your memories. When he went away.

When he went away? Seth thought of the last night he saw his father. *They had a fight, mom and dad. Why can't I see it clearly?*

The image appeared before him, the hallway of his mother's house, the doorway to the kitchen.

> *"Why does it have to be tonight?"* his mother shouted at his father.
>
> *"I've been discovered. It's not safe for me to stay here. You knew this day would come,"* Seth's father said in a very matter-of-fact way.
>
> *"That doesn't make it easier, and you know it."*
>
> *"Five years ago, when we came here, we discussed this. And I told you then that this was only temporary. I can't let him find you, and he's so close."*
>
> *"I just wish there was another way, I don't think I can do this without you."* She was crying now, Seth could hear her sobs, and it pulled at his heart making him want to cry as well.
>
> *"If he comes, use the book, and utterly destroy him..."*

The book! The spell is in the book. I need to get back to Merek. As the realization hit him, the scene faded away, and bright white light flooded around him. It took some time for his eyes to adjust, but as they did, the scene before him startled him.

He was in a large room with a single table at the center. Eight chairs surrounded the table, and each was made of a deep rich wood with a golden grain. The table was made of the same wood, but looked as if it were carved from a single piece. Seth lay sprawled out on a floor tiled with black marble that was covered with silver runes of all shapes and sizes. The walls of the room were white marble and covered with golden runes. At each chair rested a person, appearing human, but Seth had his doubts about how true that image was. Four women, and four men. One of the men, a black-haired scruffy looking character, was bound to his chair with golden braces.

A tall, slender woman with long dark hair stood up from the table, her chair gliding noiseless across the floor. She wore a long gown that shimmered with many colors, and a golden necklace with a small pendant on it. The pendant had four crescents in a circle around a dot, the symbol of Lyecha. She walked over to Seth as he tried to get up, and offered him a delicate, slender hand. "Welcome to the Crossroads, Seth."

Her voice washed over him like a soothing blanket. It made him feel at peace, joyful for having heard it. Seth lifted his head and looked into her clear blue eyes. They held nothing but love and admiration as he reached up and took her hand. Her touch brought warmth to his core and made the pain, and uncertainty, and doubt dissolve away. Tears filled his eyes, clouding his vision as he was lifted to his knees. He made no more effort than that as emotions overwhelmed him, and he broke down into fits of sobs, his tears running down his face and falling to the floor.

The woman descended to her knees before him, her gown spreading out evenly around her as she did. She laid a reassuring hand on his shoulder, which brought some comfort. Lifting his head to meet her gaze again, he got himself under control enough to speak. "Why me?"

A sadness filled her eyes as she took in his emotions. "Dear Seth, it had to be somebody. When times get dark, a hero rises to the challenge. We did not ask you to be that hero, but we saw the potential in you, and granted you our gifts. What you've made of them is your own doing."

"And if I choose to do nothing more? If I've had enough?"

"We could ask nothing more of you. You have already accomplished more than we ever thought you would."

"I want to go home," Seth said, his eyes pleading with hers. "I want to go home, and I want to live happily ever after. Isn't that how these stories always end? And they all lived happily ever after?"

"Sadly, no. Even as the goddess of time, there are some things I cannot guarantee."

"So what happens now? Where do I go, and what do I do?"

"It is your choice what you do. But I know a beautiful warrior maiden and a Kingdom who are in need of a hero."

Seth's entire demeanor changed. "Malia. How do I get back?"

Lyecha smiled, a warm and loving smile that filled Seth's heart with hope. "Back the way you came, but before you go, please, take this." She unclasped the necklace from around her neck and presented it to Seth. "For my champion, a true warrior of time." Hanging the gold chain around Seth's neck, she stood up and again offered Seth a hand. He took it and rose to his feet, the pendant glittering in the light.

All of the gods and goddesses rose to their feet except Grishtor, who remained bound to his chair. One by one they bowed before Seth, starting with Lyecha. When the last finished their bow, Lyecha smiled at Seth one last time. "Go now, the world needs you."

Seth turned and walked back toward the door he came through, wrapped his fingers around the handle, and turned it. The door swung open, and through the door he could see the driving rain just starting to let up, and the first beams of sunlight breaking through the clouds. He turned back one last time and said, "My goddess Lyecha, thank you."

Then he turned back and stepped out onto the battlefield, the black orb still in his hand.

Cedric burst from the front gates of the city only to see the carnage that lay before him. Thousands of Narshuks were burnt, hacked, slashed, or otherwise slaughtered in the defense of Findoor castle. Hundreds more still toppled over with the rest of the people. Soldiers' and wizards' lifeless bodies rested at the top of the city walls. Picking his way through the battlefield, he made his way to Merek and Malia. They too rested on the ground in a peaceful breathless sleep. He was about to run up to them when a light caught his eye. The rift on the hill outside the castle was growing faster than before, and another smaller rift was opened above it.

"What the..." the Bard said, then watched as two figures fell from the rift above, plummeted to the ground, then disappeared. When they disappeared, another light flooded out over the battlefield. Merek and Malia both gasped for air, as did many others.

Cedric ran toward Merek and helped him up. "Welcome back, old man," he said with a smile.

Merek sat up and flicked mud from his robes. "Thank you, Cedric. I am fine, but our general is wounded. Please, tend to her. Do not worry about me."

Stepping over to Malia, he heard her gasping for breath. He knelt beside her and unbuckled the left straps of her chest plate, loosening it. She gasped for air, but there was still something impeding her breathing. She opened her eyes and looked up at Cedric and whispered, "Seth..." Then closed them again.

"Merek, we need a healer here. I fear she has broken ribs that have punctured a lung."

It took a moment for Merek to process what was said, and he was about to respond when another light appeared not twenty feet away from them. A black door with a wood frame stood on the field. Cedric readied his bow in an instant, nocking an arrow and drawing the string back.

There were a few tense moments before the door opened and a bright light flooded out. A figure stood in the doorway saying something over its shoulder, then it turned and stepped through.

"Seth?" Cedric asked, lowering his bow for a split second before realizing what he was doing.

Without a word, the figure in plate armor bearing the symbol of Lyecha on his chest and wearing a glittering Lyecian pendant stepped away from the doorway and held up his left hand. Out of nowhere, the old leather-bound book appeared in his hand. He looked out at Cedric and Merek and spoke, "I need help with this, quickly."

Cedric was about to object when he saw the black orb in Seth's hand start to pulsate. He dropped his bow and ran to Seth. "What do you need my friend?"

"Take the book, hold it so I can open it."

Cedric presented the front of the book to Seth, who swiped his hand over the steel plate on the front. Seth gritted his teeth with the strain of holding the black orb that now fought against him. "Lay it on the ground, and turn it over," he said to Cedric, who did as he was told without question.

"The answer was always here. It was just hidden away," Seth said, dropping to his knees before the book. Holding his left hand over the pages, he spoke the words, "My goddess Lyecha, show me the way."

The pages of the book lifted, separated into two, and merged with their neighbors revealing a second set of pages hidden within the first. As quickly as he could, Seth flipped through the pages of silver text looking for the right spell. When he found it, he stood up and drew upon the power of death.

As he began chanting, he let go of the pulsating black orb, which floated out before him. Seth finished the words in the spell, not really sure what he was saying, but seeing the effect. The orb floated above the ground, and shattered with a burst of light.

The three men stood in a circle around a writhing mass of shadow that screeched and shouted like a thousand voices all speaking at once. It moved toward Cedric, tendrils reaching out for him. Seth held his hands out before him, his palms facing out. Summoning the power of fire to him, he brought forth gouts of flame that blasted and encompassed the writhing black mass. "Kill It!" yelled Seth as he poured more power into his spell.

Merek looked at Seth for a moment, and then at the black mass. He blinked, then held his hands out in the same fashion as Seth, pointing them toward the burning black thing on the field. Hairs on the back of Cedric's neck raised and the crackle of electricity could be heard as Merek's hands lit up. Blue lightning burst forth, blasting the already burning creature that now lay on the ground. Cedric backed up another step and dropped his bow. The mask on his face hid the fear in his eyes as the creature before him continued to reach for him, despite being blasted from two directions. A look of panic came over Seth's face as the creature drew closer to Cedric. "Now, Cedric. Blast him now!"

Shaking his head, Cedric snapped out of his stunned silence and raised his hands up in front of him. Summoning the power of water, his hands erupted with blue energy that blasted forth at the now screaming creature. The bone-chilling energy slammed into the side of it and combined with the two streams already consuming it. The perfect triangle of energy blasted the darkness that squirmed and retched on the field until the last of it was destroyed.

The three men ceased their attacks when no movement remained. A small pile of ash settled on the ground before blowing away in a gentle breeze. Cedric looked up at Seth and smiled. "Welcome back, my friend."

Seth stood silent for a minute and listened. Sounds of voices and growls could be heard from the castle--people and beasts waking up. "Where is Malia?" Seth said, looking around with a frantic expression trying to locate her. A short distance away he spotted Malia's still figure, The chest plate was dented in, crushed by the weight of the beast that fell on her. He ran to her and knelt down by her side, resting two fingers on her neck to check for a pulse.

"Not again. Not like this. You can't die like this," Seth said, tears blurring his vision. He tried to clear his mind, to summon up the power of water that he needed, but failed. Turning to Cedric, he yelled, "Go, Cedric, get a healer, please."

Cedric shook his head. "I can't, Seth. The battle isn't done yet."

A gleam in the air above the castle caught all their eyes, a golden light reflecting the small amount of sunlight breaking through the clouds above. Morganath let out a tremendous roar that shook the land beneath them, then swooped down, raining fire on the remaining Narshuks who rallied at the now open city gate.

Seth looked up, desperation on his face. "She needs help now, Cedric. The battle will be over in minutes, but that may be too late."

Merek approached the three companions, his gray robes covered with mud, but still the silver embroidery glowed in the dim light. "You can do this, Seth. I believe in you. You've opened the doorway to the Crossroads and stood in the presence of the gods. Battled and destroyed the most powerful being that ever lived in this world. This is the love of your life. Focus."

Seth dropped to his knees beside Malia and outstretched his hands above her. Closing his eyes, he blocked out the sounds of the battle around him and pushed back his doubts. In his mind's eye he saw blue, and grasped that thought, summoning the power of water. A blue light surrounded his hands and flowed down into her body. Scratches disappeared, cuts closed, and Seth could even hear the shattered ribs set with a snap and then mend. The blue light faded, but her body lay still, her heartbeat remaining weak.

"Come back to me, Malia," Seth whispered in her ear as he leaned down over her and lifted her off the ground. He cradled her in his arms, tears flowing down his face. "Come back to me, my love."

Chapter 36 – Long Live the King

The last of the books in Merek's library dissolved and drifted up before Grian to be absorbed by the dark wizard. Time was no concern as he emptied the library of its arcane knowledge, but now that he had completed his task, he looked to the window to see what light remained of the day. The first rays of sunlight broke through the clouds above the castle and streamed into the room. A wicked smile spread over his face as he stepped away from the table and said, "Perfect, still time to announce myself and claim my prize. If there's anything left to claim, that is."

Grian walked out of the now empty library and made his way through the halls. People in the castle were beginning to wake up. *Perfect,* he thought, his smile growing wider. He made his way to the throne room at the center of the castle, where the King's council convened, bickering over what they should do about the day's events. Runners, still groggy from the ordeal, came to and from the chamber carrying detailed messages about what went on outside. As he approached the doors, he stretched his arms wide and stepped into the chamber, tall and confident, his robes billowing out behind him.

His footsteps echoed throughout the chamber over the rest of the voices in the room as he walked to the far end, stepped up onto the platform, and sat down on the throne. One by one, council members stopped their discussions and turned to face the dark wizard who had the audacity to seat himself at the empty throne. One brave council member stepped forward and approached the throne. "Good sir, remove yourself from the King's throne at once, or I shall have you arrested for treason."

Grian lifted his head and looked at the man who opposed him with a wicked smile. Summoning the power of death, he said, "Mortuas victasa cadavrai." Pointing at the man, a bolt of black energy shot from the tip of his finger and pounded into the man's chest. Silence filled the room as all the other council members waited to see what would become of the one who stood up to the mysterious stranger. A gasp escaped the man as the energy worked through his body. His eyes sank into his head leaving two dark holes in his face, and a horrid moan emanated from his lips as they thinned and curled back away from his teeth. His flesh turned gray and pressed down against his bones as all of the moisture drained away from his body.

Rather than falling over dead, the living corpse lurched forward, devoid of life's grace, and took a place beside the throne, its empty eye sockets staring out at the rest of the council.

Once the hideous creature settled beside him, Grian looked out over the council and addressed them, "I hereby claim kingship over this land, and all people therein. If there are any present who contest this, let them speak now."

Silence met him as the council looked at the creature standing beside him. After a few moments of quiet, one man at the back of the chamber summoned up the courage to step into the aisle. He hesitated, but his ideals got the better of him and he approached the throne. Being a member of the council showed on him, as he was overweight by a significant amount, and he waddled, more than walked, across the room. His voice shook as he spoke, "Th-this is an aberration of nature. I think I speak for the entire council when I say we cannot allow this."

"Is that all? Can anybody else vouch for this man?" Grian waited for somebody to come forward and back him up, but none came. "Huh. It seems that you are on your own, my friend. Can I not change your mind?"

A look of shock came over the fat man's face. "Change my mind? Why this," he motioned to the creature standing beside the throne, "this is an outrage! Come now, we cannot let this charlatan, this dark sorcerer, take over our fair Kingdom!"

Grian let out a laugh at the man's description of him, then raised his hand and spoke again, "Mortuas victasa cadavrai." A second bolt of black energy fired into the man's chest. He staggered back a step, letting out a moan as his body transformed, his eyes sunk in and disappeared inside his skull and his lips drew back. When the spell was complete, the creature approached the throne and took its place on the other side.

"Now, are there any other objections? No?" Grian looked out over the council once more to be sure.

No one else spoke.

"Excellent. Send word immediately to the remains of the army and surrounding kingdoms. Findoor has a new King." The council applauded their new King, hesitant at first, but eventually mounting into a thunderous cheer. When the cheers died down, Grian spoke again. "My first act as your new King is thus: Arch-Magus Merek, any of his students, and any and all Time Weavers are to be arrested on sight."

Malia's eyes snapped open as she gasped for air, drawing the attention of all three men. She looked up at Seth, cradled in his arms. "You came for me."

"Of course, my love. But you have Merek to thank." Seth said.

Malia craned her head around to find the old wizard. When she found him, she smiled and said, "Thank you."

Merek gave her a warm smile in return and said, "Do not thank me. I simply reminded Seth of what he could already do. It was he who revived you and called your soul back. But now we have a bigger problem." He turned his head toward the growing rift in the distance. "Cy opened that rift, but as yet, my most powerful wizards have not been able to close it. I fear I must ask one final task of you Seth."

"Anything, Merek, just name it," Seth said, helping Malia to her feet.

"We must close the rift. I shall help you, but only you can freely travel between worlds without causing further damage. I fear Cy has constructed this rift so that it may only be closed by a Time Weaver."

Seth turned to face the rift just as it surged larger again. The edges of the rift crackled and arced with energy that consumed the boundaries between the two planes. Through the rift, Seth could see the blue sky of his home world. The area just beyond the rift was clear of people and things and came out onto a paved surface. Seth didn't recognize the scene in the rift, but suspected it was some kind of military compound, based on the army-green vehicles in the distance and the barbed wire fences. Looking back at the ancient wizard he asked, "How do I close it?"

"You'll have to stand at the center, and use your magic to force the rift closed. It is likely that only the power of time will now separate the two planes enough to seal the rift. Focus on that, and remember what I taught you."

Seth nodded. "Alright, let's do this."

Running out to into the field, Seth flagged down Morganath as he made his last round about the castle looking for stray Narshuks. It took only seconds for him to cover the distance, causing a great gust of air as he landed. "I'm glad you're alive. What of Gladius? I presume he is dead?" asked the dragon.

"Yes. Destroyed. I need you to get me high enough to be in the middle of that rift. Think you can handle it?" Seth asked, his tone urgent.

"Handle it? I was born for this." The dragon lowered his head to allow Seth to climb on.

Before leaving to mount the dragon, Seth turned back to the rest of the group. Malia walked up to him and placed her arms around his waist, drawing him into an embrace. "Be careful, Seth."

Seth leaned down and pressed his lips against hers. When they separated, he smiled and said, "Of course, my dear. Have I ever been anything but?"

Another pulse of energy ripped through the air from the rift, raising the hair on the backs of their necks and creating a thunderous shock wave that startled everyone on the field outside the city walls. Merek approached them and said, "Come, Seth. We must hurry."

"Alright, I'm coming." He turned to walk away, then paused and looked over his shoulder. "Malia?"

"Yes?"

"I love you."

"I love you too, Seth. Now go. Save the world."

Returning to his course, he made his way to Morganath and climbed onto his neck. The great gold dragon lifted his head and extended his wings, stretching them out. With a push of his legs, and a powerful downstroke, Morganath launched himself into the air. Circling once to gain altitude, he turned toward the rift and made his approach.

Chapter 37 - Out of Control

Within minutes Morganath had Seth positioned just outside the rift. The electric hum and crackle of the rift echoed through the sky, growing louder as they approached. Seth looked at the rift in awe. "At the rate it's growing, our worlds won't last the night."

Morganath moved in toward the rift, getting as close as he dared, with the rift throwing random strokes of lighting through the air. One stroke arced out, coming within inches of his wing. The thunder from it deafened Seth and almost shook him from his seat on the dragon's back. "I can't get any closer," said the massive dragon, hovering around the center of the rift. "If this was Cy's doing, there's no way anybody else could fix it. What's done by a Time Weaver can only be undone by one. And you, my friend, appear to be the last of your kind."

"Damn that bastard," Seth cursed. "It's Cy's ultimate 'fuck you'. If he can't win, nobody does."

The great dragon nodded his head. "We must hurry, Seth; we will not be safe here for long."

Seth nodded and looked through the rift. He could feel the waves of energy radiating away from it, and see his own world on the other side. The sun was beginning to set, creating an orange-red glow on the parking lot. There was an area cleared around the rift on the other side. Beyond the safety zone he saw military personnel milling around, and Denton beyond that, laid out across the horizon.

He stood up on Morganath's neck, his stomach jumping into his throat as he looked down to the ground. At the base of the rift, Merek was ready to cast his spells, and gave Seth a wave to tell him so. Swallowing his fear, he cleared his mind. Wave upon wave of energy rushed at him, like the rift was alive and trying to get rid of him. He silenced his mind and concentrated on his goal, visualizing the rift closing in his mind. Summoning power to him, he called upon the power of air to keep him aloft, and leapt off the dragon's back toward the center of the rift.

Electricity arced all around him, snapping and crackling even louder as he flew into the center of the rift. When he reached the threshold between the two worlds, he stopped himself on the boundary and poured magical energy into closing the rift. The power of time and space obeyed his command, and the two worlds pulled apart, exposing the aether between worlds. The rift faltered and slowed its growth but resisted his efforts.

Seth drew more power to him from both worlds, harnessing all the power he could muster and trying to force the rift closed. Still it resisted. As he floated in mid-air, suspended between the two worlds, the arcing around him slowed. He looked around to either side of the rift and saw the edges drawing in, making the hole smaller.

Malia watched Seth work, focused on his task, walking closer to the rift. She thought for sure that Seth would close it with ease, but when it didn't, she grew concerned. "What is going on Merek, why does it resist Seth's power?"

Merek turned to face Malia and said, "Something is wrong. This rift is different somehow."

Malia opened her mouth to speak again when she saw the arcs settle down and the hole begin to shrink. Hope filled her heart, and a smile spread across her face. "This is it, look, it is shrinking!"

Watching the rift shrink down to half of its size, a light appeared in the center of it around Seth. It caught her eye, but it was obvious that Seth didn't notice, or didn't care. As the rift got smaller still, the light grew brighter and began to pulse. "This isn't right, why won't it just close?" Malia asked, confused.

All at once, massive strokes of lightning flew from the edges of the rift, striking Seth in the chest and blasting him back. Seth flew through the air and disappeared on the other side of the rift. With Seth removed, the rift flared and ripped, tearing open on all sides even wider than it had started, and growing even faster.

"Seth!" Malia shouted, running toward the rift, "No!"

"Son of a bitch," Seth said as he opened his eyes. Fire raged through his chest like something burned him from the inside. He could feel the waves of energy from the rift still, and hear the thunder and arcing electricity from it. Lifting his head hurt like hell, but he managed it, and took his bearings.

There was solid pavement beneath him, and smoke rose from his smoldering chest. Pain ripped through him as he moved, and he could hear voices around him, but couldn't make them out through the ringing in his ears. His eyes teared up and blurred his vision, but he could make out dark forms standing all around him. Collapsing back to the ground he laid there for a few minutes looking at the red and orange sky. Somebody was beside him, kneeling and trying to talk to him.

Calling upon the power of water, he felt a wave of relief flow over him like the cool ocean rolling in at high tide. The ringing in his ears quieted, and the pain and burning in his chest eased. The voice of the man beside him became clear as he looked down at Seth and said, "Jesus Christ, he's healing."

Trying again to lift himself up, Seth braced his elbows on the ground and pushed. He rose up into a sitting positioned and rubbed his eyes to clear away the tears. "Where am I? Did it work? Is the rift closed?" He turned to face the man beside him and saw the expanding rift looming over them, tearing up and out in every direction.

"Boy, you're lucky you're not dead," the military man said. He offered Seth a hand. "Can you stand?"

"I think so, yeah."

Seth took the man's hand and hauled himself up off the ground. Now facing him, Seth saw his name tag which read "Mathers". He turned and looked around at the rest of the soldiers standing around him. Mathers offered him a hand and said, "General Neil Mathers, US Army. And you must be Seth Alkirk."

"Yeah, good to meet you," Seth said, shaking his hand.

"You really aren't human, are you?" Mathers asked, doing away with tact and pleasantries. "I mean, I didn't believe it at first, but now that I've seen for myself, I really can't deny it. What exactly were you trying to do up there, before you nearly got yourself killed?"

Sparing a glance toward the rift, Seth looked back at the General and said, "Trying to close it. Trying to save the world."

"Is there anything we can do?"

Seth flashed him a grin. "Yeah. Stand back, and try not to die."

He turned and broke into a run back toward the rift. The air flowed with him, and as he leapt toward the rift, the power of air lifted him up into the sky.

General Mathers watched with awe as he flew toward the center of the rift again. "God speed to you, Seth."

Malia sobbed and dropped to her knees. The edges of the rift pushed out at an alarming rate, crushing the two worlds together. The ground shook beneath them as grass, soil and pavement bunched up at the boundary between worlds. Merek walked up behind her and placed a comforting hand on her shoulder. "It's over," he said, his voice filled with sadness. "Even in death, Gladius mocks us."

All of the companions stood and watched as the rift tore into the sky and consumed everything in its path. Grass, trees, stone, even the air itself disappeared as the fabric of time and space between the worlds began to crumble and break apart.

Morganath took several long strides toward them and spoke, "We must leave. Our only hope is to get as far away as we can. Perhaps there will be something left when it is done."

"You're right as always old friend," Merek said, then turned to face Malia on the ground. "Come, Malia, we must make haste."

She lifted her head up to face Merek, tears flowing from red swollen eyes staining her cheeks. "I will not go. I will not give up on him."

"If you don't come now, there won't be another chance. Seth would not want you to die in mourning."

"You are free to go if you like. Run, hide, for all the good it will do you. And you may yet live. But I would much rather die than live without him."

Morganath lowered his neck to the ground to allow the companions to climb on. "Come, Merek, we must go now. You as well Cedric, there is room for several."

Lowering to his knees before Malia, Merek looked into her deep gray eyes and knew at once her resolve. "Very well then. If you shall stay, then I shall remain by your side. I have lived a good many years already."

She took Merek's thin, ancient hand and said, "Thank you."

Cedric was about to turn to climb on Morganath when something caught his eye. At the center of the rift, there was a figure, dwarfed by the size of the tear. "Look there," he said, pointing to the spot floating in the air. "What is that?"

Merek and Malia both turned their heads in time to see the dark spot explode with energy, like a tiny sun casting light over the entire field and replacing the fading light from the setting sun.

Leaping to her feet, Malia shouted out, "It's Seth! I knew he would not give up. I knew he could do it!"

Without a thought, Merek burst into a run toward the rift.

Seth flew through the air like a bullet, launching himself into the center of the rift. Drawing energy first from his world, and then from both at once, he came to a halt at the dividing line between them. Suspended in the sky by the power of air, he opened his body as a conduit for all of the raw magical energy he could find. It filled his body until it burned, and even then he continued to draw.

His head was struck with sharp pains like there was a fire cooking his brain from the inside out. Seth's eyes smoked and his fingers burned. The energy started leaking through his skin, heating up his armor, and still he pulled more. A great force built up inside of him, and when he thought he would die if he stored any more, he released it in a massive burst that pushed the two worlds apart. His body lit up like a star in the sky, and still he forced the magical energy through it. His armor glowed with the heat, his clothing and skin burned, and still he used the magic to restore himself while he channeled it into the task at hand.

A light glowed around him as the edges of the rift pulled in, closing the gaping hole. Seth recognized the feeling, and rather than ignore it, he latched onto the feedback of energy and used it to fuel his efforts. The glow died down and more energy flowed through him still. Burns formed over most of his body, but he ignored the fire consuming him and continued to feed the energy through his body, channeling it into closing the rift.

The tear in the fabric of both universes shrank down until they were nothing but man-sized holes, and it was then that he projected his voice out toward the Galadir side. "Merek, now. Seal the rift!"

Pain tore through his body as the energy he channeled consumed him.

Merek heard the call and began his spell, drawing on what remained of the energy around him to seal the rift closed. He chanted the words to the spell, building up in his minds eye the wall that would be required to separate the worlds. As he worked, the rift before him continued to shrink until it was nothing but a point of light, flashing and fighting to stay open.

Redoubling his efforts, he channeled more energy, and fought the force trying to keep the tear open. His chanting grew louder as he lifted his hands and funneled the energy into a pinpoint, streaming it into the light that refused to go out. As he neared the point of exhaustion, a burst of light and energy flashed back through the hole in the form of a great stroke of lightning, striking him in the chest and knocking him back through the air.

When he landed, the only thing he saw was the last fading light of their sun, and the first stars appearing in a clear sky. Everything went dark, and he exhaled his last breath.

Mathers stood back and watched as the strange portal between the worlds faltered, and then shrank down. Another soldier approached him from the left and addressed him. "General Mathers, sir."

"At ease soldier," he said, never breaking his gaze from the sight before him.

"Is there anything we should do to help?"

"I don't think so. I think he has things under control now."

As the rift closed, Mathers walked forward, but kept his distance. Light flooded from the hole, impairing his vision and lighting up the whole parking lot. He lifted a hand to shield his eyes just in time to hear a bone-rattling scream come from the tear, and then it closed. The only trace that remained of the portal was the crushed asphalt where the worlds had pressed together. He took his hat off and held it over his heart and saluted, bowed his head, and remained silent.

Cedric and Malia ran to the old wizard's side. Smoke rose from his chest, and a vacant expression covered his face. Cedric knelt down beside the body and reached out a hand to close Merek's eyes. "Rest be with you, old man. May Hadra be good to you in the next world."

Malia's tears began again. "You will be missed, old friend." Lowering herself to his side, she leaned down and kissed his cheek, then got up and walked toward the spot where the rift first opened. "And what of Seth?"

Cedric followed her, lifting and carrying Merek's body in his arms. "I'm not certain."

As they walked toward the crest of the hill, they spotted a small pile of shining metal where the rift had been. Malia broke into a run toward it, only to stop short of it, disappointed. In a neat pile on the ground were glittering armor plates. In the center of the exposed chest plate was the symbol of Lyecha etched into the crystal, and hanging from the corner of it, was a gold chain with the Lyecian pendant.

Malia reached down and plucked it from the pile. "What does it mean?"

Cedric examined it, smiled and said, "Seth wore that when he returned from the realm of the gods. I think he wanted you to have it. I don't know what's become of him, but if I had to guess, I think it means he's coming back. One does not easily part from a gift of the gods."

Lifting it up, Malia hung the chain around her neck and smiled. "Then I shall wear it, and await his return."

They both turned to walk back to Morganath when they spotted a large contingent of Findoor soldiers walking their way. One soldier leading them approached Malia and called out to her. "General Corsair! We thought you had fallen. It is good to see you alive."

"I am alive and well," she replied. "Why are you not at the castle, helping with the cleanup and casualties?"

A troubled look came over the young man's face. "Have you not heard?"

"No, what is the matter?"

"It's Grian. He's returned and arrested control of the council and the Kingdom. The dead walk, serving only him. We are the few who got away before we could meet the same fate."

Several miles east of Findoor castle, after the storm had cleared, Jaren Corsair milled about his little cottage, picking up debris and herding his animals back into their pens. The sun shone down on his gray streaked hair, its warmth reassuring him that the battle was done. Who had won, he didn't know.

Runners, making their way to the east to summon aid from neighboring kingdoms, had warned him of the impending battle and advised that he either seek shelter at the castle, or travel east with them until the war was won. Jaren refused.

When all of his animals were accounted for, he set about making any repairs to his house and the surrounding gardens. He was about to refasten a shutter to a back window when he noticed the weathered wood monument on his wife's grave had been knocked over during the storm.

He walked over to it, shaking his head. "Blasted storms have no respect for the dead," he said as he stood it back up and lifted his hammer to pound it back in. A deep rumble was the only warning he got before the ground over the grave exploded in a shower of dirt and rocks.

Jaren flew backwards and landed in the garden next to the grave on his back. "By the gods," he cursed as he pushed himself up onto his elbows. A gruesome rattling sound came from the hole before him, followed by a skeletal hand that reached up and plunged its bony fingers into the dirt. He scrambled back a step or two, his heart suddenly racing at the sight before him.

Rising out of the ground was his long-dead wife. Fleshless bones quivered as it tried to gain its feet. Small bits of fabric hung from the abomination and empty eye sockets filled with pinpoints of light stared down at Jaren. Its fingers curled into a fist as it lunged at him. He closed his eyes and cowered away from it just as he heard a strong, clear female voice ring out through the air, "Incendras."

There was a blast, and a clatter. "Grace of Anam, help me," he said, afraid to open his eyes. An unfamiliar burnt smell filled his senses and stuck to the inside of his mouth, making him want to retch.

"Father!"

The familiar voice cut through the terror and he managed to open his eyes. "Malia, my child! Thank goodness. What," he paused to take a breath and wipe his face with his sleeve. "What is happening here?"

Standing at the corner of the house was a small company of soldiers riding horses, with Malia leading them. She swung her legs to one side of the mare and dismounted, her armor clattering as she hit the ground. "Father, we must go, now. I knew you would be too stubborn to leave. Why wouldn't you listen to the runners?"

He sat up and managed a weak smile, the wrinkles around his gray eyes forming crow's feet. "I couldn't leave our home. Nor could I leave your mother. Why should we leave now, after so many generations have worked so hard to keep this land?"

Malia reached him and offered her hand to lift him up off the ground. "The dead rise. Findoor is lost. We must leave now, Father. Set aside your resolve and come with me."

"Slow down, my child. What is this you speak of?"

She let out a great sigh and started again. "Father, Findoor was attacked, and while we defeated the offending army, during the battle a dark wizard usurped the throne. He wields terrible magic, and is raising all the dead in the Kingdom to serve him. Even our own soldiers rose up against us."

A look of shock and terror washed over his face as realization set in. "Where shall we go then?"

"To the west, to Caldoor. There, we can seek the aid of our neighbors, and return to rid the Kingdom of this plague. But we must flee now, and fight another day. Survivors of the attack are already heading that way, and taking any survivors they find with them."

His face softened, and he smiled. "I wish we could have our reunion in more amiable circumstances, but I will come with you now. At the very least, it will give me some time with you."

Malia smiled back at him. "Oh father, we shall have plenty of time to catch up. Gather your things and bring them out to the horse. And be quick about it."

Jaren nodded and hustled into the house to collect some clothes and rations for the journey. By the time he made his way back outside, Malia and the other soldiers had returned what remained of her mother's bones to their proper resting place. A single tear ran down his cheek as he mounted the horse with Malia. As they turned west and rode away from the old cottage, Malia looked back in the direction of the castle one more time, hoping that somehow, Seth would find his way back to her.

Acknowledgments

If I was to say that I did this all on my own, I'd be lying. In reality, while my name is on the cover of this book, there are so many more who deserve to be there as contributors. But since there is only so much room there for names, I'll list them here instead.

First, and foremost, to my beautiful wife and children, thank you. For your tolerance and unending patience with me during long nights and early mornings of writing. I fear there were times when it verged on neglect, and I'm not proud of those moments, but without your support, I would never have made it here.

To my wife, I love you with all my heart and soul. Without your keen eye for detail, and brilliant mind for some of the steamier parts of the book, I fear this book would not be nearly as good as I think it is now. For everything you do, from proofreading and editing, to graphic design and cover layout, thank you. You worked miracles with it.

My best friend, Darren. You got me interested in fantasy on a level that I don't think I would have achieved on my own. I don't think my wife will ever forgive you for it, but I will be eternally grateful to you for all the good times we've had through the years.

To all the folks up at the Office of Letters and Light, keep doing what you're doing. Without the NaNoWriMo (National Novel Writing Month) contest, I would never have started writing. You guys do amazing work, don't ever stop.

Faith, Celine, Victoria, Peter, Caroline, Alison, Connie, Jupiter, Jenny, Dean, Jeff, Danielle, and so many others who I can't even think of all the names (sorry if I missed anyone!!!), thank you all for your critical eyes, your encouraging words, and most of all, your friendship during this long and rocky process.

Friends, family, fans, readers, reviewers, and the many other people out there who might pick up my book, and tell me they love it, even if they don't: thank you for your love and support. It really does mean a lot to me. To those who don't love it, and tell me why: thank you for helping me become a better writer and author.

Writing a novel is hard. But to anyone out there who is debating whether to take the plunge and write a book, I encourage you to do so. There is a whole world of writers out there willing to give their help, support and friendship to others taking on this same monumental task. You'll never regret it.

Visit http://thomasaknight.com for the latest news and updates on Thomas A. Knight